DEEP COVER

Praise for Kara A. McLeod

Actual Stop

"This author is new for me, but she had me at cop character."
—*Amanda's Reviews*

Worthy of Trust and Confidence

"Kara A. McLeod knows how to write a great story with characters that have strength and at the same time are vulnerable…[T]his is an action-packed adventure with two badass female leads with smoldering hot chemistry. Once I got started, there is no way in hell you could have dragged this book from me…You have a fantastic mystery, a ton of corruption, and a love story that just won't quit."
—*The Romantic Reader Blog*

Known Threat

"McLeod has become a master in writing a fantastic story with main characters that exude fortitude, strength, kindness, and underneath it all, raw vulnerability. It's hard not to be captured by this series."—*The Romantic Reader Blog*

"*Known Threat* is well written with likable characters and a good amount of drama and police procedural. There is a bit of romance, action, and even a touch of suspense thrown in for good measure."—*Illustrious Illusions*

By the Author

Actual Stop

Worthy of Trust and Confidence

Known Threat

Deep Cover

Visit us at www.boldstrokesbooks.com

DEEP COVER

by
Kara A. McLeod

2025

DEEP COVER

ISBN 13: 978-1-63679-808-0

This Trade Paperback Original Is Published By
Bold Strokes Books, Inc.
P.O. Box 249
Valley Falls, NY 12185

First Edition: March 2025

CREDITS
EDITOR: SHELLEY THRASHER
PRODUCTION DESIGN: STACIA SEAMAN
COVER DESIGN BY JEANINE HENNING

Acknowledgments

Thank you to everyone who has been patient with me while "normal" life derailed everything. I appreciate you more than words can possibly express.

Radclyffe, you continue to be the best publisher ever.

Shelley, I still don't know how you haven't strangled me. You have the patience of a saint.

Chief, you also haven't strangled me or told me to shove it. Do you and Shelley have a support group?

My Hetero-Soul-Mate, SASD, love you to bits, lady! Your words are present and accounted for. As always.

Thing One, miss you like crazy.

Glocamorra, you made it, buddy!

For Riley, my partner in crime.

Oh, and in life. That, too.

CHAPTER ONE

"Alex, what the fuck?" the bleached-blond woman at my elbow screeched.

I winced at both the pitch and the decibel level, unable to contain either my exasperated eye roll or my huff of annoyance. I was busy peering anxiously through the crowd jostling on the busy New York street, searching while trying not to appear to be doing so, and I didn't appreciate the break in my concentration. "What?"

Tamara stopped in front of me and spun on one heel, her posture and body language evidencing her ire. She popped her gum as she glared at me, hands on her ample hips, toe tapping.

I blinked at her, confused. "What?"

"You keep stepping on my fucking feet, that's what," Tamara snapped. "What the hell's wrong with you?" Her white-blond hair tumbled down over her forehead and into her heavily lined eyes, combining with her age-inappropriate dress to somehow make her seem younger.

"Sorry," I muttered, neither sounding nor feeling contrite. I rubbed at my forehead with my left hand, careful to avoid the eyebrow bar that was intended to distract from the scar there, and glanced around. Was I pulling it off? The looking while not looking like I was looking? I hoped so.

Tamara's glare softened. "She's over there." Her voice was low, and her eyes twinkled with amusement. "In the stop-and-rob across the way."

"W-what?" My heart stopped, and the warmth drained out of my face. Oops. Guess I hadn't been as sly as I'd thought. Either that or Tamara was much more observant than I'd given her credit for. Memo to me.

Tamara's bright-red lips pulled up in a knowing smirk. "That woman you've been looking at. She's across the street."

Attempting to hide my terror beneath mountains of annoyance, I shook my head and grabbed her arm, jerking her back into step beside me. "I haven't been looking at anyone."

Tamara chuckled, but I didn't hear any derision or meanness in the sound. Clearly, she didn't believe the denial that sounded feeble even to me, but for some reason she chose not to comment on it.

"Fine." A beat. "She's been looking at you, though."

I choked on the beer I was swigging out of a bottle wrapped in a brown paper bag and—after a few long, agonizing seconds of coughing and sputtering—whipped my head around to fix her with a pointed glare. "What?"

My voice was flat and toneless, and I hoped against hope it projected an air of indifference colored with just a hint of irritation. With any luck, she thought it was just because she was teasing me and not because I was petrified that after almost five weeks of what I'd like to think consisted of a flawless undercover performance, I'd just fucked up. How badly remained to be seen.

Tamara shrugged and waved one hand as she dug through her gigantic purse with the other. A dull clinking noise emanated from within it as she rummaged, but after another long moment, her hand emerged clasping a crumpled pack of cigarettes.

Not wanting to waste any more of her concentration on waiting for her to locate the matches she insisted on using, I flicked the lighter I carried with me for times like these and held it out for her, cupping the flickering flame with one hand to shield it from the gentle breeze while holding my beer protectively against my chest with my arm. Tamara inhaled a deep lungful of smoke and let it out slowly, her eyes half lidded in an expression not unlike pleasure.

"It's okay, you know," she said after almost a minute of silence. She was peering at me out of the corner of her eyes, and smoke billowed behind her in a steady stream as we walked.

"What's okay?" I chugged the last of my beer and tossed the empty bottle into a nearby trash can.

"If you wanna play with girls." I narrowed my eyes at her, but she shrugged and went on. "I mean, hey, it's not my thing, but, you know, whatever floats your boat, right?"

"I don't," I said through clenched teeth. But I couldn't seem to stop myself from letting my gaze slide back to where I'd last spotted the woman currently under discussion, and I hoped my disappointment at not seeing her didn't show. Tamara appeared too busy sucking on her cigarette to notice.

"You're not worried about Tate, are you?" she asked, letting her snort of derision voice the rest of her opinion about the man that I was, by all appearances, "dating." "'Cause you know he'd totally be into it. As long as you let him watch. Or at least provide details afterward." She grinned at me and wiggled her eyebrows.

"Nah." I gave an offhanded wave and jerked open the door of the bar, holding it ajar so she could enter.

Tamara sauntered in ahead of me, her attention now riveted to the crowd awaiting our return, the odd conversation apparently completely forgotten, leaving me time to cast one last aching glance over my shoulder before I strolled in after her.

"Hey, Alex," the bartender, Ronnie, called to me as I ambled by.

I gave a half nod and changed direction, heading toward him. People moved out of the way to make room. I unzipped my parka and shoved my hands deep in my pockets to hide their trembling. I was shaken, and I was worried it showed.

"S'up?" I was trying for casual but wasn't sure whether my attempt was passing. I shot a quick peek past the stairs and Tamara, who was jiggling her way up to the balcony where my raucous crew was making their presence known. I pulled a fist full of crumpled bills out of the pocket of my jeans and dropped them on the counter. "Beer?"

Ronnie snorted and waved at my wrinkly money. "On the house."

"Thanks," I said, accepting the icy pint glass from him and taking a long, deep pull.

The cold liquid felt orgasmic going down my throat, and I had to give myself a stern reminder not to drink too much tonight, which was a tall order, if I wanted to keep up with this group. A heavy sigh slipped from my lips, and I ran one hand through my hair, ruffling it a little, making it stand on end even more than it already did. My mind was running like a robo dwarf hamster on a wheel at the pet store as I turned over current events and attempted to figure out what the hell I was going to do about them. My life was complicated enough. I sure as hell didn't need this new development. Although—

"Yo, Alex!" someone shouted down from the balcony, and it carried across the crowded bar. "What the fuck?"

I rolled my eyes and gave Ronnie a conspiratorial little smile before tipping my head up and raising my eyes toward the sound.

"What?" I mouthed. I wasn't inclined to raise my voice to a level necessary to be heard over the din of the music pounding out of the very walls of the place. I made an impatient little gesture with my hands and raised my eyebrows.

Tate, my "boyfriend," grinned at me in what I'm sure he thought was a sultry manner, his dark eyes glinting dangerously with a palpable heat as he stared down at me from above. From his vantage point, he had to have a nice view of my cleavage, and he showed his appreciation by licking his lips. It was a struggle not to pull my coat closed in an effort to cover myself.

The smile I threw Ronnie now was tight-lipped and not the least bit amused. I pushed myself off the bar, cold beer in hand, and jerked my head in the direction of my summons. "Gotta go." Without waiting for a reply, I started making my way through the press of bodies, not in any particular hurry to reach my intended destination.

When I'd finally made my way upstairs long minutes later, a rough-and-tumble game of pool was in full swing. It looked like the guys had been at this for a while, if the apparent level of intoxication was any indication, and I managed to suppress a huff of exasperation, but just barely.

I'd just spied Tamara, whispering and giggling with someone in the corner as she played bartender with the bottles of alcohol she'd snuck in inside her purse, and had taken a step in their direction when my progress was halted. Someone forcefully grabbed me from behind and jerked me off balance until I was almost smothered in a full body hug.

"I need cash," Tate growled in my ear, scraping his two-day-old stubble across my cheek, ear, and neck as he did so. I leaned away so our skin was no longer touching, but he took advantage of our positions and possessively ran his hands down my shoulders and over my barely contained breasts.

His breath was sour, telling me I'd been right about how long he'd been there, and his hard-on was poking me in the back. As if somehow knowing I'd sensed it, Tate pulled me to him even rougher, grinding himself against me, almost humping me in full view of everyone.

Not at all surprised by this greeting, I reached back and palmed his ass with both of my hands, encouraging his movements and adding a little hip-rocking of my own for good measure. Tate groaned in my ear.

Smiling wickedly and catching Tamara's eye across the pool table, I turned my head toward him and up, his cue to bend down to me so I could tell him something. I took my time positioning my lips a hairs-breadth away from the shell of his ear.

"Something bothering you, baby?"

Tate growled again and spun me around, lifting me off the floor with one easy motion and settling me so I was straddling him and had to wrap my legs around his waist. He rocked his hips into mine, and I could feel him pressing hard against my crotch. Forcing a giggle, I wrapped my arms around his neck and ground my pelvis against his even harder, making exaggerated motions with my hips and tugging on his black, almost shoulder-length hair.

"Oh, baby, I'm going to fuck you so good later." Tate made a show of panting in my ear, not slowing his hip thrusts one bit.

He must've been really goddamn plastered to be doing this in front of everyone and their mother, but one look around told me everyone else in our little group was equally bombed, so he probably wouldn't catch too much shit for it tomorrow. A few of the guys were leering at us and laughing, cheering Tate on. A couple of the others were too busy arguing over their pool game to pay much attention to what any of the rest of us were doing, and one guy was busy being manhandled in a corner by one of the girls—I couldn't tell which one—and was therefore distracted. Whether the other couple's behavior had inspired Tate's current mood or they'd taken their cue from us was unclear.

Wanting to end this encounter so I could return to my beer and my moping, I slid my arms down around his shoulders and raked my fingernails across the broad muscles of his back. Tate growled again and dropped me.

I got my feet under me just in time to avoid landing flat on my ass, but not quickly enough to avoid the jarring stop that almost severed my tongue with my teeth. I winced and swallowed a mouthful of blood.

Tate spun me around and pressed me against the railing that overlooked the rest of the bar, all but falling on top of me in his stupor. I could feel him fumbling for his belt behind me as he continued to grind himself into my ass, and I might've been offended that he appeared set on trying to full-on fuck me in the middle of the bar if I hadn't been positive he'd never last long enough to get his own pants off, let alone mine. That was a relief because I wasn't in the mood to beat the shit out of him in front of witnesses.

Tate's breath was coming in short, feeble gasps now, little growls and what might've been words falling from his lips. I whirled back around to face him and grabbed both of his wrists, pinning our hands low between our bodies and taking a half step closer. I dug my thumbs into the little divot where his radii met his ulnae and pressed. Hard. He winced and grimaced, and I twisted, pushing my short nails into his skin. It was a message. While I didn't want to draw blood, it wouldn't stop me from trying.

I stood on my toes to indicate I wanted to talk to him and forced a smile. He leaned down and tucked his chin back into my shoulder on the far side, presumably so no one could see his expression. "Watch it," I whispered.

He nodded, and I could feel his fingers flittering against my thighs. "Sorry."

I patted his wrists and dropped a light kiss on his cheek before turning back around and wrapping his arms around my waist and holding his hands together to rest beneath mine on my stomach. He squeezed me and leaned back a bit, getting drawn into some debate about cars. I'm not sure. I tuned him out almost immediately.

Instead of paying attention to the conversation around me, I scanned the crowd, taking in every detail about each patron in sight to write up in my notes at some TBD date. And this stubborn insistence on vigilance and a possibly misplaced sense of duty made me lock eyes with the most beautiful woman ever to walk the earth at the exact moment the man behind me decided to ignore my earlier warning and started placing languid kisses on my neck.

Only Tate drunkenly sagging against me kept me pinned to the railing at that point, although I was unsure whether I'd have collapsed to the ground or made a run for it if I'd have been able to move. I became still and wire-tight as I stood there, my skin suddenly cold despite the hot press of bodies all around me. My heart thudded out of control, and the blood rushing in my ears was interfering with coherent thought as I tried to contemplate the ramifications of my current situation.

Allison Reynolds continued to stand motionless just inside the doorway of the main floor of the bar, looking even more breathtaking than ever, her inky eyes boring into mine and tinted with the barest hint of anger. Or perhaps it was judgment. I wasn't sure. But whichever it was, I could feel the heavy weight of that gaze even from across the considerable distance that separated us, and I was unable to swallow the lump in the back of my throat. I ignored Tate's murmured words—endearments? apologies? who even knew?—focusing all my attention, all my being, solely on Allison.

Though it'd been less than six weeks since I last saw her, the passage of time must've somehow muted the memory of her beauty, because she bowled me over. She was the most beautiful thing I'd seen since...well, since the last time I'd seen her.

Her black hair had been cut recently and was brushed back off her forehead, falling in thick waves almost to her shoulders. Her olive skin was flawless, and my fingertips tingled with the memory of the way it felt under my hands. Her lean hips and thighs were hugged tightly in a pair of dark jeans that flared just a little at the ankles over her black, low-heeled boots. And my mouth simultaneously watered and went dry at the way her top accentuated her figure.

"Hey, check her out." Crash's drunkenly loud statement broke into my reverie as he moved to stand next to me at the railing. "Fresh meat."

"She must be lost," Barker chimed in as he took up a similar stance on my other side. Out of the corner of my eye, I could see him scratching his chin. "Way too upscale for this place."

Crash laughed, lifting one hand to push his greasy, dirty-blond hair back out of his eyes. "I'll help her find her way," he said, slurring his words. "To the end of my cock." He handed his beer across me to his buddy and made a move toward the stairs, presumably so he could make his way down to where Allison stood, still staring into my eyes.

Shit. An icy thrill of terror slid down my throat to lodge cold and hard in my chest. *Shit, shit, shit!*

"No!" My voice broke unsolicited, colored with a hard edge I instantly wished I'd managed to rein in. Tate obviously noticed and frowned. He put his hands on my shoulders and turned me so he could see my face. Crash and Barker both froze and said nothing. I couldn't see their expressions, but out of the corner of my eye, I could see they were watching me, their undivided attention causing an unwelcome flush to blossom in my cheeks. After a long, tense moment of silence, they finally laughed.

Think. My mind raced to divine some miraculous way out of the hot mess I'd just created with my outburst. *Think.* But I couldn't think. Not really. Just one glance from Allison Reynolds had totally short-circuited every single, solitary mental function. Good to know some things never changed.

Fortunately for me, Tamara appeared just then and gave me an opening. "Here, Crash," she said as she shimmied over, lifting to Crash's lips a cup full of whatever she and Laurel had been concocting in the corner. "Tell me what you think. Too strong?" Her blue gaze roved over Crash's face and then followed his to see what'd so captivated him. "Oh, hey, Alex! Look. It's your girl."

All three guys snapped their heads back around to stare at me, clearly puzzled.

"Your girl?" Tate asked. His voice was tight. Strained.

Uh-oh. Not good.

Tamara answered for me, jerking her chin toward Allison, who'd sauntered over to lean against the bar, her dark eyes never once wavering from me. Tamara's lips were stretched into a knowing smirk. "Yeah. We saw her while we were out getting the vodka. She was practically fucking Alex with her eyes." Tamara let out a high, tinkling laugh.

I clenched my teeth together in a useless attempt to contain my considerable ire and fought with everything I had not to roll my eyes. "Oh, she was not," I replied, forcing a chuckle I prayed was passable.

"She totally was," Tamara insisted, gesturing with her full drink cup and sloshing a good portion of the liquid over the side and onto both Crash and the floor. "She followed us for, like, three blocks and never once took her eyes off you."

I couldn't seem to stop myself from gaping at her and mentally kicked myself for not being more observant. No way in hell should I have let my attention wander to the point that Tamara was more aware of what was going on around us than I was. But Allison Reynolds had always had that effect on me. Right from the very first second I'd laid eyes on her, my world had imploded, crumpling and folding in on itself until everything and everyone else became inconsequential, and only she existed. It'd always been my downfall. I stifled my weary sigh.

"You were too focused on trying to package the beer so you could get away with drinking it on the street to notice at first," Tamara was informing me in a knowing voice. "But once you guys made eye contact, you totally had amazing chemistry."

"Clearly." I took a deep breath and straightened my shoulders as an idea formed in my head on the heels of Tamara's words. If I was going to pull this off, I was going to need to get some of my swagger back. I turned to flash Tate a sultry smile.

"Your birthday's coming up," I said in a low voice, as though I intended the comment for his ears only, but I really wanted to ensure everyone was hanging on my every word. The last thing I needed was one of the guys hitting on Allison. And not just because it'd launch me into a tailspin of jealousy the likes of which the world has never seen. Although that was motivation enough.

"Yeah?" Tate replied. A light started gleaming in his dark eyes, and his expression more than indicated he was curious to see where I was going with this.

"Yeah." I wound one arm around his neck and pressed up against him. "You know I don't have much cash, so I thought maybe I could get you her instead…" I allowed my voice to drop and my words to trail off, my silence saying more than any detailed description ever could.

Tate's eyes were about to bug out of his head, and out of the corner of my eyes I could see that Barker and Crash wore matching expressions of disbelief. I concentrated all my focus on just keeping eye contact with Tate.

"You…You mean you…And her…" Tate was stammering, his breathing shallow as he glanced back and forth from me to Allison, his expression colored with the faintest glimmer of hope.

I leaned close and trailed my fingertips across the faint stubble covering his jaw and the top of his neck. "That's right, baby. If she wants to play, that is."

Tate stared at me, clearly stunned, for a few more seconds before his lips stretched into an honest-to-goodness grin. He turned to the guys with a countenance of smug triumph. "Hear that, boys? No one goes near her."

"Aw, but Tate—" Crash started to protest.

Tate cut him off with a dark glare, and Crash's mouth snapped shut with an audible click. He returned his attention to me, an almost predatory gleam in his eyes. "Go get 'er, babe." He punctuated his statement with a possessive slap on my ass.

I somehow managed not to clench my hands into fists as I walked away.

The stroll down the stairs and through the throng over to the bar where Allison stood watching me seemed to take both forever and not long enough, but it gave me ample opportunity to ask myself no less than a dozen times what the hell I was doing.

To say that this was a terrible idea was the mother of all understatements, but I couldn't think of how I could possibly have avoided my current predicament. I needed to speak to Allison without an audience. Well, without an audience that could hear me. The hoots and hollers of the gang upstairs carried over the din of the crowded bar to my already ringing ears. This seemed like the best I could do under the circumstances.

To be fair, though, I hadn't yet worked out the specifics of what I intended to say to her. Asking her what the hell she was doing here might be a good start, but I wasn't sure I wanted to know. Even though I loved her with all my heart and regardless of the reality that she affected me on a very visceral level, I was still harboring some mixed feelings stemming from some information that'd come to light the last time we'd seen one another. And now wasn't the time or place for us to get into any of that. No. I needed to concentrate on getting her the hell out of here. Everything else would have to wait.

Allison's near-black eyes tracked every move I made as I walked toward her, causing a fluttering in and around my heart I was all too familiar with. She regarded me with hostile curiosity, one hand resting on her cocked hip, her entire body radiating a barely contained ire.

"Hey," I said when I reached her, aware that my voice was scarcely audible over the music and the crowd. I had to force myself not to beam at her or touch her, though I ached to do both. We were supposed to be perfect strangers, after all, and I was pretty sure strangers didn't kiss one another breathless within the first few seconds of an introduction. Well, not outside of a *Penthouse Forum* letter, anyway.

"I'm Alex," I went on before she had a chance to reply, extending one hand in her direction as though I were introducing myself. Which, in a way, I guess I was.

"Alex," Allison said, drawing out the word as though she were rolling it around in her mouth, tasting it as she spoke it. She studied me for a beat before folding my hand into her own, pumping it twice, and then letting go.

The shock I always felt when she touched me caught me off guard, and my hand tingled where our skin had brushed only scant moments before. The corner of my mouth twitched, and my breath caught in my throat. Okay, now I positively ached to kiss her and had to rein in the impulse. I decided it was safer for both of us if I focused more on my non-desire-based feelings. That way I'd at least be able to carry on a conversation.

"Nice to meet you," I replied, trying to send her a message with my eyes.

"What's up?" She kept her question general and innocuous, completely within the realm of something one would ask a new acquaintance, and I appreciated her discretion.

I shook my head once, just a quick back and forth that could've meant anything or nothing to anyone who might've been watching. And I knew people were indeed watching. The spot between my shoulder blades tingled under the weight of their combined attention. To dispel some of my nervous energy, I used the fingers of my left hand to spin the ring adorning the middle finger of my right.

"Can I buy you a drink?" I asked, jerking my head toward the bar.

Allison shook her head. She eyed me thoughtfully for a moment and then waved at Ronnie to get his attention. She took some cash out of her pocket and laid it on the bar, regarding the hotel key card that had gotten mixed in with all her money as though it held the answers to all the questions she wanted to ask but couldn't. She tapped the edge of it once on the top of the bar, and realization flooded my brain. It was a long-unused code between us. She wanted to see me alone in an hour.

"How about I buy you one?" she suggested, taking deliberate care to deposit a dime, a nickel, a quarter, and a penny on the bar in front of her. She took her time placing them at precise intervals, stacking the dime on top of the nickel and the penny on top of the quarter. Now she was giving me a location. Her eyes were on me the entire time, boring straight into my soul, setting my heart on fire and reducing it to ash at the same time.

I squelched those feelings with great effort and took a moment to surreptitiously glance at my watch. It was my turn to shake my head. I drummed my fingers on the bar twice to indicate to her that she'd have to wait at least two hours until I could get away and shot her what I hoped was a disarming smile. She frowned but didn't comment. The longing to argue with me—or at least demand why she'd have to wait—flitted openly across her beautiful face, but she kept the impulse in check. Her restraint relieved me.

Slowly, I leaned into her so I could whisper in her ear. I paused before speaking to indulge in the desire to breathe in the scent that had always meant her to me, and I shivered, delighted against both my better judgment and my will, not to mention turned on beyond belief. Which, of course, only pissed me off even more.

"When I sit back," I murmured, recklessly giving in to the urge to brush my lips against her ear as I spoke, "you're going to slap me across the face hard and storm out of here."

She stiffened but neither spoke nor pulled away. I couldn't discern her facial expression as I couldn't see it. "Storm out of here and don't look back." I brushed my lips against her ear once more before I backed away. I stared at her for what felt like an eternity and held my breath.

The skin around Allison's soulful dark eyes tightened, and she hauled off and decked me so fast I didn't even have time to steel myself against the shock of the blow. I blinked in surprise—barely cognizant of the laughter, shouts, and groans from the group observing above— and touched a hesitant hand to my cheek and the corner of my mouth. I tried to tamp down the panic that filled me at the coppery taste of blood as I watched Allison walk away.

I was once again surprised, this time pleasantly, when she did as I asked and didn't look back.

CHAPTER TWO

For once in my life, luck was on my side. Tate was beyond wasted and passed out the second his head hit the pillow. I removed his boots and his belt to ensure he'd be at least somewhat comfortable and put a large glass of water and a couple of aspirin on the nightstand next to the bed. Then I crept out of the apartment and caught a taxi uptown, ignoring the voice inside me clamoring at me to stop. But it was almost like living in a bad dream, watching myself from outside my body. I knew this wasn't a good idea but was powerless to stop myself.

I was extremely familiar with the Sheraton New York Hotel, so I walked with a purpose toward the elevator to Allison's room. The security guard at the podium never even glanced up from his crossword puzzle as I strode by, which made me glad I'd taken the time to don a hat and a light jacket before I set off. It was a stereotype, but people who looked and dressed the way I was now tended not to stay at hotels like the Sheraton, and the less attention I drew to myself, the better off everyone would be.

The elevator ride took both an eternity and an instant, and I blinked when I realized I was standing in front of the door to room 1526, my hand poised to knock. The walk down the hall from the elevator bank was a complete blur. I took a deep breath, trying—and failing—to calm my thundering heart and still my jangling nerves. A little annoyed with my body for its betrayal, I scowled and rapped lightly on the door.

A few seconds went by—the longest few seconds of my life in recent memory—but finally the door opened, and Allison's neutral expression greeted me. Her hair was disheveled and her pajamas rumpled, as though she'd been lying down, but her dark eyes were alert, so clearly she'd been waiting for me. Her blank expression didn't indicate her current patience level, which meant I'd have to tread very carefully.

Neither of us spoke as she stepped aside, gesturing for me to come in. I slid through the doorway and into the narrow space just inside, standing in front of her. We kept our eyes on each other, silent, as she shut the door.

After a moment, not knowing what else to do, but desperately needing to do *something*, I took off my hat and ran one hand through my tousled hair, scratching my scalp as I did so. At least my current hairstyle was low-maintenance. Even when I attempted to tame it, it looked like I'd just woken up, so I no longer put any kind of effort into it. I just washed it and let it do what it wanted.

Allison smirked and followed with her own fingers the path my hand had just made. I closed my eyes and sighed, forgetting briefly my discomfort at her touch.

"Ryan," Allison whispered, her voice barely hinting at something I couldn't place.

A frisson shot up my spine, and I shuddered at the familiar heat just her words could spark. I opened my eyes and looked at her, unable to prevent my hand—that independent, stupid appendage—from cupping her cheek. I sighed again and smiled.

"No one's called me that in a long time," I said, one knot loosening while another tightened in my chest.

Allison took her time replying. In the meantime, her gaze roved over me, clearly taking in the haircut, the makeup, and the piercings, all of which were different from the last time she'd seen me. Her fingers traced the curve of my ear and trailed down my neck, resulting in a not-unpleasant tensing of my stomach muscles. I broke out in goose bumps, and my nipples tightened almost painfully as moisture pooled between my legs. I didn't even try to hide my shiver. She knew what she did to me. I had neither the time nor the energy to pretend otherwise.

Allison smiled a little and slid her hands into the lapels of my jacket, removing it while running her hands down my bare arms. The garment dropped to the floor forgotten, and Allison gazed at the landscape of my body as though seeking to lay claim to it. She really didn't know it'd always been hers?

"You changed your hair," she said, her voice slightly louder than a murmur. Her fingers, meanwhile, were wreaking havoc on my nervous system as they lightly traced the ink now visible on my arms. "And got tattoos."

"The tats are fake. They're a bitch to keep getting reapplied." I don't know why I'd bothered to add that last part. Nerves, I suppose.

Allison nodded but seemed fixated on my head, and the corners of her lips turned down as she inspected my new 'do.

My natural hair color was a honey blond streaked with both darker and lighter strands throughout. It was thick, with a subtle wave when I wore it longer, my preferred style. It'd garnered me a great many unearned compliments, and she always used to tease me about it. She'd also used to enjoy running her fingers through it. Now I wasn't sure I'd find out whether that predilection would hold now that it was short, which disappointed me.

"You remembered," Allison said finally, her eyes beginning to gleam.

I nodded, longing to drown in her gaze yet not get sucked in forever.

"Of course. A dime on top of a nickel. Fifteen. A penny on top of a quarter. Twenty-six." The coins she'd placed on the bar earlier had been our code to convey to one another where and when to tryst back when we'd been trying to keep our relationship a secret. I remembered every second like it was yesterday.

"And, of course, the hotel room key was a dead giveaway." I grinned, and she grinned back.

"Yeah, well, I was a little annoyed when you told me I'd have to wait two hours for an explanation. And even more annoyed when it was more than three."

My grin turned into a lopsided smirk, though I'd known she was irritated as soon as I'd seen her expression in the bar. And since she was a stickler for punctuality, I'd known she'd be irked when I showed up late.

"Patience is a virtue," I told her.

She looked very serious and reached out tentatively to touch the corner of my mouth, a bit swollen from her punch earlier.

"I'm sorry," she whispered.

I turned my head and pulled out of her reach before her thumb could contact my newly broken skin. Her gaze bored into mine with an intensity that tugged on my soul.

"It's okay. I told you to." My heart was clattering within the too-small confines of my chest, and I had the not-unpleasant experience of feeling hot and cold at the same time.

Allison nodded, appearing solemn. "I know. What I don't know is why."

I sighed, threaded our fingers together, and led her over to the bed. We sat side by side, and I stared at our joined hands, resting in my lap. I took a deep breath, trying to prepare myself, but she beat me to the punch.

"Who was that guy?" Her voice carried a dangerous edge of accusation.

"Allison—" I started to say, wincing, but she put her fingers over my lips. The touch was a little too forceful against the split lip she'd given me earlier, and I grimaced, both against the twinge of pain and the fear of inadvertently getting blood on her. I pulled out of her reach again.

"No," Allison said sharply, clearly expecting obedience. "No. I haven't heard from you in weeks. No calls, no texts, no emails. You didn't—" She hesitated, and something defying immediate definition flickered behind her eyes. "You barely had three seconds to speak to me on Christmas Day. And I know how the job is. I get that sometimes we're pressed for time, but I felt like an inconvenience."

I barely had time to register her hurried, quick, almost defensive words before she continued.

"It's like you dropped off the face of the earth. And when I finally do manage to track you down—completely by accident, might I add— this." She waved in front of me, an obvious indication of her as-yet-unspoken point. "Different hair, different clothes. Piercings and tattoos all over the place. Some sleazy guy practically fucking you in the middle of a bar. I don't know what in God's name mmpphhh—"

Allison's tirade turned into an indistinct mumble against the press of my lips against hers, the best way to shut her the hell up. Well, and she was just so achingly beautiful in her anger, I couldn't best the impulse to kiss her breathless. What can I say? I'm only human.

For a long moment, she didn't respond, which caused a painful pressure in my chest, but eventually she sighed. The tension leeched out of her body, and she yielded, wrapping her arms around me and letting her lips feed on mine as though I were her only source of oxygen, and she'd been unable to breathe for a very long time.

When we finally broke apart—minutes later? hours? there was no way to tell—we were both a little breathless, Allison appearing dazed, her eyes just this side of unfocused. Unable to contain my smile, I lifted one of her hands to my lips and placed a light kiss on the knuckles.

I froze then. Fuck. I shouldn't have kissed her with my cut lip. I'd been thinking about that a few minutes ago, too, yet I'd allowed her to have intimate contact with my possibly-HIV-infected blood. My heart heavy with dread, I realized I'd been right to pull a disappearing act. I had less than no self-control when it came to her.

I cleared my throat and forced myself back on topic. "Can I talk now?"

Allison nodded, her expression shuttered. She folded her arms over her chest and watched me warily.

"I'm undercover."

Allison blinked at me. "What?"

"I'm undercover," I repeated. When she didn't respond right away, I grinned and bumped her shoulder with my own. "What? You think I'd cut and dye my hair for the fun of it? Come on!"

"You're undercover," she said, ignoring my attempt at levity, her voice and her eyes both flat. Something akin to recognition flickered across the sculpted planes of her face, followed swiftly by apparent annoyance.

It was my turn to nod. "Yeah. I told you I was going to do this."

"You did *not* tell me you were going to do this."

"Sure I did. We had a long conversation about it."

"We had a conversation about you helping the counterfeit squad with something one time. That was it."

"Right. And that's what this turned into."

"You didn't think you should've warned me about being completely out of touch?"

"I did! Or at least I tried. This all blew up when you were on your way to Moscow. I couldn't get ahold of you because you were in the air, so I left you a voice mail."

Allison's brows furrowed. "You…you left me a voice mail?"

"Of course. On your work phone. I wasn't sure whether you had international activated on your personal phone, but I knew your work phone would. Why? Didn't you get it?"

"No. No, I didn't." Her tone was hard and brittle.

My insides seized up, and I swallowed, a little unnerved. Did she not believe me? Why wouldn't she? I wouldn't lie about something like that. "Oh. I'm sorry. I left one, I swear."

"I'm sure you did."

"But…"

"But nothing. I believe you. I'd suspected Beau was going through my emails somehow, so I've changed my password three separate times, but it never occurred to me that he'd been listening to my voice mails as well. Guess I'd better change that password, too."

I doubted anyone would do that, but I didn't want to appear to be just dismissing her theories. "Are you sure? I mean, maybe it was just a glitch at the phone company or something."

"No. I'm pretty sure it was him. We just had an inspection down on PPD and had to give the inspectors our passwords for everything so they could make sure we weren't falsely utilizing government resources.

Right after that, I started noticing emails were being marked as read even though I'd never seen them, especially ones from you. From there, I started checking my trash folder and noticed messages there I'd never seen. That's when I changed my password."

"Wow." I didn't know what to say. It boggled the mind. "Did you report him?"

Allison shook her head. "What would be the point?"

"Well, it wouldn't be hard to prove he'd been snooping through your emails."

"And what good would that do?"

"I don't know. Get him demoted or maybe even fired?"

She tilted her head and appraised me with a fondly exasperated look. "It's adorable how optimistic you are."

"What?"

"Surely you remember that whole disaster with Danny Ephron. How many times was he accused of sexual harassment?"

"Three, I think. Maybe four. I stopped counting."

"Exactly. And what happened to him? He got demoted, and then he got promoted again. Twice. And then after the last accusation, they just put him on administrative leave and let him ride out the last couple years until retirement sitting at home, doing nothing, and getting paid for it."

"Yeah. That was bullshit."

"And he wasn't half as well connected as Byers is. Trust me, it's just easier to let it go. I'll make sure to change my voice-mail password, and that will be that."

"Okay." I wasn't sure this was the best course of action, but it was her call, not mine.

"So back to this undercover assignment and why I haven't heard from you in over a month."

"It's been almost five weeks. And I haven't had anything to do with my real life since I went under. I haven't checked my voice mail or my email in forever. I don't have anything with me that could ever tie me to who I really am."

Saying that out loud made my heart pound because Allison was part of the life I'd been trying so hard to divorce myself from. Even meeting her like this could have dire consequences. For the investigation, for me personally, and for her if the wrong people found out I'd seen her and put two and two together... I pushed that thought away, trying to ignore the icy stab of fear splintering my heart.

"You're *deep* cover." She sounded stunned. But her tone indicated she'd already worked out that much for herself and wasn't really seeking confirmation. I nodded once more anyway, and she blinked at me again. "But we don't do that. In our agency, we don't do deep cover."

"We do now." I replied with no small amount of embarrassment, averting my gaze. "Or rather, *I* do."

"Why?" Allison's voice was a touch more heated than I felt was warranted, and I couldn't help wondering why. "Why would the agency completely break protocol and allow you to take on an assignment for which you haven't been properly trained?"

I was silent for a long moment as I waited for the pieces to fall into place in Allison's head.

"Iran," she said flatly. It wasn't a question.

Several months ago, I'd been involved in a shooting. Well, to be fair, the term "shooting" tends to imply I'd gotten a shot off somewhere during the fray, which I hadn't. I hadn't even drawn my weapon. Or known there'd been a need to.

Thorough investigation after the fact had revealed said "shooting" had been a contract hit taken out on me by my boss at the time, Mark Jennings, which I later thought gave new meaning to the term poor employee evaluation.

Mark, it'd turned out, had been in league with a group of Iranians who were printing and selling astronomical amounts of counterfeit money, as well as recirculating vast numbers of bills that'd already been submitted to our office to be logged into our vaults as evidence yet had—through his intervention—found their way back out onto the streets.

The Joint Terrorism Task Force had attempted to prove in a court of law that the group was materially supporting terrorism with the profits of their scheme but hadn't been able to make a convincing enough case. The Iranians had been smart enough to have layers to their organization and to ensure the men they'd smuggled into the United States—illegally, I'd like to point out—had no actual connection to the real heavy hitters.

It was still unclear to me how Mark had gotten mixed up with those guys, although I had my suspicions, which I'd been instructed in no uncertain terms to keep to myself. But I'd inadvertently stumbled onto one of Mark's contacts while conducting an unofficial run out for a friend in another office, and it'd been decided it was time to neutralize the perceived threat. In other words, me.

The Iranians he'd been doing business with had been more than happy to protect their commercial interests and provide the muscle. Worst-case scenario for them, the shooter got caught and either deported or sent to federal prison. Whoever they chose as the hired gun would've been expendable as far as the day-to-day operations were concerned. And if all went well, it'd look like I'd done exactly what I'd been hired to do and taken a bullet for the president of Iran. It'd been win-win for both Mark and the Iranians.

Unfortunately for all of us, things hadn't gone as planned. I'd gotten shot, yes, but I'd been wearing a ballistic vest, and none of the hits that'd connected with my skin had struck anyplace vital. I'd survived, and the attempt on my life had only succeeded in pissing me the hell off.

Also unfortunately, my very recent ex-girlfriend at the time, an NYPD Intel Detective named Lucia Mendez, had been killed by the gunman because she'd been at the absolute worst place at the most inconvenient time. And after I'd recovered enough to return to work, I'd ended up helping nab the bad guys, including Mark. It'd ended up being a losing situation for everyone involved.

After that disaster, my twin sister Rory had been kidnapped by one of our threat subjects to be used as leverage to facilitate a meeting with the president's daughter, who he'd believed to be his wife. I believed an argument could be made that it'd been our fault that'd happened in the first place, as Mark had failed to assign the subject's case to an agent for monitoring, which'd allowed him to run around unchecked for weeks. But headquarters had taken a different view of the situation, much to my considerable displeasure.

I held no illusions that the Secret Service felt bad for anything that'd happened, a belief strengthened by the fact that no one had ever come out and said anything remotely to that effect. That I'd been shot, that my ex-girlfriend and a fellow law enforcement officer had been killed, that they'd been unable to ferret out one of our own who'd turned to a life of crime, and a boss, no less—no one in any sort of position of authority had addressed those facts. It was almost as if they'd been hoping that by ignoring the issues, they'd magically go away.

That attitude had initially pissed me off—I'd even attempted to quit—but once I'd had time to calm down and think, I'd decided to use the situation to my complete advantage. When I'd been approached about assisting with this investigation, I'd jumped on it without even asking for permission from my new immediate supervisor. I sure as hell didn't bother to clear it through headquarters. If they were that upset about it, they could come pull me out. Five weeks later, I still hadn't heard a peep from anyone.

It'd worked out for me on a personal level, as well. This sort of operation, this having to be "on" all the time, distracted me from more private problems that even now caused me to break out in a cold sweat and endure pangs of guilt-induced nausea when I dwelt on them. It'd also given me the perfect excuse to avoid dealing with them. Well, until now, apparently.

Allison's eyes narrowed, then darkened even more. That was never a good sign. She wasn't even bothering to try to disguise her anger. She stood abruptly and stalked to the other side of the room, the tension rising off her wire-tight body in palpable waves. She stopped and put her hands on her hips but didn't turn around.

My heart dropped into my stomach, and a trickle of cold seeped into my now seemingly vacant chest. I hated it when Allison was upset with me. It made me almost physically ill. I swallowed hard against the bile rising in my throat and waited.

"That was really stupid, Ryan," she muttered, toneless.

"Excuse me?" Of all the things I'd been expecting to come out of her mouth, that wasn't even close.

"I can't believe you'd do something so reckless."

A spark of anger flared inside me, and I shot to my feet, refusing to have this discussion sitting down. She was calling me an idiot, and I was hurt she had so little faith in me, in my abilities as an agent. She was making it sound like this was a task I'd undertaken as a lark, without thought, and had rushed headlong into with little or no forethought.

Believe me, I knew the consequences all too well. Not a day went by that I wasn't terrified I was going to screw something up and someone else was going to end up dead. Only someone who'd already been responsible for someone else's death could fully appreciate that kind of horror. The fear gnawed in my belly, the back of my throat, behind my eyes. I was never rid of it. Ever. And the cold realization that she considered me the type of person who didn't think about those things, especially after everything that'd happened in my not-so-distant past, almost crippled me.

"I'm taking all the necessary precautions," I shot back, my voice flinty and hard. I was trying to contain my anger. And failing. Badly.

I might as well have not even spoken for all the attention she was paying to me. She turned back around, facing in my direction, but she wouldn't look at me. Her facial expression was distant and colored with a hint of something I couldn't place.

"I've got to stop this before you get yourself killed," she muttered under her breath, moving toward the desk where her cell phone sat.

I let out a short laugh, but it was bitter and completely devoid of humor. She didn't trust me, didn't think me capable, and that knowledge almost destroyed me. But she didn't know that the past several weeks spent undercover had taught me a great deal about how to control my emotions and continue to think somewhat rationally, even in the most trying situations. I'd been unable to do that when she and I had been together before, but I'd practiced since then, and those hard-learned lessons were coming in handy now.

"What?" I scoffed, my own mood just shy of furious. "You're going to call someone now? At this hour?"

Allison froze, her hand halfway stretched toward her phone, and fixed me with a murderous glare. I could see the anger in her eyes, and the sight of it fanned the ardent flames of my own.

"Who?" I asked, sarcasm dripping from my voice in heavy, poisonous drabs. "Who are you going to call? What boss can you possibly think you have wrapped that tightly around your little finger that you—a mere thirteen—can have me yanked out of an undercover investigation ongoing for more than a month?"

Allison opened her mouth, but I was on a roll and sharply waved my hand.

"What are you going to say, Allison?" I demanded, my tone brittle to the point of breaking. "Huh? To this boss that you're going to dictate how to do his job? What? That I just *happened* to swing by your hotel room at three o'clock in the morning for a visit and told you the whole sordid tale? Oh, yeah." I sounded derisive now, and biting. "That'll go over well."

Allison's eyes narrowed again, and she folded her arms across her chest and cocked her hip, two sure signs she was pissed. "I plan to point out what someone should have long ago: that you're not qualified to do this."

Something inside me snapped. Not just broke but shattered. The raw fury welling up inside me was making it difficult to see, and if I didn't get out of there soon, I was going to say or do something I'd never be able to take back. Something I'd regret.

"I can do this," I snarled at her. "I *have* been doing this. You should remember that before you start making your calls and trying to torpedo my career. I'm blond, Allison. But I'm not an idiot."

Jaw clenched against my burgeoning rage, I stalked past her toward the door. I didn't even have it in me to argue with her anymore. Girlfriend or not, I didn't need to justify my actions. And she had no business making me feel as though I did.

Allison managed to grab my wrist as I brushed past her. "Where the hell are you going?" she demanded, the hollowness of her voice bleeding away to reveal a burning irritation of her own.

Beyond livid, I jerked my arm out of her grasp with a force I wouldn't have thought possible and kept walking, pausing only long enough to snatch my coat and hat off the floor as I went. I donned them with sharp, erratic motions and ripped the door open. I was seething. It was past time for me to go.

"Ryan," Allison called out after me one more time.

Without a word, I exited her room on a tidal wave of righteous anger and slammed the door behind me, not bothering to look back.

CHAPTER THREE

Though my anger had lessened by the time I finally made it back to the studio apartment Tate and I "shared" in the West Village, it still bore a razor-sharp edge, and it took all my shaky self-control not to slam that door, too. I forced myself to shut it like a normal human and sagged against it, struggling to calm down.

"I was wondering where you'd gone." Tate's quiet voice cut through the darkness.

I jumped. I couldn't help it. "Jesus, Tate!" Adrenaline spiked through me so fast it bordered on painful. "You scared the shit out of me."

My eyes were slowly adjusting to the darkness, and through the dim gloom accented by the faint glow of streetlights outside the window, I could just see the outline of his shape half propped up in the king-sized bed that took up most of the room. If the lights had been on, I'd have been able to tell that his hair was a shambles, which made me smile a little as some more of the anger ebbed out of me.

"Sorry," Tate whispered, truly sounding like he was. I heard the rustle of sheets against skin as he shifted on the bed.

"It's okay," I murmured. I took a deep breath and sighed, tossing aside my hat and running my fingers through my own hair. I kicked my shoes off and divested myself of my jacket, which I dropped onto the floor, too exhausted, both physically and emotionally, to pretend to be neat. Relieved, I scrambled onto the bed still dressed and sank into the pillows with a sigh.

"No, it isn't," Tate breathed, his voice tinged with something I'd never heard from him before. He'd changed out of the clothes he'd been wearing earlier, which indicated that he'd been up for a while.

"Tate." I sighed again, closing my eyes and allowing the tension to seep out of me bit by agonizingly slow bit. "It's fine."

He turned onto his side and propped his head up on his elbow, looking down at me. I couldn't see his face clearly in the gloom, but I did notice his serious expression. My heart stopped, and an almost overwhelming desire to beg him to hold back whatever words were about to come out of his mouth next nearly consumed me.

"Not that," Tate said, rolling his eyes and looking annoyed.

"Then what?" I asked, not at all sure I wanted to know. I folded my hands together on my stomach and crossed my legs at the ankles.

Tate averted his gaze and looked a little embarrassed. "For what happened at the bar," he murmured, his voice so low, I almost couldn't hear it. And at this confession, his face crumpled, and he appeared faintly miserable.

I frowned, trying to determine what he was talking about. Any and all thoughts I had regarding the bar that evening were wrapped up in Allison's sudden, unexpected appearance, so I was having trouble figuring out what he meant.

"Forget it," I told him after a moment, unable to come up with anything he needed to apologize for.

"No." Tate caught my gaze for the briefest of moments before looking away. "You're a Secret Service agent and my partner. You deserve better than to have me mauling you in public the way I did." He took a deep breath, studying the sheet next to my arm with more interest than it warranted as he went on. "I'd blame it on the fact that I was drunk, but that's really no excuse. I'm sorry. It won't happen again."

The light went on in my Allison-addled little brain, and I couldn't contain my laugh. "Oh, Tate, don't worry about it. It's not a big deal."

"I'm glad you find it funny," he grumbled. "I feel like an idiot. I mean, you could have me arrested for sexual assault for what I did."

I shrugged and rolled my shoulders, bobbing my foot. "We're supposed to be a couple. Everyone expects that kind of stuff. It's not like we haven't done it before." And that was true. We'd been known on occasion to hang all over each other to keep up appearances. It'd never been an issue. I was having trouble deciphering why it'd be one now.

"I've never taken it that far before," Tate said quietly. "I mean, not when…I shouldn't have done it. I'm sorry."

I pursed my lips and focused on the ceiling as I considered his words. It was true that I hadn't been happy about what he'd done while he was doing it, and a part of me had wondered whether decking him would've blown our cover. But while his behavior hadn't been right, given the situation we were in and the fact that we had so many more important things to focus on, maybe getting wrapped around the axle about it wasn't my best plan. Besides, he had apologized, and he'd sounded sincere. Once was a mistake, and I could let it go. If he did it again, we'd have an issue. But I'd cross that bridge if and when I came to it.

"Apology accepted," I told him.

Tate's face split into a grin of his own, and I thought I saw a sparkle in his eyes. "Yeah?"

I nodded once, my own smile widening to the point that I felt the pull on my split lip. "Yeah. No worries." Hmm. Was my downplaying the issue contributing to the overall problem? I rubbed my eyes, too tired to really think about it.

Tate's face darkened, and he reached out to touch my lip. I beat him to it, making sure my own hand got there long before his did. I glanced at my fingers and frowned when I noted the faint dark smudge of blood. I darted my tongue out to lick the rest of it away, and, damn it, I blushed. Thank goodness he couldn't see that reaction in the darkness. At least I didn't think he could.

"So," Tate drawled, gazing directly into my eyes. "Are you going to tell me what that was all about?"

I sighed again and rolled onto my side. I was so tired. I didn't want to talk or share. I'd never been one to open up and spill my problems to people I barely knew, and I wasn't likely to start being that sort of person now. I just wanted to close my eyes and sleep for about a week.

"Alex," Tate whispered.

My eyes shot open at the soft sound of his voice, and I realized I'd been drifting off. I huffed and rolled my head so I could glance at the clock. "What time are we expected to make an appearance tomorrow?" I wanted to know.

"Not till after eight," he replied, his voice still low. "But you have to go to the shop first, don't you?"

I said nothing and closed my eyes. I was trying—unsuccessfully, it would seem—to get a handle on the eddying emotions that were agitating my frayed nerves. Tears stung my eyes, and I swallowed, trying to dislodge the lump forming in my throat. Of all the times for Allison to make a resurgence, now was the worst one possible. I always had that kind of luck.

The bed moved as Tate shifted his weight, and my urge to cry gained strength. I was always more emotional when I was tired.

"You never talk about yourself," Tate said quietly, sounding almost hurt at the notion. "About your life outside of this."

Surprised, I glanced at his face, taken aback by his expression.

I'd never known Tate to be so serious. I shrugged, still not willing to capitulate, though I don't think I could have articulated why. Not exactly.

"That can't be true," I murmured.

Tate half grinned and raised an eyebrow. "It is true," he insisted. "I only know that you're a Secret Service agent because my handler told me. Not you." That last phrase was almost accusatory, as though he felt I owed him.

Anger flared in me again, white hot and painful, but I managed to quell it. Barely. A small part of me knew he was right. Oh, I sure as hell hated to admit it even to myself and would never tell him out loud, no matter how much he deserved to hear the words. But I didn't open myself up to him. Not ever.

I didn't know anybody who'd ever been deep cover before. Allison had been right when she'd pointed out that our agency didn't do that sort of work. As far as I knew, we didn't. Some people did regular undercover work. I had on occasion. But it was quick. In and out in a matter of hours. This, where you lived the part twenty-four-seven for days, weeks, months on end without cessation in sight, was unheard of in my world. I didn't know the rules of interaction between partners, so I made up my own as I went along. Story of my life, apparently.

"Isn't it better if you don't know?" I asked. "Less to have to deny or pretend if our cover is ever compromised."

Tate made a small noise in the back of his throat, but to his credit, he didn't push the issue. "You know her," he said after a time.

At his words, my heart stopped, and a coldness began to spread throughout my chest and toward my limbs. When my heart did finally start beating again, it was racing, and my face was on fire.

"Who?" I asked, knowing full well my hesitation had given me away.

"Alex," Tate said, the hint of a disapproving frown on his handsome face.

"Was it that obvious?" I wanted to know.

Tate lifted one shoulder. "There was something in your eyes…" He looked at me almost expectantly.

My breath hitched. "Do you think anyone else noticed?"

Tate shook his head, and some stray tresses of dark hair fell across his forehead. "Nah. You shut it down pretty fast. Besides, they were all looking at her initially, not at you."

I wanted to feel relief at his words but couldn't. If he'd noticed it, chances were somebody else had. *Fuck.* I pressed the heels of my trembling hands hard against my eyes. What the hell was I going to do? My all-consuming fear roared inside my chest, making it hard for me to breathe.

As if in answer to my unspoken question, my cell phone vibrated from its place on the nightstand. Frowning, Tate and I looked at one another. I flicked another glance toward the clock on the cable box on the other side of the room. It was well past four in the morning.

"You expecting a call?" Tate asked, his gaze fixed firmly on my buzzing cell phone.

My frown deepened as I shook my head. "No."

"Maybe it's that woman," Tate suggested. He obviously borderline disapproved of the possibility that I'd given Allison the number to my throw-down phone. His tone said it all.

"No way," I told him, annoyed that he might have believed I'd jeopardize the mission as well as our safety. A wave of guilt buried my irritation as it occurred to me that going to see Allison to begin with had done just that. "She doesn't have this number."

"Hmm," Tate murmured, returning his attention to me now that my phone had gone silent. "Text," he mused aloud.

I continued to stare at the phone for a bit, as though if I only concentrated hard enough, it'd grow legs and rush over to the bed and into my hand. It didn't. And so, with a deep exhale of weariness and exasperation, as though I had to scale the Alps to reach it, I rolled over onto my side and fished it from the nightstand with my fingertips.

A small noise escaped the back of my throat as I settled back and pressed the button on the side to wake it, wincing slightly as the brightness of the little screen accosted my eyes. The number the text message originated from was displayed clearly, and I felt a sudden pressure in my chest. The number didn't come with an identifier attached, which only meant one person. As if things weren't already complicated enough.

"Who is it?" Tate asked, leaning near to get a peek. As my partner and the one person in this world with whom I spent more time than any other, he knew a text at this hour could mean only two things. Either someone from our little gang wanted something—which, given the state of the group when we'd left, was unlikely—or it was work. He wasn't being nosy, just trying to gauge exactly how worried he needed to be. Unfortunately, I couldn't answer that question for him. Not yet.

"It's Rico," I told him, a slight rush of fear arcing through me.

"Oh." Tate exhaled.

Rico was my handler. Sort of. Well, except we didn't really have handlers. But he was the only person in the Secret Service with whom I was allowed to have any contact until this whole thing was wrapped up and I was permitted to resurface and rejoin regular life, so it was close enough. And what contact we did have was rare, at best. That I was getting a text message from him at this hour completely out of the blue after not having heard from him in over two weeks wasn't a good sign. My heart started hammering.

"What did he say?"

I read and reread the message, frowning, feeling the slight ache in my lip again as it pulled against the cut. The message was vague, cryptic, and it was designed to be. In the event I lost my phone or someone picked it up and read a message before I could erase it, it was supposed to appear to be gibberish. A string of numbers that could mean anything or nothing, depending on who was looking.

I blinked and read again. 621 191 120 1000 1.

The 621 identified him as the sender. June 21 was his birthday and an easy enough number for me to remember. The 191 meant it was an emergency. That was supposed to look more innocuous than the more traditional 911. Personally, I hadn't thought anyone would be fooled by that ploy, but no one had felt inclined to listen to me. 120 was the street address to one of five empty, undercover office buildings we utilized in Manhattan. 1000 was a report time, and the 1 meant today.

I thumbed the power button to turn off the display and clenched the phone, feeling so many conflicting emotions that I was paralyzed under their onslaught. In a vain attempt to regain self-control, I took a deep breath, counting to ten slowly as I inhaled and then repeating the count as I exhaled. It helped. Somewhat. But not enough.

"I have to go in tomorrow," I told him, my voice hollow, flat. The irony of my empty tone wasn't lost on me as my raging feelings teemed and swirled in my gut, making me nauseous. "Today," I said after a moment. I closed my eyes, determined to end the discussion and get some sleep.

Tate sucked in a sharp breath. "And he's just telling you about it now? He couldn't have mentioned it at a more reasonable hour?"

"Apparently not."

"Why do you have to go in at all? What could've possibly happened to require your presence at the last minute like this?"

My lip twitched, though I couldn't say whether it was from fury or because I was about to burst into tears. I clenched my jaw to make the quivering stop. And even though his questions were rhetorical, I felt compelled to respond to them anyway.

"Some people just have to have the last word."

CHAPTER FOUR

At ten o'clock the next morning I strode into the lobby of the building where we rented a largely unused office, all full of piss and vinegar. What little sleep I'd managed to snag had been fitful at best and had served only to fuel my anger at the entire situation. Couple that with the complicated evasive maneuvers I always took when I reported in to ensure no one would be able to follow me should they even be inclined to do so, and I was ready to spit nails.

Something of my mood undoubtedly showed on my face because Rico, who was waiting for me at the elevator bank, took one look at me and immediately adopted an expression that always preceded him giving me a whole ration of shit. For some reason I'd never been able to determine, he'd long ago decided the best way to counteract my sour moods was to irritate me until I broke out of them. I was even less inclined to indulge him today than usual.

"Hey, Ace. You look terrible. Rough night?"

I lifted my chin once in a sort of half-assed imitation of the PPD nod. "Something like that."

My tone sounded sharp, staccato, even to me, and I felt a brief stab of remorse for my behavior. It wasn't Rico's fault we were here. I'd do well to remember that.

"Aww. Poor baby. It must be tough hanging out with your new friends at the bar all the time and getting paid to do it."

"Shut up."

"Whoa. Who pissed in your Cheerios this morning?"

I shot him a look meant to wither, but he didn't even blink.

He grinned at me in that way he'd once drunkenly admitted he thought was charming, but his grin faded when he noticed it was having no effect on me. His gaze flicked toward the main door to the lobby, and his expression fell even farther. He opened his mouth as if to say something and then closed it again. Indecision warred with discretion in his dark eyes. It was obvious he had something to get off his chest—something he knew I wasn't going to like—but nothing was coming out.

Completely robbed of all semblance of patience, I brushed past him and pushed the button for the elevator, hitching my huge black shoulder bag higher with one hand as I brushed some dust off my suit jacket with the other. The faint jingling inside of some of the more outlandish jewelry I normally wore as part of this assignment accompanied the motion, serving to remind me once again why I was there. As if I could forget.

The elevator doors slid open, and Rico and I stepped inside. He obviously had something big on his mind, but I wasn't in the mood to drag it out of him. I dug in my bag to make sure all my various piercings were present and accounted for as the doors started to slide closed.

"Hold the elevator," someone called out, slightly breathless.

I fumed at the delay as Rico stuck his arm out to stop the doors from closing but didn't raise my head. I did, however, take a step back to make room for the newcomer.

"Thanks," she said as she hopped on.

The sound of that voice finally penetrated my awareness as I caught a faint hint of a very familiar perfume and froze. I seemed to be moving in slow motion as I looked up, only to confirm what my heart already knew.

Allison, clad in a tailored black business suit over a crisp, white, collared shirt, stood three feet away from me looking gorgeous. My heart stuttered. She was facing straight ahead, clearly ignoring me, and from what I could see of her face, her mood perfectly matched my own. Desire and fury battled with one another, anxiety and guilt watching silently in the wings. It was a bloody skirmish to be sure, and I'd have been hard pressed to say who won.

"Good morning, AT Reynolds," Rico said. His voice was soft, and though the greeting was directed at Allison, he looked at me as he said it and flashed an apologetic smile as I gaped at him.

My mind reeled as I struggled to process his words. AT. As in ATSAIC. As in boss. Allison had been promoted. Realization clicked inside my head loud enough that it drowned out the other emotions clamoring for attention, if only briefly, and the pit of my stomach felt suddenly hollow. Now I knew why Allison was back in New York, a fact I hadn't had much time to consider the previous evening, what with the initial sighting and the kissing and the fighting and all.

Oh. Shit.

I was so screwed.

The doors to the elevator slid open once again, and Allison stepped off, radiating determination and purpose, her stride swift and sure. I stared after her for a moment, my annoyance taking a back seat to my incredulity and embarrassment. I followed her at a much slower pace and turned to look at Rico, hoping for answers.

"I'm sorry," he whispered as we trailed in Allison's irritated wake. "I was hoping I'd have time to warn you." He ran an absent hand through his brown hair—a sure sign he was nervous—and pursed his lips. He eyed me as though waiting for me to explode.

An icy feeling of dread had seized my heart, spreading rapidly throughout the rest of my body. I ran one hand through my own hair, feeling nervous myself, and took a deep breath.

"She's the new boss of the squad, isn't she?" But I didn't really need to ask. I already knew the answer.

Rico nodded. "Yeah. She is. Well, my squad, not yours. Are you okay?"

I sighed and tried to smile, but the expression probably looked twisted and grotesque. I touched his arm, trying to offer comfort I didn't feel. "I'm fine."

Rico gave me one last look of sympathy and led the way into the office, where our meeting was to take place.

The building we were sitting in was sort of a drop house used for private meetings or front businesses for undercover operations. It was never meant to function as a real office. As such, it was furnished sparsely, unfortunately for me. I had nothing to look at, nothing to focus my attention on, except Allison.

Well, that wasn't entirely true. The Special Agent in Charge of the New York Field Office, Ben Flannigan, was present as well, and I could've looked at him, but it didn't seem like a very good idea. My feelings toward him were even more confusing than my feelings toward Allison, and I really didn't want to get into any of that at present.

"Agent O'Connor," SAIC Flannigan said, his low, even baritone washing over me and making me scowl. His dark hair was brushed back off his forehead, and his moss-green eyes were piercing as he took us all in. Clearly, the man missed nothing.

I settled myself across from the desk behind which he sat and bobbed my head in reply. I had to force myself to address him, and the single word I spoke in acknowledgment was clipped and curt. "Sir."

Allison had sat next to him, making it a point to keep all her attention focused on a file in her lap, presumably so she wouldn't have to make eye contact with me, but who the hell knew? I had conflicting emotions about her even being there, to say nothing of the fact that she had yet to acknowledge my presence in any way. God, this was going to be a fun meeting.

"Agent Corazon," SAIC Flannigan said.

Rico made a low reply and took the last empty chair in the room, to my immediate left. He sat uncharacteristically still. I knew he respected SAIC Flannigan a great deal and figured his sudden bout of self-control was due to a burning desire to either make a good impression or call no undue attention to himself. If I were in a different frame of mind, I'd likely have thought that was adorable and smirked at the idea.

"Ladies and gentleman," SAIC Flannigan said, rolling a gold Cross pen between his fingers, "I'll make this brief. I have a teleconference with headquarters in an hour, and I need to get back to the office." He took a deep breath, and out of the corner of my eyes, I could see the look he gave me. His expression seemed speculative for an instant before he recovered himself.

"Agent O'Connor, Agent Corazon, you both know AT Allison Reynolds. AT Reynolds is now in charge of the Counterfeit Squad, which means she is now part of your direct chain of command. If any issues arise in the course of your operation, I want her notified ASAP."

I felt a pronounced flutter in my stomach as the boss uttered those words, but I tried hard to ignore it and even harder to keep my unease from showing on my face. I had no way to know whether it was working.

The SAIC continued without missing a beat. "Agent O'Connor, your protocol for this operation will not change. All communications, apart from extreme emergencies and exigent circumstances, will come to this office through Agent Corazon. Agent Corazon will assume the responsibility for keeping AT Reynolds in the loop and up to speed on what's happening."

The SAIC stood then and placed his hands palms down on the desk, which, although it might look as though it were a move of intimidation, I knew he actually did to stretch his forearms out. He glanced from Rico to Allison to me, his gaze almost stern. "Agent O'Connor."

"Sir." I sounded like a petulant teenager, which only made me angrier.

"Are you expected to report in today?" He was talking about my undercover identity, and we both knew it.

"Yes, sir. At fourteen-hundred."

SAIC Flannigan nodded once as though satisfied and moved out from behind the desk. "Agent Corazon, begin briefing AT Reynolds about the operation thus far. Agent O'Connor, if you'd walk me to the elevator bank."

Both Allison and Rico glanced at me then, and surprise showed in the eyes of both of them, but I didn't have time to comment, as the boss had already strode out of the room. With a dark glower, I got up to follow, barely refraining from slamming the door to the office behind me.

SAIC Flannigan was waiting for me in the hall. He took a moment to let his concerned gaze sweep over me. "How're you doing?" he asked. He turned and began to slowly saunter toward the elevator.

I shrugged with one shoulder and kept pace with him. "Fine, sir."

His expression—what I could see of it out of the corner of my eyes—was dubious, and I surmised that my carefully constructed façade had cracked. "You sure?"

"Yes, sir."

SAIC Flannigan sighed and fiddled with the end of his tie. Indecision was flitting behind his eyes, which made me uneasy and also irrationally furious. He and I hadn't talked very much since the night I'd slid my badge across a table to him and told him the job wasn't worth the aggravation. In fact, I think the only conversation we'd had in the interim had been the one where he'd pointed out to me how bad it looked for me to quit right on the heels of Walker's death.

On that occasion, he'd suggested that I at least stick it out until the NYPD finished their murder investigation to ensure I'd be scoped by the agency. I'd gone undercover not long after that and hadn't spoken to him since. I certainly didn't want to get into any of that now. I still had to deal with Allison. I doubted I could handle arguing with both of them back to back. Not with as little sleep as I had under my belt.

"Really, Ryan? You're still angry with me?"

I glared at him murderously. Clearly, he had no compunction about getting into this now. And being forced into this conversation against my will only inflated my ire. My chest heavy and tight, I struggled not to tell him off. "With all due respect, I don't really see how that's relevant. Sir."

He sighed, and I felt the teensiest prick of remorse. The "sir" had been intended to wound, and it'd hit the mark.

"I wish you'd try to see this from my point of view," he said softly, looking sad.

I ground my teeth together to keep from blurting out his oft-uttered adage about wishing and continued to glare at the floor in front of me. How fucking dare he? Why the hell did he think it was appropriate for him to demand that I see things from his point of view when he seemed so determined not to even consider mine? Since the whole Walker incident, he had been acting like a supervisor, and that was the last thing I'd needed from him.

After a long moment, he sighed again and held up a hand, looking resigned. "Okay. Let's talk about something that is relevant, then. Is this going to be a problem for you?"

I looked at him darkly, unsure what he was getting at. "Is what going to be a problem for me?"

We'd reached the elevator bank, but he didn't push the button, instead opting to turn and face me. The disquiet in his eyes was almost heartbreaking. Or it would've been if I weren't still so furious with him for adopting the agency's pretend-like-nothing-had-happened attitude when it came to all the people around me getting hurt because my fellow agents had dropped numerous metaphorical balls left and right. I tried not to scowl like a petulant child but apparently didn't manage it very well.

He took a deep breath, and his hand twitched like he wanted to touch me but had thought better of it. "If I push to have her reassigned," he said quietly, "people will talk. But I'll do it. If you ask me to."

I chuckled rather bitterly under my breath at the notion that he'd do anything simply because I asked for it. He hadn't seemed so inclined several weeks prior, when headquarters had decreed we wouldn't be giving any formal statements regarding any of the events that'd led us here. "People talk anyway. Nothing any of us can do about that."

"Do you want me to reassign her?"

I shook my head. "No. It wouldn't really matter anyway. She isn't technically *my* boss. She's the boss of the squad working this case. And once the case is over and I resume my regular duties in PI, whatever conflict of interest we might have will be resolved."

"You're sure."

I inhaled a long, slow breath to give myself a moment to collect my thoughts. "I'm sure."

A small smile touched the corners of his mouth then. "Stubborn," he said lightly. "Just like your mother."

Part of me resented his attempt to bridge the chasm between us by throwing my mom into the mix, but most of me was curious about how the rest of my family was faring. The second most difficult part of this assignment for me had been having absolutely no contact with my siblings or my mom.

"How is she?"

He grinned, his whole face lighting up as it always did whenever my mother was the topic of conversation. The bittersweet pressure in my chest increased. He really loved her, and we were all pretty damn lucky despite his tendency to be a complete ass where the job was concerned.

"She's fine. Pissed as hell at me for letting you do this, but she understands. More or less. She made me promise to tell you she loves you and to remind you to eat enough and get enough rest. She wants you to call when you can but understands you may not be able to. Though I suspect you have a whole lot of Irish guilt headed your way once this is over."

I rolled my eyes. Who the hell was he kidding? He hadn't *let* me do anything. I'd just charged ahead and thrown myself into the assignment without giving any of the bosses a chance to say anything about it. But the argument that was sure to ensue on the heels of me pointing that fact out to him wasn't worth the time it'd take to have.

Instead, I said, "I love her, too. Please tell her for me."

Dad nodded and finally pushed the button to call the elevator. "Of course." He reached into the pocket of his suit and brought out a plain white envelope, which he handed to me. "That's from Rory. She misses you terribly. She's less understanding than your mother in regard to this assignment. Although I suppose that's to be expected."

"Thanks." I regarded the envelope, nearly buckling under a whole slew of conflicting emotions on the heels of the announcement. "I guess that means she's back, then."

I tried to keep my tone casual, but my voice broke on the last word, giving away my dismay. I continued to stare at the envelope as though it could help me work through the crippling betrayal I was experiencing. It remained silent. Go figure.

"She got back about two weeks ago. She was pretty upset you weren't around to welcome her home."

"Well, isn't that a coincidence?" I spat bitterly, unable to stop myself from spewing the words. "Seeing as how I was pretty upset when she took off without so much as a word in the first place."

I kept my head down and my eyes fixed resolutely on the envelope in my hands as I crumpled it in my fists. I wasn't sure whether I was embarrassed by my outburst or whether I was just trying to avoid continuing this conversation. I bit my lower lip as I shoved the letter into my pocket and out of sight. Would that I could stow my feelings that easily.

The most difficult part of this assignment had been dealing with the guilt I'd been feeling and convincing myself I hadn't completely abandoned Rory when she'd needed me the most. The notion that I might have kept me up many nights, although the rest of the nights I remained awake because I was fuming over Rory's timely disappearing act. After all these weeks of back and forth, I wasn't sure I was all that eager to see what my twin sister had written.

Dad either didn't notice my emotional turmoil or chose not to comment on it. The elevator doors opened, and he stepped into the car to depart. "Be careful, Ryan."

"Always." I gave him a nod before turning to head back to the office.

CHAPTER FIVE

I took a moment to collect myself before returning to the room where Rico and Allison were busy reviewing the basics of the case. The letter from Rory had brought a whole host of unpleasant emotions to the forefront of my mind and was burning a hole in my pocket. I had to force myself not to rip it open and read it right there in the hallway. Only the knowledge that whatever my sister had to say would likely make me more upset than I already was stayed my hand. I took a deep breath and let myself back into the office.

Allison and Rico both turned to look at me, and for an instant, I thought I knew what a deer caught in the headlights must feel like. The awkward moment stretched taut to the point of breaking, and I fought to maintain a neutral expression as I took one of the empty seats in front of the desk.

Allison's gaze lingered on me for an impossibly long moment before she finally returned her attention to Rico, who was standing in front of the dry-erase board that took up the majority of one wall. I followed Allison's gaze and raised an eyebrow at the scribbles, circles, and lines that covered the board. After slumping back into my chair, I laced my fingers together over my stomach as I attempted to figure out where in the explanation of the case Rico was.

Rico hesitated for another long moment, staring at me as though seeking permission to continue. I gave him a slight nod, and he cleared his throat and returned his uncapped marker to one of the circles on the board.

"I was just explaining to AT Reynolds how we got to all the key players."

I nodded and attempted to pretend that Allison's mere presence wasn't wrecking my already threadbare nerves and that I wasn't watching her out of the corner of one eye.

"Thank you, Agent Corazon," Allison said. "I'd like Agent O'Connor to continue, please."

I snapped my head in her direction so quickly I felt a twinge and tried not to frown. "What?"

Allison regarded me coolly. It drove me batshit crazy that she was so easily able to pretend I was just another agent, and she knew it. I suspected that's why she did it half the time, but I didn't think calling her out on it in front of Rico was such a great idea. He knew we were together—it wasn't exactly a secret at this point—but that didn't mean I was comfortable getting into a knock-down drag-out in his presence. I hastened to do some damage control.

"I'm sorry. I wasn't sure I heard you correctly. You want me to continue?"

Allison pushed her chair back from the desk just enough to cross her legs. She sat back and rested her hands on the arms of the chair, still maintaining eye contact with me. Rico might as well not have even come to the meeting for all the attention we were paying him.

"Yes, please. I want to make sure you understand all the subtle nuances of the investigation. Seeing as how you're so embroiled in it."

I stared at her hard, torn between smirking and snapping. In the end, I settled for nodding. Rising, I took the marker from a very uneasy-looking Rico and motioned for him to sit down. I slowly replaced the cap and set it on the edge of the board before retrieving a laser pointer from my suit pocket. Sure, I carried it around only so I could annoy people with it and make fun shapes on the ground when I was bored, but no one needed to know that.

When I turned back around, both Allison and Rico were watching me, one appearing expectant, the other seeming sympathetic. I don't think I need to tell you which was which.

"From the beginning?" I asked Allison, already knowing the answer.

She nodded. "Please."

"Okay." I glanced at the board and frowned at some of the more cryptic scribbles. When I glared at Rico, he shrugged. Rolling my eyes, I put the laser pointer back into my pocket and grabbed the eraser. I took my time wiping the board clean, as much to irritate Allison as to give myself time to make sure I had all the facts of the case well in hand. It wouldn't do me any good to appear hesitant or uncertain. I needed to show her that I knew what I was doing.

Once the board was clear, I grabbed the marker and prepared to write, angling myself so I was facing her as much as possible. I wanted to be able to see her as I talked and anticipate any inevitable questions or concerns, so I could address them before she voiced them. As stoic as she was, it wouldn't be easy, but I had to try.

"Okay," I said as I wrote. "The investigation began several months ago when the ATF received a tip from a cooperating defendant that a group here in the city was putting out feelers in an attempt to get their hands on large caches of automatic weapons." I underlined the "CD" I'd written on the board, underscored it with a downward-pointing arrow, and dropped my arm.

"Further investigation on the part of the ATF revealed that the group goes by the name the True American Patriots. They call themselves TAP, or tappers for short." I added the group's acronym underneath the arrow. "They feel as though the government has grossly failed the American people, especially in regard to immigrants. They don't think they should have to pay taxes to support programs that provide interpreters in local schools or implement signage in the city in any other language except English. They object to the idea of immigrants who haven't completed the citizenship process being given driver's licenses or the right to vote—"

"I didn't think non-citizens could vote," Allison said.

"They can't."

Allison's brow furrowed, and I could almost see her trying to make sense of that complete nonsense. "Then why do they…?"

I shrugged. "Now you see part of the problem. They're making up things to be angry about and building a platform on misinformation. They've also recommended some sort of pregnancy test requirement— at airports maybe? it's unclear—to prevent pregnant women who're citizens of other countries from flying here at all and that tourist or visitor visas should be limited to a month to prevent women who aren't visibly pregnant from coming here and giving birth to so-called anchor babies. I guess in case they manage to fool or completely avoid their airport pregnancy test? I don't know. Basically, they're ethnocentric and want everyone who isn't already a citizen deported."

Allison's expression never changed, although she did tilt her head slightly, several locks of hair falling across her forehead. "Interesting. And?"

I had to force myself to concentrate on her words and not get completely distracted by how beautiful she looked. "In addition to their intolerance of other cultures, they're also pretty intolerant of other religions. Well, no. That's not strictly true. Other Christian religions don't seem to pose a problem for them, nor do Judaism, Hinduism, or Buddhism. At least not that we've seen. It's basically Islam they take issue with. They think the country's 'capitulation,'" I made air quotes with my fingers, "to certain specific…'outlandish' tenets of the religion will bring about the fall of the nation."

"Outlandish?"

"Their word choice, not mine, and their distorted point of view. They strongly object to any of the religious practices that they consider at odds with the standards and laws of this country. Fact or fiction doesn't seem to bother them. They've complained about states allowing Muslim women to have their driver's license pictures taken while wearing the full burka because they say that completely negates the purpose behind picture IDs. They're upset that places have been fined or reprimanded and directed not to advertise that they sell pork or have up pictures of cartoon pigs because Muslims are offended. I don't think that actually happened here, to be fair, but they're insisting that it happened somewhere in the world, and they're still citing it. They're outraged because they claim that mosques are ignoring noise ordinances so they can broadcast their call to prayer. The tipping point for them seemed to be the case where a Muslim man groomed and raped a preteen girl and wasn't prosecuted because he cited the customs of his religion's teachings as well as the fact that his behavior is completely acceptable where he comes from because he was taught that women are worthless and therefore he couldn't be expected to treat the girl with any respect."

Now Allison's expression did change. Her eyebrows rose, and she appeared appalled. "Did that really happen?"

I sighed. "Yeah. That one actually is true. I didn't believe it either until I researched it. It was pretty messed up. But it also didn't happen in the US, so—"

"Where did it happen?"

"Nottingham in the UK, in like 2013. But I guess they feel like it's only a matter of time before it happens here? I'd like to point out all the straight white men who get what amounts to a slap on the wrist or less for similar behaviors, but I suspect that wouldn't go over well."

Allison scowled and waved a hand at me to continue.

"So, anyway, I guess these guys decided to arm themselves for the holy war they think is coming. Or rather for the one they'd like to start. They'd been buying guns off the dealer the ATF popped a few months back—nothing too crazy, just unregistered handguns, the type anyone could find at a gun show, just with illegal magazines—and recently started feeling him out to see if he could get them something a little more powerful."

"Such as?"

"They'll take anything. AR-15s. M-4s. They don't seem particularly interested in MP-5s, but I heard they were talking about trying to score some P-90s the other day. They definitely want to get their hands on some grenade launchers and anti-aircraft guns."

"Holy shit," Rico whispered.

Allison's expression had darkened even further, probably because I'd basically just confirmed her worst fears about me getting myself killed. She pursed her lips and tapped the arms of the chair as she appeared to consider that statement.

I hesitated. Should I divulge the next part? Well, no sense in trying to hide it, right? Besides, she'd find out anyway at some point and then be rightfully pissed at me for not telling her. "Nothing concrete has been decided just yet, but there's been some talk of a preemptive strike."

"A preemptive strike on what?" Allison's tone was sharp.

"Mosques in the area, I think. I'm not positive." I shrugged. "Like I said, it's just talk. And I'm not far enough into the inner circle yet that they get into those kinds of things in front of me. What little they do divulge is veiled innuendo, some of which I get, some of which gets translated for me later."

"Jesus Christ."

"Yeah. It's not good."

Allison blew a quick breath out one side of her mouth, utilizing the puff of air to move the stray wisps of hair from her forehead. She tipped her head back and stared at the ceiling. Her eyes held a faraway cast, and I glanced to Rico, who merely grimaced.

"How did we get involved?" Allison asked.

"Oh. Well, they believe they shouldn't have to waste their hard-earned money funding this operation. They've recently begun to try their hand at counterfeiting as a way to raise some much-needed capital, but their product is piss-poor. I'm not sure if that means they're thinking about paying for their guns with counterfeit. I hope not." I couldn't imagine the gun dealers would take too kindly to that, and while I wasn't positive how they'd show their displeasure, I suspected it'd be in a very messy way.

"Can't we just arrest them for the counterfeiting so far?"

I shook my head. "They haven't done nearly enough to get any real time. The AUSA wants to be able to hammer them. He'd like to be able to catch them purchasing guns, and he wants taped evidence of them talking about whatever they plan to use them for. Since their contact was arrested, they obviously haven't done any business with him, but they have yet to find a new supplier, so we're kind of stuck on that score as well. And the AUSA doesn't think the testimony of a cooperating defendant will carry enough weight to be able to put too many of this group away for a significant period of time."

"Hmm." Allison drummed her fingers on the arms of her chair. "And how did you get involved?"

"I'm sorry?"

"What's your connection to the operation? How did you come to be undercover?"

"Oh." I glanced at Rico, whose eyes had widened a fraction. "Well, they thought that sending a woman in would arouse less suspicion. And there are no women in the squad currently. Since I used to be there, and since I'm now on the JTTF and this is technically a terrorism-related investigation…"

Allison pursed her lips briefly, and I held my breath, waiting for the explosion. "I see. So where does that leave us? What's the objective?"

Huh. That was a surprise. I'd thought she'd have more of a reaction. "My partner, Tate—"

"The guy I saw you with last night?" Allison said, sounding angry.

I blushed and looked away. "Yeah. Him. He's ATF. He's been under longer than I have. His cover is former military who spent too much time in country and as a result is sympathetic to their cause. He's attempting to help them find another supplier."

"And your cover?"

"I was brought in to help them turn out a better counterfeit bill. One that will float effortlessly on the open market. My cover is as a recent college graduate with a degree in graphic design who works at a print shop to supplement her freelance work. After the ATF approached us with this idea and backstopped a print shop for me to work at, they had Tate propose the idea of bringing me into the group. The group thinks he specifically chose me for my graphic design skills and seduced me to keep me in the dark until they feel they can trust me. Right now, they just think I'm his bimbo, and he's been told to eventually convince me to make these bills for them. He's supposed to wait a bit to approach me about the project until they can feel me out and get an idea of how I'll respond to the suggestion. Tate told me the other day he thinks it'll be soon."

Allison's eyes had narrowed, and the muscles in her jaw tensed. My heart thudded a little more rapidly at the sight, and a sick feeling started to pool in the pit of my stomach. I hated it when she was upset. I tightened my grip around my marker and waited as patiently as I could for her to ask another question.

Allison stared at me for a long moment, and I had to force myself to stare back placidly. It wasn't easy. Not when half of me wanted to ask her what the hell her problem was and the other half wanted to kiss her breathless. I rubbed my thumbs against the outside edges of my index fingers and willed myself not to flush again.

"Agent Corazon," Allison said eventually, taking her time before finally shifting her attention to him.

"Yes, ma'am?"

"Could you please explain to me how we're keeping track of Agent O'Connor while she's undercover?"

I winced and averted my gaze. I knew where this was going, the same way I knew it wouldn't end up any place good. I took a deep, shaky breath and tugged at the hair at the back of my neck.

"Ma'am?" Rico sounded confused.

"Do you not understand the question?" A darkly dangerous note that set me on edge underscored Allison's tone.

"Not exactly, ma'am."

"I'll rephrase. How do we know where Agent O'Connor is at any given time? Do we have twenty-four-hour surveillance on her?"

"Yes, ma'am. When she's at work, at the print shop, the ATF has eyes on her. One agent is always in the shop with her, posing as another employee, and at least two other agents are standing by in an upstairs room keeping an eye on her via a closed-circuit surveillance system. They call me when she reports in and when she leaves for the day. And we have the outside of her cover apartment wired for video, as well as having electronic sensors that log any time the door or either of the windows is opened."

"And someone is watching that video feed at all times?"

"Yes, ma'am. We set it up so it runs to the duty desk. We have dedicated agents assigned just to watch that video feed between the hours of oh-six-hundred and twenty-two-hundred. After that, the duty desk takes over. They have instructions to contact the midnight response guys if something happens between those hours. And the local area precinct is aware that we have an ongoing operation in the area, although they don't know any of the details. We've been assured they'll respond if we call them for assistance."

"Wonderful. So, considering all the surveillance, you must be aware that Agent O'Connor had returned to her apartment and then left again during the overnight shift last night. You know where she went and who she was with. You know what time she arrived back home."

Rico hesitated, and my heart sank. He obviously had no idea any of that had happened. I wasn't sure whether the duty desk guy had fallen asleep or just hadn't reported the activity, but it didn't really matter. Neither was acceptable. It was all I could do not to close my eyes and smack my forehead with my palm.

"I see," Allison said softly, each syllable enunciated carefully enough that it tripped off her tongue with a sharp crack. "And when Agent O'Connor is in transit to or from her cover job, who has her back then?"

I could feel the heavy, oppressive silence inside my chest cavity the way you can feel the rumble of a jet engine when you're standing on a tarmac or the bass of the speakers at a concert. I held my breath, praying this moment would end soon.

When Rico didn't answer, Allison went on. "And who has eyes on her when she's out at the bar with this potentially homicidal group the way she was last night? Anybody?"

Again, Rico said nothing, and I fought to keep the surprise off my face. I hadn't been briefed on the specifics of the logistics that'd gone into ensuring my safety, and I'd assumed my fellow agents had been keeping an extremely close eye on me. To learn that I'd been basically on my own for weeks was something of a shock. On the heels of that revelation, it was hard for me to argue with Allison's point of view that I shouldn't be doing this.

"Does Agent O'Connor carry any sort of tracking device with her?"

"No, ma'am. She doesn't."

"And why not?" Allison's gaze landed on me as she asked the question, and my eyes widened. I couldn't answer that. I'd asked for one, and my request had been denied. I'd just assumed there was enough manpower on me not to warrant it and hadn't broached the subject again.

Rico balked again. "Due to equipment availability and budget constraints, it was decided that—"

"What about on her phone?" Allison's voice resembled the dangerous tension of a drawn bowstring.

"Huh?"

"There are tracking apps available for phones. Does she have one enabled?"

Rico glanced at me, clearly confused and miserable. "She does, yes."

"And do the agents constantly monitor it?"

"I—I think so?"

This time I couldn't help closing my eyes and letting out a quiet, exasperated breath. Jesus Christ. He *thought* so? What the actual fuck?

"Very well." Allison's tone was clipped, and I didn't need to open my eyes to know that the skin around her eyes and lips had tightened. "Please tell the squad we have a mandatory meeting this afternoon at fourteen hundred hours in the conference room. All squad personnel—as well as all SOs who monitor the duty desk and any agents from any squad who are assigned to the supplemental overnight shift in the next couple weeks—are to attend. Call Ops to get the upcoming schedule. And make sure that every single person is at that meeting, even the ones who had midnight response last night. The only excuse for missing it is court or an ongoing protection assignment where they are actually *on* shift. If they're off shift, I expect to see them in that conference room. If they're on annual leave, I expect to see them in that conference room. If they're out of town and can't make it back in time, they're to call in. If they're on sick leave and not in the hospital, I expect them to call in. We're going to implement new surveillance protocols for this assignment."

My eyes had popped open in the middle of her monologue, and I gaped at her in disbelief. An edict like that was going to piss off a lot of people, and she knew it. But I could tell by the set of her shoulders and her jaw, by the flashing of her eyes, that she didn't give a shit.

"Yes, ma'am," Rico said, his voice small.

"Who's the AT for TOS?" Allison asked.

I grimaced. TOS, or the technical operations squad, was responsible for all the surveillance equipment in the office. If a squad needed any type of equipment to support any of their operations, they had to requisition it through TOS. That Allison wanted to talk to the person in charge there could only mean one thing. I didn't envy the conversation I knew would take place.

"AT Schultz."

"Ian Schultz?"

Rico nodded.

"Thank you. That will be all, Agent Corazon." Allison returned her focus to me.

Rico tensed and appeared uncertain, his face a living canvas of shifting emotions far too complex for me to follow. He glanced from Allison to me and then back again before apparently deciding he'd been dismissed. He gave me one last apologetic-looking glance before getting to his feet, lightly squeezing my shoulder as he slid by me, leaving me alone with Allison.

CHAPTER SIX

The room was eerily quiet in the wake of Rico's departure, and I tried not to fidget. I glanced back at the dry-erase board helplessly, as though it held the answers to questions I didn't even know enough to ask.

The stillness continued to shroud us, and I searched for a way to break it, to dispel the tension gathering in the room. "Do you want me to go over the group's members and hierarchy?"

When Allison didn't answer, I glanced at her. She'd shifted so her elbows rested against the edge of the desk and was massaging her temples with her fingertips. Her eyes were shut, her face pinched in pain and lined with something else I couldn't quite place. My heart constricted, and I had to physically stop myself from going to her, unsure how she'd react to any attempts to soothe or comfort her.

For lack of anything better to do, and to avoid making her uncomfortable by standing there and gaping at her like a fool, I refocused my attention on the dry-erase board. I set myself to the task of diagraming the group's makeup and pecking order. The only sounds in the room were the rustling of cloth, the squeak of the marker on the board, and the occasional, almost inaudible sigh.

"Can you please come over here and sit down?" Allison's low voice barely broke the strange semi-calm, but it grabbed my attention.

I capped the marker I was using and set it back on the waiting ledge so I could comply. After I turned around, I saw that she'd sat up again and was watching me intently. That gaze was like a gust of hot wind against my skin, and it did all manner of wonderfully inappropriate things to me. Slowly, I eased myself into the chair and crossed my legs at the knees.

Allison continued to study me like I was some interesting species she had yet to figure out. Her brows and the corners of her mouth pulled down in obvious displeasure. "Can you take those out?"

It took me a second to realize what she was asking, but as soon as she gestured toward my face, I caught on. I nodded, unable to speak. It took me longer than I'd have liked to rummage through my bag to find my contact case—and it felt like a damn eternity with her staring at me expectantly while I did it—but I finally located it and retrieved it from where it'd gotten stuck at the bottom of a pocket. I removed the contacts, set them into their case, and pushed it away from the edge of the desk. Then I blinked a few times to let my eyes adjust to the sudden disappearance of a foreign object while Allison studied the little brown discs with a slight scowl.

"Better?" I asked.

Allison nodded. "Much. The hair is one thing. But I couldn't stand seeing you with brown eyes. Why are you wearing those anyway?"

"I don't know. With all the press I've gotten in the past couple months, I guess I thought it'd be a good idea to look as little like myself as humanly possible. You know, in case any of these guys had seen me on the news or anything."

Allison's face darkened, and the tips of her fingers turned white as she pressed her splayed hands hard into the surface of the desk. She took a slow, measured breath and let it out just as deliberately. "Do you now see the problem I have with you taking this assignment?"

I didn't say anything. I was positive she wasn't looking for a response. Also, I was certain whatever I had to contribute would only make things worse. Instead, I concentrated on remaining still and not allowing any emotion to play out across my face.

"When you first mentioned that you were going undercover, you neglected to mention that it'd be this deep or for this long."

"It wasn't supposed to be either. Things just sort of…evolved, and I couldn't do anything once I was in except go with it."

Allison picked up my contact case and sat back, regarding it thoughtfully. After a long pause, she shook her head and placed the case on the desk again. Then she looked at me. "I realize some of the things I said last night could be construed as lack of faith in your abilities as an agent. I hope you know that couldn't be further from the truth."

I was skeptical and barely managed to refrain from allowing my eyebrows to rise. To buy myself a moment, I took the contacts back from her and put them in my bag. "Really?"

Allison shook her head. "Of course not. You're a fantastic agent. But you *aren't* trained for this. None of us are trained for this. And after talking to Rico, I'm even more concerned because it's clear you've been insufficiently monitored for weeks. If something goes wrong, no one's even going to know about it, much less be able to help you." A beat. "I'm worried about you."

A feeling of warmth not unlike the one that accompanies taking a shot of Jameson straight from the bottle started to gather in my chest. I didn't even try to hide the grin stealing over my face.

Allison rolled her eyes. "Stop it. Me worrying about you isn't something for you to grin about."

"It's kind of something for me to grin about."

"Really? You like that you're making me physically ill? Are you that much of a sadist?"

"Of course not. But I do like that you care."

"Of course I care. I love you. I was willing to leave the detail early, so I could come back to New York to be with you."

My smile softened. "I know you were. And I appreciate that. Although it looks like it wasn't necessary. Congratulations, by the way."

"Thanks. You do realize I've had countless fantasies about sexually harassing you now that I'm your boss."

I laughed, but I was unable to ignore the wistful twinge her words caused. I wasn't sure we'd ever be able to make any of those fantasies come true, and it made me indescribably sad. Instead of getting into all that, I said, "It's only sexual harassment if it's unwanted, which it definitely is not. Besides, you're not *my* boss. You're *a* boss."

Allison waved one hand. "Semantics."

"Attention to detail."

"I could still write you up for insubordination, even though you're not in my squad."

"You better buy stock in Bic. You're going to need a lot of pens if that's how you plan to try to exert your power over me. I'm not sure if you know this, but I'm something of a loose cannon."

"Hmm. Good thing I have a backup plan to inspire obedience." Allison's eyes were impossibly dark as she looked at me, her expression one of undisguised lust.

All the air in my lungs left me in a great whoosh. My mouth went dry, and my hands trembled. The logical part of me wanted to change the subject, but the rest of me was scrambled just enough to ensure I wouldn't be able to manage to. I licked my lips as my mind snagged on the memory of what it was like to kiss her, really kiss her, for hours without having to think about anything other than the exquisite softness of her lips.

Allison pushed her chair back from the desk, holding my gaze as she prowled around to my side, looking like sin made flesh. The slow, deliberate grace with which she moved hypnotized me, and the way her tailored suit clung deliciously to her curves didn't help me think any clearer.

I collapsed back into my chair and watched as she stalked me. My skin tingled with anticipation, and I pressed my legs together to try to tamp down my burgeoning arousal.

Allison stopped so her thighs brushed lightly against the edge of my kneecap, and after towering over me for a long moment, she slowly leaned down to rest the heels of her hands on the edges of the arms of my chair, pinning me in place. I tried to swallow, but my throat wouldn't cooperate. The inability to make my body obey my commands disconcerted me, as did the nearly insurmountable urge to let everything go and allow myself to be swept away by the look in her eyes.

She'd positioned herself so we were eye to eye, and her breath ghosted over my lips with each soft exhale. My pulse was racing, and I shoved my hands down to tuck them underneath my thighs, as much to hide their trembling as to keep myself from touching her.

"Ryan," Allison whispered, staring deeply into my eyes before letting her own flutter shut. Her lips brushed mine so softly I couldn't be positive she'd kissed me at all.

My heart sputtered like a lawnmower struggling to start. Breathing had become impossible, and I had to give myself a serious kick in the ass to force myself to utter the next words that came out of my mouth.

"We shouldn't."

Allison didn't move, didn't flinch, didn't give any sign that she'd heard me. I was starting to wonder whether I'd spoken aloud. The longer she stayed there, the longer we shared the same air, the weaker my resolve not to have my way with her on the desk became. The way the buttons of her white dress shirt were stretched taut across her chest distracted me, and my fingers twitched as I tried not to think about ripping it off her and sending those buttons flying to reveal her silky smooth skin.

"Why not?"

I blinked, startled. "I—I don't..."

I was unable to stop myself from running the tip of my tongue over the inside of my lip where she'd broken the skin when she'd punched me the previous evening. The resultant ache helped remind me why I'd stopped to begin with, though for some reason I was having trouble saying that aloud.

Allison shifted, pulling back just enough to meet my gaze full on.

The depth of the emotions displayed on her face turned my insides to mush. A shiver went up my spine as she lifted one hand to tuck a stray lock of hair back behind my ear and then gently traced the edge of my jaw. I felt that caress over my entire body.

"Are you ready to tell me what's wrong?"

I sucked in a harsh breath, and my lower lip quivered. "How'd you know?"

A wry smile tugged at the corners of Allison's lips, and the look she gave me was one of fond exasperation. "You're not terribly subtle, and you're a horrible liar. Plus, you've never *not* taken advantage of any opportunity to get me naked."

I sighed wearily and closed my eyes. I'd been avoiding this conversation the way I avoided those people who dressed up in cartoon character suits in Times Square. And just like in Times Square, clearly I was going to be badgered into participating whether I consented or not.

"It's about your test, isn't it?"

My blood turned to ice, and my eyes flew open. She was staring at me, and her expression showed a quiet certainty. I hesitated, torn between denying her question and just giving in and admitting she was right. "It's ridiculously creepy when you do that."

Allison smirked for an instant before her countenance became serious once again. "Was it positive?"

I shrugged and shifted my focus so I was staring at the dry-erase board. Simply having this conversation would be hard enough as it was. No way was I going to be able to get through it while looking at her.

"I haven't taken it yet."

Allison withdrew from my personal space, and I felt a keen longing to go after her, to close the distance between us and lose myself in the safety of her embrace. But if I touched her, even innocently, I'd never be able to keep my distance from her again.

"Why?" Allison asked. She leaned on the edge of the desk and watched me, evidently not upset but merely curious.

I took a deep breath and forced myself to utter the sentence I hadn't had the guts to admit silently to myself. "Because I'm afraid it will be."

Sympathy flooded Allison's eyes, and she nodded. "I can see how that might be frightening."

"And I can't…I can't be with you, you know, like that, until I know for sure that I'm okay." I swallowed. "And if it does turn out to be positive, I'm not sure if I can ever…I would just feel so…I couldn't stop worrying that…Can you understand?"

Though I hadn't said anything that made sense, Allison's lips pursed, and she appeared to be considering how to respond. "I can understand how you might be concerned, I suppose. If our positions were reversed, I'd likely entertain similar thoughts. And I don't want to push you, but by refusing to determine whether we have anything to worry about, you're effectively condemning both of us to a life without physical intimacy."

The part about worrying was true enough. And when she spelled it out like that, it did sound rather stupid, though her observation didn't necessarily alleviate my feelings on the subject. However, that wasn't the only problem I was considering. I was rather surprised she'd just glossed over what she *had* to have concluded: that if the test did come back positive, I'd have to let her go. I'd never condemn her to a life without physical intimacy and was far too selfish to allow her to seek release elsewhere while she was with me.

My insides felt full, like they were pressing on one another in unnatural ways as I contemplated a life without her. The mere notion made me sick to my stomach and despondent, and I opened my eyes wide, trying to discourage the tears gathering there from falling. I was trying to figure out how best to explain my feelings to her when her phone rang, shattering my train of thought.

Allison looked both apologetic and annoyed as she retrieved the offending device from a clip on her belt. She glanced at the caller ID, and her countenance suddenly changed to one of apprehension. "I'm sorry. I have to take this."

I waved her on and cleared my throat so I'd be able to speak despite the lump there. "Go ahead. I'll be here."

She didn't appear to have heard me, focused solely on the phone in her hand. Without a backward glance, she stepped out into the hall, shut the door behind her, and left me to navigate the murky waters of my thoughts alone.

CHAPTER SEVEN

I sat there in the tiny faux office for an undetermined amount of time, my thoughts cycling so quickly I might as well have been thinking of nothing at all. I could barely land on one track long enough to identify the subject matter and couldn't stay on it long enough to make any real progress toward deciding anything.

Groaning, I tipped my head back so I could glower at the ceiling, shoving my hands into my pockets and freezing at the feel of paper against my skin. I wrapped my fingers around the offending object and wrenched it free, the crinkling almost ominous against the silent backdrop of the room.

I regarded my sister's scribbly handwriting on the front of the envelope as though it alone had the power to convey her message to me. My insides twisted, and the vise-like grip of guilt that seized my heart momentarily drowned out all the other unpleasant emotions that'd surfaced along with the recollection that Rory had returned.

Delicately plucking at the corner of the envelope where the flap folded over the opening, tearing it a little, I had to force myself to stop. I didn't want to read it. Not here. Not now. Not when I still had unfinished business with Allison. But the curiosity was killing me.

What could she possibly have needed to say to me so badly that called for this? Was she angry? Concerned? Scolding me? Had she apologized for leaving or explained why she'd felt she had to? I had no way to tell.

Scrubbing at the hollow of my cheek with the heel of my hand, I considered my missteps in handling her before she'd disappeared. I'd told her I thought she needed to talk to someone about the rape and what she'd flippantly called the "possible abortion" that'd followed when she'd taken the morning-after pill, but I hadn't pushed her on the subject. Not really. Not nearly as hard as she'd pushed me to seek therapy on the heels of the shooting. Not as hard as I should've. And then I'd gone undercover, and she'd just gone.

But she was evidently back now. I hoped that was a good sign. I hoped that meant she'd had some help dealing with what'd happened to her, because Lord knew I'd failed her epically. Much like I'd failed her by allowing her to wind up in that situation to begin with.

The door to the room opened, cutting off my self-loathing before it could pick up a good head of steam. I shoved the envelope back into my pocket and sat up straighter.

"I'm sorry about that," Allison said as she reentered the room.

I glanced over my shoulder at her, surprised that she appeared on edge about something. I watched warily as she reseated herself behind the desk. "What's wrong?"

Her forehead crinkled, and she shook her head. "Nothing."

I raised my eyebrows. "You know, you're just about as subtle as I am and only a marginally better liar."

"Remind me not to play poker with you, then."

"Can you please be serious for a second?"

"Wow. *You* want to be serious about something? That's a first."

"Cute. I can't help you if I don't know what's bothering you."

"You can't help me at all. Not unless you can figure out a way to get out."

"Get out? Get out of what?"

"This assignment. These people are killers. You said that yourself. If they figure out who you really are, you'll be dead before anyone can get to you. Obviously, you can't just walk away. That'd be suspicious. But we need to start thinking of a plausible reason for you to sever your ties with them."

I was startled, as much at the shift in topic as my inability to believe what I was hearing. "But if I leave, they have to start over. And every day these nuts are out walking around is one more day they can plot to kill people. They have to be stopped."

"And I'm not disagreeing with you. They do have to be stopped. But someone else can do the stopping. Someone else who's been adequately prepared for this type of mission. Someone who isn't you."

"Allison, we're so close. In a few more weeks we'll have everything we need to put these guys away."

"And that's a few more weeks they have to figure out that you're a fed, pump you full of lead from their illegally obtained weapons, and dump your body in the river."

"Don't you think you're being a little dramatic?"

"Don't you think you're being a little naive?"

"Don't you care about the people they might kill?"

"Honestly? At this exact moment in time? No. No, I don't."

"How can you say that?"

"Because I only care about what could happen to you."

I let out a noisy, frustrated huff, fisted one hand into my hair so hard it hurt, and closed my eyes. "This argument isn't getting us anywhere. We obviously have completely opposite views on the subject."

"That you're even admitting that is disconcerting in and of itself."

"What the hell is that supposed to mean?"

"Can you really not see how reckless this is? Rico just told you that you're pretty much on your own most of the time. How can that not scare the shit out of you?"

"I'm not on my own. Tate's with me."

Allison snorted and looked torn between derision and despair. "What's he going to do? Blow his own cover to save you? Then you'll both die."

"We don't know that it's going to come to that."

"And we don't know that it won't, either."

"Allison—"

"Can you promise that, Ryan?" she asked hotly. "Can you guarantee me this assignment will flow to its natural conclusion without a hitch and nothing will happen to you?"

"Of course not, but—"

"But nothing."

"Oh, that's mature." I'd been unable to keep the venom from my voice. I stood up, unwilling to continue this argument from my chair.

Allison stood, too, and narrowed her eyes. "You can make snarky comments all you want. It doesn't bolster your argument at all. In fact, it just proves that you don't really have one, or you'd be making it."

"I have made it. You just don't like it."

"You haven't made anything. I haven't heard a single solution come out of your mouth for how to keep you better protected while you do this."

"Well, I need some time. Obviously I didn't realize Rico and the guys were slacking that much. An hour or two to think about this isn't too much to ask."

"And can you swear nothing's going to happen to you in that hour or two?"

"Yes, I can. Because I don't have to be at 'work' for another three hours."

Allison glared at me. Perhaps being a smart-ass wasn't helping my cause. But damn, it was like she was deliberately pushing every single button I had. One of us needed to calm the hell down and try to steer this conversation back to a more rational place, or nothing would get accomplished.

"This discussion is over," Allison said. "Find a way out. That's an order."

I blinked at her. "Did you just issue me a freaking directive?"

She continued to stare at me.

"Are you kidding me?"

"I've never been more serious in my entire life." She watched me intently and took half a step closer. We were now standing so near one another that we were breathing each other's air again. "I've almost lost you twice in the past couple of months, and in both those instances, you were surrounded by other agents who could've or should've helped you. What do you think your odds of survival are on your own like this?"

"I'm not thinking about my survival," I shouted. I put my fingers over my lips as soon as the words were out of my mouth. I hadn't known what I was going to say before I'd said it, and my outburst surprised even me.

The corners of Allison's mouth twitched, her resolve apparently wavering, but she was clearly trying hard not to let it go at the same time. And underneath that determination, I would've sworn I saw pain and sadness. Fuck. I'd just put my foot in my mouth, apparently.

"Is that what this is? Some sort of suicide mission?" Her voice as she spoke was whisper soft, and my heart constricted.

"Of course not."

"But if you're not thinking about your survival, how can you expect to actually survive?"

"You're deliberately twisting my words to arrive at the worst possible conclusion!"

Allison swallowed hard and cleared her throat. "No. I get it. If you get killed on this stupid assignment, you don't have to deal with the possibility of being HIV positive. You won't have to figure out how to live."

"It really isn't like that." I furrowed my brow as I tried to come up with a way to convince her that she was off the mark, but nothing was coming to mind.

"Then what is it like, Ryan? Huh? Tell me?" Allison's eyes were near pleading now, the faintest hint of desperation coloring her tone.

"I don't know. It's just...Not like that."

"Rory. Your parents. Me. Do you even care what it would do to us if something happened to you?"

My own resolve weakened, and I felt like an air mattress with a slow leak. "Of course I care."

"But not enough to do the one thing that could ensure your safety, huh?"

"Allison." Her name was a soft sigh falling from my lips, but I had nothing more to say. I longed to make her see this dilemma from my point of view, but declarations about the big picture and the greater good sounded flimsy on the heels of what she'd just asked me. Because if our positions had been reversed, no force on earth would've convinced me she should see this thing through.

Allison stared at me expectantly for a long moment—during which I held my breath and stared back miserably—before her eyes widened a tad, and she whirled around and stalked out of the room, leaving me to stare after her.

CHAPTER EIGHT

I stood motionless, staring at the door Allison had just disappeared through. I knew our conversation had been traversing some pretty rough terrain—hell, I hadn't been all too keen on participating in it myself—but I didn't think that was any reason to just bolt from the room.

I continued to frown at the door as I considered what'd just happened and measured it against what I knew about Allison and her normal reaction to stress. I'd never seen her back down from a challenge, and she sure as hell had never shied away from a fight with me. It was almost like a sort of foreplay, pushing one another's buttons. I couldn't imagine that'd changed.

Something was wrong. I wasn't positive she'd welcome me checking up on her, but I was just as stubborn as she was, which meant I refused to let her cut our conversation short without even an explanation. Yes, I had done that to her the night before. Yes, I do know the definition of hypocrisy.

With equal parts apprehension and irritation, I crept down the hall toward the only direction she could've gone. My irritation vanished and the apprehension flared as I heard someone retching in the ladies' room. And once I realized she was sick, I was definitely checking on her.

I eased the door open, slunk into the bathroom, and could just make out the shape of Allison's knees underneath the walls of a far stall. The forceful sounds coming from within it told me she hadn't even heard me come in and wouldn't finish soon.

My irritation and hurt evaporated as I watched and listened to her. Wanting to help, I tiptoed into the stall behind her. Seeing her slumped over with her forearms resting on the toilet seat as she heaved made my own insides clench in sympathy.

I grasped the silky strands of her hair. If I'd had a rubber band, I would've bound them back out of her face, but since I'd cut my own hair for this op, I no longer used them.

Allison visibly tensed, either due to the surprise of my touch or the strength of her stomach's contractions. Yet I continued to hold her hair with one hand and rub her back with the other, trying to comfort her.

After forever, the tension drained out of her, and she sagged. She let out a huge sigh of what I assumed was relief and slid sideways so she sat on the floor to one side of the toilet. When she reached up to brush a few stray locks of hair from her face, her hand was shaking.

I handed her some toilet paper so she could wipe her mouth and flushed for her when she tossed the used scrap into the bowl. Then I held out my hand to help her up.

She stared at it for a moment like she didn't know what to make of it before glancing up to me with an adorably confused expression. A small smile tugged at the corners of my mouth, and I rolled my eyes before I leaned down to loop one arm around her waist and position one of hers across my shoulders.

With a tiny grunt, I managed to haul her up from the bathroom floor. Taking it nice and slow, I walked her over to the chair in the corner of the restroom near the sinks and sat her down. I then wet a paper towel, squeezed out the excess water, and placed it on the back of her neck.

Allison tipped her face up to look at me, and her expression nearly broke my heart. I tried to pull my hand away, but she snagged it and began tracing the ridges of my knuckles with her thumb.

"Thank you," she whispered, keeping her eyes trained on my face.

"You're welcome," I whispered back. "You okay?"

Allison continued to stare at me, and for a long moment, I forgot that I'd asked her a question. Tears started welling in her eyes and making slow tracks down her cheeks. When I reached up to wipe them away, she let out a heart-wrenching sob and abruptly dropped my hand, using both of hers to hide her face.

My stomach sank. I could probably count on one hand the number of times I'd seen her cry and still have fingers left over. That she was borderline hysterical now only meant that something big was bothering her. Surely the vague possibility of something happening to me on this undercover assignment couldn't make her break down like this, though I couldn't imagine what could.

I made small shushing sounds as I pulled her into a hug. She wrapped her arms around my waist and buried her face in my stomach.

Her grip was almost painful, but I didn't ask her to ease up, not when she was so distraught.

It took all my willpower not to pester her to tell me what was wrong. Instead of asking my numerous questions, I held her as close as possible while making what I hoped were soothing tracks through her hair and across the plains of her back with my hands.

When she'd finally exhausted either all her energy or all her tears, she sat back—not enough to break our embrace, but enough to tip her head up to look me in the eyes.

"I'm sorry," she murmured.

It was my turn to be confused. "Why are you apologizing? You have nothing to be sorry for."

Allison sniffled, and I reluctantly untangled her arms from around my waist so I could retrieve a tissue for her from the vanity next to the sink. As I handed it over, I knelt next to her so we'd be at eye level.

She sniffled again and took a second to dab at her eyes before blowing her nose. She crumpled the used tissue into a ball and tossed it in the vague direction of the trash can, making a small noise in the back of her throat when her shot missed. She moved as though to get up, but I stopped her with a gentle hand on her thigh.

"Leave it. We'll get it later."

Allison nodded, though it clearly pained her to do so. I couldn't help smiling at her predictable reaction. She was much more type A than I was, which I found utterly endearing.

Allison took in my smile, and her expression clouded, which caused my blood to run a little cold and my heart to do an awkward sort of Irish jig. She licked her lips in a gesture I recognized as nervousness, and the skin around her eyes tightened.

"I'm sorry. I've been a little emotional lately."

"That's okay. We all have our days."

She huffed in obvious irritation. "I don't. At least not like this."

"You've had some doozies." I tried to grin at her to take the sting out of my words, but I'm afraid I appeared to grimace.

Allison's eyes narrowed, and some of the fire I was used to seeing sparked in them. "You're one to talk."

I shrugged. "I know *I* can act like a gigantic baby. I've never pretended otherwise. Unlike some people."

Allison's face fell then, and an immediate stab of remorse with a heaping side of irritation at my apparent inability to take something seriously for two consecutive minutes at a stretch assaulted me. I didn't mean to make her feel bad. I'd been shooting for a smile or an eye roll. Damn. I was an ass.

Trying to fix the hot mess I'd just made, I squeezed her hands and waited until she looked at me. Her despondent expression almost killed me.

"I need to tell you something."

My mouth went dry, and my heart ceased to stomp and splashed unceremoniously into the area normally occupied by my stomach. No good conversation had ever started with those words. At least not any I'd ever been involved in.

"Okay," I said, wincing when my voice broke on the word.

Hesitantly, Allison took my hands, pulled them into her lap, and stared at them for a long time. Each second that dragged past with her not speaking felt like an eternity, and my heart—which had clawed its way back to its proper position within my chest—felt like it was working overtime to pump blood that had taken on the consistency of mud.

"You're not making me feel any better." I was trying for levity, which was always my go-to in any emotionally charged situation, but I failed miserably.

Allison appeared startled and looked up at me with newly formed tears in her eyes. Now I felt like I might need to throw up. I clenched my jaw tight against the nausea bubbling up inside me and swallowed hard.

"Whatever it is, it can't be that bad." My voice sounded rough, like I'd spent all night screaming at a concert and smoking cigars, and my statement did nothing to convince me that my words were even remotely true.

Allison favored me with a bitter smile that looked altogether wrong on her face. She squeezed my fingers and narrowed her eyes again as she studied me. "Do you love me?"

"You know I do." The answer was automatic, but that didn't mean I'd expected the question. "Allison, you're starting to scare me. Please, just tell me what's wrong."

She shook her head, and her gaze slid away from mine to focus on some point on the floor behind me. "This is a lot harder than I anticipated."

"Whatever you're afraid of is probably a helluva lot worse than what's actually going to happen."

"Sage words, O'Connor."

"I have my moments. Few and far between though they may be." I hesitated a beat, hoping I was about to say the right thing. It wasn't what I wanted, but it was what I thought she needed to hear. "You don't have to tell me if you're not ready. I'll be right here to listen when you are."

"It's just that...If I do this...If I say the words out loud...It—it makes them real."

"Oh. Well, that doesn't sound good."

Allison met my gaze again, and too much was going on behind her eyes for me to get a good sense of exactly what she was feeling. "I'm not sure if it's good or not."

I took a deep breath, an attempt to calm my jittery nerves, but a feeble one at best. And it did not work even a little bit. "Whatever it is, we'll get through it."

"Do you really mean that?"

I nodded, not trusting myself to speak.

Allison's expression softened, and she looked at me with such love and adoration I almost forgot how to breathe. My stomach fluttered, but this time it was for a different reason.

"I'm pregnant."

It took a second or two for her words to penetrate my awareness, and as soon as they did, my entire world ground to a complete halt. My heart, my mouth, my brain—none of them were working, although that might've been a good thing. I had no way to know what my reaction would be, so perhaps it was best that it was delayed.

The light in Allison's eyes dimmed as the silence stretched between us, and still I failed to react. She frowned. "Aren't you going to say anything?"

"Congratulations?" I didn't mean to sound so unsure, but apparently I couldn't do much about that. Not when my body felt like a discarded old pumpkin whose insides had been scooped out and then left to rot on a porch for weeks on end.

Allison's expression combined pain and anger. "Gee, thanks."

I forced myself to swallow past the lump in my throat and tried to ignore the hollow feeling in my chest. "No, really. It's great. I'm just surprised. I didn't even realize you wanted kids. You've never said anything." And that also seemed like a conversation we should have had. Right? Was I overthinking this situation? Being selfish? I wasn't sure.

Allison looked away from me again, appearing distant. "I'd honestly never really thought about it one way or the other." She spoke softly, almost as if that were the first time she'd ever admitted that fact and she was afraid to say it too loud lest the baby hear her and be offended.

I considered that fact. If she'd never thought about having kids, then how the hell had she—? My eyes flew open wide, and I had to force myself not to scramble to my feet or pull my hands out of hers too roughly. I took a long, slow, deep breath and let it out as I counted to five.

"This is *Beau's* baby?" It felt like a stupid question, but I wanted an answer.

Her face crumpled, and she appeared mildly ashamed and a lot nauseous, though that could've just been the morning sickness. She sucked the corner of her lower lip between her teeth and nodded.

I nodded, too. Because mirroring her actions seemed innocuous and also maybe somehow supportive in some way? I nodded for so long I started to feel like a bobblehead as I tried hard to think beyond the agony knotting my insides. The unpleasant tingling feeling that'd enveloped me wasn't helping.

My mouth was watering the way it does just before I get sick, and I turned my head slowly so I could study the bathroom stalls. I was having a hard time deciding whether I wanted to throw up or pass out or if both of those desires would become reality. Then I started contemplating which might occur first. Was it possible to do both simultaneously?

A gentle hand on my shoulder and a cool towel on the side of my face brought me out of my internal musings. I blinked and noticed Allison standing in front of me, looking worried. Shouldn't I be doing the cool-towel thing for her? I probably should. Oops. I needed to get a grip here. This was not what Allison needed. I took a deep breath, determined to wrangle my skittering emotions into some semblance of order.

"You need to listen to me," she said. Her hand left my arm and settled lightly on the other side of my face. "I know what you're thinking, and you need to stop. I did not cheat on you."

I glanced toward her stomach, where it would appear evidence said otherwise, but didn't reply.

With an annoyed-sounding huff, Allison took my hand and placed it on the damp paper towel, forcing me to actively participate in keeping it pressed to my overheated skin. Then she reached into the pocket of her suit jacket and brought out a small slip of paper. She held it in trembling hands for a long moment as she stared at it. Then she handed it to me with a tentative expression.

"Look at the corner," she said. "Look how far along I am."

I didn't want to take it from her, didn't want to see the

incontrovertible proof that life as I knew it was about to change, but she took my other hand and forced the paper into my grip.

The image was grainy, but there was no mistaking the shadowy figure in the center of the picture. A baby. Allison's baby. I continued to stare at it as my thoughts whizzed around my head the way a comet speeds around the solar system. And like comets, all of them were moving far too swiftly for me to catch.

Not sure exactly what to think or how to feel, I handed the picture back to Allison and nodded. I tried to smile, but the result was shaky at best. "Is it too soon to ask if it's a boy or a girl? I'm sorry. I don't know much about pregnancy."

Allison ignored my question. "You saw it, right? I'm thirteen weeks along. That was right before you and I got back together." Her words had a desperate edge to them that normally would've moved me to want to comfort her, but now they bounced off me like so many pieces of dandelion fluff.

Still feeling nauseated yet numb, I took her face gently in both of my hands, staring deeply into her eyes. I smiled and inclined my head toward the exit before I let her go. I'd managed to make it all the way over to the door, open it, and take a step into the hall before I realized that Allison hadn't followed.

Frowning, I turned back to see her still standing in the middle of the bathroom holding her ultrasound picture in her hand. She was staring at it with the most heartbreakingly despondent expression as tears forged new tracks down her face. I frowned more deeply.

"Aren't you coming?" I asked, unsure why she was still standing there. Maybe I hadn't been clear that I'd wanted her to follow me. Normally, a head tilt was the only invitation she needed, but these were unusual circumstances.

Her head snapped up, and her eyes widened. She stared at me as though she didn't understand the question. I held my hand out to her, wiggled my fingers, and inclined my head again, this time in the direction of the hallway.

"Come on," I said, trying to make my tone light as I forced a smile. "I refuse to have the rest of this conversation in a damn bathroom."

I waited for an impossibly long moment for her to take my hand, and as she did, I thought that soon it would be cradling a child. For a second, I considered whether it'd be a boy or a girl and if it would have her silky dark hair and dazzling smile.

Forcing that notion away, I pulled her behind me into the hall.

CHAPTER NINE

The walk back to the office was silent, and I tried to focus on the warmth of her hand in mine and the way our fingers fit together perfectly. I needed those few seconds to cling to the life I'd become accustomed to. As soon as this conversation ended, I'd never be able to look at anything the same way again.

We entered the room, and I shut the door. Allison stood for a long moment staring at the chairs, looking as though she were trying to decide where to sit. I looked, too, and after a moment, I pulled the one I'd occupied earlier away from the desk a bit for her. She glanced up at me, surprise written on her features. I tried to smile as I gestured for her to take a seat.

Once I was sure she was settled, I turned the chair next to hers slightly so I could face her, sat down, and watched her. She appeared small somehow and somewhat broken. I wished I could do something for her. I wished I could begin to piece together what that something could even be.

After a near eternity, Allison let out a noisy sigh and rubbed the side of her neck. She cut a side glance at me. "I'm reluctant to admit this, but I immediately thought when I found out that this had to be some kind of terrible after-school special."

"Why's that?"

"Because in those stupid things, the girl automatically gets pregnant the first time she has sex."

"You got pregnant from the first time you had sex with him?"

Allison shook her head. "No. It was the last, actually. But that was the only time we did it without a condom." She dropped her head so it rested in the palm of her hand. "God. How could I be so stupid?"

I wasn't sure how to respond. I didn't know anything about the circumstances surrounding that night. Maybe she'd thought it wouldn't come to this. Maybe she'd been plastered and hadn't been thinking at all. We'd all been there. Most of us not with men, but still…

"So what happens now?" I asked.

Allison turned her head so she could look at me out of one eye. "What do you mean?"

"Well, I assume you don't want to…terminate it."

Allison dropped her hand and pinned me with a dark look. "Of course not. I'd never be able to forgive myself."

My thoughts strayed to Rory. Had taking the morning-after pill been a tough decision for her or had it simply been a knee-jerk reaction to the rape? I knew she'd rationalized that she'd never really known for certain whether she'd been pregnant to begin with, so there was nothing to "forgive," but I wondered whether she believed that or whether it was something she said to try to convince herself.

"This isn't like what happened with Rory," Allison said, doing that creepy mind-reading thing she was so fond of.

"No. I guess not." I hesitated. "So, are you thinking about giving it up for adoption?"

Allison's glare on the heels of that question combined disbelief, betrayal, and loathing, and it hit me like a cannonball to the gut. "I can't believe you'd even ask me that. You know how I feel about it."

Inwardly, I scolded myself. I did know how she felt about adoption, which was why I couldn't believe I'd been insensitive enough to even suggest it. But given how career-driven she'd always been, it hadn't occurred to me that she'd consider keeping it. We didn't have a lot of mothers on the job, but we each knew a few, and their situations seemed difficult and complicated. Though she had to have thought of that reality already. I opened my mouth to reply but closed it again. I needed to think about what I was going to say before I said it and inadvertently made things worse.

"I'm sorry. I do know. I guess I just didn't consider it because I know that you ended up with the greatest parents on the entire planet," I said.

"You're right. I did. And that still didn't make up for the fact that my real parents gave me away. It still didn't stop me from wondering why they didn't want me. I'd never do that to a child. I'd never condemn anyone to the self-doubt I struggled with growing up. That I still—" She looked away.

My insides roiled and writhed on the heels of that near admission. One she'd never made before. I'd assumed she was over all that— she'd certainly never mentioned it in a present-tense context—and it had always felt insensitive of me to mention the circumstances of her childhood, so I never did. But maybe you never really get over it. I was lucky enough that I didn't know. My heart ached for her that she did. "You're right. I'm sorry."

"And how would I even be sure it went to a good home?" Allison went on as though I hadn't just admitted she had a point. "Not all kids are lucky enough to get adopted, let alone by parents as great as mine. Some kids grow up in group homes or get bounced around from foster home to foster home until they're old enough to be on their own."

"That's true. I shouldn't have asked. I apologize. Truly."

"I'd always wonder," Allison admitted quietly. Her eyes were red-rimmed as she stared at me. "If I gave it up, I'd look at every kid roughly that age for the rest of my life, and I'd always wonder."

I placed a comforting hand on her arm. "No adoption."

My capitulation didn't appear to reassure Allison. She seemed worried as she looked at me. "Do you want kids?"

I raised my eyebrows in surprise and tried not to panic. "Do I?"

Allison's brow wrinkled, and she nodded.

"I, uh…I don't know. I've never seen myself having them." When her face fell, I hastened to do damage control. "But I've never seen myself not having kids either."

She looked at me suspiciously. "Really?"

"They've never been on my radar, one way or another." To be fair, I thought that said a lot, but now didn't seem like the time to bring it up.

Allison shifted her attention to the top of the desk in front of us, her eyes taking on a faraway cast. She was definitely deep in thought about something. While I waited for her to decide whether to say whatever she was mulling over, I considered what she'd just asked me.

Kids were okay. I liked them well enough, I supposed. I mean, I'd babysat when I was a teenager, like just about every other girl in America, and I hadn't hated the experience. But I hadn't had a ton of interaction with any children in years. I got to play with my cousin Katie's kids during family get-togethers, and the handful of times I'd seen my brother Aiden's little boy when he'd visited from Oregon had been fun. I just wasn't sure how I felt about having one around on a permanent, full-time basis. It seemed like a lot of work, and I was fairly certain it'd have a negative impact on my *Law & Order: SVU* marathons.

Now that I was thinking about it, having kids somehow felt as though it signified the end of the long journey into adulthood, and I wasn't particularly keen on reaching that ending point just yet. Despite my age—and the fact that I'd carried a gun for years—I still didn't feel like an adult. Not really. I didn't have a pet. Hell. I didn't even own a plant. I was still getting used to navigating all the subtle nuances of an honest-to-goodness relationship and clearly making an epic, never-ending mess of it. How in God's name could I be a parent when I barely had a handle on life?

I glanced at Allison then, and that's when I finally recognized her glow for what it was. I'd noticed it when I'd seen her the night before at the bar, but I'd just chalked it up to the fact that I hadn't seen her in forever. Now that I knew, though, it all made sense. And I couldn't help admitting that it looked good on her, even when she was obviously miserable and confused.

"Kids have never been on my radar either," Allison finally said, her voice a low murmur that made me wonder whether she was speaking to me or to herself. "I mean, I don't dislike them. I just...I'd just never thought about them before, one way or the other."

I nodded, realizing that she understood my take on the subject. The knot in my chest loosened a tiny bit. "Yeah."

A twisted, gruesome sort of smile contorted her lips, a shadow of regret in her eyes. "I have no idea what to do. With my life, I mean. I just...This was never part of my plan."

I hesitated before replying. "If anyone can shift on the fly like this, it's you."

Allison blinked as if startled and met my gaze as though she'd just realized I was in the room, even though we'd been having a conversation. "Just me?"

My heart stuttered to a stop with all the grace and finesse of an engine that'd run out of gas, and my blood felt ice cold, which was an interesting contrast to the sudden fire painting the surface of my skin. Holy shit. Was she asking me to raise a baby with her? No. That was crazy. Wasn't it? I mean, we'd only just gotten back together a few months ago. We couldn't possibly be there yet. Could we? I didn't want to assume. Because if I misinterpreted what she was saying and answered a question she hadn't actually asked—if I jumped to the rest of our lives before she'd reached that chapter—I could potentially ruin everything.

Allison's expression became colder by noticeable degrees the longer I remained silent until it was a complete mask. My stomach felt like a suddenly deflated balloon, and I struggled to find something—anything—to say to make any of this better. I decided to just go for it. Because whatever her reaction was bound to be, that had to be better than this.

"Allison, are you saying—"

I never got any farther than that. She stood abruptly, and the scraping of the feet of the chair against the tiled floor sounded loud in comparison to the relative quiet we'd been sitting in. I winced at the sudden intrusion as my words died on my lips.

Allison looked down at me as I continued to sit there like an idiot, and I would have given anything to wipe that non-expression off her face. Or to inject some sort of feeling into her eyes.

"Until we figure out how to extract you from this mess, keep Rico better updated on all your movements. I won't have you killed because we failed to do our due diligence."

"Just because you failed to do your due diligence?" I asked, unable to help myself.

I'm not sure what reaction I'd hoped to provoke from her, but I was disappointed on all counts because she didn't even blink. She merely fixed me with a pointed look.

"Just do as you're told, Agent O'Connor."

Then she walked out, leaving me to once again stare after her.

CHAPTER TEN

I was shaking as I stepped out of the office building and onto the street, and the blast of wintry air felt fantastic against my overheated skin. Once I accepted the fact that Allison was nowhere to be seen, I slumped against the wall a few steps past the door to the building and bowed my head. I focused on the pavement by the toes of my dress shoes and allowed my thoughts to simply drift for a long moment.

I wasn't sure what to make of what'd just happened, of the news that Allison was pregnant or of the conversation that had followed. I felt somehow lost at sea yet completely weighed down and didn't know what to do. I didn't even know what I was supposed to want to do, let alone what I wanted. I tugged the hair at my forehead as I worried.

My phone buzzed inside my bag, interrupting my directionless wallowing and forcing me out of my head and back into the real world. After pushing myself off the wall with a low groan, I fished it out and looked at it. The words on the screen made me frown, yet my heart leapt, and I had to force myself not to snap my head up. Instead, I made myself read the message again.

Look across the street and to your right.

I sucked the corner of my bottom lip into my mouth and ran my tongue over the cut there. Then I lifted my gaze and casually scanned the street, trying not to look like that's what I was doing. After a few long seconds of searching, I spotted Rico leaning against a lamppost on the corner, his face shielded somewhat by the brim of a baseball cap. You'd think a guy wearing a suit with no tie and a baseball cap would attract attention, but here in New York, that was the least interesting outfit on the street. One of the many reasons I loved this city.

I tried to tell myself not to be disappointed that it wasn't Allison—that it made no sense for her to text me, nor would she have been able to do so since she didn't have my number—but the admonition didn't dampen the regret that blossomed when I realized it wasn't her who'd reached out to me.

As soon as Rico recognized that I'd seen him, he inclined his head to one side a bit, indicating he wanted me to follow him. I glanced around to make sure no one was watching us, and when I'd confirmed that no one appeared to be, I lifted my chin in acknowledgment.

After shoving my phone back into my pocket, I allowed my hand to linger there as I strolled. Nervously, I tapped a staccato rhythm against the edge of the phone with my ring. My heart beat out a matching tempo, and a shiver shot up my spine.

I ambled in the direction I'd seen Rico go and ended up following him into a crowded coffee shop. When I walked in, he was standing in line looking up at the menu, appearing to be a regular guy trying to score a caffeine fix.

I took my place behind him in line and studied the menu also, dragging my gaze away to occasionally regard the other patrons in the shop or the people walking along the sidewalk. Though I was well away from my own neighborhood and the neighborhoods of any of the investigation's targets, I still wasn't about to drop my guard.

"I'm *so* sorry," Rico said softly out of the corner of his mouth, not once looking away from the board detailing the establishment's offerings.

"For what?" I murmured back. I ducked my head and made a show of counting out my money.

Out of the corner of one eye, I saw Rico had bowed his head, too, and adjusted the bill of his ball cap. "I thought we were on you better."

My heart did a little flip, either at the admission itself or the public venue of it. I glanced around again. "It's cool."

"It's not."

I shrugged. He was right. It wasn't. Not even a little bit, but I couldn't do much about it. I hadn't yet figured out how to time travel to rectify any of life's mistakes, and if I ever did, this would be the absolute last on a very long list of stops for me. No sense getting all fired up over something I couldn't change.

"I just got back from CAT school," he said, taking a step forward to keep close enough to the patron in front of his as to maintain his cover as a caffeine addict. It was obviously both an explanation and an excuse, and knowing the proverbial ball hadn't been dropped on his watch made me feel a whole lot better about the entire situation.

"Good." I had to fight not to grin at him as I offered the only form of congratulations I could, given our situation. He'd been wanting to go to Counter Assault Team school for as long as I could remember. His name had been on the list for years. He'd even been tapped to go a couple of times before budget cuts had necessitated the training class be canceled. I was thrilled he'd finally gotten his wish.

"I'll fix it."

"Thanks."

It was his turn to order, and I waited patiently while he flirted with the barista, who giggled like she was thirteen. I rolled my eyes and tried not to laugh. I also tried not to push him to hurry him along, but it was a struggle. Once he'd tired of making the woman behind the counter blush and I'd ordered my own vat of coffee, we shuffled down the line to wait for our drinks.

"You in trouble with the missus?" Rico asked.

"You sure that's how you want to refer to your boss?"

A small smile played at the edges of his lips. "Fair point. You gonna answer my question?"

"She's not happy with either of us. But if I were you, I'd be more worried about myself."

"Because you have ways of making it up to her I can only dream about?"

Now I had to struggle not to punch him. "Because I don't have to see her every day. She'll have had plenty of time to calm down before we cross paths again. You, on the other hand, get to weather that particular storm constantly. Starting this afternoon. Good fucking luck."

He paled and swallowed hard. "Shit."

I grinned and then pulled out my phone and opened a game app so I'd appear engrossed in it and less like I was talking to him.

"Any advice?"

"On?"

"On how to get back into your girlfriend's good graces?"

I paused as I swiped at my phone screen a few times, wincing as I realized I'd overlooked several obvious moves. "Don't argue with her."

Rico snorted. "You do."

I shrugged. "Yeah, but that's our dynamic. It isn't yours. And now seems like a bad time to try to start that, don't you think?"

He grimaced and nodded for me to continue.

"Don't offer excuses. Just have a plan to fix whatever problem she has. And if you don't have one, get one. Fast."

Rico's drink order came up, so he went to retrieve it and then lingered over by the creamer station for me to join him with mine.

"That's it?" Rico said as soon as I reached his side.

I rooted around for the sugar container and started pouring. "That's it."

"Come on. There has to be something else."

I glanced at him out of the corner of one eye without lifting my head. "Nothing else *you* can do."

"I'm so screwed."

I hid my playful shoulder bump beneath reaching across him for a handful of napkins. "Just try to make sure I don't get killed, okay?"

Rico glared at me. "That's not funny."

"Who says I was joking?"

"Ryan."

"Shhh." I scowled at him and glanced around nervously. Sure, I hadn't noticed anyone paying attention to us, but that didn't mean nobody was.

"Sorry." He looked around, too, and dipped his head before lowering his voice. "I'll figure something out, okay?"

"I know you will."

"I don't suppose you have any ideas."

"Besides getting me the tracking device I asked for and assigning someone to specifically monitor it and the phone app at all times? No. I'm out."

"I'm pretty sure your girl is going to take care of that."

I smiled at the thought of her ripping AT Schultz a new one. "Mmm."

"Oh, my God. You're turned on right now, aren't you?"

I blinked. "What?"

Rico was smirking at me. "Imagining your other half going all 'I am woman, hear me roar' is getting you hot and bothered."

I wrinkled my nose at him and made a rude noise in the back of my throat. "Don't be gross." He wasn't wrong, but that didn't mean we needed to discuss specifics.

"Hey, we all have our kinks. Me, I really like it when Paige—"

"I am *begging* you not to finish that sentence."

"I'm just saying."

"Well, stop saying. Please."

He shrugged. "Okay. So does that mean you don't want a play-by-play of how the meeting went down?"

"No. I don't need one. But I do need for you to get your ass back to the office and figure out how to convince your boss not to rip *you* a new one."

He swallowed hard and glanced at his watch. "Yeah. I'd better get going."

"Good luck," I told him as he started to go.

He stopped and turned back to toss a balled-up napkin into the trash can next to me. "Be careful," he whispered.

"I will be."

Chapter Eleven

After Rico left, I settled myself onto a stool in the corner of the cafe and stared out the window, moving only to sip my coffee occasionally or run my fingers along the seam of my paper cup. I tried not to let myself think about how much further we had to go in the operation or all the things that could go wrong before it was finished, but I'm afraid I didn't manage very well.

I shifted, needing to burn off some of my nervous energy, and slid my hand into the pocket of my suit jacket yet froze as my hand hit paper. The envelope Rory had given my father to give me. I fingered it for a long moment as I glanced at and then dismissed random passersby as they wandered past the window where I was sitting. Did I really want to get into this now? Would I be able to concentrate on my fake job if I didn't? I sighed and retrieved the envelope, slowly flattening it out on the counter in front of me.

I stared at it for a long moment before sliding my thumb underneath the corner of the flap and tearing. The paper gave way, and I slipped my finger into the newly made hole so I could rip the envelope along the seam. Tension coiled between my shoulder blades as I captured the edge of the single piece of paper with my thumb and forefinger and pulled it out so I could look at what my sister had written.

On it, in my sister's barely decipherable hand, was a single, unfamiliar phone number. I frowned and turned the paper over, hoping for another clue: a word, a phrase, a drawing of a ladybug wearing a top hat, anything. Nothing. I turned the paper back over and devoured the number for a bit before I stuffed everything into my pocket and pushed the stool away from the counter.

The scrape of the legs against the tile floor was loud, and I winced against the noise. I grabbed my half-empty coffee cup and made my way outside. The gust of wind that hit me the instant my feet touched pavement made me gasp, and I clasped the lapels of my coat tight against my chest with one hand as I tried to keep a firm grip on my coffee with the other. Between the intermittent drafts and the pedestrians jostling me as I tried to make my way down the street, it was tough, so I swallowed the remainder of my drink in one long gulp and tossed the empty cup into the trash.

I shoved my hands into my pockets and curled my fingers around the envelope as I wandered along. I gazed restlessly around the street as I strode, trying to take in people and storefronts all at once. After walking about two blocks, I spotted what I was looking for and let out a deep breath. Then I tightened my grasp on the envelope and quickened my pace.

The quiet of the shop felt thick after the hustle and bustle of the street, and it unsettled me. I tried not to fidget or bounce on the balls of my feet as I conducted the transaction, but it was tough. I couldn't refrain from glancing repeatedly at the clock on the wall behind the salesman, even though I was certain he'd noticed. I clenched my jaw against my rising frustration and forced myself not to snap at him. The entire experience took way longer than I'd hoped, and I was barely able to avoid snatching my purchase out of his hand and darting out the door.

Once I was back on the street, I hurried down the block to a small park and sat down on a vacant bench. My fingers were clumsy as I struggled to extract the crumpled paper from my pocket, and in my awkward fumbling I dropped it twice and had to jump to retrieve it before it blew away. I took a deep breath and told myself to calm the hell down as I dialed the number on the paper from my brand-new burner phone with trembling hands. My heart was pounding, thudding out those deep, hard, forceful beats that drowned out the world around me, the ones that almost hurt.

"Hello?" My sister's voice floated over the line after barely a ring.

"Hey," I said.

"Hey! You got my note."

I looked at the paper in question and debated tearing it into tiny pieces, wanting to ensure no one else would be able to decipher it. Not that it'd matter much, I supposed. But I wasn't about to take any chances.

"Yeah," I said, tilting my head to hold the phone between my shoulder and my ear to free up my other hand to shred my sister's note and the envelope it had come in. "Very cloak-and-dagger."

"Well, I know the stakes. I watch plenty of IDtv." She paused for a long moment, and I thought I heard her sigh, but it was tough to tell over the wind and the roar of my own blood rushing through my ears. "I wasn't sure you'd call."

"Of course I called."

"So you're not mad at me?" She hesitated again. "You know, for taking off."

"I'm not thrilled that you did it, but I guess I get why you felt you had to."

"Do you?"

"Yeah. I really do."

"I guess I'm not mad at you either. You know, anymore."

I smiled and stood, taking care to cup the shrapnel that was the remains of the note and the envelope in the palm of my hand so they wouldn't blow away. I wandered over to a nearby trash can and dumped some of the pieces in, watching them float down to land atop old banana peels, discarded coffee cups, day-old newspapers, and baggies that I assumed were full of dog crap. I put the rest of the pieces back in my pocket and started walking aimlessly.

"How are you doing?" I asked, half afraid of her answer.

"I'm hanging in. You?"

"I'm okay. Better now."

"Now…"

"Now that I know you're back. Now that I know you're safe."

This time I was sure I heard her sigh. "Ryan, I told you before, what happened with Adam wasn't your fault."

I swallowed and closed my eyes to run the knuckle of my thumb across my eyebrow. "Let's not do this now. Please."

"Then let it go."

"Sure." I didn't even try to keep the bitterness out of my tone.

"Did you…" The silence that descended in the wake of those words lasted so long I took the phone away from my ear to confirm we were still connected.

"You still there?"

"Yeah. Did you take the test?"

She didn't elaborate on which test she was talking about. She didn't have to. "No. Not yet. Did you?"

"Why not?"

"Why didn't I take it?"

"Mmm-hmm."

"Because."

"Because you're afraid of what it will say."

"Well, that, and I'm afraid I can still test positive for it down the line. The incubation period hasn't elapsed yet." A strong gust of wind punctuated my statement, and I ducked my head and tucked my chin into my coat, thrusting my hands as far into my pockets as they would go. My left eye had started to water, but I let the tear trickle down my cheek, unwilling to expose my fingers to the cold long enough to wipe it away.

"You completed the PEP regimen?"

"I did. It fucking sucked."

"Side effects?"

I snorted. "All of them. You?"

"Yeah. It wasn't pretty."

"Yeah." The side effects had made it difficult for me to do my job at times, but I'd managed. Barely. It'd been better than the alternative, which'd been sitting alone in my apartment and letting my thoughts consume me.

"So what're you worried about?"

I started to say her name but stopped myself. I glanced around as my nerves skittered and sparked. No one appeared to be paying me any mind, but that didn't mean no one was. I tossed a few more pieces of Rory's note into another trash can as I passed it and scrubbed at my watering eye and my now-wet cheek before tucking my hand back into the relative warmth my pocket provided. "You know that's not one hundred percent effective."

"It increases the odds, though. That's better than nothing."

"True." I didn't have it in me to argue with her. I didn't want to infect her with my special brand of pessimism on the subject. If she needed to believe the post-exposure preventative medication would ensure we didn't get sick, who was I to take that away from her? "Have you been talking to someone?"

"Have you?"

I had to bite my lip again to keep from saying her name. God, she was frustrating. "No, but my experience was different than yours."

"You mean because you weren't raped."

I cringed and dug the fingers of one hand into the meat of my palm as I used the other to move the phone to the opposite ear. "I wish you wouldn't say that."

"Why? Because not saying it out loud will make it less true?"

"Of course not."

"Well, for your information, my therapist told me I needed to start saying it aloud. She said it would help me get over the shame that accompanies the stigma as well as aid me in accepting what happened."

Oh. It'd never occurred to me that she'd been ashamed about it at all. Angry, sick, and confused, yes. But not ashamed. Personally, I didn't think there was anything to be ashamed about. But I guessed everyone processed differently. "Is it working?"

She was quiet for a long moment. "I don't know. It's too soon to tell."

"Are you…Is there like a group or something?"

"A what?"

"You know, like other survivors and stuff."

"Oh. Yeah."

"Have you been?"

"A couple times."

"Are they helping?"

"Again, it's hard to say."

My insides quivered and clenched, and I looked around helplessly. God, what I wouldn't give to be able to shoulder this burden for her. "Well, if there's anything I can do…" I didn't even know how to finish that sentence.

"There's not."

The lance of pain that cut through me on the heels of her words burned worse than anything I'd ever experienced. "I'm sorry," I whispered. Now both eyes were watering, and I opened them wide to get the moisture to dry.

"Just like there's nothing I can do to help you," Rory said.

"Help me with what?"

"The fact that you killed a man."

I turned right at the corner and made my way up the block toward the subway stop. "Why would I need help with that? I don't feel bad about it."

"You don't?" She sounded skeptical. Or maybe a little afraid. I wasn't sure.

"Not even a little bit." And I wasn't lying to make her feel better. I hadn't lost a wink of sleep over his death. Though I'd occasionally wished I'd made him suffer more.

"I do."

"You feel bad that I killed him?" It occurred to me a second after the words left my mouth that anyone listening might interpret that the wrong way and become alarmed. I looked around to see whether my declaration had garnered any reaction. No one had even paused. After all, this was New York. Who knew what people thought I was talking about?

"Not exactly. I feel bad that you had to, if that makes sense."

"Well, don't. I can promise you, it hasn't fazed me."

"And sometimes…" She took a deep breath and let it out slowly.

I slackened my pace to stall my arrival at the subway stop. "Sometimes…?"

"Sometimes I think about the pill I took after."

Her words stole the air from my lungs. "And you get upset about that?"

"No. But sometimes I think about it, and I feel bad that I don't feel worse. Does that sound crazy?"

My lower lip trembled, and I leaned against the side of a building and closed my eyes. "I think that whatever you feel or don't feel is just right."

"I mean, I never even knew for sure that I would've gotten pregnant. I might not have," she said, as though she hadn't already told me this a dozen times, as though she were trying to convince me because I was arguing with her.

"I know." My thoughts drifted to Allison, to her glow, to the life growing inside her. I opened my mouth to tell Rory about it, but then I stopped. This definitely wasn't the time.

"I should probably be upset," Rory said, re-covering ground we'd been over. "Because there's always that slim possibility that maybe… But I'm not."

"And that's fine," I said. My voice sounded small, my tone hollow. "You don't have to feel anything. Nothing's wrong with you."

"I would never have been able to look at it without remembering what'd happened. You know. If there'd been an *it*."

Allison's expression as she told me she'd never forgive herself if she terminated her pregnancy flashed behind my closed eyelids. My throat was suddenly tight and my tongue too big for my mouth. "Then you did the right thing."

"You're not just saying that? You're not just telling me what you think I want to hear?"

I paused as I thought about how Allison would look gently cradling a newborn in her arms. The serenity and joy I imagined radiating from her as she gazed down at her child made my heart shudder and swell and ache. "Of course not," I mumbled, blinking against the tears the stinging cold was bringing to my eyes.

"What if I can't have kids?" Rory blurted out, surprising me.

"What?"

She took a deep breath and let out a weary sigh. "Well, if I end up HIV positive, I can't exactly have unprotected sex with anyone to get pregnant. So what if taking that pill—if ensuring there was no chance for the rape to result in a pregnancy—meant I ruined my last shot to have children?"

"Oh." Not being in a position where that was either a problem or an option for me, I hadn't considered the possibility. "You don't know that you are, though. You said yourself you'd taken the meds." And she'd just been trying to convince me I had nothing to worry about, but I decided it was better not to bring that up. She had something on her mind. I needed to let her get it out. "Besides, you can always do in-vitro if you want to conceive."

"Yeah, I guess. But what if I pass it along to the baby?"

"I don't know. You'd have to do more research about that. But I think I remember hearing that it's possible to have a child when you're HIV positive. You still don't know that you are, though, so…"

"No. I suppose not."

"Wait. You're a doctor. Shouldn't you know all this stuff already? Or at least have easy ways of finding it out?"

Silence. "Well…yes…"

"But you're still afraid that somehow, some way, things just won't be that easy for you."

"Yeah."

"*If* you're even positive. Which you probably aren't." Strange that I was trying so hard to convince her that she was going to be okay, yet I couldn't entertain that possibility myself. Ah, the mysterious curiosities of the mind.

"Yeah," Rory said, her voice low.

We both lapsed into silence then, and my mind drifted back to Allison and her unexpected pregnancy. No, this definitely wasn't the time to discuss this development with Rory. I closed my eyes again, wishing I had a time machine so I could make everything just stop. Just for a minute. Just so I could get my bearings. Just so I could breathe.

"Are you okay?" Rory's voice broke into my pointless yearning.

I opened my eyes and pushed off the wall, shaking my head to banish the image. "Yeah. I'm fine. It's just been a long couple of days. A long couple of weeks, really."

"You're okay with this operation? You're being careful?"

"Of course. But I have to go now. I have to get ready for work."

"Your cover job?"

"Yeah. I need to go home and change."

"Stay safe. That's what you guys tell each other, right?"

I smiled. "Yeah. We do."

"Okay, then do it."

"I will."

"Call me when you can. Day or night. I'll leave the phone on."

"Okay."

"I love you, Ryan."

"I love you, too."

I hung up before she said anything else. Then I dropped the remaining pieces of her note along with my new burner phone into the nearest trash can and headed down the steps to catch a train back downtown.

CHAPTER TWELVE

It was a good thing the print shop I "worked" for was just a cover and that the majority of the people wandering in and out of it were federal agents who were either helping make the operation look good or were there to talk to one of the guys upstairs, because my mind definitely wasn't on my job. The handful of regular civilians who'd moseyed in thinking it was an actual store hadn't brought me anything too complicated, for which I was grateful. I didn't have it in me to convincingly pretend I knew anything about design.

The last client had thrown me for a loop. It'd been a woman inquiring about custom invitations for her child's first birthday party. As far as I was concerned, her timing couldn't have been more unfortunate. After all the talk about babies I'd already endured, the last thing I needed was to be confronted by one. But there it was, staring at me sleepily from its mother's arms. They'd left more than fifteen minutes ago, but their presence still lingered in the shop the way the aroma of homemade tacos stains your kitchen, and my stomach was still in knots.

My distraction had made me clumsy, and I'd just knocked over the cup of ballpoint pens that the set team had placed on the counter next to the computer monitor. I sighed and bent down to gather them up just as the doorbell chimed, indicating that someone had entered the shop. Crouched behind the counter, I couldn't see who it was, so I called out, "I'll be right with you."

"Take your time," a man replied.

I finished cleaning up the mess as quickly as I could and stood, my blood turning to ice-cold sludge in my veins, and the operation of all my internal organs grinding to a halt. Seth Gatsonis, the number-two guy in the terrorist organization we were trying to stop, was standing an arm's length away, looking at me intently. Of course, I wasn't supposed to know who he was since Tate had yet to introduce me. Fuck. I needed to play this off.

I flashed him my best shop-girl smile and prayed to whatever deity might be listening that he hadn't seen the flash of recognition that had to have flickered behind my eyes. I also prayed that the gaggle of agents upstairs was paying attention and would wait until this conversation ended before completing their shift change. I had no idea how I'd explain it if they all came piling out of the back—where the stairway was located—now.

"What can I do for you?" I asked, pushing the toe of my shoe against the underside of the counter to force myself to focus on the present and not look like I was listening for footsteps I hoped I'd never hear.

Seth rested one forearm on the counter and smiled back. "Well, that's the million-dollar question, isn't it?"

"Sure is. You looking for something particular?"

"I might be. You guys do custom work, right?"

I gestured to the art the ATF had provided when they'd set up shop—courtesy of whatever their version of the Visual Information Branch was, no doubt—and hoped he didn't expect me to mock anything up for him now. That'd blow my cover for sure. I could work PowerPoint to a great enough degree to produce site diagrams, but that was about the extent of my artistic expertise. "Absolutely. On the wall, you can see some examples of past jobs we've done, and I have a book around here somewhere if you want to look at it."

"That's okay," he said, interrupting my search. "I've got something specific in mind."

"Okay. Lay it on me." I grabbed a pad of paper and one of the pens I'd just retrieved from the ground so I could take notes for the guys who'd actually be doing the work, biting my lip when I noticed my hands were trembling. I hoped he'd just think I was overcaffeinated or strung out and wouldn't recognize my behavior as nervousness. Part of me had debated keeping my hands hidden behind the counter, figuring the ATF guys could just listen to the tapes to get the details—this place was wired better than Nixon had wired the Oval Office—but I was afraid it'd look suspicious if I didn't at least jot something down.

"Can you guys do money?"

"Excuse me?"

"Fake money, can you do it?"

I hadn't expected him to be so direct about it. "Not legally."

He laughed. "Of course not. I didn't mean fake money to pass off as real money. I meant like a joke."

"A joke," I repeated, allowing my lack of comprehension and skepticism to color my words.

"My buddy's turning fifty this year, and I'm organizing a black-tie, casino-themed party. I want to make some phony bills with his face on them for the guests to play with. You know, like party favors."

Ah. Clever. That was quite a story. I had to give him points for originality. I also had to be careful not to fuck this up. My heart was racing, and it was a trick to keep my breathing even. "Oh, sure. I can do that. You want all denominations of bills or just fifties to mark the occasion?"

"You mean you do the work yourself?"

"Most of it. What? You thought I was just here to look good and take the orders?" I grinned at him. At least I hoped it was a grin. But it felt more like a grotesque imitation.

He laughed again, so it must've been passable. "I won't argue with the looking-good part. I plead the Fifth on the part about just taking orders."

"Smart man."

"I know how to make a woman happy."

"I'll bet you do." *Ew. Just ew.* "So, do you have a picture of your friend for the bills?"

"Not on me. I can email it to you later, if that'd help. Do you have a card?"

I leaned over and plucked one of my fake business cards out of the holder on the edge of the counter and tried not to frown when his gaze dropped to my chest at the motion. "Here you go."

"Alex Travers," he read aloud before slipping it into his pocket.

"That's me."

"Well, let me ask you something, Alex Travers."

"Only if you stop saying my full name like that. It makes me feel like I'm back in high school being called to the principal's office because I'm in trouble."

"You? In trouble? A cute little thing like you? I don't believe it for a minute."

Could I play it off if I gagged? Probably not. "You'd be surprised," I said with a smirk, because at least that part was true. A great many things about me would likely surprise him. "What'd you wanna ask me?"

"Well, this guy whose birthday it is, he's my oldest friend in the entire world. And we always go all out for one another's celebrations. It's like a contest to see who can top the other."

I nodded and tried to look interested. "Sounds like fun."

"Yeah, well, obviously I need these to look good."

"You're already insulting my work, and I haven't even done it yet?" I said teasingly. "Ouch."

"No, no. I'm sure it'll look great. But will it feel like real money?" When I just furrowed my eyebrows at him, he went on. "You know how real money has texture to it? I want that."

"Oh. So, you want me to actually use a press instead of just a printer."

"Is that how they make real money?"

I had to fight not to roll my eyes. As if he really didn't know. "Yup."

"Can you do that?"

I shrugged. "It'll cost more because it'll be more work for me, but sure. I can do that."

"Oh, money's no object."

I raised an eyebrow. "This guy must be a really good friend. I haven't even told you what the damage is yet."

"He is. Besides, no matter what I spend, it still won't top the year he flew ten of us on a private charter jet to a fantasy hockey camp."

"Wow. That sounds awesome."

"I'm still trying to top that one. But I think with your help I'll be on the right track."

"How much time are we talking? Is this a rush job? Because that'll cost extra."

"Not too much of a rush. The party's not for a few weeks."

I wondered whether he was thinking of a specific timetable and, if so, what might be the significance behind it. The next Muslim holiday wasn't for several months. Could they be planning on marking a Christian holiday? I thought the next one of those was several months away, too. I'd have to remember to ask Tate later if he'd heard anything that might fit with this schedule.

"Okay, well, why don't you think about what denominations of bills you want, what you might want them to say, and how many we're talking about. And let me know when you email me the picture. Then I'll send you over some mockups, and you can decide which ones you like best. You need chips, too?"

He stared at me blankly for a long moment. "Chips?"

"Like casino chips." He still didn't say anything. "To go with your casino-night theme?"

"Oh. Right. Chips. You can do that, too?"

"Not me personally, but I know a guy who'll put something I design onto some. I can make a call if you want. Get you a good price."

"Let's just start with the bills, and I'll let you know about the chips."

"Fair enough. Just so you know, for something custom like this, there's a design fee. If you decide you want to proceed with the actual product, it'll be applied to your total."

"Sounds fair."

"When you send me your friend's picture, I'll hit you back for a method of payment before I begin the work."

"Okay. I'll send that over to you as soon as possible."

"Have a great night," I told him.

He smiled at me and left the shop. Once the door had swung shut, I let out a relieved breath and slumped over the counter. Closing my eyes, I rubbed at my temple with trembling fingertips.

"That was unexpected," a voice said behind me, causing me to jump.

I whirled around, ready for a fight, but it was just one of the ATF guys. Pike was his last name. I don't think I'd ever heard his first. I cast a wary glance toward the door to the shop but didn't see any sign of Seth. "Yeah. It was. You guys heard all that, right?"

He nodded and stepped up so he was standing next to me. "We did. Guess that means the case is finally about to take off."

I swallowed against the giant lump that'd lodged in my throat and tried to ignore the resulting discomfort. "Tate said he thought it'd be sooner rather than later." My voice wavered.

"You ready for that?"

If it'd been a guy from my own agency asking me that question, I'd have quipped back that it didn't matter whether I was ready or not because we were about to go anyway. But I didn't want to appear unprofessional. And I really didn't want to seem scared. So I settled for nodding. "The sooner this starts, the sooner it ends, and I can get back to my life."

He clapped me on my bad shoulder, and I hissed quietly at the contact. It didn't hurt nearly as bad as it had when I'd first been shot—it was more of a dull, annoying ache at this point—but that didn't mean I was comfortable with people manhandling it. "I think you'll get your wish sooner than you think. I'm gonna go call this in. You okay here?"

I nodded even though he'd already turned away. "I'm good," I said softly to his retreating form, thinking about how right Allison had been earlier about what a terrible liar I was. That statement didn't convince even me.

CHAPTER THIRTEEN

Y ou okay?" Tate asked, hooking the elbow of my good arm with his hand just as I was about to reach for the door to the bar. When I looked up at him, he used his grip to gently guide me out of the way. "You've been quiet all evening."

"I've just got a lot on my mind. That's all."

"And not all of it's the op, is it?"

I sighed and raked my fingers through my hair, scratching my nails hard against my scalp. "Not all of it, no."

"That woman?"

I shook my head a little and rolled the earrings adorning my left ear between the pads of my forefinger and thumb. "I don't want to talk about it. Especially not here."

"What are you guys doing?" someone said from behind me.

I froze, my heart lodged behind my eyeballs and pounding furiously, before I turned around to see Crash and Barker grinning at us. Fuck. I really hoped they hadn't heard any of that. Or that if they had, they'd just think I was nervous about a threesome.

Tate wound an arm around my waist and pulled me into him. "Just talking."

Crash made a face. "You'd better not be thinking about ditching to go fuck somewhere."

"Wouldn't you, if you were me?" Tate said, wrapping his other arm around me.

Crash let his gaze wander down my body and then back up, and I had to force myself not to squirm under the attention or punch him to make him stop. "Probably. But you might want to stick around anyway."

"Why's that?" Tate asked.

"Rumor has it Seth's coming tonight. Maybe Nathan, too."

I sucked in a harsh breath and turned my face so it was buried in

Tate's neck. The move was intended to hide my expression, but I was counting on Crash mistaking it for disinterest. After all, as far as he knew, I had no clue who either Seth or Nathan was. I needed to make sure it stayed that way.

"Really?" Tate dug his fingers into my hips as I dug my own into his lower back. "They almost never come out."

"True," Crash said. "But tonight's special."

"It is? Why?" Tate obviously wanted to know. I could feel the vibrations of his voice against my cheek.

"You'll see."

Tate didn't reply.

"So, whatever you guys are going to do, you better hurry up and do it. You're not going to want to miss this."

"We'll be right in," Tate said, ducking his head to brush his lips against my throat.

"Whatever," Crash replied, but his voice sounded farther away, so I assumed he was leaving.

"Is he gone?" I whispered into Tate's ear after a moment.

Tate nodded and pulled back, leaving me room to glance around. He and I were more or less alone on the street, and far enough away from the bouncer at the door that he wouldn't be able to hear us. But I doubted it'd stay that way long, so I resolved to be more on my guard. I tilted my head up so I could look into Tate's eyes and saw worry mixed with curiosity lurking there.

"What's wrong?" I wanted to know.

"Something doesn't feel right."

"You mean about Seth and Nathan? Or about this special night?"

"Both."

"Any idea why tonight's different from any other night?"

"Not a clue."

"They didn't say anything?"

"Nope."

"That's weird."

"Yeah."

"Hmmm." I rubbed my lips. "And you can't think of anything that would bring Nathan or Seth out tonight?"

Tate shook his head and took a step back, releasing his hold on me completely. I shivered at the loss of his body heat and pulled my coat tighter around myself. "No. I've got nothing. They've never come here. Not once. Not in all the months I've been hanging out with these guys."

"So why now?" I asked.

"It makes you wonder."

"And why here? Why someplace so public?"

"Exactly. It doesn't make sense. Unless…"

"Unless they're not worried about people seeing them because this group is even bigger than we first thought."

"Are you thinking that this isn't just a bar? That it's a peripheral base of operations?"

"I dunno. Maybe it's nothing. Maybe this really is just a party. But if it's not, that means all the people we haven't been paying too much attention to, we should've been." I mean, I'd been sort of tangentially looking at them, but more as witnesses than perpetrators. Fuck.

Tate's brows bunched, and the corners of his mouth pulled down in a small frown. "Crash was being unusually cryptic, too, don't you think?"

My mouth was dry, and I licked my lips. "Hmm. He's normally a lot more bluster and bravado, yes."

"Any idea why the change?"

"You'd know better than I would. You know him. I don't. I'm just the arm candy, remember?"

Tate was staring at the door to the bar, deep in thought. "Mmm."

"What is it?"

"It's just…" His frown deepened, and he started fiddling with the leather cord he wore around his neck. "No one else said anything about Seth or Nathan coming out tonight."

"So?"

"So how would Crash know?"

I considered that question. "Are you thinking maybe he's closer to the inner circle than we originally thought?"

"He must be, though I haven't seen anything so far to indicate that."

"Who have you been dealing with when you've been talking about getting weapons and such?"

"A different guy. John Smith. He reports directly to Nathan and Seth."

I rolled my eyes. "That cannot possibly be his real name."

Tate smiled. "Believe it or not, it is. We've verified."

"Huh. Interesting."

"It's a goddamn clusterfuck is what it is." Tate closed his eyes and rubbed the space between his brows with the knuckle of one thumb. "We haven't seen anything to indicate that Crash is in regular contact with either Nathan or Seth."

"But we both know that doesn't mean he's not," I said, thinking of how I'd talked to my sister earlier today, and it was likely no one would ever know about that conversation. "Prepaid burner phones are a godsend to criminals. I don't have to tell you that. Besides, we aren't monitoring anyone's phones in real time yet. We're still waiting on the court orders to come through for that, right?"

He nodded.

"So maybe Crash is in this thing up to his eyeballs and just hasn't let that fact slip in front of you yet."

"The entire point of me being here is so we don't get blindsided by this sort of stuff." Tate's voice was a low grumble, and his entire body was wire tight.

"And now we know."

"Fuck," he said and banged his fist against the side of the building.

I glanced at the people streaming by us on their way to the party to see whether anyone was watching us. A few people had seen Tate's display and were trying to pretend they weren't staring, but that was to be expected when someone started punching walls. I put one hand on Tate's arm.

"Hey. Calm down. You're starting to attract attention."

He ran the fingers of one hand through his hair while he inspected the bloody knuckles of the other. He lifted his injured hand to his lips and took a long moment to suck on the newly acquired cuts. When he was finished, he favored me with a lopsided smile. "Sorry."

My pulse was racing, and I struggled to keep my hands and my voice steady. "Nothing we can do about any of this now. We're expected to make an appearance tonight, and it'll look weird if we don't show."

Tate nodded. "Yeah. I guess you're right."

"Well, then let's just stick with the original plan and see what happens." I didn't feel good about it. Not at all. But what else could I do? This was a great chance to glean some new intel, and my first opportunity to actually put Seth and Nathan in a room with anyone associated with this group. I wasn't about to pass that up. When Tate didn't move right away, I held out my hand, waiting for him to take it. After a beat, he did. "You ready to go in?"

"As I'll ever be, I suppose."

I tugged him along behind me. "Okay. Then let's get this over with."

The bar was even more packed than usual, which I found odd, considering the sign on the door announced the establishment was closed for a private party. There were a lot of faces I recognized as well as a lot of faces I didn't. I scanned the crowd as I threaded my way through it, trying to memorize as many details as I could. I planned to break away to the relative solitude of the bathroom and text Rico some of the specifics at the earliest opportunity. But right now, I needed to blend in and try to be as inconspicuous as possible.

"Tate," Crash shouted over the din. "Alex. Over here."

I rolled my eyes. So much for inconspicuous. Tate nudged the small of my back with the heel of his hand, and I started making my way over to where the group of people I knew was gathered. Emma handed me a beer when I sidled up next to her, and we engaged in idle chitchat as I tried to casually survey the crowd.

My nerves spooled tighter and tighter the longer the party went on, and I was having trouble making myself stand still. I needed to move, to pace and flail or at least talk out some of my nervous energy, but my situation prevented that, and it was driving me nuts. I smiled and nodded at whatever Emma was going on about and took a shaky sip of my beer. Either something needed to happen or I needed to get the hell out of here, and soon. Maybe now would be a good time to go to the bathroom.

I handed Emma my beer—my third of the evening, or was it my fourth?—and had started to excuse myself when I heard raised voices across the room, followed by the sounds of shushing being carried back through the crowd. The hissing noises of people trying to quiet one another continued for a long moment, and I exchanged a puzzled glance with Tate. He shrugged and fixated his attention on where I could see two people standing on a raised platform that normally served as a stage on nights there was live music.

I tapped Emma on the shoulder, motioned for her to hand me back my beer, and focused on where everyone else was looking. A few whispers and murmurs sounded from folks nearby, but I couldn't decipher them, so I settled for waiting impatiently for the show to start.

The squeal of a microphone emitting feedback accompanied the illumination of a spotlight, and everyone groaned and winced in unison. Now that the stage was lit up, I could see that one of the people occupying it was Seth, and he smiled a little as he lifted the mike to his lips. A gigantic American flag hung at his back on top of the red velvet curtain that usually graced the stage. I raised an eyebrow and looked around, but no one seemed to find the flag noteworthy.

"Testing, testing," Seth said, his expression indicating he was expecting more feedback. His posture eased when his words carried without incident, and he smiled wider. "Welcome, everyone. Thank you all for coming."

The hissing and murmuring died down, and the crowd grew silent except for the occasional cough or rustle of fabric as someone shifted.

I glanced around again and noticed everyone staring at the stage with rapt attention. I bumped the edge of Tate's free hand with my own, and he fluttered his pinkie finger against mine.

"As many of you probably already know, I'm Seth Gatsonis, and this is Nathan Scoles. He and I go back a lot of years. I'm not going to tell you exactly how many"—the crowd chuckled—"but suffice it to say this man here is my best friend in the whole world."

Nathan gave a sort of halfhearted wave but didn't look at Seth, and he didn't smile. My chest contracted, and I clenched my teeth and took a deep breath against my building unease. My pinkie tightened around Tate's, and he shuffled closer to me.

"Nathan had a son, my godson, Bobby, and today would've been his twenty-sixth birthday. Sadly, Bobby was killed serving this great country almost three years ago." Seth paused and took a moment to clear his throat. "I know a lot of you in this room tonight knew him, but for those of you who didn't, I'm sorry. You missed out. God never created a finer human being. He's been sorely missed, and he'll continue to be sorely missed for the rest of our days on earth."

Murmurs of agreement rippled through the throng, and the grip around my heart tightened. Nathan was tough to read. He was scanning the gathering, but it was hard for me to tell whether he was so emotionless because he was trying not to break down in a room full of people over the loss of his son or whether he was too busy sizing everybody up to even register what Seth was saying.

"Anyway, Nathan and I wanted to thank you all for coming tonight to celebrate Bobby's life. And if anyone has anything to say about Bobby, well, we'll leave the mike on. Just come up and start talking." Seth stopped and moved as though to walk away before turning back quickly. "Oh, but keep it clean. Bobby's grandma is here somewhere. No need to traumatize the poor woman. You can tell the raunchy stories among yourselves."

Several people laughed, and Seth grinned before leaning in to murmur in Nathan's ear and clapping him on the shoulder. Together, the two of them left the stage as other people jockeyed to get up onto it.

Conversation started to pick up around us again as Tate and I exchanged a glance. He seemed tense, on edge. I studied him, noting his rigid posture and the tightness around his lips and eyes. It seemed a shadow had darkened his soul, and I opened my mouth to ask him what was up, but before I could get a word in, he wrapped an arm around my shoulder and pressed his lips against my ear. "Give it a few minutes. Then we'll slip out for a bit."

I nodded and turned to ghost my lips across his jaw, then tucked my head under his chin. With my ear resting flush against his chest the way it was, I could hear his heart galloping, thudding against the hollow of my cheek. It pretty much matched mine beat for beat. I took a deep, shaky breath and let it out in a count of six. The move didn't help calm me, but it did give me something else to concentrate on.

"Did you know Bobby, Crash?" Tate was asking, his voice a low rumble that tickled my ear. I lifted my head and rubbed the now-tingling skin. I would've sworn I'd heard a tremor in his voice and was dying to ask him about it, but now wasn't the time.

Crash was gulping his beer, so he took a second to answer. "Mmm. Yeah. We grew up together."

"Were you close?"

"You could say that."

The silence that fell between them then landed with all the subtlety of a bowling ball being dropped from a third-story balcony. I wrapped my arm around Tate's waist and slipped my fingers under the hem of his shirt so I could touch his skin. Then I pushed. Hard. Tate tapped me on the arm, and I eased up a bit.

"Well, we're very sorry for your loss."

Something dark flickered in Crash's eyes, and he exchanged a glance with Barker, who turned away. "Thanks. He was a good guy. Which reminds me, I want to go say hi to his grandma before she leaves. She never stays at these things long. I'll be back."

Crash turned to follow Barker, and Tate and I took the opportunity to slip away to a relatively unoccupied corner of the room. Tate leaned into me, pressing me up against the wall and blocking me from the rest of the crowd with his body. I could see how tense he was, which only wound me up more. What was going on with him?

"Okay," I said in a low voice close to his ear. "Was any of that new information to you?"

"All of it, actually."

"How? Didn't you guys run checks on Nathan when this all started?"

"We did. But we didn't find anything about a son."

"Did you find anything at all? Credit history? Soc? Parking tickets? Anything?"

"I'm pretty sure the guys working up that part of the case did find something. What, I can't remember."

"So what are you thinking?"

"Maybe Nathan Scoles is an alias?"

"Or maybe Bobby's mom left Nathan when Bobby was small?"

"Maybe she remarried, or they never married at all, and Bobby's last name wasn't Scoles." Tate finished my thought.

"We've got a lot of maybes."

"We do. And no way to check any of them right now."

"Then let's focus on what we do know. A man who would've been twenty-six today died overseas serving in the military."

"I'm sure it won't be too hard to figure out which branch. Someone here has to know. And that's not a strange question to ask."

"It might explain why Nathan and Seth are so radical in their beliefs. They obviously harbor some resentment over what happened to Bobby."

"It's very likely."

"We're going to need specifics."

"I'll see what I can get out of the guys tonight. And once we leave here, I'll pop this new intel over to the squad and see what they can run down."

I hummed and gripped the hem of Tate's shirt just above the waistband of his jeans. If someone happened to glance our way, I wanted it to look like we were doing more than just talking, like we were wrapped up in one another. "Seth said Bobby died almost three years ago, didn't he?" I asked.

Tate nodded. "Yeah. Why?"

"Well, you said there's been talk of something going down pretty soon."

"That's the word. I've been told to step up my efforts to find us a sympathetic contact because they want the firepower ASAP. But they're being pretty tight-lipped about the specifics. I suspect that's a CYA move on their part. I mean, obviously, they're still keeping certain things from me. Why do you ask?"

"I've been trying to figure out roughly when they might make their move, but I've been stumped because I've been focusing on religious holidays, and there aren't any for several months, which doesn't seem to fit with that timetable..."

"But they might be planning something for the anniversary of Bobby's death," Tate said, picking up on my thought.

I swiped the palm of my hand across my forehead to slick away the beads of sweat gathering there and wiped them on the leg of my jeans before threading my arm around Tate's waist again. "It's my best guess. We need to find out exactly when he died."

"I'm on it."

"There's something else."

"What?"

"Seth came into the shop today." When Tate's expression darkened and his body tensed, I frowned. "Your counterparts who spend the day there with me didn't tell you."

He shook his head. "No. But I haven't had time to check in. Until I met up with you, I was with Dixon all day. What did he want?"

"He had some story about needing fake money for some party he's throwing. Wanted to know whether I could do it and how realistic I could make it look." I paused as something occurred to me. "Come to think of it, the timetable he gave me was only a couple weeks."

Tate sucked in a swift breath. "That's not a very big window."

"No. But now that we have some clue, it should be enough for us to get our assets in place to stop whatever they have planned, shouldn't it? I mean, they can't sell a large volume of counterfeit money *that* quickly. Especially if they're trying to avoid drawing attention to themselves. They'll need some time to raise the capital they want before they'll have enough to pay for the guns. It buys us a little time." But the specifics of their plan still didn't make a whole lot of sense.

Tate's eyes held a faraway cast. "Yeah." He blinked slowly and then looked around once before brushing his lips against my cheek. "I'm going to see what I can find out."

"Okay. I'll do a little subtle digging of my own."

"Be careful."

"You, too."

CHAPTER FOURTEEN

While Tate made his way through the crowd to go who knew where to talk to God only knew who, I snagged an empty stool at the bar to see what I could glean by eavesdropping on nearby conversations. I flagged down Ronnie to order a beer, and as I watched him pour it, I wondered whether he'd known Bobby and if he knew anything about this group. He could've been a part of it, for all I knew. We didn't have the entire membership list, which made it tough to tell who I needed to watch out for.

Ronnie set the beer in front of me, and I'd just taken my first sip when I heard someone say "Alex Travers" behind me.

Startled, I spun around and came face-to-face with Seth. I didn't even try to mask my surprise. "Hey. Of all the gin joints in all the towns in all the world…"

Seth smiled and leaned heavily on the bar next to me. "I believe it was you who walked into mine."

"So I did. But in my defense, I didn't realize it at the time."

"So you're not stalking me."

"'Fraid not. Relieved?"

"Disappointed."

"Well, how about I buy you a beer to make it up to you?"

Seth raised an eyebrow and looked me up and down. I held my breath and tightened my grip on my glass as I tried to force myself to act like I was enjoying the inspection. Or at least like it didn't make me want to wrinkle my nose and beat feet out of there.

"Girls today sure are forward. I can't decide whether I like that or not."

"Well, how about a drink while you think about it? I'd offer to let you buy me one to preserve your masculinity, but Ronnie just set me up, so I'm good for a bit yet."

Seth looked amused. "Okay. But only if you let me get the next round."

"I won't say no to free beer." I waved at Ronnie and signaled to him that I needed another before turning back to Seth.

"Are you sure you're old enough to drink?"

I scoffed. "I know a woman likes to be told she looks young, but she doesn't like to hear she looks like jailbait."

"And a man doesn't like to buy drinks for a woman who actually *is* jailbait."

I lifted my glass in salute to his sentiment. "Fair enough. I'm twenty-four." I wasn't, actually. Not even close. But I could almost pass for it, which was one reason they'd thought I'd be perfect for this assignment. Even leaders of a radical, fringe, pseudo-militia group dropped their guard around a girl who looked like she was barely out of college.

He narrowed his eyes as he studied me, presumably trying to determine whether I was telling the truth.

"Do you wanna see my ID?" I asked, reaching for my pocket.

"No. I believe you. I was just thinking about how you'd have been exactly Bobby's type. He'd have been all over you if he were here. And you must not have known him, because I'm sure he'd have mentioned you."

"No. You're right. I didn't know him. I came here with someone tonight. But I've been listening to people tell stories about him. He sounds like a great guy. I'm very sorry for your loss."

Seth took the glass Ronnie set in front of him and stared into it for a long moment before taking a sip. "It was hard."

I let that statement settle between us before I spoke again. "You wanna talk about it?"

He took another deep swig and smacked his lips. "Not much to say. He was a good kid who died too soon in a pointless war." He sighed and went back to staring at his beer.

"Lot of wars are pointless," I said.

He shifted his gaze so he was looking at me out of the corner of his eye. "You lose someone?"

"My dad," I said, feeding him a cover story Tate and I had constructed ages ago for just such a situation.

"When?"

"In 2003. IED."

"I'm sorry."

I shrugged. "It was a long time ago. A lot longer ago than your loss."

"Still. The pain never really goes away, does it?"

"No. Not really." I paused. "You serve?"

Seth shook his head. "No. Not me. Nathan did, though."

"So heroism runs in the family, then."

Seth's expression on the heels of my statement was odd. Like a mixture of pain and regret shot through with tiny slivers of fear. "Guess so. You remember him? Your dad?"

I smiled. "Not much. I was really small when he left. But my mom likes to tell a story about how he wanted to try to teach me to fight. Said he wanted to make sure I'd be able to put the boys in their place till he came home to make sure they stayed there. Like I was even old enough for that."

"But he never came home."

I allowed my smile to fall. "No. He didn't."

Seth's gaze flickered down to my lip. "That's not from a guy failing to keep his place, is it? Maybe that guy I saw punching a wall earlier?"

Fuck! I knew some people had seen that, but I hadn't realized Seth had been one of them. Yeah, flying under the radar was so off the table. I cocked my head as I studied him, trying to appear as though I were attempting to figure out what his interest was rather than freaking out while trying to simultaneously determine why he'd decided to pretend he didn't know Tate. "That's a pretty personal question, don't you think?"

"Is that a yes?"

I shook my head. "No. It's not."

"It's not a yes? Or that's not what happened?"

"Planning to avenge my honor?"

"Do you need me to?"

I laughed. "Do I really seem like the kind of girl who'd let a guy beat on her?"

"Lots of women say they'd never allow it. But somehow it ends up happening anyway." Something dark flickered behind his eyes, and his jaw tensed. He took another long gulp of his beer. "A man shouldn't hit a woman. Ever."

"Sounds as though you're speaking from experience," I said lightly, wondering whether I was going too far. "Your mom?"

It was Seth's turn to smile. "Not *my* mom. My mom was a pistol. Even if it'd occurred to my dad to knock her around—which it didn't—she'd have given it right back to him. And won."

"So someone else then." My mind worked overtime to try to make the connection, as this was obviously an important topic to him and might give us some insight we'd need down the line. Something about the way he'd emphasized "my" a minute ago stuck with me. If it wasn't his mom, it was someone else's. And who had we just been talking about? "Bobby's mom?"

The muscles in Seth's forearms bunched as his grip tightened on the glass he now held in both hands. He didn't say anything for a moment. But then he relaxed and turned his head to smile at me. "No. But you know what? You were right. This stuff is far too personal, not to mention depressing, for an already dark day. How about something lighter?"

Interesting. Seems I'd touched a nerve with my question. Seth's "no" just now was less than convincing, which made me wonder. Had Nathan knocked Bobby's mom around? I'd seen the man for only a few scant minutes, and while he'd seemed a bit broody, that didn't necessarily mean he was prone to beat on women. But that didn't rule it out, either. Tate said they hadn't found any indication of a wife or a son, which suggested she'd been out of the picture for a while. Was that why? Had she left because Nathan had been violent?

And what of Seth's reaction to my suggestion? Just how close had he and Bobby's mom been? He'd said Nathan was his best friend, so he must've known Bobby's mom. A flashbulb went off inside my brain, and it was an effort for me to keep my eyes from widening or my gaze snapping to where Seth was ordering us another round and chatting with Ronnie while he poured. Was it possible he and Nathan's ex had been lovers? Was he Bobby's dad? It would explain why he was so invested in this subject.

"Here you go," Seth said, setting a fresh beer in front of me and interrupting my thoughts. "Fresh drink, fresh conversation. No more talk of why your lip's split open, deal?"

I held up my glass. "Deal."

"You wanna know why her lip's busted?" a voice said from behind us. "I'll tell you."

Seth and I both turned to see Crash standing there grinning at us. His eyes were a touch glassy, and his cheeks were flushed, which led me to believe he'd been pounding shots, and hard. I glanced around for Tate, but he was nowhere to be seen.

Seth shifted his attention from Crash to me. "I see you two have met."

I rolled my eyes and nodded. "Can't say it's been a pleasure."

Crash narrowed his eyes. "With a mouth like that, it's no wonder she popped you. What'd you say to her anyway? I never did ask."

Seth's eyebrows shot up into his hairline. "She?"

I shrugged. "Told you I wouldn't let a man hit me."

"But you let a woman?"

"I wouldn't say let, exactly." Not only was that just what'd happened, but I'd asked for it. He didn't need to know that, though. "She caught me off guard."

Crash laughed. "It was priceless."

"Weren't we going to change the subject?" I said to Seth.

"We were. Let's see. What would be a safe topic for mixed company?"

"Did you see that fucker Carmichael is coming back here again?" Crash chimed in.

My heart stopped beating, and I held my breath. Of course they'd shift the topic to the president. Because that was just the kind of luck I had. And I could tell by Crash's tone and Seth's expression that this wasn't going anywhere good. Suddenly, I wished I'd entertained the questions about my lip. "Aren't politics, religion, and sex supposed to be off the table if you want to ensure a conversation stays civil?"

"Where'd you hear that?" Seth asked Crash, his brows pulled down into a scowl.

I cast my gaze heavenward and took a long, deep drink to overpower the urge to sigh. No way did I want any part of whatever they were about to say, but the way we were all configured left me sort of blocked in. Would it be too obvious if I excused myself? I glanced around for Tate again, hoping he'd come to my rescue.

"Saw it on the news," Crash was saying. "Some campaign fund-raiser. Like the guy isn't up here every other week."

I pursed lips. He wasn't wrong. President Carmichael, code name Harbinger, did spend a fair amount of time campaigning in New York, but I suspected my annoyance with the president's frequent visits stemmed from a different reason than his.

Seth's reply got lost beneath my own musings, but I did rejoin the discussion just in time to hear Crash say, "Fucking bullshit."

I looked from Seth to Crash and back again, my heart shriveling at their expressions. *Oh, please, don't say it.* My heart winked out of existence altogether, and the space where it'd been flashed a burning sort of cold that gave me goose bumps. I held my breath. *Oh, please, please, please, don—*

"Cocksucker deserves a bullet to the head," Crash said.

I closed my eyes, let out the breath I'd been holding, and bowed my head. *Fuck. He said it.*

"Don't worry," Seth said. "He'll get it."

My head snapped up, and I inhaled so fast I choked. I doubled over and started coughing uncontrollably as Seth pounded me on the back. *Great. Fucking great. Like I needed to start a PI investigation on these mopes on top of everything else.*

"You okay?" he asked.

I sputtered for what felt like three or four lifetimes before I was finally able to choke out, "Wrong pipe." I took several greedy, gulping breaths and hoped with everything I had the explanation was plausible.

"She can't hold her liquor," I heard Crash tell Seth.

I rolled my eyes and shot Crash a look meant to wither. After a few more coughs and several attempts to clear my throat, I said, "You really don't want to go there with me. Not unless you want me to tell Seth about—"

Crash lunged toward me and slapped one hand across my mouth. I let out a muffled cry at the sting of having my split lip manhandled and dug my thumb and first two fingers into the fleshy part of his palm as I effortlessly plucked him off. I eased my tongue out to test the edges of the cut, relieved beyond words he hadn't broken it back open.

"Did you even have any idea what I was going to say?" I wanted to know.

"No," Crash admitted. "But I'm sure whatever it was wasn't good."

I gave a half shrug and murmured, "Eh."

Crash looked to Seth, then to me, then back again. "So, Seth, you got a minute?" He gave me another furtive glance and shoved his hands deep into the pockets of his jeans while shifting on the balls of his feet.

I smiled a little at Crash's inability to be subtle and stood, guzzling what was left of my beer in record time. "Guess that's my cue to leave." I wiped my mouth with the napkin that'd been sitting under my glass and tossed a couple of bills onto the bar.

"I'll be seeing you, Alex Travers," Seth said with a grin.

I waited until I'd walked away before whispering a reply. "You certainly will."

CHAPTER FIFTEEN

Alex," Tate whispered, shaking my shoulder.

"Mmm." I buried my face deeper into the pillow and threw one arm up over my ear. My head was pounding, my mouth tasted like week-old burritos that'd been left too long in the trunk of a car on a sizzling summer day, and my stomach was rolling around and around in an obvious attempt to find a way out of my body. It was far too early for me to be conscious.

"Alex," Tate said again, louder.

"What?" I mumbled into the pillowcase.

"Your phone?"

"What?"

He wrapped his fingers around my shoulder and pulled, forcing me to roll over. I squeezed my eyes shut and groaned against the daylight that started battering my lids. The thud of a small object being dropped in the center of my chest caught my attention, and I fumbled for it halfheartedly.

"It's been buzzing nonstop for the past twenty minutes."

"Fuck," I whispered to myself as I eased one eye open to look at the screen.

Tate flopped back down onto the bed beside me and closed his eyes. "Who is it?" he mumbled, not sounding particularly interested.

I opened the other eye, hoping it'd help me focus, and squinted at the word "unavailable" displayed across the screen. "Dunno."

Only the sounds of traffic from the street below and the incessant buzzing of someone trying to get in touch with me broke the silence between us.

"You gonna answer it?" Tate asked. He shifted around to get into a more comfortable position but didn't open his eyes.

"Dunno." Not many people had this number, which meant I didn't get a lot of calls. Whoever was so hell-bent on stalking me at the moment was obviously determined not to be recognized, so I was reluctant to pick up.

The phone fell silent, and I regarded it for a long moment before tossing it onto the nightstand and burrowing back into the covers. I let out a contented sigh and closed my eyes, eager to go back to sleep. I had the day off from my cover job, and none of my plans included getting out of bed for longer than it took to answer the door when the delivery guy brought my takeout. But that was still a long way off. For now, I only wanted to—

The phone started buzzing again, causing both Tate and me to let out identical groans. "What the fuck?" I groused, smashing my face into the pillow. Even that small motion caused my head to throb, and I tensed against the pain before forcing myself to relax.

"Answer it," Tate mumbled, his command muffled beneath the comforter he'd pulled up over his head.

"Uhhh." I didn't feel like moving, let alone talking to anyone. Without opening my eyes, I fumbled around the nightstand for an eternity before I located the phone. Unfortunately, I needed to look at it in order to answer it. I eased open one eye as little as I thought I could get away with, which was just enough to be able to see the blurry "unavailable" and locate the "accept" button. I thumbed it and slammed my eye shut as I put the phone to my ear.

"Hello?" I somehow sounded thicker and scratchier than I had a second ago.

"It's me," a familiar voice said in my ear.

My eyes flew open just long enough to get speared by the daylight before I slammed them shut again and rolled over so my back was to the window. "Hey," I tried to say. It came out all garbled, so I cleared my throat and tried again. "Hey."

"You okay?"

"Mmm. Sure." My brain was sluggish, and it took several long moments of slogging through the fog for something to occur to me. "Wait. How did you get this number?"

My question caused Tate to yank the blanket down and push himself somewhat upright. I opened my eye to find him staring at me, probably waiting for me to tell him who I was talking to, but I ignored him.

"How do you think?"

"Oh. Right." Stupid question. Rico gave it to her. That made sense, though I still wasn't sure why she was calling. I scrubbed at my eyelids with the knuckles of my index fingers and then massaged my temples.

"You busy?"

"Now? Uh…no? Not really. Why?"

"Can you meet me at the place on Eighth?"

"What? Right this second?"

"The sooner the better."

A small keening noise escaped the back of my throat. The mere idea of moving to the bathroom, let alone leaving the apartment, made my head scream and my stomach flip in revolt. Lord knew what reactions that doing it would produce. "Do I have to?"

"Are you going to make me issue you a freaking directive?" Allison asked, throwing back the words I'd spoken to her the day before. Her voice was tight.

I sighed and dropped my forehead into the heel of my hand. I shook my head, wincing at the sudden shooting bursts of pain before I remembered she couldn't see me. "No. I'll come."

"Good."

"How much time do I have?"

"Get here ASAP."

"Okay. I'll see you soon." I hung up before she could reply and tossed the phone toward the foot of the bed. It landed on the blanket between Tate and me with a dull thump.

"Was that her?"

I nodded without looking at him. I was too busy staring at the clock and trying to make my brain work enough to figure out how long it'd take me to get uptown. Allison had said "get *here* ASAP," which led me to believe she was already there. While I wasn't inclined to rush, I definitely didn't want to keep her waiting longer than necessary. Besides, the sooner I went up there, the sooner I could come back and take a nap.

"How'd she get your number?"

"Rico gave it to her."

Tate sat up all the way and angled his body so he was more or less facing me. "Rico?"

I started making my way to the foot of the bed. Every millimeter I moved caused my body to scream at me in protest. I was debating whether I was going to throw up. This assignment needed to end soon. I wasn't sure how much more of it my liver could take.

"Your handler, Rico?" Tate asked.

"Handler? Oh. Yeah. Sure."

I'd made it to the edge of the bed and managed to swing my feet over it and stand, but my head had now added spinning to the mix, and I was unsteady. I took a deep breath and concentrated on making sure I had my footing before I started weaving over to the closet.

"Why would he give that woman your number? Does he know her, too?"

"You could say that." Where the hell were my favorite jeans? I tore the closet apart twice trying to find them. It wasn't until I dropped my head in defeat that I noticed I had them on. Oh. Right. I'd worn them to the party last night and apparently forgotten to take them off. Stupid. I began scouring the closet for something else to wear.

"How?" Tate asked after a while.

"Hmm?"

"How does he know her?"

"Oh. She's his new boss."

"She works with you?" He sounded part incredulous, part alarmed.

"Mmm-hmm." I'd located another pair of jeans as well as a T-shirt and moved on to finding some underwear and socks.

"What was she doing in the bar the other night, then?"

"She'd seen me on the street and recognized me. She'd wanted to find out what I was doing."

"You mean she didn't already know?"

I shook my head and immediately regretted it. My grip tightened around my balled-up socks as I waited for the pain to subside. "No. She'd just transferred in. She hadn't been briefed yet."

"Is that why you had to go in yesterday?"

I started to nod but stopped myself just in time. "Yeah."

"So, she's up to speed now."

"Yup."

"Then why does she want to see you again today?"

Good Lord, the man asked a lot of questions. I wouldn't have had the patience to endure this inquisition on a good day. Now, I was downright surly about it. "Guess I'll find out, won't I?" I said, my voice clipped. I didn't even have the energy to speculate about her reasoning. I was too tired and way too hungover.

"Guess so."

I turned to face him. "Are you planning to report in today?"

Tate nodded and ran his fingers through his hair, which was already sticking up all over the place. "Yeah. I wanna pass along the intel we gathered last night. Hopefully, it'll help them find something new on Nathan."

"That reminds me. I forgot to tell you that Nathan served. Did you already know that?" I glanced at the ceiling as I tried to recall whether he'd mentioned it before. It didn't sound familiar, but my brain wasn't firing on all cylinders.

"I don't think so. Which makes me even more certain that Nathan Scoles is an alias."

"Mmm. Do you think your guys can find out what branch and whether he was deployed and when?"

He shrugged. "They can certainly try. Why? You got a theory?"

I thought back to my conversation with Seth and my curiosity about whether he could be Bobby's biological father. "I do. But it's a little out there. That info would help me decide if we need to follow up on it."

"Okay. Then I'll add it to the list of things we need to talk about."

"Good. Also, just FYI, both Crash and Seth made threats toward the president last night." I started making my way toward the bathroom with my clothes clasped in my arms.

"What?!"

I cringed at the volume of his exclamation, which felt like knives being scraped against the inside of my skull. "I know. Morons."

"Our president? As in the president of the United States?"

"That's the one."

"Holy shit!"

I cringed again. "Yeah. Obviously, we'll handle it because that's what we do, but I just wanted to make you aware. POTUS is supposed to be up here next week for a fund-raiser, so I need you to keep an ear out and let me know if you hear anything that indicates they're going to try to hit him when he's in town. I'll find out today who the PI Advance will be for the visit and tell them to be on the lookout."

"Fuck, this is bad."

I turned back around and raised an eyebrow at his distraught expression. I'd been upset when they'd made the initial threats because I hadn't wanted to add another layer to an already complicated investigation, but the threat itself hadn't concerned me. We were good at what we did, and knowing about the possibility of an attack beforehand gave us an enormous edge. "It's fine. Like I said, we'll handle it."

"You can't tell them."

"I can't tell who?"

"Your agency. If you tell them, you'll blow our cover."

I let out a huff and threw up my hands, waving my clothes around, which made me feel stupid. "I can't *not* tell them there could be an imminent attack on POTUS. They need to know."

"But then you guys have to do an investigation, right? Isn't that what happens next?"

"Yeah. We'll interview each of them, as well as everyone they've ever spoken to in their entire lives and most of the people they've been in a room or a subway car with."

He startled and stared at me. "Really?"

I laughed. "No. Not really. But we do talk to some of their associates."

"And how long do you think it'll be before Seth figures out exactly why the Secret Service is interviewing him about that? Even if he doesn't think you're an agent, he'll think you're a traitor."

"I've already thought of that. I'm just going to tell them to make sure they hold the follow-up until we're out. I promise."

"They'll do that?"

"Of course. They don't want to see me killed."

He still seemed skeptical. "You're sure."

I nodded and refrained from rolling my eyes. "Absolutely."

Tate frowned and scrubbed at his right eye with the heel of his hand. Then he yawned and flopped back down. "Okay. If you're sure."

I turned back toward the bathroom. "I'm sure," I called over my shoulder.

"Indian tonight?" he yelled back as I shut the door to take a shower. "We can go over everything over samosas."

"Sure," I replied. The combination of the effort required to answer at such a volume coupled with the echo of my voice bouncing off the tile walls and ricocheting into my eardrums caused a sharp lance of pain to shoot through my head, and I groaned.

I touched my forehead and closed my eyes. When I opened them again, I yanked open the medicine cabinet and started rooting around for some aspirin. I grimaced as I choked down the pills with a handful of water I'd scooped from out of the tap and shut the cabinet door. As it swung closed, I glimpsed myself in the mirror and gasped. I looked awful. I was pale—well, paler than normal—and my eyes were red-rimmed and bloodshot and underscored by dark circles. I made a face and turned away.

I twisted the handle to the faucet to start the shower and sank down onto the closed toilet lid to wait the necessary few minutes for the water to get hot. My heart was racing, and my skin was slick with a light sheen of sweat, though it was tough to tell whether that was my body's reaction to the excessive amounts of booze I'd consumed the night before or whether it was nerves due to my impending meeting with Allison. Maybe it was some sort of terrible blend.

I sat there on the toilet seat with the hollow of my cheek resting in the heel of my hand staring blankly at the running water for a bit as my mind shuffled through topics as quickly as a professional dealer rearranges cards before a poker game. Only I was pretty sure that dealers were more deliberate in their actions. I felt like my mind was shuffling on autopilot, and I was sort of half watching. I wasn't sure why. Even if I'd been able to land on a subject to mull over, I didn't have the energy for any serious introspection.

Heaving the world's most dramatic sigh, I struggled to my feet and fought through my dizziness to undress. The sooner I got a move on, the sooner I could come back here and pass the fuck back out. I hoped.

CHAPTER SIXTEEN

"You look like shit," Allison said as soon as I set foot in the office ninety minutes later. "What took you so long?"

"I had to make a stop first," I said, my answer coming out on the waves of another bone-weary sigh as I flopped down into the chair opposite the desk she'd seated herself at and tossed the bag I'd brought with me onto its top. "And thanks. You look beautiful, as always."

The sentiment had tumbled out automatically, and I froze as I realized what I'd just said. I eyed Allison, attempting to get an accurate gauge of her mood from her expression and her body language. It didn't work. She'd taken care to make herself as unreadable as possible. Normally, I'd try to do the same, if only to give her a taste of her own medicine because I was childish like that, but now I was far too exhausted to make the effort. Instead, I reached into the bag, wincing at the crumpling noise it made, and withdrew a powdered doughnut.

"You know I don't eat those," Allison said.

I tried not to smile at the familiar protest. "Uh-huh."

"I don't know why you always insist on buying them."

"Because they're delicious. Which I know you know because you always steal them from me." A beat. "And I needed something to soak up the alcohol."

"Rough night?" she asked, her voice strained, her gaze straying to the treat in my hand. She'd threaded her fingers together on top of the desk, and parts of them were turning white, presumably from the force with which she was clamping them together. Her gaze darted back and forth between my face and my breakfast.

"I've had better." That wasn't a lie. Though I was hopeful this snack would help. I took a big bite, not caring that powdered sugar was flying everywhere.

"Must be tough, getting paid to spend your nights drinking like a college kid."

"Mmm," I hummed around my mouthful. I chewed and swallowed the bite as quickly as possible. "It's no picnic, I assure you. The hangovers are killer, and I don't bounce back the way I used to. I'm getting too old for this."

"I forgot to ask. Where do you sleep?"

Something about the way she'd asked the question, the tone she'd used, the look on her face, made my nerves spark and smoke, which did nothing for my headache. I tried to stall the inevitable by taking another bite and chewing it a little more slowly. When I swallowed, it was a struggle to choke it down. "What?"

She tilted her head to the side and adopted an air of forced innocence that didn't fool me for a second. "Well, you can't go back to your own apartment, right? You're deep cover. It isn't safe. So, you must have a crash pad. Where is it?"

My heart wilted. I knew where this was going. I looked at the doughnut and sighed as I slipped what remained of it back into the bag. I wasn't as hungry as I'd been a minute ago. "Um...it's in the Village."

Allison, wearing her nonchalance like a cheap thrift-shop wig, spun the bag around so the opening was facing her and retrieved the remainder of my half-eaten doughnut. She gave me a warning look, daring me to say something about what she was about to do, and then took a much more delicate and restrained bite. "And you sleep there alone?"

"You want to know if Tate sleeps there with me," I said, cutting through all the bullshit and straight to the point.

She swallowed, dabbed at the corners of her mouth with the pad of her thumbs in turn, and placed the rest of the doughnut back in the bag. "Does he?"

I nodded, dreading her reaction. "Yes. But only because the ATF didn't want to pay for two places. And they thought it'd lend to our cover story that we were shacking up if we went home together. If any of the group stops by what's supposed to be Tate's place, they'll see some of my stuff lying around and hopefully think Tate's doing his job as far as I'm concerned."

Allison bit down on the inside of her lower lip and took a deep breath. "So can I assume there's only one bed?"

My heart lurched from beat to beat, and my breath was held hostage in my lungs. I nodded again. "Yeah. But it's a king, and we build a pillow wall in between us at night to make it slightly less awkward."

That'd been Tate's idea, not mine. I honestly hadn't cared enough to worry about it, but he'd felt it was necessary, so that's what we'd done.

"I see."

I waited a long moment for her to say something else, and the suspense almost killed me. "If you think any part of me likes this arrangement—"

"It's fine. It's just something I needed to know."

"I'm not having sex with him," I told her. The way she'd been looking at me made me think she'd been entertaining the notion, and I wanted to disabuse her of that suspicion.

"Okay," she said. She ducked her head and retrieved a black velvet box from the top drawer of the desk. She hesitated for a split second before setting it on the desktop and pushing it over to me.

My lurching heart stopped. "What's this?"

"Open it."

I did so, warily. Inside, nestled against a black velvet backer, was a diamond pendant set in silver on a silver chain. I glanced up at her from underneath my eyelashes without lifting my head. "It's beautiful. Thank you."

Allison bobbed her head once. "It's your new tracking device."

Now I did lift my head, so I'd be able to gape at her more effectively. "Since when do we have tracking devices like this?"

"NYFO doesn't. Not yet. But one of the headquarters divisions does. I had someone drive one up yesterday."

A distinct warmth pooled in my chest and began to ooze out to flood the rest of my extremities the way the gooey chocolate center trickles out of a lava cake. "You must've had to pull a lot of strings to set that ball in motion."

She looked away. "Well, I can't have you dying on my watch. Not when I could've done something to prevent it."

I studied the pendant with interest, turning it over and over between my fingertips, trying to glimpse the technology it contained. "How does it work?"

"IRMD installed a tracking app on my phone. I can see where that necklace is at all times. That way, if you lose your phone…Well, hopefully you won't lose the necklace, too." She paused. "I have the alerts set to both audible and visual every five minutes, so even if the guys drop the ball, I'll be able to pick it up."

"Won't that get annoying?"

She shrugged and glanced away.

"It's cool. Thanks." I lifted it from its cushy bed and held it up.

The corners of my mouth turned up in a small smile, and I favored her with a flirty look. "Put it on me?"

Allison rolled her eyes. "I'm sure you're more than capable of putting it on yourself."

"I know I'm capable. I just wanted you to do it for me."

Allison rolled her eyes even harder and let out an annoyed little huff. Her movements were jerky as she stood, and she grabbed the pendant out of my hand a little more forcefully than necessary, but her touch was gentle as she brushed against the sensitive skin at the nape of my neck. I shivered in delight and tried not to look as disappointed as I felt when she finished and resumed her seat on the other side of the desk.

"Thanks," I said after a long moment, my voice shaky.

Allison nodded but didn't reply.

The silence that settled between us was all kinds of awkward, and I was equipped to deal with it for only about ten seconds before I cracked. "So…How are you feeling?"

"Why do you care?" she asked, but the question lacked any real bite. Mostly she just sounded defeated.

"Of course I care." She didn't reply, and as the quiet pulled between us, I started twisting the ring on my finger. "Look, about yesterday—"

"I don't want to talk about it."

"Well, that's too bad because we're going to." Allison's head snapped up, and her eyes widened, but I rushed on before she could retort. "I'm sorry I didn't respond the way you wanted me to, but it was a lot to take in."

"I know the feeling," she said bitterly.

My head throbbed. "Okay. Well, you've had some time to process everything. I really hadn't."

"And now?" The question was tentative and highlighted her vulnerability in a way she usually never allowed.

"And now…" I still wasn't sure. I mean, I adored her, and the thought of life without her made me want to crawl under my bed and curl up into a ball and wait for existence as I knew it to end. But the idea of motherhood made me want to run screaming in the other direction. It wasn't easy for me to form any sort of acceptable answer to her question in the face of such two opposite notions paralyzing me. "And now I've decided to take my HIV test before I can think about anything else."

Okay, that had come out of left field, and maybe I'd said it to buy myself a little time, but it wasn't a total lie. I did feel like I needed to settle that issue one way or the other before I could even begin to plan my future.

"You're still on that?" Allison asked, her tone an interesting mix of irritated and gentle.

I shrugged. "Maybe."

"Next I suppose you're going to tell me that if you test positive, we're over."

I opened my mouth to deny it, but that would've been pointless. She was right. That'd been what I planned to say. Well, maybe not right that second, but it would've come up at some point. My mouth snapped shut with an audible click, and I bit my lower lip and nodded.

Allison closed her eyes and rubbed at the lids for a moment. "You're an idiot, you know that?"

It was hard not to be offended, so I didn't even try. "What?"

"Have you even done any research on HIV, transmission, and prevention? At all?"

"Some," I lied. It'd been irresponsible of me, but I'd been trying very hard not to pop the little denial bubble I'd constructed for myself, and a large part of that had been to avoid anything to do with research on the subject.

"So you know it's extremely unlikely that you even have it? That it's more likely Rory contracted it than you?"

At her words, my insides flash-froze and then cracked and crumbled the way you'd see in a cartoon. I'd been trying not to think about that, too. I cleared my throat to offer the only defense I'd been able to come up with on the rare occasions I'd allowed myself to even think of the subject. "Normally, that'd probably be true. But there are mucous membranes in your mouth, and not only were mine all sliced up, but he more or less bled directly into them."

Her eyes clouded. My logic had evidently given her pause. I swallowed hard and concentrated on breathing around the heavy knot in the middle of my chest. Something about the fact that she hadn't argued with me made me ill. I guess part of me had been hoping she would.

"Okay," she said, dragging out the word. "Well, then, are you aware that it is extremely unlikely you could transmit it to me? *If* you even have it?"

Okay, she had me there. Like I said, I hadn't done much research on the topic. And by not much, I actually meant none, if I were being honest. Because the way my mind worked overtime to worry about nothing, all the statistics in the world wouldn't do anything to ease my fears. All I'd ever be able to think about when we were together would be the possibility of her getting sick, remoteness notwithstanding.

I was pretty sure that answer wouldn't fly, though, so I didn't bother to mention it. Not now. I figured we could talk about it later—much later—like after my hangover had abated, or after this op ended...or after hell had frozen over. One of those. I mean, it wasn't like she'd have the chance to put the moves on me anytime soon anyway. So, yeah, stalling seemed like the way to go.

Except that the way she was suddenly looking at me, the heat and intensity in her gaze made me freeze like an antelope at a watering hole when it hears a rustle in the brush. I was feeling very much like prey in that moment, and it confused the hell out of me.

"A—Allison?" I stuttered as my heart seemed to collapse in on itself, making the pounding in my head exponentially worse. God, what I wouldn't give for a drink of water. Did this office have vending machines? I couldn't remember.

"Mmm?"

"Why are you looking at me like that?"

"Like what?" The innocence in her tone didn't fool me for a second.

"Like you're starving, and you can't wait to eat—wait! That came out wrong!"

Allison's lips curved into a mischievous grin. "Freudian slip?"

"No!" I winced. My protest had been a tad too loud and far too shrill for my sensitive ears.

"Hmm. Whatever you say. Although, to be honest, I hadn't thought of that."

"What were you—nope, never mind. I don't want to know."

Her grin widened. "Don't you?"

I shook my head, hoping to convince at least one of us. "I don't."

"Okay." Her intonation indicated she didn't believe me in the slightest, and she leered at me again.

My entire body was humming, but I tried to keep the conversation on track. "Allison, seriously, what is with you?"

"What do you mean?"

"You were just pissed at me like ten seconds ago. Now you're thinking about getting me naked?"

She shrugged. "No matter what else is going on, a part of me is pretty much always thinking about getting you naked."

I goggled at her, flabbergasted. That wasn't like her. She was the down-to-earth one. *I* was the one who was always thinking about one or both of us being naked. I couldn't have her acting like me. Nothing would ever get done. I had to snap her out of this. "Allison, really. What's going on?"

Something about the seriousness of my manner must have gotten through to her because she rubbed her hands down the length of her face and sighed. "I'm sorry."

"You don't ever have to be sorry about something like that. It's just…not like you. Which means something's up. What is it?"

She frowned, silent for a moment. "I *think* it's just one of the side effects of my weird pregnancy hormones."

"Oh." I hadn't considered that possibility, and now that she'd mentioned it, I wanted to smack myself upside the head for not taking it into account. "What can I do?"

"I don't know, Ryan. I honestly don't. I feel like I'm going insane. My thoughts are all over the place, and they seem to change every thirty seconds."

"But…that's normal, right?" I wasn't sure. I didn't have a lot of experience with pregnant women. I was still a kid the last time my mom had been pregnant, so I didn't remember much about how she'd behaved. And the few friends I had who had kids had experienced pregnancy long before I knew them.

Allison nodded. "Yes. It's normal. But that doesn't mean it's pleasant."

"I suppose not."

We sat there in silence, looking anywhere but at each other for a long time before she cleared her throat. "So."

"So."

"Do you have anything else to report?"

Wow. Suddenly she was all business again. I tried to pretend her abrupt mood shift didn't sting and shifted to catch up. "I do, actually. Seth and some of the other members of the group showed an unusual interest in the upcoming POTUS visit."

Allison's expression became grave. "How serious?"

"Threat-level serious. But I don't have any specifics yet."

She shook her head and ran one hand through her hair before looking at the ceiling. "Of course." She pursed her lips. "I'll tell the PI Advance for the visit."

"Thanks. If I can get any more info on exactly what they're planning, I'll let you know. All I have is ominous, vague statements about Harbinger getting the bullet to the head that he deserves."

"Great."

"I can't imagine they really intend to do anything. Not this trip, anyway. It'd be foolish of them to split their focus like that."

Allison shook her head and stifled a small yawn.

I wanted to ask her how she'd been sleeping or make some remark about needing to get her rest, but I was afraid she'd blow a gasket, so instead I just went on. "Can you do me a favor and tell whoever it is not to start conducting interviews just yet? Not many of us were present for that conversation, and I don't want my cover blown."

Allison nodded. "It's Meaghan. And of course. I'll make sure she gets the message."

"Thanks," I said again.

"What are you doing for the rest of the day? Do you have to report to your cover job?"

I shook my head. "No. I have the day off."

"So you don't have to rush off?"

"No. I have some time. Why? Did you have something in mind?"

Allison's expression now was unreadable. "I did." She drew the words out in a way that made me uneasy.

I was as intrigued as I was nervous. "What is it?"

She suddenly looked guilty. "Well—"

A knock on the door interrupted her, and I whirled around in a blind panic, staring at it as though I were trying to see through it. Who the fuck was that? Had I been compromised somehow? Were we about to be gunned down in a hail of bullets? My mind raced as I tried to consider all the possible tactical responses to whatever threat might be on the other side as I eased my hand down toward the weapon I had holstered on my ankle.

Allison's hand landed heavily on my shoulder, and I flinched. "Easy," she said as she breezed past me toward the door. "It's okay."

My heart and head continued to pound, and I ignored her hollow-sounding reassurances as I broke leather, eased the gun out of its holster, and held it down near the floor.

Allison glanced at me over her shoulder just before her fingers brushed the doorknob, and she rolled her eyes. I swallowed hard and tightened my grip on the gun, making sure I'd be ready in case shit was about to break bad.

Allison opened the door, and I held my breath, poised to level the barrel at whomever was about to come through it.

"SAIC Quinn," Allison said, stepping aside enough for me to see Claudia standing in the doorway. "Thank you for coming on such short notice."

I stuffed the gun back into its holster and leaped to my feet, as confused as I was mortified. "Claudia?" What was she doing here?

"Hello, Allison. Ryan." Claudia stepped into the room and unbuttoned her coat. "It's nice to see you again."

I gaped at her. Literally gaped. My mouth was hanging open and everything. I felt like a damned cartoon character. Claudia and Allison chatted, ignoring me, but that was fine. I couldn't hear much of what they were saying anyway. I tried to figure out what was going on. It took a near eternity, but finally my attention snagged on what Allison had just said in greeting. *Thank you for coming on such short notice.*

I snapped my jaw shut with an audible clack, and every muscle in my body tensed for a fight. I narrowed my eyes and leveled a glare at Allison, who looked as though she were waiting for me to snap at her. She was right to worry. I was furious.

"I'll leave you two alone," Allison said after a bit, her gaze still boring into mine.

I wanted to call after her, to express my disbelief and disappointment that she'd sold me out, but she'd slipped through the door and pulled it shut behind her before I had a chance to open my mouth.

Gritting my teeth, I shifted my attention to Claudia, who was watching me with no discernible expression. The silence stretched between us like taffy, and underneath its heavy pressure, I could hear the low buzz of the overhead fluorescent lights.

"So," Claudia said after a long moment. "I hear we need to have a chat."

Shit.

CHAPTER SEVENTEEN

I didn't know what to say, so I just watched Claudia as I waited for some sort of direction. She glanced around the room before settling into one of the chairs on the near side of the desk. And then she situated herself and looked up at me before gesturing to the other. "Please. Sit."

Despite the "please," it wasn't a request. I sighed and tried not to flop or flounce like a petulant teenager, but it was tough considering I felt like I'd been tattled on. I crossed my legs and folded my arms across my chest. My body language was telling, but I didn't care.

"What are you doing here?" I asked when I couldn't stand her scrutiny any longer. A beat. "I thought you'd been transferred to DC."

Claudia raised her eyebrows slightly. "I was. But my family wasn't, so I'm back and forth often."

"Oh."

Her continued silence was probably part of an interviewing technique, and I was determined not to be the one to break it. After a while, she said, "Allison has told me some of what's been going on. Why don't you tell me the rest?"

I counted to five in a deliberate attempt to avoid snapping at her. "I'm not sure what else there is to tell. I'm sure she filled you in thoroughly." Oops. That'd come across snarkier than I intended.

Claudia nodded. "She did."

"So what do you want to know?"

"Why you thought this was a good idea, for starters."

I considered how to respond. I hadn't thought this was a good idea per se. It'd been more of an opportunity that I'd seized out of desperation. I sucked on my lower lip for a second. "You know I didn't think that."

The corners of Claudia's mouth quirked like she wanted to smile. "No?"

I shook my head. "No."

"Why did you get involved, then?" When I didn't answer right away, she went on. "I don't have to tell you that you haven't been properly trained for this sort of operation."

"Trust me, you'd have to get in line to impart that kernel of wisdom."

"So, that had occurred to you, then."

"I'm aware, yes."

"Yet here we are."

"Here we are."

I tried to relax my muscles. It didn't work as well as I'd hoped, but nothing in my life ever did. Trying to distract myself from the awkwardness shrouding the room, I wondered whether I could get away with checking my watch. Not that I had anywhere to be, but it would give me something to do, and I so badly needed something to do.

Claudia continued to watch me with a contemplative expression. Then her demeanor softened. She leaned forward. "I'm worried about you, Ryan."

I sighed, feeling like an ass, and ran one hand through my hair. "Yeah. Sorry." What else could I say? Nothing could undo my situation; no magical genie was standing by to wrinkle her nose on command in order to extract me from this op. I had to see this through.

"What do you need?" Claudia asked, surprising me.

"Huh?"

Now she did smile. "In order to be safe. What do you need? What can I get you?"

I considered the question, rubbing my lower lip with the side of my index finger. Half a dozen different things sprang to mind, but she couldn't give me any of them. "Will you keep an eye on Allison?"

Claudia blinked. "Allison? Why? She's not the one in danger. You are."

She wasn't wrong, but I wasn't about to tell her the real reason I'd asked. Allison's pregnancy was her own business, as was when or whether she chose to tell anyone about it. Instead, I said, "I don't want her to worry about me."

"I don't think she can help it."

"Probably not," I whispered more to myself than to her.

"I see you have the tracking device on," Claudia said, nodding in the direction of the pendant nestled against my collarbone.

Realization jabbed me hard between the ribs. "*You* drove it up?"

Claudia nodded. "When Allison told me what was going on, it was the only thing I could think of to do."

My chest tightened. I was stunned and touched and annoyed. I tried to swallow again, and when that didn't work, I inhaled sharply. "Thank you."

Claudia pinned me with a hard look. "You're determined to stick it out, then? Nothing I can say will change your mind?"

I shook my head. She couldn't be serious.

Claudia's shoulders sagged, and she looked defeated. "I figured as much. If Allison couldn't talk you out of it, I didn't know what hope I had. But I had to try."

"You realize that me pulling out now without warning is probably more dangerous than me just hanging in till the end, right?"

Claudia sighed and nodded, wiping the tips of her fingers across her eyes. "I do. But that doesn't mean I have to like it."

"That makes two of us."

"What's the plan, then?"

"I hang around until they either tell me something I can use to get them arrested or they do something monumentally stupid that I can testify to. Hopefully that thing isn't murdering a whole bunch of people in cold blood." Hmm. Boiled down like that, it did sound like it might border on the worst plan ever.

If Claudia agreed with my inner assessment of the situation, she chose not to comment on it. Instead, she said, "Got anything useful?"

"Almost."

"Think it'll be anytime soon?"

"God, I hope so." I just wanted this to be over. My desire to escape my life had waned over the past five weeks, and I was eager to resume normal existence. Not to mention I was looking forward to not having to worry that the people I'd surrounded myself with were actively plotting to kill someone every minute of every day. Or that the someone might be me.

"Well, if you need me to run anything down, let me know. I have a long reach." Claudia smiled as though she found the idea amusing.

I laughed. "That's an understatement. And thanks. I appreciate that." I paused. "I'd like to think that one day I won't always be coming to you with some crisis or another."

Claudia's smile softened. "I'd like to think that, too. In the meantime, stay as safe as you can, and call me if you need anything."

She reached into her jacket pocket and took out a small square of folded paper, which she then handed me. I accepted it and unfolded it, surprised to see an unfamiliar telephone number. "What's this?"

"The number to an untraceable phone. I have it with me and always keep it on. Don't be afraid to use it."

I studied the neat writing as I tried to decide how to respond. "Thanks. But I don't want to bother you. I mean, you live in DC and…" I left the "what are you really going to do for me" part unspoken.

"I do. But I told you, Evie doesn't. I've been told she has a long reach as well. Say the word, and the entire NYPD is at your disposal."

I blinked at her. What the hell was she talking about? "Evie?"

The wattage of Claudia's smile was turned up a bit, and I could tell my cluelessness tickled her. "My wife. Evelyn." When I didn't say anything, she went on. "Beneroya." Still nothing. Now her eyebrows went up. "The police commissioner."

My eyes went wide. Claudia was gay? And married? And her wife was the commissioner of the NYPD? How the hell had she managed to keep *any* of that quiet? No one has secrets in the Secret Service. Everybody talks about everyone else all the time. Shit, people were talking about me and Allison almost before a me and Allison existed. How the fuck did no one know this?

"I don't talk about my private life." Claudia answered my unspoken question. "It's nobody's business."

"Huh. Guess I know why the Intel Detectives had to go to special motorcade training," I blurted out without thinking.

Claudia laughed. "That's exactly why. I was tired of them taking lanes whenever it suited them and not waiting for the motorcade to shift first. It drove me insane."

"And you didn't want to take credit for that? Everyone was thrilled when they stopped weaving in and out of traffic like they were racing the devil. Why not capitalize on it?"

Claudia scoffed. "And have every agent within a fifty-mile radius giving me a list of things they wanted addressed with the NYPD? And giving everyone else something to fantasize about? No thank you."

"Why did you tell me, then? Aren't you worried I might blab?"

"Not even a little bit."

"Why not?"

"You, of all people, know better than anyone what it's like to be the subject of gossip. I can't imagine you'd want to inflict that hardship on anyone else."

She wasn't wrong, but her blind trust of someone she didn't really know still stymied me. I cleared my throat. "Well…"

Claudia must have sensed my embarrassment because she shifted the conversation back to the topic at hand. "Aside from the tracking device and the app on your phone, what measures do you have in place to ensure your safety?"

"Are you asking as a boss?" Not that it mattered. I was just stalling for time. Now that I knew exactly how little stood between me and discovery—me and pain or death—my penchant for denial was kicking in hard.

"No," Claudia said, surprising me yet again. "Criminal investigations aren't in my purview. You know that. I'm asking as your friend."

My cheeks flushed, and the surface of my skin tingled. While I was touched by her assessment of our relationship, thrilled that someone I looked up to held me in such high regard, we were edging a little too close to the touchy-feely-squishy areas that I tended to avoid with anyone except Allison.

I bit the inside of my lower lip and reached up to finger the tracking device, feeling the hardness of the diamond as I pressed it into the pad of my forefinger. "Allison told you that, too, didn't she?" My voice was quiet, almost a whisper.

Out of the corner of my eye, I saw Claudia nod. "She did. And she's working to fix the manpower oversight. What I want to know is what you, personally, are doing to secure your own safety. Because let's face it, you'll probably need to save yourself long before anyone else will be able to."

I swallowed hard and tried to ignore the stutter of my heart or the lurch of my stomach. "I have a gun on my ankle at all times. I'm not quite as proficient at drawing from there as I am from my hip, but it's better than nothing."

"Mmm. Okay. Good. What else?"

"Just the regular stuff we all know, I guess. Fighting, subduing a suspect, escaping restraints, things like that. And my running game is pretty strong. So I'm prepared to flee, if it comes to that. I wish I'd followed through on taking some sort of parkour course. That might've come in handy."

Panic was rising inside me, threatening to blot out all reason or rational thought or hope. This wasn't the first time I'd been afraid since I'd gone under. The feeling seemed to come in waves, and while its appearance had never been predictable, I'd always been able to overcome it eventually. Of course, I hadn't been aware of just how alone I was before. It certainly made for a new twist.

"What else can you do?" Claudia asked. "Before you're in a situation that's life or death. What can you do to make sure you don't end up there to begin with? How can you guarantee that you won't have to fight or run?"

Or die? I forced myself to focus on her question, made myself consider it. "I can make sure I'm never alone with anyone who might want me dead should they find out I'm undercover. I can always insist that we meet in a public place and have Tate with me whenever possible."

I glanced up at her and saw her nod. "Good. What else?"

I frowned and stared at the foot of the desk. I was drawing a blank. "Um…"

"How about you text someone your location at all times? Just be sure they have a vague idea where you are?"

"I thought we had decided that I needed to save myself. What good will that do?"

Claudia's expression was grave, and my heart dropped. I knew what she was thinking. That if shit went pear-shaped, they'd at least have a place to start looking for my body. I sighed, wishing I could swallow. Hangovers sucked.

I pressed on, not wanting to give her a chance to expound. "I can try. But I'm not sure how easy that will be. I don't want anyone getting suspicious."

Claudia hummed under her breath. "Would they be suspicious? Or would they think you were an internet-obsessed Gen Z-er exercising her need to document every single facet of her life?"

"I'm not sure. Don't you think they'd be annoyed?"

"Perhaps. But is 'annoyed' better than you getting caught out somewhere with none of us having any idea where you are or even where you most recently were? Better safe than sorry, right?"

"Right," I said, even though I was still skeptical. Besides, wasn't the necklace I was now wearing supposed to take care of that? And what about the app on my phone? It was supposed to let the team know where I always was without me having to tell them. Not that it'd mattered much, apparently. No one had been watching it anyway. The throbbing in my head became more insistent, and I winced, unable to ignore it any longer.

"You look tired," Claudia said.

I sighed. "You have no idea."

"Do you have to report to your cover job today?"

I shook my head and regretted doing it as the pounding became worse. I stilled and let out a sigh. "No. I'm off."

Claudia bobbed her head once. "Good. Go home and get some rest." She pointed one index finger at me. "That's an order."

I smiled and nodded back. "Yes, ma'am."

Claudia stood and squeezed my shoulder lightly on her way out the door. I sat there for a moment, slouched down in the chair, trying to scrape together enough energy to propel myself to my feet. This place had to at least have a water fountain, right? Though the idea of having to bend over to take a drink made me ill. Hmm. Was there a way to scoop the water from my cupped hand into my mouth? It'd be messy, but I'd avoid the inevitable head rush when I stood back up. My stomach, however, didn't appear too keen on having anything new introduced to it any time soon. I closed my eyes and rubbed them with my fingertips. God, I hoped this wrapped up in the not-too-distant future. I couldn't take much more.

I heard the door open again behind me, so I dropped my hands and struggled to sit up straight. Allison circled the chair and held out a cup of water. I mumbled a grateful "Thanks" before downing it in four gulps. I let out an "ahh" that soda commercials would pay top dollar for before wiping my damp lips with the back of my hand.

"Thanks," I said again, smiling up at her.

Allison didn't reply. Instead, she held out a second glass that I hadn't noticed before, and I took it with trembling fingers as she reached into her pocket. She then offered her closed fist to me, and when I extended my palm, she dropped two aspirins into it. I popped them into my mouth and used the entire second glass of water to wash them down. Then I leaned forward to place both cups on the edge of the desk.

"Better?" Allison asked, her voice low.

"Much. Thank you."

She stared at me before reaching out again, wiggling her fingers when I merely continued to sit there. "Come on."

I took her hand and allowed her to pull me to a standing position. Without a word, she led me out the door and into the hall.

"Where are we going?"

She didn't answer. I got only an enigmatic glance over her shoulder and what might have been the beginning of a smile. I followed her, confused, until she stopped in front of another closed door at the far end of the hall. I started to ask her what we were doing there but thought better of it. I doubted she'd answer.

Allison opened the door and led me inside. To my surprise, it was home to a small double bed, a nightstand, and a mirror on one wall. I turned a little too fast to look at her, and my head spun. Allison appeared almost nervous as she led me over to the bed.

"Allison, what are we doing here?"

"You look exhausted. I thought maybe you could get some sleep." When I opened my mouth to chime in, she rolled her eyes. "Oh, good God. Just sleep, Ryan. I'm not going to try anything. Jesus."

I grinned, somewhat embarrassed, but then I realized something. "You're going to stay with me?"

Allison nodded. "I mean, if that's okay."

"I'd love it."

We took off our shoes in silence, sneaking little glances at one another from underneath our lashes. I set my phone down on the nightstand and removed my ankle holster as Allison took off her suit jacket and her gear, and then we settled down together on the bed. I rolled over onto my side and reached back to take her hand, pulling it across my waist. After letting out a long sigh as the tension drained from my body, I closed my eyes, utterly content. Allison shifted so that she was snuggled up behind me, gave me a forceful squeeze, and deposited a soft kiss behind my ear before whispering that she loved me.

I drifted off to sleep with a smile on my face and a lightness in my heart.

CHAPTER EIGHTEEN

Allison was right. I'd been exhausted. So much so, in fact, that I slept away the entire afternoon and all through the night without stirring. I woke in a panic late the next morning with no immediate idea where the hell I was with a groggy and slightly cranky Allison at my back. Panic sliced through me so quickly it was painful, and I leapt out of bed and scrabbled on the nightstand for my phone.

My guts twisted when I saw the countless calls and texts from Tate and Rico. Fuck. This was bad. Stupid interior room with no windows making me think it was still night.

"What's wrong?" Allison asked, running her hands through her hair trying to tame it, her voice thick with sleep.

"We should've set an alarm," I said as I started texting Tate back without bothering to read any of his messages.

"What?" She sat all the way up, swung her feet over the side of the bed, and stretched.

"It's morning. Tate's been looking for me."

Allison shot to her feet, her eyes wide. "What?"

"Fuck." I stuffed my feet into my shoes and wiggled them, trying to get them all the way on. "I've got to go. I should have been at the shop over an hour ago."

Allison blinked several times and yawned, shaking her head. She waved one hand toward the door. "I'm sure it'll be fine. Go."

I started to dash through it, but then I stopped. I turned back to Allison and smiled. "Hey."

She glanced up from putting on her own shoes, clearly puzzled. "Yeah?"

"Thanks. Last night was really nice. And I obviously needed it."

Allison smiled back. "I'm glad. Now go. You're already late. Check in with me later."

I darted over to her to drop a quick peck on her cheek and breezed out of the room before my impulse to crawl back into her arms or to overanalyze our current situation became too overwhelming.

I stopped into a Duane Reade on the way to the shop to pick up some deodorant, toothpaste, and a toothbrush and used a bottle of water to rinse my mouth after I brushed my teeth. What little of the liquid I had left went to being splashed on my face and dumped over my head. I ruffled my now-damp hair with my fingers. It wasn't perfect, but it would have to do. I didn't have time to stop at the apartment to get ready properly.

My phone had been buzzing like crazy the entire trip, but I ignored it, not in the mood for the well-deserved telling-off I was sure was coming my way. I barreled into the shop like a bull stampeding through Pamplona and skidded behind the counter, tugging at the hem of my T-shirt as I went.

Hopkins, the ATF guy who'd been covering for me, did not look amused. He inspected me from head to toe and pursed his lips.

"What?" I said, my heart still racing.

"You're okay, then?" His tone was edging toward condescension, and it rankled me.

"I'm fine."

He narrowed his eyes and leaned on the counter. "Tate was worried."

"I've already texted him."

He continued to stare me down, and I had to bite the inside of my lip to keep from snapping at him. "If you can't handle the stresses of this assignment, maybe we should make other arrangements."

I snorted as ire raged through me. "Yeah. Good luck getting the okay to pull me out and insert a new undercover into this operation at this stage." He scowled at me, and I waved him away. "Get the fuck out of here. Let me do my job."

He opened his mouth, obviously to say something else, but the bell over the front door chimed, cutting him off. He shot me a dark glare meant to wither as he stomped away in the direction of the back room, where I knew he was probably going to head right upstairs to talk shit about me to the rest of the cover team, and I rolled my eyes.

"Rough morning?" Seth asked with a knowing grin as he approached the counter.

I shook my head. "Nothing I can't handle."

He nodded in the direction Hopkins had just gone. "That guy giving you a hard time?"

I forced myself to smile instead of what I really wanted to do, which was to groan. "Always the knight in shining armor, huh?"

He shrugged. "Only when necessary."

"Well, don't worry. I can handle him, too." I paused. "What are you doing here?"

"I was in the neighborhood, and I thought I'd stop by in person to tell you that I loved the mock-ups you did."

Oh, shit. I hadn't seen those yet. I hadn't been aware that he had either. The ATF team must have done them and just emailed them off. After all, it was their email address, not mine. I cursed myself for not reading all of Tate's messages. If I had, I might not've been caught out just now. Oh, well. No undoing it. Hopefully the alarm that'd sliced through me at his words hadn't shown on my face.

"Yeah? So you want me to go ahead with the project?"

"Absolutely."

I nodded and snagged a notebook and a pen, then went about accessing the email account through the terminal on the counter so I could try to get some idea what the hell we were talking about. I scanned it quickly and clicked the pen open, poising the tip above the top sheet of paper. "Great. So which of these did you like best?" I turned the monitor so he could see the options.

Seth leaned in, and his brows pulled down as he studied the images. After a bit, he tapped the screen with his index finger. "That one."

I made a note of it on my pad. "Okay. Did you want different denominations? Or just fifties?"

"Just fifties."

I raised my eyebrows. "High stakes."

He grinned at me. "It's the only way to play."

I smiled back. "I agree. Any idea how many you want?"

His smile faded a bit, and he leaned one elbow casually on the countertop. "How many can you make?"

Interesting. "How much time do I have?"

Seth glanced at his watch. "Three weeks. And a couple of days."

I nodded as my mind raced. Had Tate had a chance to figure out when Bobby had died? Was that the timetable we were working on? Or did the group have some other nebulous date in mind? Would it even help us if we knew? So many questions, so few answers.

"Okay. Well, do you want it to resemble the color palette of older money, or did you want the newer money with all the other colors in it?"

"The older bills would be easier to replicate, right?"

I nodded. "Definitely."

"Those will be fine."

I scratched my scalp as I tried to recall any of the discussion I'd had with the ATF guys about how we were going to pull this off and what equipment they had available. I'd discussed the possibility of needing an intaglio press, but they'd looked at me blankly then, so I wasn't super-confident they'd had any idea what I'd been talking about, let alone taken steps to procure one. "The most time-consuming part will be making the master die, and I'll have a computer to help me with that. Once that's done, it's just a matter of cranking out the bills and then letting them dry."

"Tell you what. You get to work making the die thing, and I'll hit you up in a couple days with a final number. How's that?"

I shrugged. "Works for me."

Seth studied me for a long moment, his gaze scouring my face. I forced myself not to fidget under his scrutiny but instead meet his gaze with a challenging one of my own. After a bit, he shook his head a little and smiled apologetically. "Sorry. I was just thinking."

"Do I want to know what about?"

"I was just wondering whether you'd be up for another project?"

"After this one, you mean?"

"Maybe. Yeah."

I lifted one hand in a careless gesture that didn't at all match how I was feeling. "Sure. What is it?"

Seth started measuring me again. "I'll let you know. I don't want to distract you from this one. But I promise you, it'll be worth your while."

"Okay, well, when we're done with this one, I can draw up the paperwork for that one."

"Uh, no!" Seth said quickly. "No paperwork."

I cocked my head and gave him what I hoped was a puzzled look. My insides were jumping around, and I wanted to scream. This could be it, the in I'd been waiting for. I clenched my one hand into a tight fist beneath the counter and out of sight. "Huh? What do you mean? I have to draw up specs so I know what to charge."

"This one would be more like a freelance gig. All the proceeds to you. We wouldn't go through the shop. So, no paperwork."

"Hmm," I murmured, pretending to consider his terms. "My freelance gigs normally don't come via the shop. I could get into trouble if my boss finds out."

Seth grinned at me again, but this grin was sly. "I won't tell if you won't." I hesitated once more, not wanting to make him suspicious by appearing too eager. "Think about it," he said.

I nodded. "Okay. I will."

He rapped the palms of his hands on the edge of the counter twice. "Good. I'll be seeing you, Alex Travers."

That seemed to be his favorite parting line where I was concerned. "Later," I called after him, shaking my head.

Okay. What had I just learned from that little encounter? Three weeks seemed to be a sticking point for him, although I didn't yet know exactly when this whole mess would go down. Just because he wanted the money in about three weeks didn't mean anything. They'd still need time to sell it. I made a mental note to ask Tate how much the type and number of weapons they were looking to get their hands on went for so I could calculate how much capital they'd need to raise. Then I'd have a better idea what sort of window we were looking at.

The bell over the front door chimed again, but this time much louder, as though the person entering had slammed the door open rather than simply pushing it. I glanced up. Uh-oh. Speaking of Tate, he was storming across the shop with the darkest scowl possible on his face. I swallowed hard and grabbed the edge of the counter with both hands.

"What. The fuck. Is wrong with you?" he scream-whispered when he stopped in front of me.

I looked out the front door, half afraid I'd see Seth lurking outside watching us, but he was nowhere in sight. Still, that didn't mean he wasn't around. "Hey, Tate. Seth was just here."

"I *know* Seth was just here," he snapped.

My intestines snarled. "Did he see you?"

Somehow, his scowl darkened. "No. He didn't see me. And what difference would it make if he did? I'm supposed to be keeping you close, remember?"

"Oh. Right."

His brows pulled down even farther, and his eyes flashed. He placed his own hands on the counter and leaned in. "So, do you want to tell me what the hell happened last night?"

I twisted my lips against the stab of guilt that pierced my side. "Tate, I'm really sorry. I fell asleep. It was an accident."

Tate huffed, took a few steps away, and then whirled around again and stalked back, running his fingers through his hair. He pointed at me. "It was inexcusable. Get your shit together."

My thoughts flickered to the guys upstairs—his colleagues—who were likely watching this exchange like it was some sort of juicy, real-life soap opera, and my cheeks burned. Yes, I'd been wrong. But it wasn't like I'd done it on purpose! I sure as fuck didn't appreciate being scolded like a child.

I drew myself up to my full height and crossed my arms over my chest. "I said I was sorry!"

He flung his arms out to his sides. "Do you have any idea how worried I was about you? I had no idea if you'd had an accident, or you'd been compromised, or what."

Some of the air went out of my anger. I clenched my teeth and counted the pens in the cup next to the computer twice before I responded. As much as I wanted to fire back at him, I could see his point. Plus, I didn't want to give the voyeurs upstairs anything to talk about.

"Look," I said, making sure to keep my voice low and even. "You're right. I'm sorry I worried you. It won't happen again."

Tate deflated as well. Now that the ire had left him, I noticed the dark circles under his eyes and the tight lines at the corners of his mouth. Also, I saw that his hand was shaking. He must have realized it at the same time because he shoved it into his pocket and ran the other through his hair again. "I'm sorry, too. I shouldn't have yelled at you."

"I get it. You were worried. If you ever disappear like that on me, you're going to get a lot worse."

He favored me with a small smile and dragged a nearby stool over so he could plop down in front of me. "So, really, what happened?"

Bursts of anger sparked inside me like fireworks at the Disney World nightly show, but I did my best to snuff them out. "I told you. I fell asleep. I had no idea I was going to fall out like that."

"Where?"

"One of our throw-down offices has a bunk room. I only intended to take a quick nap."

"You must have really been out of it to have not heard any of my calls or texts."

"Yeah."

The silence that settled between us then was awkward and threaded through with the possibility of a renewed argument, so I cleared my throat and changed the subject. "Did your guys get anything on Nathan or Bobby?"

Tate blinked at me, then shook his head. "Uh, not yet. They're working on it. They've got some calls in to some of their military contacts. They're just waiting for some sort of response."

"Mmm. I'm sorry. I'm drawing a blank. Did you ever figure out what branch of the military Bobby served in?"

Tate's brow furrowed, and he scratched behind his ear. "Not exactly. Reports differed. Some of his friends said he was a Marine. But others swore he'd been a Navy SEAL."

It was my turn to frown. "That's possible, though, right? I mean if he finished his Marine tour and then enlisted in the Navy?"

Tate shrugged. "I guess. I don't really know. But at least it excluded a few branches of the armed forces. That's something."

"Any idea when we'll have an answer?"

"None," he said with a small shake of his head.

"Fuck. We definitely need his KIA date."

Tate cocked his head at me. "You got something?"

"Not really. Seth insists on this order being ready in about three weeks. But they'll still need to sell the counterfeit money. How much scratch are they looking to score?"

He shrugged. "Beats me. They still haven't narrowed down exactly what weapons they're looking to purchase. They've been having me put out feelers for several different types."

"Ballpark. What's the most we're talking?"

Tate blew out a breath and shifted his gaze to the ceiling. "Most? I'd say about three million?"

My eyes almost bugged out of their sockets, and I shook my head. "Do you have any idea how long it'll take them to sell almost six million in counterfeit currency?" At his puzzled look, I went on. "The price point is point-six-on-the-dollar. So, for every dollar someone buys, they pay sixty cents."

"So they need to sell almost twice what they want to earn."

"Exactly."

"Fuck."

"We have to be missing something."

Tate slumped over, resting his elbow on the counter and dropping the hollow of his cheek into his hand. "I know. But what?"

The bell to the front door chimed again, and this time an almost-too-normal-looking couple who never glanced my way before they started looking around entered.

Tate pushed himself to a standing position and returned the stool to its previous place. "That's my cue. I'll see you later, right?"

"I'm coming straight to the apartment after, I swear." I held up my right hand in a poor imitation of a Scout's promise.

Tate smiled. "Good. See you then."

He rapped the knuckles of one hand twice on the counter before turning to go, leaving me to ponder over what we could possibly be missing.

It was going to be a long day.

CHAPTER NINETEEN

The plan is stupid," I said to Tate hours later as I was still in the process of hanging my coat on the hooks that decorated the wall just inside the door to the apartment.

Tate looked up from the laptop he had balanced on his knees as he sat on the small loveseat that took up an entire corner of the room. "Huh?"

"I've been thinking about it all day," I said as I went to the refrigerator to grab a beer. I held a bottle up to him, and he nodded. I retrieved the bottle opener from the drawer and popped off the tops, then paused to review my thoughts again as I took a sip while handing the other beer to him.

"Thinking about what?" he asked, watching me with a puzzled expression.

I flopped onto the floor opposite him and folded my legs, resting the bottle on the area rug in front of me. "The whole buy-a-bunch-of-assault-weapons-to-shoot-up-a-mosque plan. It doesn't make any sense."

Tate's lips twisted in a wry smile. "A group that's planning mass murder not making sense? Come on."

I rolled my eyes. "You know what I mean. Even for a homicidal group, this plan has huge holes in it." I lifted my hand so I could start ticking off the points one by one. "First, they need to find someone to procure these weapons for them, which is no easy feat. Second, they need to pay for them, which apparently they plan to do using proceeds from the sale of counterfeit currency."

"Maybe they have no idea what the going rate is for either," Tate suggested. "Maybe they have unrealistic expectations around both."

"Still, though, even if we set that possibility aside, making the exchange for both the money and the weapons involves a huge risk. Their chance of being arrested during either seems like it'd make someone rethink the idea."

"True," Tate said, his eyes glassy as he stared off into space.

"And then they're risking getting caught carrying out the shooting. How do they expect to charge into a religious institution with assault weapons without attracting attention? How do they expect to get away clean? Have they thought about surveillance cameras on-site or in the neighborhood or surrounding areas? How do they expect that none of them is going to get caught in some kind of crossfire and end up wounded and in need of serious medical attention or, worse, dead? There are far too many ways for this situation to go sideways. And I can't see a viable way to mitigate any of them. Not really."

"Plus, neither Seth nor Nathan is stupid. They have to have considered at least some of that."

I took a deep breath and another long drink. "So, what do you think? Are we operating off their original plan not knowing they've changed it?"

Tate looked lost. "I don't know. Maybe none of that was ever the plan. Maybe this whole thing is a test of my commitment. Maybe they want to see if I'd actually be willing to risk arrest for this cause. Maybe they don't want weapons at all."

"We're back to a shitload of maybes. And then what's my part in all this? If they never intended to procure counterfeit currency, why bother having you bring me in at all?"

Tate shrugged. "I really have no idea."

"Does any of that worry you?"

"A bit."

"How are we going to find out?"

"I have no thoughts on that, either."

"Shit. Well, what do you have thoughts on, then?"

"I have thoughts on Bobby's military service and KIA date."

I sat up straighter. "You do?"

He nodded at his laptop. "Yup. Hopkins just emailed this over to me. Looks like Bobby was a Marine. He was killed during some sort of reconnaissance op that ended in an ambush by members of the Taliban. Details are sketchy. But there's an indication that something was off about the mission."

"Off how?"

"Hard to say. No one's been forthcoming with answers, though there have been a lot of questions."

"Like what?"

Tate glanced at the screen. "How did the Taliban know the team was even there? Why were they in the area as long as they were? Why did it take them so long to call for backup? Was all of their equipment working properly? Why did it take reinforcements so long to arrive? Things like that."

"Hmm."

"They're still working on getting to the bottom of it. But the military doesn't exactly have a reputation for complete transparency or full disclosure when it comes to talking about specifics regarding operations. Especially botched ones."

"They do not."

"We did manage to get his KIA date, though."

"And?"

"And it turns out you were right. His last name wasn't Scoles. It was Seabrook."

I frowned. "What? Seabrook? Who the hell is that?"

Tate shrugged. "Don't know. Maybe a stepdad. Maybe it's his mom's maiden name. The guys are running that info now to see what they can get on him. But he died in August."

I threw up my hands. "Then what's the significance of the date they're planning on? What freaking date *are* they even planning on? Surely they aren't looking to push this off until August." Jesus. I couldn't stay in this assignment until then. I'd go insane. I was already climbing the walls as it was.

"Maybe there isn't one. Maybe they just picked a random date. Maybe it's a scheduling issue. Who the hell knows?"

"That's one of the things we have to find out. And sooner rather than later."

"I know," Tate said with a nod, closing the laptop and putting it on the cushion next to him. "And we will."

I took another sip of beer and rolled it around in my mouth for a second before I replied. "Do you think we'll be able to stop this? Before anyone gets hurt, I mean."

"I sure hope so."

"Yeah. Me, too."

"Having doubts?"

I nodded. "Yeah. You?"

He nodded back. "Yeah. Some."

A knock on the door interrupted my next thought, and I jumped like I'd just been bitten by a greenhead, but when I glanced at Tate to determine whether I should be alarmed, he seemed relieved, almost happy.

"Pizza," he said with a grin as he got to his feet and headed for the door. "And wings."

As if somehow recognizing the word, my stomach let out an audible growl, causing Tate to raise his eyebrows as he reached for the knob.

"Shut up," I grumbled. "I haven't eaten since yesterday."

"That's not good for your metabolism," he said. He pulled open the door and reached into his pocket for some cash. I watched the exchange of pleasantries, money, and food, thrilled to see that he'd gone ahead and ordered several pies and a couple of sides.

I hopped to my feet, guzzling the rest of my beer on my way to retrieve another. "You want one?" I asked him.

He nodded. "Thanks."

I uncapped both bottles and grabbed a roll of paper towels before resuming my seat on the floor in front of the coffee table where he'd spread out all the delivery boxes. "Yum," I said without thinking.

He pointed to the box closest to me. "That one's yours. Chicken, red onion, garlic, and basil. Good thing your girl isn't here. I'd feel bad for her having to kiss you after that."

I rolled my eyes. "Ha ha. Very funny." I tore off the point of the biggest slice in the box with my teeth and closed my eyes with a contented sigh as I chewed. God. It tasted amazing. And I didn't even care that it was a little too hot for my comfort. I finished that mouthful and took another, bigger bite. I hadn't realized how hungry I was until now.

When I opened my eyes, Tate was staring at me, looking amused and a little impressed. "Good?"

"Mmm" was all I could muster around the huge wad of gooey, saucy cheese I was devouring before going in for a piece of the crust. Yes. I eat my pizza backward. Yes. I know it's weird.

He smiled and took a bite of his own pizza.

I chewed for a while before forcing the food down my throat so I could speak. "Thanks for dinner. Why'd you order so much food? Are we expecting company?"

"No, I thought that—" His phone rang. He dropped his slice back into the box, wiped his hands on a paper towel, and fished around in the couch cushions for a bit before coming up with the device. "Hello?"

I shrugged and took another bite of my pizza before returning it to its box. Then I pushed myself up on my knees so I could open all the other containers one by one and inspect their contents.

"Oh, hey, baby," Tate said.

Baby? My examination of the rest of our dinner faltered for a second. I hadn't realized Tate had a significant other. I wondered who it was and what they thought about him being undercover. I also wondered whether it was a good idea for anyone from his regular life to be contacting him. But he did this more than I did, so I supposed he knew what he was doing.

Offering Tate the barest illusion of privacy in the studio apartment we shared, I stood and went to the kitchen area to grab some plates. So far, I'd uncovered two different types of wings, some French fries, some garlic knots with sauce, and several cannolis. That type of spread required an actual dish. After some consideration, I retrieved one for Tate, too, then got the ketchup out of the fridge and moved back to my spot on the other side of the coffee table.

"Yeah," Tate was saying, not appearing ill at ease or concerned about having a private conversation in my presence, though he did glance at me. "She's okay."

I raised an eyebrow. Was he talking about me?

"I'm sure," he said. A pause. "She fell asleep."

Okay. That was definitely about me.

"I don't know," he said, his voice rising. "I haven't had a chance to ask."

Hmm. Not sure I liked him talking about me to someone I didn't know. Or even someone I did know. To anyone at all, really. I narrowed my eyes at him as I placed his plate on the couch cushion beside his leg and put the ketchup on the floor before loading my own with a little bit of everything. Once no more ceramic was visible, I settled back down to eat like a savage, being careful not to dump anything in the process.

"I know," Tate said as he balanced his empty plate on his knees and leaned forward so he could fill it. He tilted his head, trapping the phone between his shoulder and his ear, and used both hands to start piling items onto his dish.

"Yeah. You, too. I'll call you later," Tate said before hanging up. He tossed the phone onto the floor and resumed choosing his fare.

I waited as long as I could for him to speak—which was about twelve seconds—before prompting him. "Well?"

"Well, what?" he asked, not looking at me.

"What the hell was that?" Why was he making me drag this out of him? Wasn't he the one who'd been giving me shit about not talking to him about myself? Was he being difficult on purpose as some sort of payback? Was this about to become a tit-for-tat situation?

Tate slumped back onto the couch and shoved a handful of fries into his mouth. I made a face at the sight of him doing so without even a drop of ketchup. He took his time chewing, all the while staring into space, appearing thoughtful. After he'd swallowed, he wiped his mouth before saying, "That was my wife."

I inhaled sharply and ended up choking on the mozzarella stick that I'd shoved into my mouth a second earlier. I coughed for what felt like an eternity, using a paper towel to catch the spray of breading and cheese that would've otherwise ended up all over the room. When I was finally able to breathe normally again, I fixed him with a dark glare meant to singe off all his eyebrow hair. "Your what?"

His relaxed attitude and slow chewing indicated that my glare had not had the desired effect. "My wife."

If this had been a cartoon, my eyes would've started spinning like the dials of a Vegas slot machine. And when they finally stopped, instead of indicating Tate had hit the jackpot, he'd have gotten slapped with "You've been giving me a hard time about not opening up when all this time you've been hiding a wife?" And then I decided to voice my earlier concern and followed up with "What the hell is she doing calling you when you're undercover?"

Tate took a swig of beer and made a face. "Relax. She's on the job, too. She knows when and how to call me without getting me—us—compromised."

I mulled that tidbit over while I took another enormous bite of pizza. Huh. Tate was married. To an agent. Who presumably knew exactly what sort of assignment this was. I coughed again. "And she's cool with…?" I wasn't sure how to articulate what I was asking so I just waved a hand back and forth between us.

Tate stared at me for a minute, looking lost. Then he grinned and started to laugh. "Yes, Alex. She's fine. She understands how these things go. Besides…" He hesitated. "We have an arrangement."

I lowered my now crust-less pizza. "An arrangement."

Tate nodded, tore off a small chunk of garlic knot, dipped it in some sauce, and tossed it into his mouth. "Yeah, well, when you go undercover for as long as we do, things are bound to happen. She gets it. So do I."

I was glad she did because I sure as hell didn't. I repeated the words to myself in my head, trying to get a handle on what he was telling me. I was even too stunned to be grossed out by him talking with his mouth full.

Tate must have seen my confusion because he clarified, "Our relationship is sort of…open."

Oh. Open. Got it. I bobbed my head once in acknowledgment. "Mmm."

Tate shrugged. "I know it doesn't work for everyone. But it works for us."

"Huh." I had a whole slew of questions, and I had to shove a hunk of chicken wing into my maw to ensure that none of them would come flying out.

Tate smiled again. "It's okay. You can ask."

I shook my head, concentrating on the spiciness of the wing sauce to distract myself. "No. That's okay. It's none of my business."

Tate's smile turned sly and knowing. "Go ahead. I can see you're dying to."

"No, really. I don't need to know."

But he must have needed to talk about it because he went right ahead. "Most of the time, we're together when we engage in extracurricular activities. The only time it's acceptable for either of us to have solo playtime is when we're undercover like this."

"Hmm." Maybe if I stuck to noncommittal murmurs, I'd be able to make it out of this conversation unscathed. It was worth a try.

"We had a long talk about it," Tate went on, obviously mistaking my mumbling for interest. "We're under for weeks, months, years at a time. It didn't seem fair to either of us to go without on those long assignments."

So did that mean that while he was here with me, she was out getting some? No, no! Ryan. Do not ask him that question. You don't need to know. You don't want to know. Besides, exhibiting any inclination toward participation would most likely end up with me hearing things I never wanted to. Well, *more* things I never wanted to. Nope. Best to stick to the plan. I nodded and hummed under my breath.

"That's part of the reason why things went the way they did the other night in the bar."

I stared at him, trying to rally my brain into figuring out what he was talking about. It didn't work.

"You know," he said when it became clear that I was clueless. "When I had you against the railing…"

"Oh!" Right. That. So much for making it out of the conversation unscathed.

He had the grace to look embarrassed and palmed the back of his neck as he glanced away. "Yeah. I'm just sort of used to things going in that direction with my cover partners. I'd even sort of gotten the impression that you might be into it somehow. So…"

"Wait. What? Why would you think I was into it?"

Tate shrugged. "I don't know. You never seemed uncomfortable pretending to be sleeping with me."

"And that translates to me actually wanting to do it?" Was he kidding me with this? We had only ever pretended that in public. When we were back here, it was all business. How, then, did that indicate to him that I wanted to go to bed with him? Were all guys this deluded?

He shook his head. "No. It definitely doesn't. When not putting on a show for the group, you've never been anything but professional. Maybe it was just wishful thinking on my part. I don't know. And again, I'm sorry."

"Ah. Okay." Well, it was more of an explanation for his motivation than I'd had before. On some level, I appreciated his candor, even though I didn't fully understand it. On another, I wanted to pretend it'd never happened and move on.

Tate seemed to sense my feelings because he reverted to his story. "Anyway, the one rule Christina and I have is that if any feelings start to develop, we have to put the brakes on and have a discussion about it."

He stopped then, thank God, and lapsed into some deep introspection, which gave me an opportunity to try to figure out how to school my face into a non-expression. I wasn't a prude. I mean, sure, that sort of arrangement would never have worked for me and Allison because we were both too jealous. But I knew a few people who made relationships like that work. And good for them. It's just that I barely knew Tate. Our friendship level hadn't progressed to the stage where he should be hitting me with revelations like this. Not by a long shot.

"That's only happened once," Tate said out of nowhere, surprising and horrifying me in equal measure.

"Huh?" I said before I could stop myself.

He looked pained, and it was clear his mind was somewhere else. "I started messing around with a woman on another assignment. I'd been under for a little over a year, and I ended up falling for her. We carried on for a while after the assignment ended, and I was even considering leaving Christina for her, if you can believe that." He met my eyes then, appearing sad.

I didn't know what to do or where to look. For some reason, he seemed to need to get this off his chest, and while I wasn't sure I wanted to hear it, I made myself nod and say "Wow." That his wife had just called had to have meant they'd worked through it, right? Or was this a different wife? No. It had to be the same one. Otherwise, why tell the story? When he didn't say anything for a moment, I cleared my throat. "What happened?"

He sighed. "It got complicated."

"More complicated than ignoring your rule and having an affair and falling for this broad and thinking about leaving your wife?" I blurted out. I grimaced and lifted one hand to my lips, horrified that I'd revealed my thoughts.

Tate smiled, an undercurrent of sadness laced through it. "Yes. If you can believe that. She got pregnant."

The skin on the right side of my body started tingling, and I suppressed a shudder. If he could've possibly known about Allison and her situation, I'd have sworn he was messing with me. But the odds of that were nonexistent, which meant he had to be telling the truth. Somehow, I'd have guessed the odds of that—of him having a pregnancy-related story that he just had to unburden himself about right this second—would've been even slimmer than none, but here we were.

I didn't have anything to say to that revelation, but he must not have required anything because he just barreled ahead. "Yeah. That's where things got really messy. See, I don't want kids. Never have. Can't imagine I ever will."

"Oh." Okay. I changed my mind. He had to be fucking with me. This whole exchange would be too spooky otherwise. I glanced down at the food still piled on my plate and frowned. I removed it from my lap and set it down on the floor next to me. I was suddenly no longer hungry. In fact, I felt kind of queasy.

"She wanted to keep the baby. I wanted her to get rid of it. Things sort of fell apart after that. She said she couldn't imagine spending her life with a man who'd want to kill something we'd created together. I couldn't imagine spending my life with a woman who disregarded my feelings on the subject so completely that she'd make a unilateral decision without even considering my opinion."

He lapsed back into silence then, his gaze riveted to a spot near the baseboard in the corner of the room, and I let out a soft, shaky breath. I realized I had a death grip on the neck of the bottle in my hand and glanced at my beer, but that, too, was unappealing. What would the appropriate reaction even be? I licked my lips before asking, "Where is she now?"

"Hmm?" Tate was startled out of his reverie. He blinked a couple of times and then shook his head. "Uh. Don't know. She transferred, and then she ended up quitting. I haven't spoken to her in several years."

"Jesus," I whispered. I swallowed hard. "Does that mean…?" I couldn't bring myself to finish the sentence.

"Does that mean she had the kid?" Tate said for me with a sad smile. He nodded, and my already quivering guts rolled. "Yeah. A little girl."

"But you don't know where she is?"

"Nope. I've never seen a picture of her. I don't even know her name."

"She never told you?"

"No. She just texted me when she had the baby to let me know it was a girl, and it was healthy."

I was having a hard time wrapping my brain around everything he was telling me. "And that was it?"

"That was it."

"You've never tried to find them?"

Tate's expression darkened. "What for? If she wanted me to know where they were, she'd have told me. And it isn't like I suddenly have some burning desire to be a present, involved father. What purpose would finding them have served?"

Did those words make him a complete jerk? Did not caring at all about where his child even was say something horrible about what kind of person he was? I couldn't tell. It was a tough situation, no matter what angle you viewed it from. And I didn't think there was an easy solution. The parallels made me wonder about Beau, though. About whether he had a right to know, about whether Allison planned to tell him, and about whether he'd use this baby as a way to stay involved in Allison's life. Or whether he'd actually want to be a father. Maybe he was already a father. I didn't know.

"Did she ever hit you up for child support or anything?" I asked.

"Nope. I keep expecting her to—have even been saving money just in case so it won't be so hard to cover the back pay I'm sure a competent lawyer would ask for—but so far, nothing."

I picked at some loose threads on the carpet with my fingernails. That was a lot of information in a very short time span, and not only had I not needed to know any of it, but I also wished I could *unknow* it. I rested my elbows on my knees and dropped my chin into my hands.

That Tate had just given me an opening to talk about the debacle that was my life wasn't lost on me. I pursed my lips and wiggled them back and forth as I considered the pros and cons of unloading my emotional baggage onto him. At the very least, he'd be able to empathize with my position better than anyone else I knew.

In the end, I chickened out. The words were poised on the tip of my tongue, locked and loaded and ready to be unleashed upon the world at large. But I couldn't bring myself to utter them. "What made you think of that?" I asked instead.

"The other night, when we were at the bar and they were talking about Bobby, it just reminded me that we're coming close to the day I found out."

"About your daughter's birthday?"

"Well, about the fact that she'd been born. I don't know for sure when her birthday is."

That was...wow. That was something. I had no idea what to say.

Turns out I didn't need to say much of anything because Tate went on. "It's for the best. She deserves a much better man than me to act as her father."

"Oh."

Tate's eyes widened as though he'd just realized exactly what he'd been sharing with me, and his cheeks turned pink. He cleared his throat, wiped his mouth with a paper towel, and balled it up inside one white-knuckled fist. His gaze dropped to the remainder of the food left on the table, and his mouth twisted like his stomach had gone sour.

"We'd better get this cleaned up," he said, still not looking at me. He pushed himself to his feet and started closing and gathering boxes. "We're going to be late."

I followed his example and began helping restore the room to order. "Late for what?"

He froze, and after a second, he did look over at me. Something in his expression that I couldn't quite place made me uneasy nonetheless. "We've been summoned."

"Summoned?" By whom? For what? What the hell was going on?

The look he gave me said it all, and when my heart resumed its regularly scheduled beating program, I took a deep breath, nodded, and squared my shoulders. If this group wanted to get this show on the road, I was more than happy to play along. At least that's what I was telling myself. The dread pooling low in my gut said otherwise.

Tate and I continued our cleanup in silence, and I couldn't guess what he was thinking, but I was trying to convince myself that this was a good thing. The sooner we got this ball rolling, the sooner I could go home. It was what I'd been waiting for all along, right?

So why did I feel like I was going to throw up?

CHAPTER TWENTY

Tate and I arrived at the bar later that evening underneath a faint layer of strain. Not only did neither of us want to be there, but we were still raw from our earlier conversation. I sighed and tried not to roll my eyes as he held the door open for me, and the familiar sounds and smells of the bar that'd become something of a second home these past five weeks washed over me. Once this operation ended, it'd be a *long* time before I set foot inside a liquor-based establishment again.

We wove our way through the press of bodies up to the balcony where we all usually hung out. By unspoken agreement, we didn't stop at the bar on our way, for which I was grateful. I'd already had two beers that evening and was tired of keeping rigorous tabs on my alcohol consumption. I'd struggled to ensure that I'd be seen drinking enough so the group didn't get suspicious while at the same time trying not to end up too drunk to do my job. Or, worse, inadvertently revealing something I shouldn't. Plus, the hangovers were a fucking bitch. I wasn't as young as I used to be, and this assignment constantly reminded me of that fact.

We climbed the stairs—Tate behind me with one hand on the small of my back—and saw that most of the group had already arrived. Crash was in deep conversation with a couple of the guys on one side of the room, while Tamara and Emma giggled and played darts. A few other regulars were noticeably absent, and I wasn't sure whether we should be concerned. But the weird vibe hovering in the air *did* concern me.

Everyone turned to look at us, and the hair on my arms stood up. I swallowed hard and tried not to look as uneasy as I felt. "Hey, guys."

Crash ambled our way. "You're late." He sounded gruff, his voice low and gravelly. He was obviously displeased.

I forced a laugh and stepped around him. "Late for what? Since when does drinking and fucking off have a start time?"

He glared at me coldly, and I stared right back, refusing to be intimidated. He stepped closer and ended up a lot farther inside my personal space than I liked. "Seth doesn't like to be kept waiting."

I'd have loved nothing more than to put him on his ass. But I wasn't sure I could come up with a convincing reason why Alex Travers could down a grown man without breaking a sweat. Nor did I think doing it would endear me to anyone. So I widened my eyes at him, hoping to look as innocent as possible. "Seth? He's coming here? Why?"

Crash towered over me for another few heartbeats before his face twisted into a disgusted sneer. "Of course he's not coming here. We have to go to him."

I glanced at Tate then. I couldn't help it. He looked as surprised as I felt. We were going? Going where? And why? Was this the break we'd been waiting for? But I couldn't ask most of those questions without looking like I was fishing for information, so I bit my lip.

Though finally being brought into the inner circle of this operation would be fantastic, my gut kept telling me that being taken to another location to do it wouldn't work out well for me. My Krav Maga instructor's voice echoed inside my head. "Never let them take you from point A to point B. Whatever their reason is, you aren't going to like it."

I hooked my thumbs into the pockets of my jeans and rocked back on my heels. "Oh, okay. So where are we going?"

I was playing the dumb-girl card to the hilt, hoping it wouldn't raise any flags with any of the guys. I allowed my gaze to drift over to the crowd, wondering which of them were innocent bar-goers and which were part of this group. If I needed to make a break for it, would they hinder my escape? I couldn't be sure.

Crash looked to Barker and Dixon, then to Tate, then back to me. "Well, Tate is going with them. You're coming with me."

An alarm reminiscent of the movie sign in *MST3K* started blaring inside my head, and I had to fight not to wince or widen my eyes or anything that would give away just how distressed I was. I couldn't stop myself from digging my fingertips into my hips. "I am, huh?"

"Yes," Crash said. He looked back to Barker and bobbed his head sideways once. Barker whistled through his teeth and snapped his fingers once, and Emma tossed her last dart and then abandoned the game, moving to stand by his side.

"You still haven't told me where we're going."

A beat. "We're doing a scavenger hunt," Crash said, not sounding even a little bit convincing.

"A scavenger hunt?" I had to force myself to keep my tone closer to intrigued than to suspicious or disbelieving.

"That's right."

"Why?"

Crash shrugged. "It's what they wanted to do. Thought it'd be fun."

"Is there a prize?" I wanted to know.

"There is," Crash said almost before I'd finished speaking. "But the prize changes depending on what place you come in and how long it takes you to finish if you win."

"Huh. Fun." I turned to Tate and smiled. "We're going to kill this."

"Actually," Crash broke in, "Tate is on Seth's team with Barker and Emma. You're going to be with me."

Okay. After these two pronouncements it'd become crystal clear that at least part of the goal was to separate me from Tate. Hmm. Why? Were they finally about to let Tate in on some of the finer points of their plan that he and I had only been able to speculate about thus far, like the date they wanted to kick off their little war? And if that's what they wanted with him, what did they want with me? It couldn't have been as simple as just keeping us apart, unless our cover had been blown and they'd realized it'd be easier to deal with us separately. Was it cold in here? When did it get so chilly?

I hid my shudder as I frowned and pretended to pout as I looked up at Tate. "But I want to go with you, baby."

"It'll be fine," Tate told me, sounding unconcerned. "I promise not to gloat too much when we win."

I narrowed my eyes at him. Either he was an amazing actor—in which case, I was jealous—or he really hadn't grasped the implications of the situation. "Win, my ass."

Tate grinned before stepping closer to me, positioning himself so he was standing directly in front of me and blocking me from everyone else's direct line of sight. He cupped my face in his hands and stared at me for a beat, his expression as serious as I'd ever seen it. Then he bent down and placed a light peck on my lips.

"I'll see you soon," he said under his breath.

"Be careful," I whispered back.

"You, too."

Okay. He got it. And while he didn't seem as nervous as I was, at least he was a little uneasy. Good. Hopefully that would put him even more on guard. Tate, Barker, and Emma disappeared down the stairs, and I wanted to watch them go but made myself walk over to Tamara instead. No use showing my hand just yet. Not until I had some more information.

"Hey, lady. What's going on?"

Tamara glanced at me and then went back to playing darts, squeezing one eye shut, squinting the other, and poking the tip of her tongue out of the corner of her mouth as she waved the dart back and forth, trying to line up her shot. Without a word, she held out the beer in her other hand, and I took it and helped myself to a sip. It took another few moments of prep before she let the dart fly, and she groaned in disappointment when it glanced off the edge of the board and clattered to the ground.

"I suck at this game," she said, taking her beer back and tipping her head for a long swallow.

"Kind of," I said as I retrieved the darts from the floor and gathered them into my left hand. I lined myself up to take a shot. "But who cares? It's all in good fun, right?" I let my dart fly, and while it did manage to stick into the board, it wasn't in any place impressive. I handed her the darts and stepped out of the way to give her room to take her turn.

Tamara went through the rigmarole of lining up her shot again, but she wasn't any more successful this time than the last. Her shoulders sagged, and she huffed as she thrust the darts back in my direction.

I tapped the flights against the palm of my other hand as I considered whether trying to get information out of her would be a) a good idea and b) even remotely fruitful. Over by the stairs, Crash had received a phone call and had turned his back to me, so I took the opportunity to lean closer to Tamara. "Any idea what the deal is with this scavenger hunt?"

Her expression changed, her features became more pinched, and something dark flitted beneath her eyes. "Oh. Uh. I don't have a ton of details."

"You don't? So you're cool with just engaging in an activity you know nothing about?"

"I know stuff about it. I just don't want to spoil the surprise." She averted her eyes and focused on the dartboard.

Uh-huh. Right. And if I bought that, she had a bridge to sell me. It was an effort not to roll my eyes. "What if I'm not into scavenger hunts?"

"It'll be fun," she said, a tremor in her voice. "Please just…don't argue, okay?"

"Why not?" I'd blurted that out and hadn't meant to say it aloud. But I didn't regret it, either.

The skin around Tamara's eyes had tightened, and she had her lips pressed into a thin line turned down at the corners. Her posture straightened, and she began wringing her hands in front of her hips. My heart lurched at the sight of how uneasy she was, but I didn't have a chance to ask her any questions because Crash called, "You ladies ready to go?"

Surprised, I turned on my heel, intending to stall or engage him in some sort of discussion about this whole thing, but he'd already started down the stairs behind Dixon. I swallowed hard, took a deep breath, and followed, Tamara on my heels.

I made it to the bottom of the steps in record time, but it wasn't fast enough to catch up to Crash, who'd already started threading his way out of the bar. I could just make out the top of his head through the press of bodies and kept my eyes on it as I tried to weave my own way toward the exit.

He stopped to have brief conversations with a few people I didn't know—hadn't even realized that he knew—and my stomach churned as I was again confronted with the reality that I hadn't been privy to a lot about this operation, and any of it could get me killed. I glanced at the people he'd spoken to on my way by and made mental notes regarding their features and clothing to run by Tate later.

You'd think that emerging from a stuffy, overcrowded bar into the cool night air would've made me breathe a sigh of relief. Instead, the cold had taken on a biting quality that pierced my lungs and made my throat burn. I sniffled as I shoved my hands into my pockets and tried to ignore the thundering of my heart and my gut's attempts to collapse in on itself until it winked out of existence.

Crash and Dixon were waiting for us with two guys I didn't recall seeing before. They were older—closer to Seth and Nathan's ages; closer to my actual age than to the one I was pretending to be—their features weathered and hard. Both sets of eyes narrowed as they locked onto me, and I could feel their speculation and their judgment as easily as I felt the wintry air stinging my cheeks.

What it must feel like to careen down a class 6 rapid in an inner tube washed over me then, and I struggled to maintain a neutral expression and fight an instinctive desire to tense. Fuck, this was bad. Not only was I being taken to another location, but I was severely outnumbered. Could I get out of this trip without arousing suspicion? I was racking my brain but wasn't coming up with anything.

Whatever hope of a viable escape from this nightmare I might have been clinging to shattered when, without speaking, the guys moved as one to a dark SUV with blacked-out windows. I flashed colder than the air and tugged at the ends of my spiky hairdo. Had we been compromised? Had splitting me and Tate up been just for show so we wouldn't cause a scene before being taken someplace secluded to be killed? Was I being paranoid? Probably. But I couldn't be sure. And that uncertainty made my blood run cold.

"Oooh," I said to Crash as he rounded the front of the SUV toward the driver's seat. "How very cloak-and-dagger. And me without my trench coat." In this case, as in most others, I determined that snark was the way to go.

He rolled his eyes and made a rude noise in the back of his throat that ended up sounding like a hiss when he let his breath whistle out from between his teeth. "Just get in the car," he said.

"There's no need to be an asshole about it," I shot back.

Crash bit down on his lower lip. "The other team's already left. I don't want to lose any time we don't have to."

Wow. They were going all in with this scavenger-hunt ruse. Was that the best thing they'd been able to come up with? Or had he just pulled that out of his ass because I'd been asking questions? Curious.

I watched with some dismay as Tamara disappeared through the door and made her way to the very back of the vehicle. One of the new guys stood holding the door open for me, while the other got in on the other side. So, now I could either take the middle seat and end up sandwiched between them or join Tamara in the back. Hmm. Did I want to make possible escape even more difficult by requiring myself to climb over the seat to reach the door but have easy access to eyes, ears, and throats? Or did I want to position myself so I'd only have to leap one dude to access the exit and put myself within reach of sensitive parts like stomachs and groins? Decisions, decisions.

In the end, I opted for the far back. For one thing, it'd allow me to use surprise, while still keeping a buffer between me and the guys in the front seat. For another, I could always shoot out the rear window if it came down to it. I was hoping it didn't.

I glanced over at Tamara as I took my seat, and she gave me a shaky smile before turning her head toward the window. In the dim light, the lines of her face were tight and her eyes hollow, haunted. At least she had some idea what the hell was going on. And she didn't seem one hundred percent on board with the plan.

"So, what's our first clue?" I asked, partly to break the silence, but also to see Crash scramble.

"Huh?" one of the guys in the middle seat asked as he twisted around to look at me.

"For the scavenger hunt. What's our first clue?"

"Dixon and I figured out our first clue already. We know where we're going."

"Where?" I asked.

Crash huffed and shook his head. "You'll see."

"And we'll get the next clue when we get there?"

"That's right," he said. "But we're going to try to divide and conquer. A team has to have all the clues back at the home location before they can be declared the winner. Once someone retrieves the clue, we're going to send them back and take off for the next one."

Good thing it was dark in there. Schooling my expression so I didn't look skeptical or irritated was tiring. With all the faces I was making, it was tough for me to pretend I believed any of this nonsense. "Are we allowed to do that? We don't have to arrive back together to win?"

Crash shook his head. "Loophole."

"Oh. Shrewd."

The truck descended into silence save for the occasional sigh or rustle of cloth. Crash didn't turn on the radio, and no one spoke. The oppressive atmosphere was giving me the creeps. I tried to be sly about inspecting the rest of the vehicle's passengers. While their attitudes didn't comfort me at all—how did they expect me to buy this scavenger hunt bullshit they were selling being all broody and sinister like that?—I was relieved that none of them appeared to be paying any attention to me. Well, except for Crash, who now and again caught my eye in the rearview mirror. Each time it happened, I smirked at him as though I found everything about this scenario amusing. I wasn't sure he found me genuine, but I was sure he wouldn't call me on it. That would've meant copping to this stupid ruse, and he'd never do that.

Crash took us on a very winding, circuitous route through the city that I was positive doubled back on itself several times. Hopefully the guys who supposedly monitored my movements were taking copious notes on our path because no way would I be able to take my own. I was even afraid to text Tate. Someone might have a problem with it and try to pass it off as me cheating at this nonexistent game. So I simply tried to get a vague sense of where we were so I could report the destination to the ATF guys, if not the journey.

The section of the city where Crash finally stopped was dark and the textbook definition of sketchy. I glanced out the window, trying to see as much as I could and memorize it. The tint on the windows made that a challenge.

"You know where you're going?" Crash said out of nowhere.

I looked up, trying to determine who he'd been talking to.

"Yeah. I got it," Dixon said.

"And you know what to do once you're done?" Crash asked. He caught my eye in the mirror again and rushed on. "You text us that you got it and head back. We're going to keep on going. Okay?"

"Yup. Don't worry."

"Okay," Crash said. "See you back at the clubhouse later."

There was a *clubhouse*? Did Tate know this? Or was that just some stupid name they used to refer to the bar? I couldn't be sure. Jesus, why did it have to be so dark in here? And why didn't I have a pen to write some of this stuff on my arm? I slumped farther back into the seat as one of the guys from the middle row got out and moved up to the front to sit next to Crash.

On a whim, I scrambled over the back of the seat in front of me and took his place. I wasn't thrilled about having Tamara behind me, but I was pretty sure I could take her if she got a wild hair and decided to get squirrelly. Plus, I wanted to be closer to the conversation, should there be any.

"So," I said, making my tone annoyingly bright. "What's the next clue?"

The muscles in Crash's jaw tensed as he pulled away from the curb. "We need to wait for Dixon to text it to us."

"Oh. Makes sense. But then how do we know we're driving in the right direction? Shouldn't we wait until he tells us where we need to go?"

"I don't want to sit here," Crash told me. "In case one of the other teams is in the area. I don't want them to know they have the right spot if they haven't figured it out on their own."

"Ah," I murmured. If I'd been a different person in a different sort of situation, would I have believed that? I doubted it.

The car was quiet once more, and Crash resumed his slow weaving through the streets of New York while I tried to figure out what the hell we were really doing. No way was this a scavenger hunt, though I did think we were retrieving something. Or, more likely, several somethings. I just didn't know what or why. Nor could I see any reason why one person couldn't have just done all this on their own. Unless it was a CYA thing and the group was trying to make sure that no one person held too much information. That might make sense, sort of, if we'd been operating as a sleeper cell, which, I guessed, this technically was.

Crash's phone lit up from its place in the cup holder in the center console. Showing no regard whatsoever for the law, he checked the text and nodded once. "Tamara." The sudden summons was loud in the stillness.

"Yeah?" she called, her voice trembling.

"Dixon just texted me the next clue."

"Ooh," I said, feigning enthusiasm and leaning forward, half expecting to get an elbow to the face. "What is it?" They knew that I knew this was bullshit, right? They had to. I'm not that great of an actress.

"Huh? I mean, he did?" Tamara said. "Great?" Her tone indicated that she did not, in fact, think it was great.

"Yeah. Looks like you're up. You know how you're getting back to the clubhouse?"

"I know."

I glanced over my shoulder. Tamara looked like she was going to be sick. She had no direct access to a window that opened and no quick way to get out of the car, so if she blew chunks, we were all going to suffer. I searched my surroundings for something for her to yak into but didn't see anything. Crap.

I cracked my window a bit, hoping some cool air would help settle her nerves or her stomach or whatever part of her was preparing to throw up all over the back of my neck. Crash was making turns and weaving all over the place, so there was no telling how soon we'd stop— or what sort of impact any of this was having on Tamara's stomach—so I just held my breath and prayed that we made it to wherever we were going before Tamara's jitters got the best of her.

For lack of anything better to do and because I wanted to be an epic pain in the ass, I went back to grilling Crash regarding this faux game, knowing full well that I was stressing him out. "Do we get to play, Crash?"

"What?" His unblinking eyes were fixated on the road, and his knuckles were white from his death grip on the steering wheel.

"The scavenger hunt. Do we get to participate? If I wanted to sit in a car full of people I don't know and not speak, I could share a cab back home."

Crash inhaled, long and slow and loud, which left no mistake that I was irritating him. I ducked my head and made a show of running my hands through my hair to hide my face so the nameless guy sitting next to me wouldn't see me grin.

"You know what, Alex? You're right," Crash said, surprising me.

"Huh?"

"You're right," he repeated. "This probably has been pretty boring for you. I'm sorry. I thought it would go faster if we solved the clues, because a lot of them are based on inside jokes, and you probably won't be able to help. But I can see how you'd feel left out. Tell you what? How about you oversee keeping track of everyone's progress?"

Okay. That threw me. My brain spun as I tried to figure out how that would work, how he would allow me to participate while still keeping me in the dark. "What would I have to do?"

"Well," he said as he passed a double-parked car and then eased his way down the street and pulled up in front of a fire hydrant. "What if Tamara texts you when she's retrieved the item and then again when she makes it back to the clubhouse?"

I furrowed my brow and bit the inside of my lower lip. I hadn't figured out what his angle was, but I couldn't see any harm in playing along. "Okay. Thanks." A beat. "Will I get to retrieve one of the items?"

Crash nodded. "Yeah. The last one. That way you won't have to go back on your own. I can take you."

Being in a car alone with him didn't thrill me, but if it came down to it, I'd be able to do more damage to him than he'd be able to do to me. At least I hoped that was the case. And maybe I'd have a chance to peek at whatever the item was and tell what it was for. "Cool."

Having placated me temporarily, Crash glanced back to Tamara. "Here's your stop," he told her. "Text Alex when you've got the package and again when you're back safe. Okay?"

She didn't even bother to speak, just nodded and ran a trembling hand across her eyes. I opened my door and got out so she could push my seat forward and exit the vehicle more easily. I held out one hand to help her, and when she took it, I almost winced at how clammy her palms were. I could feel the vibrations of her body through that one appendage. Wow. She was wound up.

"You okay?" I asked her.

She nodded again and started walking on shaky legs deeper into the massive housing-project complex. I watched her go for a few seconds before getting back into the car.

Crash pulled away without a word, and I took my phone out of my pocket and clasped it between both hands on my lap, waiting for Tamara's text. Once again, we resumed what seemed to me to be aimless wandering, but this time I didn't bother to comment. I just stared out the window like everyone else and tried to memorize some landmarks.

I felt like an epoch had passed—I'd been about to try to get the two strangers' names by introducing myself to them—when my phone buzzed. I was so startled, I jumped, and then I laughed at myself. The two nameless guys exchanged a glance, and the one sitting next to me stared at me like he thought I was contagious.

I smiled and then glanced at my phone. It was a message from Tamara. The knot in my chest loosened, and I reined in my audible sigh of relief as I opened it. The word on the screen made that knot cinch right back up again. I scoured my brain, but I couldn't conceive of any scenario where receiving that response would've been welcome.

"Uh, Crash?" I said, unsure how I wanted to word my next question. "Any chance the next clue is SNAFU?"

His head whipped around so fast I almost felt the twinge he had to have gotten. His eyes were wild. "What?"

I held up my phone so he could see it. "That's what Tamara texted me. SNAFU."

"Fuck," Crash muttered under his breath as he turned back to the windshield. He punched the gas hard, and the SUV lurched as it took off.

"That's not the clue, is it?" I asked.

"No, Alex," Crash replied, his voice uncharacteristically even and measured. It gave me the creeps. "That wasn't the clue."

"Oh." I waited a few beats before speaking again. "That's not a good text, is it?"

Crash took the next turn faster than necessary. "No. It's not good."

"Did we lose?" I asked, sticking fast to the stupid scavenger-hunt cover he'd started.

Crash was silent for so long I was beginning to think I wouldn't get an answer. So I was surprised when he said, "Not exactly. Not yet."

And since I didn't have anything to say to that, for once, I kept my mouth shut.

CHAPTER TWENTY-ONE

Though I had no freaking clue where we were going or why we needed to get there in such a hurry, Crash seemed to. He drove with a purpose, maneuvering just over the speed limit—fast, but not fast enough to call attention to us—and alternated between glowering at the road ahead and texting someone with one hand. I tried to see who he might be communicating with or what they were talking about, but I didn't have a great angle from where I was sitting, and I doubted that he would have appreciated me leaning forward.

Since texting appeared to be okay, I turned my phone back on. Out of the corner of my eye, I noticed the guy to my left glance at me. Okay, so maybe texting was okay for everyone who wasn't me. How to get around this, because we appeared to be leaving the borough and heading into Brooklyn, and I wanted the guys supposed to be monitoring me to know that. On the bright side, I'd be close enough to the office that the response agents could come help me if I needed it. But I had to make sure they knew where I was without these yahoos knowing I'd done it.

I was staring at the message from Tamara when it hit me. "Hey, Crash?"

"What?"

"Do I need to tell her anything?"

"Huh?" He glanced at me over his shoulder before returning his attention to his other two tasks.

"Tamara," I said, holding up my phone even though he wasn't looking at me. "Should I give some sort of response? Do I need to tell her where to meet us or anything?"

He didn't say anything for a long moment, and I grabbed for the oh-shit handle as he took another turn without slowing down. Then

I slammed against the door as he swung the car the other way at the next corner. Jesus Christ. I was no longer worried about these wackos figuring out who I was and killing me. I was pretty sure Crash was going to get the whole lot of us killed first.

"Yeah. Make sure she goes back to the clubhouse."

His words broke into my question about whether I needed my seat belt, and it took me a second to realize he'd been answering me. "You got it," I said, before sucking in a harsh breath and holding it as Crash slammed on the brakes to avoid hitting the car in front of us. The SUV rocked forward and then back with the force of the sudden stop, and I decided that, yes, this would be a good time to strap in. I had no idea how much longer this roller-coaster ride would go on, but if it was for longer than half a mile, I suspected I'd be glad for that choice.

Once the belt was fastened, I crossed my left leg over my right and rested my phone in my lap, hoping my thigh would block most of the screen from the guy sitting next to me. I didn't need him to see what I was up to. Taking another deep breath, I opened a new message to Rico and quickly fired off the words "track map" to him before I deleted it and then started to text Tamara. Thank God I'd managed it because when Crash punched the accelerator and took the next turn, the guy next to me—who I decided to call Elmer because it'd just struck me that he kind of reminded me of Elmer Fudd—took the opportunity and leaned way closer to me than necessary and tried to peek at my screen.

I smiled at him. "You okay?"

Elmer nodded and grumbled something under his breath.

"You might want to put on your seat belt," I told him, tugging at my own for emphasis. Then I started telling Tamara what Crash had said. I debated whether to ask her if she was okay but thought better of it. That didn't seem like something one would ask if we were only playing a game.

My breathing became shallower as I waited for her reply. All I got for my worrying was an "okay." I rolled my eyes.

Crash turned down a dark, narrow street, lined on both sides with residences that weren't quite brownstones, and pulled over to one side, cutting the lights and the engine almost before the car stopped. After all that racing around, the sudden quiet seemed heavy and oppressive. I wanted to clear my throat but was afraid to call attention to myself.

Instead, I tried to figure out where we were. Down the street in one direction, I could see some kind of apartment building that was under either renovation or construction, and across from it there were buildings that appeared to have no function but were not residential. Up the street the other way, I glimpsed some kind of church, but it was tough to tell what denomination it was. I wasn't positive what street we were on, but I was fairly certain we weren't too far from NYFO. I uncrossed my legs and pressed my right one against the length of the door, comforting myself with the feel of the gun strapped to the outside of my ankle. It was nice to know I wasn't totally defenseless.

We sat there for a while, Crash texting, the guy sitting next to him—Sam, I'd decided—leaning in to see what he was doing, and Elmer staring out the window while I tried to unobtrusively keep an eye on everyone's hands. Wasn't anybody going to say anything? Someone had to say something. They had to have realized that their scavenger hunt ruse had broken down long ago and for us to just sit here in silence after that driving display was nuts.

As if reading my mind, which didn't give me the creeps at all, Crash said, "Okay. Slight change of plans." His voice sounded weird: strained, almost shaky. He ran one hand through his hair, brushing it back off his forehead. "Tamara didn't get her clue, but that's okay. That's okay," he repeated more softly, as if speaking to himself. Was he trying to convince us or reassure himself? I couldn't tell.

"Okay," I said, trying to help him along with his delusion. "So, what now?"

Crash glanced out the window and then back at his phone. "Now we wait here for a bit. Someone might be able to bring the next clue to us."

It took a colossal effort not to huff or roll my eyes or shake my head. Should I call him on this? Or continue to pretend to play along? Nope. This was stupid. "Isn't that cheating? Having someone bring the clue to us. Don't we have to go get it? After figuring out the other one? How are we going to say we even got to this one to begin with?"

He didn't answer me right away.

"You know I don't believe this is a scavenger hunt, right?" I blurted out, sick of this charade.

He still didn't reply, and neither Sam nor Elmer must've felt the need to chime in because they, too, remained silent.

"Okay," I said to no one, under my breath but still loud enough to be heard in the close confines of the car. "Guess we're not addressing that subject."

And we didn't. We sat there in silence for a while. I tapped my fingertips against the tops of my thighs and jiggled my legs to try to burn off some of my nervous energy, but it didn't work. When I got bored of staring out the window at nothing—because the street was deserted and nothing and no one had moved on it since we'd screeched to a halt—I unbuckled my seat belt and started to open my door.

All three heads in the car swiveled in my direction, and six eyes locked onto me. I paused. "What?"

"What the hell do you think you're doing?" Crash asked, sounding half angry, half disbelieving. The darkness inside the car lent a sinister air to his countenance that made me break out in goose bumps.

"What does it look like I'm doing? I'm getting out of the car."

"But...why?" Now he just seemed confused.

I shrugged, trying hard to look casual. "It's hot in here, and I need to stretch my legs and my back."

"Oh," Crash said. I thought he might've been searching for a valid argument against my plan, but since he didn't say anything else, I guess he hadn't been able to come up with one.

"That okay?" I asked.

"You're not going to go wandering around?"

I made sure he could see the face I made at him. "Where would I go? I don't even know where we are." That part, at least, was true.

He bobbed his head once. "Sure. Go for it."

I shook my own head and widened my eyes in irritation before stepping outside of the car. The cool night air felt good on my overheated skin, and I tugged at my shirt collar a few times to try to circulate a breeze under my clothes. I hadn't realized until that moment that I'd started to sweat, and I swiped at the moisture dotting my face and neck and wiped my damp palm on my pant leg.

I took a few steps away from the car and spread my feet wide, twisting my torso back and forth as though trying to loosen tight back muscles, but really I wanted to gain a better idea of our surroundings. It didn't help. I pursed my lips and furrowed my brow as I bent at the waist and allowed my upper body to hang. Now what was I gonna do? My options seemed limited. I could either stay with Crash to see what he was up to and risk dying in a horrible car wreck. Or I could tell them I was done with these shenanigans and take off, hoping to catch a cab or find a subway nearby. Or I could— The sounds of the other car doors opening interrupted my waffling. My heart catapulted up to slap my uvula, and I shot back upright. My lungs seized as my mind spun, trying to gain enough traction to at least think of some reason why they would've all needed to get out onto the street just then. One that didn't involve me.

It didn't take long to realize that they weren't even looking at me; they were all staring down the street. I let out a relieved sigh and bit back a soft chuckle. Fuck, I was paranoid. I really needed to get a grip and stop constantly assuming the worst. I'd have a nervous breakdown if I didn't.

Wait. What were they looking at? None of them had spared me even the barest glance. They were all focused on what was down there. I squinted as though I could force my eyes to penetrate the darkness. I shouldn't have been surprised that it didn't work, but I still felt a pang of disappointment.

I stepped closer to Sam, which didn't help either, so I murmured, "What are we looking at?"

Without blinking or even turning his head, he said out of the corner of his mouth, "Rag heads."

My eyes bugged out before I could stop them, and my eyebrows shot up into my hairline. I blinked several times and then shook my head roughly, as though trying to clear water out of my ears. I'm sorry. He couldn't possibly have just said what I thought he'd said. Because I thought he'd said—

"Fucking sand rats," Elmer said, startling me by coming up behind me to stand at my side. He spat on the ground for emphasis and folded his arms across his chest.

Okay. So that was a thing that happened. What the actual fuck? Wait, no, who was I kidding? Why did those statements shock me so much? These loons wanted to kill people. Like actually kill people. Gun them down in their mosque just because they worshipped in a different way. I was convinced that everyone worshipped the same deity, just with a different name and different dogmas, but that was just me, and it was neither here nor there. I should've realized that for a group like this, racial slurs would be par for the course. This was the first time any of them had uttered anything like that in my presence, and I couldn't shake the icky feeling that'd settled in the bottom of my stomach like oil coats the bottom of a bowl. God, these people were gross.

Somewhere during my introspection, Crash had come around to our side of the car to stand with us, and I spent several long minutes watching them while they all stared intently down the street. They looked tense and wore identical scowls. Occasionally, one of them grunted or muttered something under his breath. But their attention remained fixated.

I glanced to where they were all glowering, afraid of what I would see. My heart deflated like a poorly made soufflé, and the oil coating the bottom of my stomach curdled. A man and a woman were strolling along the street, minding their own business, unaware that they were on a collision course with a bunch of bigoted assholes. The woman was pushing a stroller, and given that I couldn't see a child in it, I surmised it contained a tiny baby. Fuck. Fuckity fuck fuck.

I opened my mouth to try to distract the guys but froze when I saw their expressions. They were dark and dangerous, borderline hungry. That was not a good look. It made me feel like someone had forced an ice cube down my gullet. It promised violence and screaming and pain. It promised blood. No one should ever have that look.

"Whaddya think?" Sam asked, his low voice sinister. He glanced at Crash, looking for something. And while I found the dynamic interesting, given their obvious age differences, I filed it in the back of my mind to analyze another time. For now, I needed to focus on what he was asking. Clearly, he had something on his mind. But what? I really hoped it wasn't what I thought it was.

Crash narrowed his eyes at the couple and stroked the edge of his chin with his forefinger. "It's risky," he said after a long moment.

The relief that swelled inside me was borderline painful. Thank God. I suddenly felt like an idiot. Of course they weren't going to do anything crazy. Not in the middle of a Brooklyn street. Not so out in the open where they could so easily get caught. Not before they had time to put the finishing touches on their ridiculous reverse-jihad plan. Not without Seth's okay. That would be ludicrous.

"But I think we can get away with it," Crash said, shattering my good mood and winding my guts into a tight, painful knot. He cast around, assessing the street in a glance. "If we're quick and careful."

His gaze landed on me then, and all my internal organs seized and shrank into a leaden ball. His expression became appraising, and my skin itched. I didn't know what he was looking for, so I had no idea how to ensure that he found it. On a whim, I decided that appearing angry and defiant was the way to go. I cocked one hip and rested my hands near the waistband of my jeans.

Crash's inspection of me lasted a lot longer than I wanted it to—a lot longer than I was comfortable with—but finally he nodded as if to himself and turned back to Elmer and Sam. I tried to make sure the shaky exhale that escaped once his back was turned was too soft for any of them to hear.

None of them spoke. They barely looked at one another before they set off down the block in the direction of the poor, clueless couple.

Oh, hell.

CHAPTER TWENTY-TWO

My heart gave a punishing *kaTHUNK* against my breastbone before settling into a rapid-fire *kaTHUNKkaTHUNKkaTHUNK-kaTHUNK* that rattled my rib cage. My lungs adopted a similar pace as I struggled to breathe and think at the same time. It wasn't going well.

Not knowing what else to do, I followed the guys, balling my hands into fists and digging my nails into the flesh of my palms. This was bad. This was so, so bad. I couldn't think of any legitimate reason for approaching these people, and I didn't want to dwell on the illegitimate ones. I needed to figure out a way to deescalate this situation before someone got hurt.

The guys had picked up their tempo and hurried ahead of me, and though I debated increasing my own speed to catch up, part of me wanted to hang back a bit. Maybe I hoped it'd give me more time to think of something. Maybe I hoped I'd see some way out of this clusterfuck before it was too late. Maybe I was wishing that an intergalactic wormhole would open on the sidewalk in front of me and that I could use it to escape the situation altogether. Swing and a miss on all counts.

Crash and his band of very racist men were on a collision course with this poor, defenseless family, and they had no idea what was headed their way. Should I call out? Yell something to warn them that they needed to change direction or call someone or just be more aware of their surroundings? Would it even do any good at this point? Fuck it, I had to try.

I had opened my mouth, not sure what I was planning to say but counting on an adrenaline-induced bolt of inspiration to see me through, when one of the guys shouted first. Sam? Elmer? I couldn't tell, and I supposed it didn't really matter. All that counted was that the hate-laced stream of epithets that rolled out from between his lips was so foul that it made my insides shrivel and all my hair follicles prickle and burn. It also left no mistake about what was going to happen.

The expressions on the couple's faces were almost comical, and my gaze locked onto them. Unable to look away, I got to see the moment when surprise melted into confusion and then soured into horror. I saw the exact second when it clicked for them how much trouble they were in. It made me want to throw up.

The man rushed to put himself between Crash and company and the woman who I assumed was his wife, and my heart ached at the pointless gesture. That he was willing to meet the mob and try to save her was admirable, but somehow I doubted it would matter. I didn't put it past a group of men who were willing to commit a hate crime on a New York street to beat a woman. It didn't seem like that far of a stretch.

Time slipped then. It did this sort of movie-magic phenomenon thing where it sped up and then slowed down and then seemed to reverse somehow. My world narrowed to the tableau being played out in front of me. The grunts and labored breathing of Crash, Elmer, and Sam as they swung over and over mingled with the unmistakable sound of fists landing on flesh and was underscored by the groans and oofs of the pitiable man who was getting his ass handed to him.

This had to have been the worst atrocity I'd ever witnessed firsthand, and I couldn't land on the best way to stop it. I'd had practice subduing multiple assailants, so I was pretty sure that with a little bit of work, I'd be able to get them off the guy long enough for him to make a run for it. But then my cover would probably be blown, and the group could potentially go deeper underground. Then we might never be able to stop them before they carried out their nefarious plan. Okay. That avenue was out.

I had a gun, so I could shoot them, which held some appeal. But then I had the same problem regarding my cover, so that wouldn't work. Plus, I might miss and hit the woman or the baby or some unsuspecting soul watching TV in their house. No, I didn't want to take that risk.

I could fire a round or two into the ground to get their attention. I might be able to pull that off if I could sell them on the idea that I'd been looking to do much more than just beat the guy and that the shots had been accidental discharges. But I had no guarantee they'd buy that. Shit. What the fuck was I going to do?

The shrill sounds of the woman's screams broke into my mental tailspin, and I winced at their sheer volume. I wasn't sure how I hadn't noticed them before—maybe they'd just started; I couldn't be sure—

but now that I'd heard them, I realized it would only be a matter of time before the guys became aware of them, and of her, too.

Something clicked inside me as I realized what my course of action should be, and I took off around the thick of men like a shot. On the way, I heard Crash shout like he was in pain, and I gave a silent, internal cheer that the man had managed to land at least one good blow. I was proud of him for attempting to fight back.

I had no time to examine the situation, though. The concept of time had taken on a whole new meaning for me, and I realized I'd wasted a bunch of it and had no clue how much more I had. So I button-hooked around the pack like a star running back and dashed toward the terrified woman.

When she saw me, her eyes went wide and wild, and her shriek could've popped eardrums. Guilt socked me hard in the stomach for frightening her, but if I played this right, it could save her life, so I struggled to push past it. I ran at her pell-mell, waving my hands, trying to shoo her in the opposite direction. She screeched again and threw herself over top of the stroller.

Come on, lady, I thought with a huff. Help me out here. I can't do this by myself. She was still howling and crying and shaking when I reached her, which wasn't at all what I'd wanted. I'd needed her to run away so I could pretend to give chase. And now I was more or less on top of her with no backup plan.

Not certain whether the guys were paying attention and not wanting to chance a glance over my shoulder to check, I realized I'd need to make this look good. Trembling all over, I had half a second to worry that I'd be sick all over the mother and child I was terrifying. Well, on the bright side, it'd probably make them run away.

I stutter-stepped to a stop in front of her and tried to ignore the way my stomach clenched and rolled at the look in her eyes. The way they glistened with tears made my own eyes prickle and burn. I blinked and pretended to shove her. Did that look convincing? I sure as hell hoped so.

"Run," I said under my breath.

She continued to gawk at me from her hunched position protecting her child. I made a show of grabbing at her clothes, plucking at her colorful abaya and the hijab covering her head, not hard, not enough to dislodge any of them, but enough to alarm her, if her expression was any clue.

"Run," I said again, trying to gesture with my hand but still keeping it hidden from the guys should any of them be looking. "Please."

Her face crumpled, and her watery eyes now held confusion. To emphasize my point, I pushed her shoulder and pointed again. "Go on. Get out of here. Run and call the cops."

She remained frozen for the longest time, and I was starting to worry that she didn't speak English. Shit. I couldn't tell what language she spoke, and even if I knew, it wasn't like I had time to whip my phone out of my inside jacket pocket and look up how to tell her to beat feet online. The guys might have been preoccupied with pummeling this woman's husband, but I was pretty sure they'd notice that.

"Please," I whispered again, putting one hand on her shoulder and the other on her wrist, shaking her. It was a last-ditch effort. If she didn't heed my warning, I didn't know what to do. "Please, go. Please."

I don't know whether she understood anything I'd said or if it'd finally clicked with her that I could be hurting her and I wasn't, but she spun out of my grasp. I was impressed by how swiftly she moved, and even more impressed by how fast she ran, considering she was pushing a stroller.

Behind me, one of the guys shouted, "Hey!"

"On it," I shouted back. Again, I wasn't even sure if they were talking to me or someone else, but I really wanted them to stay the hell away from this woman.

I hesitated before I started to pretend to chase her, scouring the sidewalk in front of me as I ran. I knew the guys wouldn't buy it if a lady with a stroller outran me. But I thought I might be able to make it convincing if I took a hard fall while I gave chase. At least I hoped so because, outside of that, I was devoid of ideas.

I tried to run slowly, but not too slow, to give her time to get far enough ahead of me. And about halfway down the street, I spotted what I'd been looking for: a jagged, cracked section of sidewalk jutting skyward, dislodged by the roots of an adjacent tree. Perfect.

I couldn't run directly over the spot—that would look weird and likely make the guys suspicious—but I ran as close to it as I thought I could get away with. As I screamed in its direction, I sucked in a harsh breath and held it. My lips twisted in a grimace. This was going to hurt like a bitch.

Making sure to keep my feet near the ground as I ran, I knew the tip of my shoe would catch on something. And catch it did. Harder than I'd meant it to. I gasped and let out a small cry as I went airborne, flapping my arms as though they'd be able to soften my landing.

They weren't. I hit the pavement with a bone-shuddering thud and felt a white-hot stab of pain in my ribs as my breath was knocked out of me. Jesus fuck, that hurt. What the hell had I landed on? I tried to suck in air, but nothing was happening. It was tough not to panic, even though I'd been through this before and was always able to breathe again eventually.

I rolled onto one side as I attempted to force my lungs to work, wrapping one arm around my ribs as though I could soothe the agony by cradling them. I lolled my head in the direction of the woman and was relieved to see that she was still booking it up the street. I didn't think the guys would want to give chase. Not with as big a head start as she had. I prayed that she had someplace to go, someone to take care of her. She was going to be traumatized for a long time.

A hand on my arm hauling me to my feet startled me, and I jerked. Crash was looking at me with a weird mixture of emotions that I couldn't begin to name. Anger didn't seem to be one of them, though, so at least that was something.

"You okay?" he asked.

I nodded and tried again to inhale. This time it worked. Sort of. The breath was shallow and gasping, but it was better than nothing. "Yeah," I croaked. "Sorry."

"We gotta go."

He let go of my arm and jogged back in the direction of the car. I limped after him at a much slower pace. Now that I wasn't so focused on not being able to breathe, I noticed that I hurt in a lot more places than just my ribs. I didn't think I'd done any permanent damage, but I was going to have bumps and bruises tomorrow morning for sure.

I shuffled past the man, who was lying in a crumpled heap on the ground. What I could see of him through the streetlamp-broken darkness indicated he'd been through the wringer. Bile rose in my throat at the sight of blood glistening on his face, which was barely recognizable. He wasn't moving. He wasn't even moaning. Dear God, they'd fucked him up. I clenched my teeth against the urge to vomit. That wouldn't look good, and if I wanted this monstrous hate group to let me in on their plan, which I did if I had any hopes of stopping them, I needed to look good. The needs of the many and all that. It made sense, but it didn't make me feel any better.

What was I going to do? I couldn't leave him here like this. Lord only knew the extent of his injuries. If he wasn't dead already, he might be soon. And the cold couldn't have helped anything. Or would it? I wasn't sure.

I fumbled for my phone, which was nestled inside my interior coat pocket. I had no idea where we were, but since the guys had the ability to track it, if I left it on him, they should be able to find him and get him help. But when I got it out, the screen was shattered. I thumbed the buttons to see if it would turn on, but the screen remained dark. Goddamit. How was I going to get this guy help now? I glanced up and down the street, but it was late, and nothing and no one moved. Of course. I rolled my eyes. If no one had come outside during that free-for-all, I don't know what'd made me think anyone would come outside now.

"What are you doing?" Sam yelled out the front window of the SUV. "Let's go."

"Souvenir," I said, holding up my phone so he could see it. I thought I heard him huff, but he didn't try to hurry me along.

I turned so that my back was to them and reached up to the necklace I was wearing, the tracking device Allison had given me. Since leaving my phone on the guy wasn't an option, this was the only thing I could think of. I pretended to try to take a picture as I yanked on the necklace with my other hand. The sensation of the chain snapping burned against the back of my neck.

Then, to hide the gesture as best I could, I wound up as though I were giving the guy a kick, swinging my arms as though I were attempting to build up some momentum to put behind it. My heart was racing, and even though it was cold, I was sweating. God, I hoped they didn't see this. Because if they did, I was going to have some serious explaining to do. And I wasn't sure any amount of verbal tap dancing would be able to excuse this in such a way that they ever trusted me again.

I led with my hip as I jutted my leg out toward the guy, dropping my arm at the same time. When my hand reached the bottom of its swing, which should've been hidden from the guys by my body—please let that be true—I opened my fingers to allow the necklace to fall. My heart soared for a brief instant as I watched the diamond and chain land on the ground next to his crumpled form, but it plummeted back to earth almost immediately as I registered the dull thud of my foot meeting the guy's bicep.

It wasn't hard. It certainly wasn't enough to cause him any more damage. But I'd misjudged the angle and depth of my kick and had hit him by accident. The urge to vomit intensified. My head swam, and my ears started to ring. I stared at him for another second before the deliberate revving of an engine behind me broke into my self-flagellation. I blinked and spun, hobbling off toward the car as quickly as my bruised and battered body would allow.

I held my breath as I eased myself inside the SUV and buckled myself in. My internal organs were slithering around like the blobs inside a lava lamp. I clenched my teeth together and wrapped my arms around my waist and stared out the window, hoping Rico would find the guy and trying not to think about him at the same time.

The guys were laughing and chattering and cuffing one another on the shoulder as they congratulated each other on ganging up on a man and beating the shit out of him in front of his family. If I hadn't felt sick before, their mutual accolades would've done the trick. I concentrated on the spinning inside my head so I wouldn't have to listen to them anymore.

"Aw, Alex," Crash said, snagging my attention. "What's wrong? You pissed you didn't really get to join in on the fun?"

I glanced up to see that he had tilted the rearview mirror so he could see me, and the sparkle in his eyes was disconcerting. He'd enjoyed himself back there. I fought not to sneer in disgust, and I clenched my hand tight against the broken phone I was still clutching. Instead, I bobbed my head once and forced myself to say, "Yeah."

"You scared that lady real good, though," Elmer said, giving me a sympathetic look as he tried to reassure me.

In the seat in front of me, Sam chuckled. "Yeah, you did. I thought for sure she was going to keel over before you even touched her."

"Too bad you tripped while chasing after her," Crash said, his eyes flickering back and forth between mine and the road as he sped away from the scene of the crime.

My heart gave a violent *kerTHUNK*, and I was glad it was dark and he wasn't staring directly at me because I was sure I paled. Had I imagined it, or had his voice held a measure of disbelief as he'd said that? I swallowed hard and forced what I hoped was a disgusted-sounding snort. "Yeah. Stupid fucking sidewalk."

"Right? I bet you'd've fucked her up good, huh?" Crash pressed, still stealing little glances at me.

"Totally," I said. "Maybe next time."

Elmer and Sam didn't seem either concerned by or interested in me or whatever my thoughts might've been. But Crash appeared to be studying me, measuring me. Was he attempting to figure out whether I subscribed to the same crazy belief system he did? Was this it? Had he just cracked the door? If I pulled this off, could I be invited in?

My heart was thudding so hard and so loud I was afraid that everyone else in the car would be able to hear it. But hopefully they'd chalk it up to adrenaline and the aftermath of the chase rather than the fact that I was almost shitting my pants right now. If I messed this up… *No. Don't think about it!*

"They deserve that and more," I muttered, as though I were speaking to myself. "The whole fucking lot of them."

That'd been hard to say—though it'd been the least offensive thing I could think of that might still lead these nutters to believe I was as racist as they were—and my mouth almost burned. I held my breath for a beat and then made myself let it trickle out from between my lips slowly. I assumed Crash had been talking to Seth. It didn't seem implausible that Seth would've told him about what'd happened to my nonexistent military father. And if he hadn't yet, I imagined he would after Crash told him about this debacle. Maybe, just maybe, he'd buy that I'd really meant that.

Crash started to say something, but he broke off when his phone buzzed with another text. The next few seconds of him looking more at his phone than at the road ahead were precarious, and several times I was convinced he was about to sideswipe a parked car, but we made it unscathed. However, I kept both my feet planted on the imaginary brake on the floorboard beneath me, just in case.

"Okay," Crash said as he tossed his phone into the cup holder next to him. "Change of plans. We're headed back."

I frowned, confused. What about our errands? What about the packages we were supposed to pick up? Why the detour? Had something happened? Was it related to what we'd just done? I had a whole lot of questions and zero answers.

"Is the game over?" I asked. It wasn't what I'd wanted to know, but I figured it was more innocuous than any of the other things I'd been wondering.

"This one is," Crash replied after a beat. "For now."

I nodded and directed my attention out the window, watching as we made our way back into Manhattan and listening intently for the sounds of sirens in pursuit. "Who won?"

"No one," Crash told me. "Not this time."

He sure as hell had that right.

CHAPTER TWENTY-THREE

I had no idea what time it was when Crash finally dropped me off in front of "Tate's" building, but it was late. I waved over my shoulder as the SUV pulled away from the curb and let myself into the outer door of the lobby, pausing in the vestibule to watch the taillights disappear down the street. Then I made my way through the inner door and lowered myself carefully onto one of the stone steps.

Letting out a slow, painful sigh, I leaned against the wall. I didn't know where Tate was, and I hoped he was okay. I also didn't know how I was going to verify that in the immediate future, aside from going upstairs to check if he was there. But I *did* know I wasn't going to be able to go to sleep. Not now. Not after that mess.

My gut was as snarled as New York traffic at the peak of rush hour on the Friday of a holiday weekend, and I had to fight to keep the contents of my stomach inside it. At some point on the ride home, I'd begun shaking, and not just because I was cold.

I struggled to my feet and started pacing the first-floor hallway. God, this was horrible. Images of that man lying crumpled and bleeding and motionless on the pavement kept flashing in my mind, making me wish I could get in there with a scrub brush and some bleach and eradicate the memory. My skin crawled, and I didn't think any amount of hot water would make me feel clean ever again.

Okay, I told myself, this wasn't helping. I needed to act. Sitting here beating myself up—and the irony of the word choice there wasn't lost on me—over something I couldn't change wouldn't accomplish anything. Neither worrying nor wallowing would alter the fact that I'd let those animals do that to that poor man. Before I did anything else, I needed to make sure the guys had sent someone to help him.

After a quick trip upstairs to confirm that Tate was indeed still in the wind, I dashed back out into the frigid night. I glanced around to determine whether anyone was watching me. No one appeared to be, but that didn't mean anything. Now more than ever, I needed to be cautious.

I made my way up the street, my muscles tight, straining to pick up the sounds of cloth rustling or quiet footsteps behind me on the street, my reflexes locked on high alert. I was trying to look casual as I scanned my surroundings at intervals, and while I wasn't certain I'd managed it, I did know that I hadn't picked up on anything unusual.

I caught a cab at the corner and gave the driver the cross streets closest to Allison's hotel. He probably thought I was a nut job with the way I kept turning around and looking over my shoulder the entire time, but he was polite enough—or terrified enough—not to ask any questions.

That paranoia stuck with me throughout the duration of the ride and continued to cling to me even after the cabbie had dropped me off. I'd become so nervous that someone might be following me—even though I'd watched each car that'd driven on the street anywhere near us like a hawk until they'd gone in another direction—that I'd had him drop me off a few blocks away. Then I'd taken a very circuitous path to the hotel's front door that included a lot of stopping, a ton of inspecting reflections in darkened windows, a handful of double-backs, and pop-ins to two separate establishments to either spot or lose a tail, should I even have one.

I lingered in the lobby for a bit, checking my watch and my phone often, pretending to be waiting for someone for the benefit of the security guards and front desk staff. Really, I was just making a last-ditch effort to get eyes on anyone who might've been following me. After a great deal of aimless meandering and weaving around chairs, pillars, and potted plants, I made my way to the elevator.

I held my breath as I waited for the elevator doors to slide closed, anticipating the sudden appearance of someone, anyone, who looked interested in what I was up to. My heart was still rammed up underneath my breastbone even after the doors had closed, and I put the heel of one hand to my chest as I sagged against the back wall.

The respite was too short-lived, and soon the telltale ding of the car arriving on the desired floor assaulted my ears. I shot up, body ramrod straight, muscles tightly wound, prepped for whatever fight-or-flight scenario might befall me in the hall. I didn't see anyone in either direction, which I took as a cue to speed-walk down the hall to Allison's room. The sooner I was inside and away from prying eyes, the more relaxed I'd feel.

Still looking up and down the hallway and half expecting someone to leap out at me at any moment from one of the other rooms or the utility closet, I rapped my knuckles against Allison's door. Seconds dragged by, and it was a struggle not to focus on the sensation of my insides being wrapped tighter and tighter around a lightning rod while besieged by the knowledge that my grounding wire had been cut. I knocked again, this time a little harder.

Again, my efforts were greeted with silence, and I blew out a breath from between my pursed lips and furrowed my brow as I thought. If my phone hadn't been smashed to bits by being pinned between the unstoppable force of my weight and the immovable object of a jagged slab of concrete, I would've called her. I could try the key she'd given me, but that would only work if she hadn't engaged the privacy bolt, which after her experience with Beau in Hong Kong she wouldn't have neglected to do. I also wasn't positive that letting myself into her room without her knowledge at this time of night wouldn't result in me getting shot, and I wasn't at all eager to sign up for that again.

I scoured the hallway for a house phone that I could use to ring her room, but I didn't see one. Fuck. Why did everything have to be such a goddamn production? I wanted to avoid going back down to the lobby the way I wanted to avoid Thanksgiving at my aunt's. Or Peeps. Or getting eaten by Glocamorra. But sometimes those things were unavoidable. Especially that middle one.

Before admitting defeat, I made one last-ditch effort at getting Allison's attention. I pounded on the door, making my raps twice as loud and lasting three times as long. I rocked on the balls of my feet as I waited for a response, my heart pounding too hard for me to hear much of what might've been going on inside the room. I'd just decided to begin a thirty-second countdown as a precursor to my getting back on the elevator and making the trek back downstairs when I heard the click of a bolt being shoved out of the way.

Allison flung the door open with some impressive force and stood there scowling at me for an instant before she realized it was me. Her expression morphed from angry to confused in an instant. "Ryan?"

"Hey," I said, feeling like an idiot. I glanced down the hall again. "Can I come in?"

"Sure. Yeah. Of course." She stepped aside to allow me adequate room to slip past her and rubbed at her eyes sleepily. "What are you doing here?"

I rounded on her as she shut the door. "Why did you look so surprised just now?"

"Huh?" She brushed by me and turned on the light, blinking

against the sudden brightness. Then she sat on the edge of her bed and peered at me.

I took a seat on the bed opposite her. "When you opened the door just now, you seemed surprised to see me. Didn't you look through the peephole first?"

She stared at me for a moment as though trying to figure out what I was asking her—or possibly trying to figure out how to get away with smacking me—before rolling her eyes. "Of course I did. It's not my fault you were standing too far off to the side for me to be able to see you."

"Still. You should ask who it is before you open it. Especially this late at night."

She raised an eyebrow at me. "Is that why you came over here? To criticize me? Because I'm going to need caffeine before we go any further."

I studied my hands and sighed, shaking my head. "I'm sorry. You're right. Of course that's not why I came here."

"Good. Because I'm not allowed to have caffeine." A beat. "So why did you come?"

I frowned as I considered that question. I hadn't thought too much about why I'd needed to see her so badly. I'd just…gone. At any other time, under any other circumstances, the idea would've made me smile. Today, it just made me want to cry.

Allison folded her legs under her and pulled the comforter over them. Then she balled the pillow up under her side and reclined on it, resting her temple in the heel of her hand. I could feel her impatience from where I was sitting, but she didn't rush me, for which I was grateful.

"Can I use your phone?" I blurted out as something occurred to me. I really should have done this before now—maybe asked a patron in one of the diners I'd popped in to or begged a bartender to let me use the bar's phone—but my thinking had been muddled. My stomach knotted as I realized how much precious time I'd wasted.

"Sure," Allison said. She nodded to the nightstand between the beds where it rested. "What happened to yours?"

"It got broken." I picked it up and dialed Rico's number from memory; his actual number, not the number to the burner phone he used when he communicated with me. I held my breath as I waited for him to answer and thought about how often on this assignment I'd put a hold on my oxygen intake, wondering whether it'd be detrimental to my health in the long run.

"Hello?" Rico said after a few rings.

"Rico? Please tell me you found him." I prayed that when the tracker for my phone cut off, he'd switched to monitoring my necklace, and that when it'd stayed in one place too long, he'd gone to investigate.

"Yeah," Rico said. "Don't worry. We found him. As soon as I got your text about checking the map, I started heading in your direction. I must've missed you by less than a minute."

I let out the breath I'd been holding and sagged as I recommenced trembling. I closed my eyes and hung my head, aware that Allison was watching me but not wanting to look at her. Not yet. Not until I knew how bad this was.

I licked my lips and opened my mouth. It was a struggle to force the question out. "And?" Part of me wanted to say more, but I'd been unable to make myself do that. There was a limit to things I could strong-arm myself into doing.

Rico was quiet for a long moment, and my heart joined my lungs in their momentary cessation of normal function. "It isn't good."

I swallowed and started scraping the fingernails of my free hand over the denim covering my knee. "How not good?"

Rico let a long, slow breath seep from between his lips. I heard some rustling on his end before he spoke. "He's in critical condition. There's a lot they won't know until after they do some tests and scans."

My chest was tight, and my stomach felt like an inflatable pool toy that'd gotten caught on the ladder at the edge of the deck and been torn open. "But surely you have some idea…"

"It's bad," he said, his voice low.

"Oh." Was the room spinning? I glanced up at Allison, and she was watching me with concern.

"If he makes it, it'll be because of you."

Oof. That was a fucking kick to the gut, considering I could've done more to prevent him landing in that position in the first place. My scalp directly over my forehead began tingling, and my face flushed. I doubled over and wrapped my arm around my midsection.

"If you hadn't reached out to us, if you hadn't left the tracking device on him, there's no telling how long he would've lain there before help arrived."

Again, neither helpful nor comforting. Though I supposed I couldn't blame him for trying. He wasn't working with all the pertinent information and was doing his best with what he had. I probably would've done the same in his position. Still, I wished he would just stop talking. He'd told me what I'd needed to know. Anything else was unnecessary.

"Where are you?" he asked. At least I think that's what he'd asked. The ringing in my ears made it tough to tell.

"Don't worry. I'm safe."

"Good. Because I definitely don't want to have to explain to your girlfriend how we lost you—again—but you did somehow manage to lead us to a guy who'd had the shit kicked out of him."

"Thanks, Rico," I said, wanting the conversation to be over. "Keep me posted."

"Ryan—"

I didn't wait to hear what the rest of that sentence was going to be. Instead, I cut him off with the push of a button and placed the phone back onto the nightstand. I fisted my fingers in the comforter at the edge of the bed and took a deep breath.

"Do you want to tell me what happened?" Allison asked softly.

The backs of my eyes prickled and burned as I fought to keep the tears from gathering there, and my throat ached. I shook my head. No. I didn't want to tell her. I didn't want to have to witness the moment when her love for me curdled and she wondered what kind of person I was, how I could've done what I'd done, how she could ever again allow me to touch her with these hands that'd done nothing to save someone's life. Losing her was the least of what I deserved. Maybe it was for the best. If she left me now, I wouldn't have to leave her later. My head said that made sense, but my heart still shattered at the idea of existence without her.

"Will you please tell me anyway?" she asked, her voice as tender as I'd ever heard it.

I nodded as the tears started trickling down my cheeks. "I did something bad," I said, the words stilted and choked.

Allison sat up, swung her legs to the floor, and took up a position at my side. She slipped one arm around my shoulders and pulled me close. "Whatever it is, it'll be okay."

The lump in my throat had gotten bigger, and the ache that accompanied it grew. I sniffled, stifling a wail. I shook my head as I leaned into her. "No. It won't."

"What did you do?" She rested the hollow of her cheek against the top of my head. The arm around my shoulders tightened.

I laughed—a bitter, broken, jagged sound—and swiped at my damp cheeks with the cuff of my shirtsleeve. "You were right," I said after a long moment. "This is an unmitigated disaster. I don't know what I'm doing. I'm in over my head."

Allison took a deep breath, and I steeled myself for the "I told you so" that I was sure was about to escape her lips.

But she surprised me. "I'm sure it's not that bad. Why don't you just tell me what happened?"

In the face of her kindness, the urge to allow myself to dissolve into sobs almost overwhelmed me. I blinked a couple of times and swallowed several more to try to control the impulse. "The guys I was with tonight jumped someone."

Allison tensed, but her voice was low and even when she finally replied. "Is he okay?"

I shook my head.

"I see." A beat. "And you were with them when it happened?"

I nodded and squeezed my eyes shut tight. The need to break down became stronger somehow, and I was losing the battle to keep myself in check. I tried every trick I could think of to keep myself in the present and not get mired in memories of what'd gone down tonight, but I was failing at that, too. I clasped my stomach harder and rocked back and forth.

"Hey," Allison whispered into my ear. "Shh, shh, shh. It'll be okay."

I shook my head again. I didn't believe her. How could anything ever be okay? How could I go on knowing that I'd let those assholes do that? How could I go on knowing *I'd* terrified someone? It didn't seem possible.

My stomach rolled and my esophagus twitched as if preparing for what was to come. I glanced over my shoulder, making sure I had a good gauge of where the bathroom was. I might need it in the not-too-distant future.

"Ryan," Allison said, her voice the picture of patience and calm. "There wasn't anything you could've done."

"I could've stopped it," I said. Even now, as I revisited the list of reasons I'd given myself not to get involved, the excuses seemed flimsy knowing the man might not make it through this. Were any of them worth someone's life? It'd been a snap decision, but now, looking back, I didn't think so. God, I hated twenty-twenty hindsight.

"You could have. But then you would've blown your cover. You could've ended up blowing Tate's cover. And if you'd done that, these past few weeks would've been for nothing. This group would've gone deeper underground, and who knows whether anyone would've been able to stop them from killing a bunch of people."

I refused to be appeased. "I could've told them to stop it. I could've tried to get them to leave. They could hardly assume I'm a federal agent just because I don't want to beat the shit out of a stranger on a street corner."

"True," Allison replied. "You could have. And you're right. That probably wouldn't have tipped them off to your real purpose there per se. But it would have made the group doubt your commitment to their cause. Someone still might have been able to stop them, but it wouldn't have been you. Which again would have negated your presence in this operation."

I didn't say anything. I just lapsed into silence, held captive by my memories and my guilt.

"Besides," Allison said after a moment. "You couldn't have known they'd take it that far. How could anyone?"

I shook my head. "They're all crazy. They want to shoot unarmed people for no reason. How could I not have known?" My mind flashed back to the look in Crash's eyes as he'd stared at the couple, and the remnants of my shredded heart went up like flash paper, igniting in a brilliant blaze and leaving nothing in its wake, not even ash.

"Crazy, yes. But until now, they've seemed well organized. They've been planning and biding their time. What happened tonight was… not. It was an anomaly. It makes me wonder what's really going on?"

I sat up so I could look at her. "What do you mean?"

"Well, either there's some sort of power struggle, or it was a test. A test of you and your convictions. Of your value system. Of your willingness to keep quiet in the face of violence."

I'd sort of been thinking the same thing earlier, but it hadn't seemed quite realistic enough to be plausible. "Maybe."

"You did the right thing."

I was shocked, and it didn't even occur to me to try to hide my surprise. "Really?"

Allison nodded. "Of course. You stayed safe. You survived."

"Yeah, I did. But at someone else's expense. How can I ever look at myself in the mirror again? How can *you* stand to look at me? I'm a monster."

Allison used the pad of her thumb to wipe away the residue of tears left staining my cheeks. "You're not a monster. And I can look at you because I love you."

I wanted to argue, to tell her that I didn't deserve her love or anyone else's. Not after what I'd done. But the events of the evening had taken their toll, and I was spent. I just wanted to close my eyes and forget everything for a while. If I fell asleep and didn't tell Tate where I was again, he might murder me, but I was willing to take that chance for a moment of peace.

I swatted at her legs a bit until she complied with my unspoken request and scooted back from the edge of the bed. Then I lay down on my side with my back to her, curled my hand under my cheek, and closed my eyes. I half expected her to move back to her own bed— half wanted her to so I would have an excuse to get upset, start an argument, and leave—but she snuggled up behind me without a word and wrapped her arm around my waist, pulling me close.

"I'm sorry," I told her.

"For what?"

"For always talking about me. I know you're having a rough time, too. I haven't even asked how you're feeling lately."

"Don't worry about me."

I turned my head, intending to fix her with a dark glare, but the angle was wrong, so I gave up and settled for pressing my fingernails into the flesh of her forearm. "I can't help it. I love you. I want to make sure you're okay."

"I'm fine."

The answer was too quick to be believable, not that I would've bought it even if she hadn't blurted it out the way she had. "Allison, come on. Please."

"I'm serious, Ryan. I'm fine. Tired and nauseous, but fine."

"Allison."

"Ryan."

I sighed and closed my eyes again. No amount of pleading or cajoling would make her give me something right now. I hated it when she closed herself off like this. But I also wasn't in the mood to fight about it. Not after the night I'd had. "Okay."

Allison pressed her lips to the spot just behind my ear, then tucked her forehead into my shoulder blade. I waited for her to say something else, but she remained quiet and held me.

"I don't know what I'm going to do, Allison," I whispered after a time.

She stayed silent for a bit, and I was thinking about slipping out of her embrace without waking her when she spoke. "You're going to do the only thing you can do. You're going to stop those bigoted assholes before they kill someone. And then you're going to come home."

I wanted to point out that they might have already killed someone, and that I might've let it happen, but thinking about forming the words made me want to cry. Instead, I nodded and bit my lower lip, squeezing my eyes shut against the tears.

Home sounded really good.

CHAPTER TWENTY-FOUR

I broke my promise to Tate. I'd told him I'd never worry him by staying out all night and not calling him, but that's what I did. I probably would've felt guilty about it, too, but I was too busy raking myself over the coals for helping terrorize a family. Not enough room in my battered heart to feel remorse over anything else.

My sleep had been fitful at best, and my eyes burned with the lack of rest. I rubbed them before turning over to face Allison, making sure I didn't groan in pain. Her eyes were still closed, her breathing deep and even, and if she woke up when I stirred this last time, she was doing a really good job of pretending she hadn't.

I studied her face as I weighed my options. She looked so peaceful, so relaxed. She'd been stressed lately, and I wondered how often she got a good night's sleep. Probably not as often as I'd have liked, but she'd never admit it. How could I wake her? Yet if I snuck out without saying good-bye, there'd be hell to pay. Fuck. I didn't see an easy way out of this.

I may have lain there a lot longer than necessary—gazing at her face, stroking her hair—trying to land on the best course of action. Some might call it stalling. I preferred to think of it as considering all possible angles. And when I finally decided to let her sleep, I opted to think of that as putting Allison's best interests first rather than acting like a complete coward. It was all in the spin. And I could spin with the best of them.

With one last longing glance and a soft, lingering kiss on Allison's forehead, I slipped out from underneath the comforter, moving slowly and gingerly, being careful because of my bruised ribs and also watching for any signs of disturbing her slumber. I felt a burst of relief when I made it out of the bed without waking her but continued to hold my breath as I scribbled a note on the bedside notepad and didn't release it until the hotel-room door swung shut behind me.

I ruffled my hair with my fingers and scrubbed my face with my palms before I made my way down the hall toward the elevator. Part of me wanted to go back into her room, wrap her in my arms, and stay there forever. But that wasn't practical. I had to face the day—and what I'd done last night—whether I wanted to or not. Hiding wouldn't make it go away.

On the way back downtown, I kept my eyes peeled, both for people who might be following me and for pay phones that hadn't been destroyed and might actually work so I could call Tate. Despite my searching, I found neither.

Tate wasn't in the apartment when I arrived, which ratcheted up my tension even more. Had he already been there and gone? Or had he not even made it back? Was he still with Seth? Was he okay? What would be the best way for me to figure it out? His ATF counterparts were the first option that came to mind. I assumed they were tracking him the way my guys had been tracking me—though it'd be ideal if they were doing a better job of it than mine had—or that he'd at least checked in with them to let them know he was okay. With my broken phone, I couldn't tell if he'd even bothered to reach out to me.

I'd just flung the door to the apartment open so I could head up to the print shop when I ran into Tate, who had his arm outstretched and looked to be putting his key into the lock. I jumped, startled, and put one hand to my chest. "Jesus, Tate. You scared the shit out of me!"

Tate didn't say anything. He only blinked at me. I blinked back and wrapped my hand around his forearm to yank him inside. He didn't resist. And he still didn't say anything. I cocked my head to look at him, and my heart did a backflip that an Olympic diver would be envious of before it landed with a splash on top of my diaphragm. His coloring was paler than I was used to, his face seemed to have more lines than I remembered, and his eyes were vacant and haunted, underscored by dark circles. He stopped in the middle of the room and just stood there, not saying anything, and not really appearing to see his surroundings.

"Tate?" The words was tentative, and I wanted to tell myself that was because I hadn't wanted to startle him, but it was because I was afraid. I didn't know what'd happened to him, but it couldn't have been good.

It took a long time, but when he turned his head to look at me, the gesture was forced, like the tendons in his neck weren't cooperating and he was muscling them into performing the way he wanted them to.

He smacked his lips once and ran his tongue along the lower one, but he didn't say anything.

Not knowing what else to do, I took him by the shoulder and led him over to the sofa. "Here," I said, coaxing him to sit down. He did but had lapsed back into staring into space. I narrowed my eyes as I studied him for signs of physical trauma, but didn't see any. Whatever he was going through was evidently psychological or emotional. Crap. I was okay dealing with that when it came to PI subjects, but with people I knew, it wasn't my strong suit.

Stalling for time, I went to the kitchen area to fetch him a glass of water. When I got back, he didn't take it—didn't even seem to notice it or me—so I knelt in front of him and clasped his hand, wrapping it around the glass and then enveloping it in both of mine.

"Tate," I said again. "What happened?"

He looked more unsettled than I felt, and the images of possible reasons that sprang to mind made me queasy. I squeezed his hand and nudged his boot with my knee. "Hey."

He blinked and dragged his gaze over to meet mine. But he didn't speak.

"You okay?" No answer. My blood pressure spiked. "Do I need to take you to the hospital?"

He jerked, pulling his hand out of mine and sloshing some of the water out of the glass, spraying both of us. That seemed to bring him out of his stupor. "What? No. No. I'm fine."

I rocked back so I was resting my weight on my heels. "Did you just get home?"

Tate nodded and widened his eyes as though trying to wake himself up. He combed the fingers of his free hand through his hair and shook his head. "Yeah," he said after a moment. "It was a long night."

"Yeah? You wanna tell me about it?"

He sighed, and his body sagged as he sank back into the cushions of the couch. His drink rested forgotten on the top of his thigh. "Well, I now know what the plan is."

I gasped, and for an instant, I was overjoyed. But then it registered that he didn't sound even a little happy about that, and my delight soured. "What is it?"

"Did you finish the 'scavenger hunt' last night?" He used his fingers to make air quotes as he spoke, though he managed to avoid spilling any water with the gesture.

"No. Why?"

"So you don't know what you were gathering?"

I shook my head. "Nope. I didn't want to ask. I was afraid to seem too curious. So I just kept acting like I was interested in the game itself. I don't think anyone bought it, but…" I shrugged.

Tate nodded. "You were right the other day when you said that the mass-shooting plan seemed risky and implausible."

My skin chilled, and goose bumps formed on my arms. "I was?" Crap. I hadn't wanted to be.

"You were. That is no longer the plan."

"So then what do they—?"

"They want me to get military-grade explosives," Tate said. "They want to build a bomb."

"What?!"

He nodded. "Yeah. Seems they were thinking some of the same things you were regarding visibility and exposure and escape. They decided planting a bomb was the way to go. That may have been the plan from the beginning. I don't know."

"Holy shit." I shifted so I was sitting on the ground and had my legs tucked next to me.

"Yeah. The 'scavenger hunt' last night entailed picking up several different components they'll need to build the device to their specifications. I think they're hoping that sending multiple people to retrieve equipment from several sources will somehow shield them or conceal what they're doing." A beat. "They've been watching too many movies."

"For sure. But wait. Where does the counterfeit money come in? Surely they don't plan to try to pay for their stuff with fake money." That was just asking to get killed.

Tate shook his head. "No. It's supposed to be an exchange. A trade. They're planning to offer the money to the guys who provide the explosives so they can sell it on their own later."

"That seems strangely convoluted."

Tate shrugged and seemed to notice the glass in his hand for the first time. He paused to take a long drink. "No more so than the rest of the plan."

"I guess." I paused. "I mean, to their credit, if they do it that way, there's no money trail to speak of."

We were both silent for a bit before Tate said, "There's more."

"More?"

"It's worse."

I snorted. "How can it be worse than a bomb?" As soon as the words were out of my mouth, I knew, but I was really hoping I was wrong.

"They want to lace the bomb with toxins."

Damn it. I hadn't been wrong. I also didn't want to ask this next question, but I needed to know. "What kind of toxins? Specifically?"

"Probably tabun. Maybe sarin. Someone was tossing around the idea of weaponizing standard industrial chemicals like chlorine. Those would probably be easier to get. But I think they're still working that part out."

I chewed on my lower lip and pulled at my earlobe as I mulled that over. "That's not good."

"No," he said. "It isn't."

"Do we have a date yet?"

Tate shook his head. "No. Not yet."

"Do you think it's because they don't have one? Or because they're not quite ready to disclose it?"

"I think they're not quite ready to disclose it."

"And we're no closer to figuring it out."

"Nope."

"Shit." I took a deep breath. "So what do we do?"

"Same things we've been doing, I suppose. Nothing much has changed. They still plan to hurt people. We still want to stop them."

He wasn't wrong, but somehow it felt as though the stakes had been raised. I didn't know what it was, but the idea of them utilizing chemicals and explosives rather than just guns put me even more on edge. Perhaps it was because I'd used guns myself, and I understood them. Maybe it was because gun violence took longer to carry out, and I had a false sense that I'd be able to minimize the collateral damage. Whatever it was, I was most likely just kidding myself, but the knowledge didn't do anything to diminish the uneasy feeling that'd swept over me.

I shifted, pulling my knees up against my chest and resting my forearms on them as I thought.

"So, we just keep going along as we have been," Tate said, picking up the thread of the conversation that I'd discarded. "We watch. We listen. We gather as much intel as we can and hope it's enough and that it's timely so we can stop them before they kill anyone."

I scrubbed at my scalp with my fingernails and then fiddled with some of my earrings. "Who's going to actually be building the bomb? You?"

Tate shrugged. "They haven't said. Though that'd be the best outcome for us because I can construct it so it's inert and won't go off."

"Who's the one driving this crazy train?" I blurted out.

"Huh?" He blinked at me, appearing confused by my abrupt change of subject. Allison must've been rubbing off on me.

"Who's running these meetings? Who's doing all the planning? All the organization? Is it Seth or is it Nathan?"

"It's definitely Seth. Nathan just sort of lurked a lot and glowered at everyone. He didn't say much."

"Wonder why the intel we got said that Nathan was in charge?"

"I don't know. I mean, that's definitely the image they portray. But from what I've seen, Seth is the one running the show."

"What do we know about him?"

"A little more than we know about Nathan. But not much." He leaned forward to place his glass on the coffee table. "Grew up in North Carolina. Earned an associate's degree in liberal studies, whatever the hell that means. Runs a garage on the west side. Had minor brushes with the law over the course of his life. Nothing crazy. Nothing violent. Certainly nothing to indicate he'd end up driving a radical, ethnocentric terrorist group."

"He said he and Nathan go back a long time. Any chance they grew up or went to school together?"

"It's possible. We haven't had a chance to interview a lot of people from his past because we didn't want to risk any of those people tipping him off that we were asking questions about him. So we don't know a whole lot about who he spent his time with during his formative years."

"This sucks."

Tate looked at me, his face a mask of questions. "What does?"

"This whole having-to-tiptoe-around-the-suspect thing you need to do when you're undercover. It's prohibitive. How the hell do you ever get anything done?"

He chuckled. "You don't think that just makes it more of a challenge?"

"I think that makes it more of a pain in the ass."

"Speaking of being a pain in the ass, I heard what happened last night."

The blood rushed from my face so fast the nerves tingled. I'd been making it a point *not* to think about what'd happened last night, and the sudden reminder made my insides congeal and quiver. I tried to swallow, but it didn't work. Not with my mouth as dry as it was. "What did you hear?"

"I was still with Seth when Crash came back. He told us what went down with that family. He said you did all right."

I was stunned. I hadn't been sure I'd made it convincing enough. I couldn't decide whether the notion that I had was a good thing or a bad thing. "He did?"

"Yeah."

"Was that whole bit at the end planned? Or were those people just targets of opportunity?"

"A little of both, I think. Crash has been wanting to 'test your mettle'—his words—for a little while now. So he's been keeping his eyes open for chances to do so. Guess he got what he wanted."

"Swell."

"He said he doesn't quite trust you, though."

My heart stuttered. "He doesn't? Did he say why?"

"He thinks you ask too many questions, and you're too flip. He's not sure that's a good combo, considering what they're looking for, what they want to do."

Shit. That wasn't good. Of all the things I'd been worried about ruining this for me, my sarcasm hadn't even made the list. "What does Seth think?"

"Seth didn't seem concerned." Tate pinned me with a serious look. "Before he dropped me off, he said it was time."

"Time to bring me in?"

"Time to at least start feeling you out to see whether it's something you'd be interested in."

I took a deep breath. "He's sure? He doesn't think that just asking me to help him make counterfeit without getting into the weeds about why is the way to go?"

Tate shook his head. "Apparently not. Something about the volume they want produced. He seems to think that you'll be more on board and less difficult if you understand the purpose of what they're trying to do. Guess you convinced him. Or maybe he also thinks you ask too many questions, and he feels it's just easier." He shrugged.

"Yay for me," I said. This was a good thing. Right? I mean, it was what we'd been waiting for, what we'd been working toward for weeks now. This was the beginning of the end. So why wasn't I happier about it? Oh. Right. Because it meant we were that much closer to them trying to off a bunch of people. That was probably why. Or because there was that much more of a risk of them wanting to off me. One of those.

Tate shot me a wry smile. "Yeah. Yay for you."

"So what's our next step?"

"Nothing. Just wait for Seth to approach you."

I rolled my eyes. "Patience isn't my strong suit."

Tate's sardonic smile became a grin. "Why am I not surprised?"

CHAPTER TWENTY-FIVE

The next several days were like one continuous stress test that just kept getting more and more strenuous until I was pretty sure I was going to scream. Not taking Seth or Crash or someone aside and declaring that I was ready to serve their fucked-up cause in whatever way they saw fit was an exercise in restraint, and it was wearing me out.

A few times, I wondered whether that was part of it. Were they evaluating my patience or maybe still struggling to make up their minds about me? Whatever it was, I was on edge. Allison had been right. This sort of thing, what Tate did all the time, was way out of my league. And I was frazzled enough to resolve to make Allison promise to remind me of this if I had an idea this stupid ever again. I wasn't built for this kind of constant pressure, and worrying about cracking was only making things worse.

It didn't help that Tate hadn't heard anything new. Like nothing at all. No one had been talking about it. He hadn't even seen Seth or Nathan since the night of the scavenger hunt. As far as he knew, no one had. And while I generally believed that no news was good news, in this instance I didn't buy it.

In addition to trying not to scream at them to just fill me in already, I was struggling to maintain my overall cover. I'd never pretended to be a naive piece on the side before—either in life or for an op—so having to endure night after night of drinking and ridiculous small talk and pretending to be Tate's flavor of the month was tedious at best. Especially when I'd been trying to slyly cut down on the amount of alcohol I'd been imbibing without arousing suspicion. Though I'd decided that, if questioned, I'd claim I was trying to get pregnant. In addition to being sort of plausible, that cover story could also spark a big, dramatic "blowout" between Tate and me, which would hopefully distract from any suspicions about me. It wasn't a great plan, but it was the best I'd come up with. Was that because I had babies on the brain? Who knew?

The monotony of the whole situation made me reflect on my life, and not in a good way. It'd been years since I'd been so enmeshed in the whole party scene, and I hadn't for a second regretted leaving it behind. Now, having to re-experience the whole "work to play, play to live" thing from my older, wiser perspective was bringing up painful and embarrassing memories I'd just as soon stayed buried.

I sighed and looked around the bar, trying to watch everyone without appearing too exasperated. When I thought about it, I supposed I could sort of understand hiding in plain sight, but did they have to do it at the same place every night? Was a change of scenery too much to ask for? Even back when I was hitting the town hard, I'd liked to change it up now and again.

I took a teeny sip of the beer I'd ordered out of fear that the bartenders were all in on it and reporting my movements back to whoever was really running this show. I was determined to memorize all these faces and create detailed links analysis charts if it killed me. Which, it occurred to me, it might. I made a face.

"Uh-oh," Crash said from over my shoulder. "Looks like someone's in a mood."

"And yet you still thought it was a good idea to come over here and jump up and down on my last, frayed nerve. Bold move." I faced him and stared up defiantly. Okay, so maybe getting on Crash's bad side wasn't a great idea for a number of reasons, but I was still pissed at him for beating the shit out of a man. He could interpret that however he wanted.

His interpretation must have been off because he only laughed and clapped me on the back. "Come on, Alex. You can't still be upset about the other night."

Hmm. Interesting. He was at least somewhat right. I bobbed my head once and took another sip of my beer. "What if I am?"

He shrugged. "Look. It wasn't your fault you tripped. It was dark. That broken sidewalk was tough to see. It could've happened to any of us."

I grumbled, playing along as though that were the reason for my pique. "Yeah. I guess. But still. It fucking sucked. And it hurt like a bitch."

Like the gentleman he was, Crash avoided any further questions regarding my well-being and moved right along. "You were pretty ferocious there. You know, for the time you stayed on your feet."

He grinned at me, and I rolled my eyes. "What do you want, Crash? To make fun of me for my clumsiness? I get it. Very funny. You should quit your day job and try standup."

He held up his hands. "Hey. No offense intended. I was just teasing you."

I took a deep breath and forced myself to let it out slowly. It was high time to do some damage control. I wouldn't get anywhere by being a complete bitch to him all the time. Even if he did deserve that, plus my foot up his ass.

"No. I'm sorry," I said. "I'm just embarrassed. And kicking myself. It wasn't your fault I didn't get to…Well, anyway, I shouldn't take it out on you."

Crash studied me with narrowed eyes and a contemplative expression for long enough that I was starting to wonder whether I had something on my face. "I was talking to Seth about you the other day."

My heart did a somersault at his words, and I hoped none of my apprehension-laced excitement showed on my face. To hide my expression as best I could, I took another long sip of beer. "Oh, yeah? Should I be worried or flattered?"

Crash didn't answer my question. Instead, he said, "Is it true? About your dad?"

I hesitated, which is what I assumed someone who'd really lost her father in wartime would do upon being confronted about it so bluntly by someone she barely knew. "About the IED?" I nodded. "It's true."

Crash shook his head. "Damn. That sucks. I'm sorry."

"Thanks."

He was quiet for a bit, but I could tell he was choosing his next words. "It piss you off?"

"Mmm. At first, I was just sad. Then I was angry all the time. Now, it sort of comes and goes in waves."

"Do you ever wish you could get revenge?"

His gaze was so intense, it gave me chills, but I tried not to show it. "I used to. But I suppose those are the kinds of things a teenage girl fantasizes about under those circumstances."

"Why did you stop? It can't be a simple matter of just getting older. I mean, being without your dad can't get any easier."

I shrugged. "Who would I get revenge on? Besides, I like to think that the bastards who set that roadside bomb are roasting in the fieriest pit of hell, and the seventy-two virgins they thought they were going to get to defile are mocking them while enjoying a gang bang across the molten lake."

Crash laughed. "That's one thing to hope for."

I smiled and held my breath as I waited to see where he was going with this. I didn't want to risk an entrapment charge by leading him.

He waved at the bartender for a drink of his own and greeted a few people who called his name before resuming the conversation. "And if there were another way?"

"Another way for what?"

"Another way to serve up a little of the just desserts that people like the ones who're responsible for the death of your father have coming to them?"

"You mean like I didn't manage the other night? If that taught us anything, I'd say it was that physicality isn't my strong suit."

Crash shook his head, and some of his hair fell into his eyes. He brushed it back with an impatient jerk of his hand. "No. I was actually thinking something more subtle. Something more in line with your specific talents."

"What do you know about my talents?" Let's be honest, if he were even half right about what I was good at, I was screwed.

He smirked at me like he had a secret. "Just answer the question. Would you be interested?"

I pretended to think about that possibility. "I might be. It would depend on the details. The devil's in them, and all that."

He nodded and rapped his knuckles twice on the top of the bar, grabbed his beer, and looked toward the door. I followed his gaze and saw Seth making his way inside, Tate and Nathan hot on his heels. My heart clamored up inside my throat and clung there for dear life. I tried not to fret about why Tate hadn't told me Seth had contacted him, tried to rationalize all the plausible reasons why he hadn't mentioned it, but nothing was making me feel any better.

Crash took his beer and made a beeline for Seth, but I hung back. This wasn't a conversation I wanted to rush into. Not as edgy as I was feeling now. So I retained my place at the bar, turned my back to the room, and went back to my beer as though everything were hunky dory and I wasn't the least bit interested in Seth's presence.

It wasn't long before Tate pushed his way through the crowd and appeared at my side. He bent down and pretended to drop a kiss on my cheek while whispering, "I'm so sorry. He showed up out of nowhere this afternoon. There wasn't time to call you."

"And...?" I asked softly. My hands were trembling a bit, so I wrapped my fingers around my pint glass and squeezed.

Tate sighed and ran his hand through his hair. "And we're not much further along than we were before. I have no idea where he's been these past few days or what he's been up to. What little conversation we did have was mundane, at best, and unrelated to why we're here."

"I wouldn't say we're not *much* further along. Crash and I just had an interesting discussion."

Tate fidgeted, and I could tell he wanted to glance over his shoulder, but he continued looking at me and smiling. "Oh, yeah?" He hooked some hair behind my ear.

I nodded. "Yeah. I'm not sure we have much longer to wait now. He was hinting at some things, asking me if I wanted to get revenge and such. Nothing specific. Certainly nothing we can use to lock them up. But it was enough to make me think they're about to get the ball rolling."

Tate looked thoughtful as he turned his back on the rest of the room to face the bar. "I still can't figure out what date they're looking at. I've been racking my brain trying to think of anything significant that might be coming up, and I've got nothing."

"Maybe that's our problem. Maybe there isn't anything significant attached to the date they've chosen. Maybe they picked something completely at random."

Tate paused. "It certainly would explain a lot."

"How do you think they did it?" I asked.

Tate's brow furrowed as he looked at me. "Huh?"

"Chose the date. Do you think they picked days out of a hat? Played pin the TNT on the calendar? Threw a dart?"

Tate grinned. "When this is all over, we'll have to remember to ask them. Heads up."

I pasted my best girl-in-love smile on my face and wrapped both hands around Tate's arm. "Please? I know you think it's a chick flick, but you'll like it. I promise."

Tate rolled his eyes and heaved a dramatic sigh. "Ugh. Fine. But if I watch *Easy A* with you, you have to watch *Die Hard* with me. And no running commentary. You ruined *Uncommon Valor* with your chattering."

"Hey!" I said.

Seth's hand came down on Tate's shoulder just then, which was good because I was having trouble coming up with an argument for something that hadn't happened.

"She got you watching sappy movies?" Seth asked Tate.

Tate shook his head. "I don't know how I let her talk me into these things. Those things are so boring!"

Seth laughed. "Let me tell you something. There's no greater joy in life than being able to make your woman happy. Except maybe making your kids happy. But you guys aren't there yet."

"Ha," I said to Tate. "See?" I turned to Seth and smiled. "Thank you."

"You're welcome. Listen, I haven't had a chance to let you know what an amazing job you did on the favors for my friend's party. Everything looked fantastic."

"I'm glad you think so. Hopefully, he feels the same way. When's the big day?"

"In a couple of weeks. But I was wondering, do you remember that other job I mentioned to you?"

My fingers tightened on Tate's arm, and I sucked in a small breath, praying Seth hadn't noticed. "Of course. Why?"

"You interested?"

"I might be. What is it?"

Seth glanced around. "Tell you what, let's not get mired in shop talk here. How about we meet tomorrow and discuss details?"

"Sounds good. Just let me know where and when."

"I'll text Tate the details." Seth glanced over my shoulder and indicated to someone to wait a minute before refocusing on me. "I'll see you tomorrow."

I held my breath until I was sure he was no longer in earshot of us before letting it out in a shaky sigh. I blinked and swallowed, tugging on the ends of my hair at the nape of my neck. "Okay. So we might be even farther along than we thought."

Tate was frowning. "I don't like it."

I snorted. "I don't like *any* of this. But here we are."

Tate shook his head. "Huh? No. I mean the timing of this request. I don't like it. I told Seth I had to work tomorrow."

"You think he deliberately set it up this way to get me alone?"

Tate's brow pulled down, and his lips twisted. "Hard to say. I mean, our cover seems solid. We've bugged both his phone and his apartment, and no one's heard him say anything to indicate we've been made…"

"But…?"

"But I don't like it."

I patted his hand and tried to project a sense of courage that I didn't feel. I didn't want him to know that his concerns had set me even more on edge. "Everything's going to be fine."

Which, now that I thought about it, I was pretty sure had been said by someone just prior to every single disaster in history. Famous last words.

CHAPTER TWENTY-SIX

Claudia's words from the other day echoed over and over in my mind during the hours leading up to my meeting with Seth, and I spent every spare second thinking about what I could do to save myself. I got a new phone. I gave Rico all the information I had at my disposal. I cleaned and reloaded my weapon. Then I checked it about eighteen more times to make sure it was fully loaded. I tried to think of the angles I hadn't covered and then tried not to obsess over the ones I couldn't think of.

Tate had promised that his guys would be watching me closely and that he'd be lurking as near as possible. And Rico had assured me that the squad had me covered, and I had nothing to worry about. All that manpower did nothing to alleviate my tension, but I still appreciated the pledges.

Before leaving the crash pad to meet Seth, I'd donned my comfiest jeans, my softest tee, and my most well-loved sneakers. Hopefully the day wouldn't end with me making a run for it or fighting for my life, but I didn't want to leave anything to chance. As usual, Claudia had been right, and I needed to stack the deck in my favor on the off chance I got dealt into the game.

Seth had asked me to meet him at a restaurant in NoHo, and I left way too early, so I ended up grabbing a table and drinking a ton of soda while I waited for him to join me. On the plus side, I had plenty of time to conduct a quick site advance on the place and text Rico and Tate all the info they could ever want about it and about eight texts' worth beyond that. I also had time to play spot-the-agent, and I'd picked out several people who I was pretty sure were there only to keep an eye on me. On the minus side, all that waiting just gave me extra room to spin myself up, and I needed to work that much harder to calm down. It didn't help that I had deliberately sat with my back to the door and had to fight to keep from whirling around every time anyone entered the eatery.

"Sorry we're late," Seth said as he came up beside me. He slid into a chair on the opposite side of the table, and I hadn't finished processing his words before Nathan sat down beside him.

It took everything in my power not to show my surprise, and even more beyond that not to look at Nathan like I knew him. Because while I had seen him on the stage at that party, we hadn't been introduced.

"No problem," I replied. "I've just been killing time."

Seth jerked a thumb toward Nathan, whose face appeared frozen in a permanent scowl. "I don't know if you two have met. This is my friend Nathan."

Despite the less-than-stellar reception, I held my hand out across the table. "Nice to meet you."

Nathan glanced down at it, and for a split second, it looked like he thought it was poisonous or covered in slime. It also looked like he was considering not taking it, but eventually he returned my handshake. "You, too."

I couldn't help the smirk that pulled at my lips at his reaction to me, though as amused as I was, I did wonder at the exact cause. I met Seth's gaze and saw that he was grinning. "I'm going to grab a coffee. You want anything, Nathan?"

"Beer," Nathan said, never taking his eyes off me.

"You got it. I'll be right back."

Seth ambled off, leaving Nathan and me alone and staring at one another. Small talk—especially with people I didn't know—was one of my own personal circles of hell, and I wouldn't have been comfortable with this scenario if Nathan had been someone I liked. That he was someone who would probably want me dead if he knew who I was and what I was doing here didn't make the words come any easier.

"So…" I said after the silence and the staring contest had become unbearable. I didn't have any follow up. I'd just wanted to say *something*, even something useless.

"So," Nathan said back, his tone clipped.

"Uh…I'm sorry about your son."

A shadow flitted beneath Nathan's eyes, and he ducked his head, averting his gaze and leaving me the undisputed victor in our little showdown. "Yeah. Thanks. Sorry about your dad." He nodded in the direction of the counter. "Seth told me."

I winced, trying to look sad. I took a sip of soda, trying to hide my expression a bit. "Did he?"

Nathan bobbed his head and glanced toward the entrance and

then out the large picture window to the bustling city street. "Lots of fucked-up shit going down over there."

"You don't have to tell me."

"No. I suppose I don't."

The awkward silence settled between us once again, and I chewed on the tip of my straw as I tried to decide what to do next. Did I ask him about his experience? No. I don't think I was supposed to know about that, and I couldn't recall whether they'd mentioned it at the party. I'd just about decided to launch into a ridiculous joke I knew when the bell over the entrance door clanged, and two turbaned, bearded men walked into the restaurant.

"Fucking hajis," I heard Nathan mutter under his breath while I still was looking away.

I felt my eyes go wide but tried to cover my shock and horror. After all, if I wanted these people to bring me in on their plan, I needed to appear sympathetic. But it was tough enough for me ignore the face of blatant racism.

Unable to help myself, I smiled and said in my most genial tone, "I think they're actually Sikhs."

Nathan's expression darkened. "So?"

"So, Sikhs are a completely different thing. In fact, I think I remember reading somewhere that two of their gurus refused to convert to Islam."

Now Nathan was glowering at me. "And? What's your point?"

I shrugged and mentally kicked myself for my argumentative nature. I should've kept my mouth shut. When would I learn? "No point. Just saying that anyone who's that determined not to become a Muslim is okay in my book."

Ugh. The words had somehow felt slimy as they'd slipped off my tongue, and I wanted to gargle to rid my mouth of their sour taste. God, how did they say such horrible things all the time and not gag?

Nathan continued to stare at me for a long time, and the entire time I held his gaze, my skin was trying to crawl off my body. But then his expression softened, and he broke out into a grin. "You've got some balls on you. Seth was right about that."

I blinked, but I was afraid to relax completely. "Is that good or bad?"

Nathan laughed. "It's good. Is that true? What you said about those guys?"

"What? About refusing to convert to Islam? Pretty sure."

"How did you know that?"

"One of the electives I took in college was religion, but only because everything else was already full by the time I registered. I only paid enough attention to be able to pass the tests, but that was one thing they talked about that did interest me."

Seth returned then, thank God, and set their drinks on the table before resuming his seat. Nathan started guzzling his beer without so much as a thank you to Seth for getting it for him, and I struggled not to raise an eyebrow at his behavior. It wasn't even noon yet, for crying out loud.

"So," Seth said, stirring sugar into his coffee before taking a small sip. "What did I miss?"

"Not much. We were just talking about religion."

"Mmm. That's a coincidence, since that's sort of the reason you're here."

My breath hitched, and I coughed, trying to cover my reaction. I lamented the fact that I'd never been able to secure a wire. The next several minutes of conversation were probably about to get good. And while my testimony to the discussion would be sufficient to secure an arrest warrant, I'd have felt a whole lot better about everything if I'd had whatever crazy thing they were about to hit me with on tape.

Playing dumb, I rolled my eyes. "Yeah. I'm not much of a joiner. Especially of organized religions. But thanks anyway."

Nathan choked on his beer, and Seth chuckled and shook his head. "No. We're not trying to recruit you to some kind of church."

"That's a relief. Because I haven't set foot in one in over a decade." I think that was the only true thing I'd told him since we'd met. That fact horrified my mother no end.

"No," Seth said. "Don't worry. None of that. Not exactly."

"Then what is it, exactly?"

Seth and Nathan exchanged a glance, and I wondered whether they were trying to decide if including me in this group was a good idea. I played with the ice in the bottom of my glass with my straw and tried to look as innocent and unthreatening as possible as I waited for them to reach a conclusion.

After a pause that was a lot longer than I was comfortable with, Nathan nodded, and Seth looked back at me. He wrapped both of his hands around his mug, threading his middle finger through the handle. I mirrored his body language to the best of my ability by enfolding my glass in my hands as well.

"What happened to your dad was a tragedy," Seth said.

"What happens to all soldiers in war is a tragedy."

Seth nodded. "True. But some wars are needless and shouldn't even be fought."

"I'm sure many people would agree with you. But I don't see what that has to do with anything."

Seth glanced around, and I assumed he was sizing up the customers closest to us and gauging their interest—or lack thereof—in our conversation. So I glanced, too, and noted that no one seemed to be paying any attention to us. Which didn't mean anything. The agents who were here to keep an eye on me wouldn't look like they were watching. And I hoped their skill was enough to keep Seth from recognizing any of them for what they were.

"We've all lost someone," Seth reminded me.

I nodded. "I know."

The lines etched in Seth's face suddenly seemed deeper, and his expression was grave. "And we've all tried to move on from it as best we could. But sometimes, people need a little help getting over that hump. People need a little push."

"I don't follow."

"Don't you ever want to make the people who killed your father, who took him from you, pay?"

I sat back in my chair and folded my arms across my chest. "You've been listening to Crash too much. And I'll tell you what I told him: There is no *one* person to get even with. So where would I even start?"

"Exactly," Seth said, sounding triumphant. He jabbed a finger in my direction to emphasize his point, which was still a little murky, even though I knew what he was getting at.

"Huh?"

"It's like you just said. There is no *one* person."

I blinked at him, not having to play at being confused. "You've lost me."

"I showed Nathan the results of the project you just did for me," Seth said, taking a different tack.

"Yeah," Nathan said, wiping his mouth with the back of his hand. "You did some good work there."

"Thanks." I wrinkled my brow. Jesus, the man had a hard time getting to the point. I hoped he made it there sometime soon. I wasn't as young as he thought I was, and I wasn't sure I had enough time left on earth to ride out this roundabout line of questioning.

"Remember the other day how I asked you about doing something off the books?"

"Yeah."

"What do you think about helping me with another, similar project?"

"Similar how?"

"Similar in that I want you to do almost the exact same thing."

"You got another buddy with a birthday coming up?"

Seth shook his head. "No. This time, I need you to make it look like actual money."

I paused and narrowed my eyes at him, like I imagined a regular person being asked out of the blue to commit a crime might do. "You want me to make actual money," I repeated, drawing out the words and attempting to color my tone with something akin to disbelief. Tough, since I'd known the request was coming, but I must've done a passable job because neither Nathan nor Seth appeared suspicious.

"I do, yes."

I took another sip of the watery soda lingering at the bottom of my glass and glanced around distrustfully. "Is this some kind of setup?"

"Of course not. Why would you think that?"

"Well," I said, leaning in and lowering my voice. "What you've just asked me to do is a crime. If I get caught, people will make a federal case out of it. Like an *actual* federal case."

Seth leaned in as well. "You don't think I'd have just as much to lose? Relax."

"That's exactly what you'd say if this was a setup."

Seth rolled his eyes while Nathan laughed. "I heard what happened the other night."

I figured that any normal person—well, any normal person who wasn't a sociopath—wouldn't be too proud about what they'd done, so I didn't try to put on that air. Instead, I allowed them to see the shame and guilt I felt over the incident and ducked my head. "Yeah. It wasn't my finest moment."

"Are you kidding? Crash said you were amazing."

"What?" That hadn't been the impression I'd gotten from Tate. Also, it was still somewhat jarring to hear anyone describe that train wreck as anything other than what it was.

"Oh, is this because you fell? Don't worry about that. It's not a big deal."

"Hmph."

"Did you think *that* was a setup?" Seth asked.

"I don't know. Was it?"

"Think of it as more of a test."

"What were you testing exactly?"

"We were just trying to get an idea what you'd be willing to do, if the opportunity presented itself."

Well, that was cryptic. "I see." I didn't see anything because he still wasn't being clear. The only reason I had any idea what the hell he was talking about was because of my previous conversations with Tate. Otherwise, I'd have been lost.

"And given the results of that test, it sounds like you're the perfect person to help us out with our little project."

Hmm. That was one way of putting it. Perhaps I'd been wildly overestimating their humanity. Or perhaps I'd been hoping they still had a shred of decency left. I don't know why. They were talking about blowing up a building full of people, for God's sake. But for some reason, I'd been holding on to the notion that they were at least going to feel a *little* bad about it. Nope. Apparently not.

Okay, so now I had to pretend that my clumsiness was bothering me, not the fact that I'd terrified an innocent woman while I let a bunch of wackos beat up and almost kill her husband. "What does the other night and my still being pissed about my dad have to do with this project?"

"What if I told you that by doing this, you'd be playing a very important part in an operation we have in the works to…serve up a little divine retribution."

I pretended to consider that statement while trying not to look like I was freaking out because he was able to utter those words so flippantly despite the gravity of the situation. "Divine retribution on who exactly?"

He held my eyes with a solemn stare. "On those who would gladly do the same to us if given half the chance."

"How can you be sure you've got the right people?" I asked, playing along. "I don't want innocent people getting caught up in anything."

"Don't worry," Nathan said, finally deciding to participate. "We've got the right people."

"And how does my making money for you factor into this divinely retributive plan?"

Seth's eyes twinkled, and he looked almost amused. I supposed that, given the age I was portraying, he saw my questions as endearing. Like a child trying to run with the grown-ups. That was fine. He could think that all he wanted. It was better than him knowing why I was really asking.

"It's probably a good idea if you don't know *too* many of the specifics," he said. "But let's just say that your part is the catalyst that allows the whole plan to be set into motion. You're the crank in the game *Mousetrap*, if you will."

I had to hand it to him, that was a smooth move, luring me in but not giving me quite enough information to be able to take him down. It was something I might've done if I'd been in his position. So how would I have outsmarted me? I acted like I was still mulling his proposition over for another few seconds before I nodded. "Okay. I'm in. How much do you need, and when do you need it?"

Seth grinned, and Nathan downed the remaining few swallows of his beer in one gulp. "Great. We're looking to—" Seth's phone must've vibrated in his pocket because he stopped speaking and pulled it out. I didn't know what was on the screen, but seeing how his brow furrowed and his knuckles went white, I doubted it was good news. Damn it. I'd been about to get some more of an idea of when they were looking to do this. Figured.

He took a deep breath as he read—a text? an email? who could really say?—and when he was done, he tipped the phone toward Nathan so he could read it as well. I tried to study them from underneath my lashes to see if I could decipher their body language, but it was tough.

"I'm going to get another beer," Nathan said and got up and left.

I watched him go for a second before turning back to Seth, who was frowning at his phone. I waited a bit for him to speak and told myself that the world didn't revolve around me, so I had no reason to panic or be paranoid. But the reassurances did nothing to calm my thundering pulse. I swallowed and wiped my damp palms on my jeans.

"Everything okay?" I asked when I'd stood as much of Seth's distraction as I was able.

"Hmm?" he said, glancing up from his phone. "Oh. Sure. I mean, something's come up. But it's nothing I can't handle."

"Okay. Well, if you need to go take care of whatever that is, we can finish this another time."

He pinched his lower lip between his thumb and forefinger, and his brow lowered as he returned to studying the text. He didn't appear to have heard me, and I wasn't sure whether to call attention to myself or slip out. While he frowned and brooded and punched at his phone screen with his thumbs, I stirred the remnants of ice at the bottom of my glass and had just decided to take off, when he spoke.

"Actually, I could use your help with this, if you don't mind. Do you have to work today?"

I hesitated. I had a bad feeling in the pit of my stomach about this situation and wasn't sure of the best way to proceed. What had Tate told him about my schedule? Anything? And did it even matter if what I said now contradicted what Seth thought he knew? I decided it didn't and made a show of checking my watch. "I do. I have a little time, but not much. Why? What do you need?"

"One of my guys was supposed to pick something up for me, and he didn't show. I just need you to run in and grab it. In and out. It'll take ten minutes, tops. It's just down the street."

Alarm bells were clanging so loudly in the back of my head that it was tough to hear the ambient noise of the restaurant over the top of them. Something about this wasn't right. "Why can't you go in and grab it?" I asked, not caring if I appeared nosy.

Seth rubbed his knuckles across his jawline. "Well, the guy I'm getting the package from doesn't like me. Long story. And he doesn't know it's for me. If he did, he wouldn't let me have it. So I just need you to run in and pick it up."

Hmm. On the one hand, I wasn't at all keen to be taken to another location. On the other, I wanted to see what I'd be picking up. And a veritable swarm of agents was in the area. It should be easy for them to follow me and make sure nothing crazy went down. I hoped.

I took one last sip of what was left of my soda, making sure to suck as much liquid out of the glass as noisily as possible, praying it would signal whoever had eyes on me that we were getting ready to move. Then I stood, deliberately scraping the legs of the chair against the floor. I put my jacket back on. "Okay. Let's go."

"Great." Seth stood as well and started to leave.

"Wait. What about Nathan?" What the hell was I saying? The last thing I needed was to have more people in a position to hurt me.

"He'll catch up," Seth said. "You don't want to tell Nathan he can't finish a beer."

"Oh. Okay."

And with a racing heart, I followed Seth out the front door, forcing myself not to look around to try to make eye contact with someone, anyone, who could offer me nonverbal reassurance that they had my back.

It was one of the hardest things I've ever had to do.

CHAPTER TWENTY-SEVEN

I tried to get away with trailing a step or so behind Seth as we walked, but that didn't work. He slowed his gait until we were even and then chatted with me about nothing in particular as we headed God knew where. My dislike of this whole scenario grew with each step we took away from the restaurant, and the assurances I'd given myself before departure to remain convinced that this wasn't the worst idea ever—that it was broad daylight, that we were in the middle of Manhattan, that we were surrounded by agents—were shrinking in direct proportion.

My Krav Maga instructor's voice echoed in my head yet again, reminding me of what I already knew but had chosen to gloss over in favor of trying to stay on Seth's good side: if they want to take you to a secondary location, you don't want to go there because the reason they have for wanting to take you there is never going to be good. *Damn it, Zach. Do you always have to be right?* I made a mental note to admit that to him next time I saw him. Assuming I made it out of this alive.

But I was being ridiculous, right? And overly paranoid, surely. *Someone* had to be on us. I'd been promised a swarm of agents. It wasn't like we were moving at warp speed, and the crowd on the street wasn't exactly on the level of Times Square on New Year's Eve, so it wasn't like we were hard to keep track of. Yup. I was fretting more than I needed to. That's why my intestines felt like steel pipes all snarled and melted together. Because I was inventing things to worry about. Sure. That was it.

Still, it was becoming more of a struggle not to look around, not to try to spot one of the agents who was supposed to be keeping me safe. The last thing I wanted was to alert Seth that I was on edge about anything. I didn't need him asking questions or starting to think too deeply about anything connected to me outside of what I could do for him and his unholy mission.

While I was sort of successful at not scouring the street for my backup, I couldn't prevent my hand from curling around my new phone inside my pocket. I was itching to text Tate, and I chewed on the inside of my lower lip as I debated whether Seth would be suspicious if I tried it. I mean, Tate was supposed to be my man, right? So texting him wouldn't be a crazy thing to do, would it?

We passed one of those shops that sells lotions and bath bombs and such, and I stopped and stared into the window like it was the most fascinating display I'd ever seen. Not that I didn't love a good bath bomb. I did. Who doesn't? But at the moment, pampering was the farthest thing from my mind.

Seth continued a few steps and then doubled back to stand next to me at the glass. I'd hoped he'd have walked a little farther before noticing he'd lost me—every millisecond felt like it counted at this point—but the short amount of time I did gain was better than nothing, I supposed.

We stood there for a few long moments before he said, "We're kind of on a clock here. This guy has things to do, and he won't wait around forever."

"Huh? Oh. Right. Sorry. I saw an ad online for something I wanted, and I would've sworn it was from here. Just a sec." I took my phone out of my pocket and dialed Tate. He picked up after a ring and a half.

"Hey," he said. "What's up?"

We both knew this wasn't a social call, but I appreciated his playing along so much I could've kissed him for it. You know, if I weren't attached and he weren't a dude. I wasn't sure whether Seth could hear him or not, but it was better to be safe than sorry.

"Hey," I said back. "I'm outside that store with all the bath stuff down in NoHo." I glanced up at the sign as though checking to verify which store, even though I knew damn well where we were. "Lush. Do you remember the other day when I was talking about that sale? Was it here? Or somewhere else?"

"I think it was somewhere else," he said. "But I can't really remember. You know I get all those stores confused."

"Mmm. Right. I figured as much. But I thought I'd check anyway. See you later."

I hung up and put the phone back in my pocket. It hadn't been much. But I prayed it had been enough to give Tate a vague idea where I was so he could make sure his guys at least were on me. I couldn't do anything to clue in my guys that wouldn't tip Seth off to the fact that something was up. At least nothing I could think of. And while Rico should've been coordinating this with Tate's guys, I no longer had any faith that anything related to this mess would go according to plan.

I grinned at Seth and shrugged one shoulder. "Sorry. I don't make a ton of money, so I've gotta get this stuff on sale when I can."

He grinned back. "If this project goes well, you could make a ton of money."

I laughed. "I suppose that's true." I looked around and took a step closer to him. "I am a little nervous. I mean, what if we get caught?"

He put one hand on my arm. "Hey. I get it. It's scary. But don't worry. I promise, no one will have any idea you had anything to do with it."

I eyed him with as much skepticism as I felt at that moment. "And what would motivate you to protect me like that? You barely know me. So if you go down, what's to prevent you from taking me with you?"

"Hmm. Let's call it patriotism," Seth said with a secretive smile that made me want to shiver or gag. Or both. I hadn't even come up with any type of witty retort before he stopped in front of the door to some kind of eatery. "We're here."

I frowned and stared up at the sign. "Hot dogs aren't really my thing."

Seth's smile became even creepier somehow, which made all my bones start to ache and try to leave my body through my skin. He raised his eyebrows once and held the door open for me, gesturing for me to proceed inside. This time, I couldn't resist making one last, longing sweep of the sidewalk before I left the relative safety the public setting afforded. That final look did nothing to reassure me that this was going to turn out okay.

Swallowing hard, I went inside, blinking against the sudden dimness. Losing my vision so abruptly was almost painful, and I didn't bother attempting to hide my wince. After Seth had entered and shut the door, I glanced warily around the shop and its many patrons. I turned and leaned in a little so no one else would be able to hear me.

"Is it a good idea to do this here?" It didn't make any sense that he would risk arousing suspicion—*any* kind of suspicion—by allowing witnesses to his nefarious undertakings.

Seth chuckled under his breath and shook his head. "Of course not. We're not doing anything in here."

I frowned and looked around again. "Then what the hell are we doing here?"

Without answering my question, Seth strode the length of the room like he owned the place, not bothering to make eye contact with anyone. Though, to be fair, this was New York, so no one was paying him much attention either. When he reached a replica of an English phone booth tucked into the far back corner, he stopped and smiled at me over his shoulder as he pushed the door open. He stepped inside and peeked his head around the corner. "Coming?"

My insides were cold and slithery as I forced my feet to move. I didn't want to know where this was going. I didn't have to see to know that it wouldn't be anywhere good. I sidestepped a patron who was barreling out of the eatery and used the few extra seconds the move gained me to rack my brain for some sort of way out of this that wouldn't throw up any red flags. Unfortunately, I was coming up empty.

I took my phone out of my pocket as I shuffled and sent Tate a quick text telling him where I was now. However, it was tough to say whether "hot dogs, phone booth, secret exit" were going to be enough for him to go on. Because it'd taken me right up until Seth had stepped into that booth to realize just how much trouble I was in. I needed Tate to get those agents inside this building, and I needed them here now.

My mind raced as I made my way over to where Seth had just disappeared as slowly as I thought I'd be able to get away with. I wasn't sure he'd buy the curiosity act I was putting on as I pretended to be fascinated by the decor and memorabilia, but at this point, I was just about done caring what looked plausible.

I sent Tate one last panic-stricken message as I stepped into the phone booth, hoping with every fiber of my being that he'd received it and was scrambling his team to my location as I disappeared into the darkness.

I'd half expected to emerge in some sort of dank, musty, dungeon-esque room with a dirt floor and a single, flickering lightbulb dangling from a bare wire in the ceiling. Imagine my surprise when I realized we were in a posh, cozy bar of sorts. Only a handful of people were present, but it was the middle of the afternoon on a weekday. This place seemed like it catered more to a nightlife type of crowd.

"Wow," I said, not having to fake anything. "Cool. What is this place?"

Seth looked around, and it was unclear whether he was being wowed all over again or whether he was seeing it for the first time. "During Prohibition, secret speakeasies like this popped up all over the city. They fell out of fashion after a while, but a handful are still in business. They're popular now for their novelty."

"I can see why. Does your friend own this place? He must be making money hand over fist."

"He doesn't, no. And I think *friend* is a strong word. But he hangs out here a lot."

"I have got to bring Tate here sometime," I said, thinking of what it might be like to spend time here with Allison. Inwardly, I was disappointed that I'd likely never get to. It didn't seem like a good idea to ever return. Not if anyone who knew Seth might be hanging around. Shame. It was a neat place.

Seth pointed to a narrow booth in the small corner. "Go sit over there."

I glanced at the booth and then back to him. "And then what?"

"And then wait. He was supposed to meet my guy there. So now he'll meet you instead."

Mmm. This didn't feel right. "And how am I supposed to handle it when he asks where your guy is?"

"Just tell him Benny has the shits and couldn't make it. And if he still gives you a hard time, tell him you're wholly committed to the renaissance. That should be enough to sway him."

If it were me, and I'd been taking part in criminal activities that required me to meet with a specific person and that person wasn't the one who was there when I arrived, I'd turn right the hell around and beat feet out of there. But that was me. Maybe I was too paranoid. I almost certainly watched too much IDtv. Either way, the chance to stay in one place for a bit meant the guys would have a better opportunity to catch up with me. So I wasn't going to argue.

I was, however, going to ask another question. "Where are you going to be?"

"What do you mean?" Seth asked.

"Well, you said this guy hates you, right? And if he knew the package was for you, he'd never hand it over. So you can't just hang out in plain view. What if he sees you?"

Seth's lips twisted into a chilling facsimile of a smile. "Don't worry. I'll be around."

That didn't make me feel any better. I let out a shaky breath and nodded before leaving him to his own devices so I could take my place in the booth. By the time I'd gotten settled and turned back around, he was gone. Part of me wondered where he was, but most of me was glad to have a little room to breathe.

I did a quick once-over of the space, trying to locate him, but wherever he'd holed up, it was good because I didn't see hide or hair of him. That didn't mean he wasn't watching. He probably was. But it did mean he wasn't close enough to be able to tell what I was doing while I waited for the exchange.

The sides of the booth were high, which afforded me a measure of privacy that I was grateful for. I took my phone out of my pocket, intending to text Rico, but I frowned when I noticed that I had only one bar of service. The unease I'd been feeling in the pit of my stomach exploded and spread out to all the adjacent organs like buckshot.

I texted Rico anyway. And from what I could see, the message had gone through, but I had no real way to know for sure. I'd gone for the cheapest prepaid phone I could find, and that meant I lacked all the message-tracking capabilities I'd have had if I'd sprung for a more expensive one. It was a bitter pill to swallow, especially now. But I couldn't do anything about it.

The phone vibrated in my hand, startling me so much that I dropped it on the table, where it landed with a loud clatter. I fumbled it a little as I picked it back up, cursing my nerves. I made myself stop and take a deep breath before I opened the message.

It wasn't from Rico, which was disappointing. But a note from Tate was just as good. And the content made me exhale a huge sigh of relief. His guys had eyes on me, and he'd been coordinating with someone else from the Counterfeit Squad in my office, so they were somewhere on-site as well. Thank God.

Without lifting my head, I glanced up from underneath my eyelashes and did a quick sweep of the room. There weren't a ton of people in the bar, but I did pick out the two new ones right away: a man and a woman. I didn't recognize them, so they must've been Tate's colleagues. The slight nod the man gave for the split second we made eye contact confirmed my hunch, and whatever residual tension I'd been harboring melted away.

Feeling almost euphoric in the face of my relief, I sat back in the booth and waited. To pass the time, I counted the number of people in the bar twice, played a handful of games, tried unsuccessfully to surf the internet, debated ordering something to drink, immediately discarded the idea because I didn't want to have to go to the bathroom, lamented the fact that I didn't have my own phone so I couldn't listen to any of the podcasts I enjoyed and was now behind on, and longed for a manicure kit so I could address the nightmare my cuticles had become.

Time dragged by kicking and screaming, refusing to be rushed, and I was in the middle of wondering at what point I'd be able to get away with giving up on this foolhardy mission when Seth wandered back into the bar. I narrowed my eyes at him as he took a seat across from me.

"He's not coming?"

Seth shook his head and sighed, leaning far back into the leather cushioning on his side of the booth and lacing his fingers together on top of his head. "No. We're going to have to try again another time."

"I'm sorry," I said, though I wasn't. Not even a little bit.

He shrugged. "Not your fault." He let his arms fall and rapped twice on the top of the table with his fingertips. "Come on. Let's get out of here."

He got up from the table, and I followed suit, but he didn't head back toward the way we'd come in, which surprised me. "Where are we going?"

Seth glanced at me over his shoulder, and if my inquiry irritated him, he gave no indication. He bobbed his head in the direction of a small, dark hallway in the back corner of the bar. "We can't go out the way we came in."

I did not like the look of that hallway. "Why not?"

"Because it isn't done. Helps uphold the mystique of the place. This is the exit. It'll pop us out into a little side alley. Come on."

He didn't look back as he strode in the direction of that sketchy-looking hallway, but I looked lingeringly at the agents who were watching as I reluctantly followed. The hallway wasn't very long, maybe six paces, which was a relief. Seth opened the door for me and gestured with his free hand.

"Ladies first," he said.

"Thanks," I replied through the lump in my throat.

I took two steps and was still more or less inside the door frame when I turned to smile at him. Out of the corner of my eye, I registered a dark blur, but my heart didn't skip a beat nor did my adrenaline spike before the world went even darker.

CHAPTER TWENTY-EIGHT

Swimming back to consciousness was an exercise in agony, one I'd have put off indefinitely if I could've. My head was somehow both throbbing and spinning, so it was probably a good thing I was having trouble lifting my chin from my chest. Opening my eyes was also an ordeal I didn't have the energy for just yet. I decided to postpone them both for a moment.

The skin on several patches of my face burned, and I gingerly moved the muscles there, taking stock of the resultant pangs. God, that fucking hurt. I tried to recall how I'd ended up injured, but I was coming up empty. I couldn't even remember the last thing I could remember. That's how scrambled my thought processes were.

I licked my lips, dismayed to discover the sharp tang of blood. I tried to lift my hand to wipe it away, and to explore my forehead and cheeks to assess the damage, but I couldn't move it. A rough pull told me that my hands were bound behind my back, and a quick investigation with my fingertips let me know they were kept that way by handcuffs. Adrenaline spiked through me hard enough to hurt, and my head snapped up, but the wave of dizziness that enveloped me made me immediately drop it again.

The specifics of my situation took a long time to assemble themselves into anything recognizable, but when I grasped the fact that I'd been beaten and handcuffed to a chair, I inhaled. A low groan bubbled up in the back of my throat as I winced against the pain that inhaling sparked. I froze and held my breath, as much to lessen the torment as to catalogue my aches. I allowed the air to slowly seep out of my lungs and then inhaled again at a languid pace. I clenched my teeth against the moan clawing to escape and let the breath out again. A few of my ribs felt broken. I didn't think my lung had collapsed again, but it was tough to tell. What the hell had happened?

I tried to force my eyes to open, but only one would open all the way. The left one this time. The right one was almost swollen shut. I sighed, forgetting about my ribs for the fraction of a second it took me to do it, then hissed. I licked my lips again and waited for my vision to sharpen. The front of my shirt was covered in blood, and this time I couldn't stifle my groan. Great. I'd have to throw it away. No way would I be able to get all the blood out. I supposed that's what I got for wearing something I liked to a meeting with a domestic terrorist group.

I lolled my head to the left and allowed myself to look around. My head was still spinning like I'd just gotten off a crazy amusement-park ride, which made assigning meaning to the shapes I was seeing more difficult than usual. I blinked a couple times before frowning and raising my head all the way.

Seth was sitting a few feet in front of me, casual as you please, with his forearms resting across the top of the chair, which he'd turned backward. He was lazily holding a pistol in one hand. Wait. Was that *my* pistol? I subtly shifted my leg so that the outside of my ankle brushed against the leg of the chair. Sure enough, the holster was empty. Damn it! Seth appeared content to just watch me try to get my bearings, so I didn't say anything. I tried to force my eye to open wider and hoped the vertigo would subside soon.

We appeared to be in some sort of dimly lit warehouse, which didn't help me retain the tenuous grip I had on my calm. This wasn't good. Warehouses tended to be located in sparsely populated, industrialized parts of town. That meant that even if I could gather the energy necessary to scream, no one would likely hear me. Not in time to offer any assistance, anyway. And I no longer had that tracking device Allison had given me, so I had no hope there. I assumed the agents from the bar would figure out something was wrong sooner rather than later, which I hoped would lead to someone pinging my phone. But if I'd been here long enough to be beaten the way it felt like I had, chances seemed slim that help was on the way. Fuck! This was bad.

What little of the enormous room I could see was empty, which was another clue of sorts. The group apparently wasn't using this place for anything now. Though it didn't tell me whether they'd been using it previously or whether they were about to. Actually, as far as clues went, it kinda sucked. But I didn't see a bunch of other people milling around, which seemed like a point in my favor. Then again, maybe not. Fewer witnesses couldn't bode well for me.

In fact, aside from Seth, only one other person appeared to be present at this impromptu little meeting. I spotted Crash, who was standing behind Seth and a little off to the right. He was alternately making his hands into fists and massaging his knuckles. I wasn't sure whether he was attempting to look menacing or soothe an ache. But my heart lurched when I was finally able to focus enough to realize he was covered in blood, too. Blood that was probably mine.

I licked my lips once more and swallowed against the bitter, coppery taste that clung stubbornly to my tongue. I opened my mouth to try to speak, but all that came out was a hoarse, pathetic-sounding sort of squeak. I cleared my throat and tried again.

"So much for 'a man shouldn't hit a woman ever,'" I said.

Seth shrugged. "What can I say? I'm a hypocrite."

"So I see." I glanced back over at Crash. "You're going to want to wash your hands," I mumbled, my voice just above a whisper. I started using the tip of my tongue to prod at my teeth, reassuring myself that they were all there and trying to decide whether I needed to be alarmed at the few that seemed a tad loose. Then I ran it across the inside of my lips, wincing at the sting. Goddamn it! Just once I'd like to get out of one of these things without a split lip.

Both of them stared at me for a long moment before Seth asked, "What's that?"

I tried to nod in Crash's direction, but I'm afraid it looked more like an uncoordinated spasm. "Wash your hands."

"The only woman who can tell me to do that is my mama," Crash said with a sneer.

I shrugged and tried not to wince at the lance in my side. "You wanna expose yourself to HIV, it's on you." Okay. I didn't know for sure that I had it, but they didn't need to know that. I didn't know for sure that I didn't, either. That seemed like a good enough reason to bring it up. That and the mere possibility that his gut would take over, and he would panic and leave to follow my suggestion, despite all medical evidence confirming the likelihood of him contracting it that way was slim.

As I'd suspected, Crash's eyes widened, and he looked from me to his hands and back again. Seth continued to watch me thoughtfully. I focused on keeping my breaths shallow enough that they didn't jostle my ribs too much, but knowing I couldn't inhale deeply only made me want to that much more. I stilled and braced myself before I sucked in a giant, greedy breath. It hurt like hell and made my eyes water, but it helped calm me a little.

"You're bluffing," Crash said. But he sounded uncertain and kept glancing down at his hands again, his brow creased in obvious concern.

"Because that would help me so much with my predicament," I said, rolling my eyes.

Crash took a step toward me and stopped. He opened his mouth but frowned and shut it again before clenching his hands into fists. He stood there staring at me for a long moment before giving in to the urge to wipe his knuckles on the legs of his jeans.

"Go wash your hands," Seth told Crash without taking his eyes off me. "And change your clothes while you're at it. Burn those."

Crash bolted without having to be told again, and I watched him go with interest. The warehouse didn't have any windows, so I couldn't be sure what time of day it was. But I was hoping maybe he'd open a door or something and give me some sort of idea. No such luck. He disappeared into the darkened part of the room, and his footfalls continued long after I'd assumed they'd have stopped. The place was bigger than I'd thought. The icy fingers that wound their way around my heart at the notion squeezed hard, making it seize, and my lungs followed suit.

Eventually, the footsteps faded, and Seth and I were left alone as far as I could tell. I strained to pick up the telltale sounds of another person but couldn't hear anything. Just in case, I rolled my head to the left and twisted around as far as I could to see if anybody was behind me. There didn't appear to be, though I wished I could see out of my right eye so I could turn the other way to verify.

Seth's expression remained impassive as he continued to stare at me. Whatever he was thinking was carefully concealed, and he didn't appear to be in any hurry to reveal any of it. The tension in my body spooled tighter and tighter, as though I were a violin string being tuned too forcibly. I suspected that was more than half the point.

"Special Agent O'Connor," Seth said.

I wasn't the least bit surprised he knew who I was—my current quandary made it clear my cover had been blown. What I was having trouble figuring out was how. And when. Still, the bottom layer of my skin flashed cold as a new wave of adrenaline slashed through me. I struggled to force myself to keep quiet. But whether I reacted to anything that happened here was the only power I had left. It impacted nothing other than my own sense of control over the situation, and right now, that felt like a lot.

Seth resumed his creepy staring, and I returned to controlling the depth of my breaths and trying to figure out how much damage had been done during the beating. My stomach was tender and ached when I moved my torso, and my shoulders burned, but I suspected that was more due to their position than anything else. My wrists were raw from where they'd fastened the cuffs too tight, and I clenched and unclenched my fingers a few times to try to get the blood flowing to them.

"Funny," Seth said, breaking into my mental assessment. "I'd've thought you'd have more questions for me."

I shrugged, or tried to. My injured shoulder twinged with the motion, and I swallowed hard. "You know what they say about curiosity."

"You should've thought of that before you pulled this little stunt. You wouldn't be here now."

"I never was very good at doing the sensible thing."

The corners of his lips twitched like he wanted to smile. "Apparently not."

I narrowed my eye, trying to direct my focus so my head would stop swimming. It didn't work, so I shifted my attention to combating my nausea instead.

"You're not really twenty-four, are you?" Seth asked out of nowhere, taking me by surprise.

"No. I'm not."

He nodded once, almost to himself. "That's good. I'd hate to think they'd send in someone so young. Though I can't say I necessarily expected them to send anyone in at all."

I didn't bother to reply.

He continued to stare at me while he appeared to mull something over, and I began working to ease my ring off my middle finger. The ring I specifically wore for just such an occasion, which contained a tool that could possibly help me get out of these cuffs. I held my breath, hoping he wouldn't notice the motion. I certainly didn't need for him to realize what I was trying to do. It would no doubt piss him off, and that would be very, very bad.

I'd just gotten the ring clear and was starting to ease the shim out of the inside of it when Seth startled me by moving suddenly. Keeping the hand holding the gun planted on the back of the chair, he leaned to one side and retrieved something from the ground underneath the seat. I almost gasped when I realized I'd missed seeing it sitting there before. But the knot in my chest loosened when I saw it was only a laptop.

Seth regarded the device for a moment before tucking the pistol into the back of his waistband. He flipped open the laptop, punched a couple keys, and then turned it around so I could see it, resting it on the top of the chair. I stopped what I was doing and cast a wary glance at it.

It was a news article about what had originally looked like an assassination attempt on the president of Iran. A front-page one, from the looks of it. I had avoided the papers in the wake of all of that, so while I'd heard the rumors that the press had managed to get their hands on a photo of me to run with their story, I hadn't seen it myself. But there it was, clear and sharp.

I had obviously been working at the time the photo had been taken because I was in a suit, and my lapel pin and earpiece were both visible. My hair was a lot longer, and it was its normal blond color, but it was unmistakably me. I had no idea where or when it had been taken, but I supposed that didn't matter, given the predicament I was in. I'd never been a huge fan of the press, but at this moment, I outright hated them.

Allison had been right to worry about me. God. She was going to be so smug when she found out about this, although I might not be around to see it. I sent her a silent little mental message not to be too upset with me and to move on and find someone who'd treat her and the baby as well as I wanted to. I bit the inside of my cheek and made myself look away from the picture and into Seth's eyes.

My heart plummeted, and the uninjured parts of my body flashed ice cold. Seth flipped the laptop around again so he'd be able to see it, and I studied his expression. He was alternately looking at the screen and at me, and I was having a hard time controlling my internal panic. The only upside to having my face bashed in was that he likely wouldn't be able to correctly interpret my own expressions through the carnage. At least that's what I kept telling myself.

Seth took his time fiddling with the laptop, though what he was doing was anybody's guess. I sat still while I waited anxiously to see what his next move would be. I was too nervous to even consider continuing my escape attempt. Instead, I clenched my hand so hard around the ring it was sure to leave an indentation.

"You heard our conversation at the bar the other day," Seth said. "About the president coming to New York."

I swallowed hard and nodded, wincing because of the ache the action produced.

Seth nodded, too, and returned his focus to whatever was gracing the screen of the laptop. He looked contemplative. "Crash has been doing some digging. Gathering intel, as it were. Trying to figure out what sort of tactics and numbers the Secret Service use to protect our commander-in-chief, what sorts of attempts have already been tried and failed, you know, so we could use that information to determine when and where might be the best time to strike. The first thing that comes up when you search 'Secret Service and assassination attempt' is this." He paused so he could look at me, and his expression caused all my internal bodily functions to grind to an agonizing halt.

I gulped again and tried to find the perfect balance between clenching my teeth enough to alleviate my nervous tension but not ignite the agony in my jaw, which I assumed had recently been used as some sort of boxing practice. A million questions started battling for dominance in my mind, and I struggled to keep them off my face. I wasn't sure whether I'd done a good job.

"Imagine our surprise." He pursed his lips and shut the laptop before placing it back under his chair. Then he recrossed his forearms on the back of the chair and leaned forward to rest his weight on them.

I forced myself not to scoff or roll my eyes. Or burst out laughing. Of all the ways I'd imagined my cover being blown, this hadn't once crossed my mind. But of course it was the way everything played out. With my luck? How could it not have been? "Must've been quite a shock."

"Not a good one, I'm afraid."

"No. I suppose not."

He paused to tap the fingers of one hand against the opposite forearm. "I must admit I'm disappointed in you."

"Well, you're definitely not the first."

Seth ignored my quip in favor of pushing himself to a standing position. He moved the chair out of the way and began prowling around me. I clenched my teeth and my hands as I tried to tamp down the discomfort that burgeoned as he circled around me and out of my line of sight. I tensed, waiting for a blow to the back of the head with the butt of the gun that never came. Seth paused directly behind me, but he started walking again and circled back around.

When he reached my right side, he began speaking again. "I assume you're familiar with the definition of treason."

"Are you?" I shot back, unable to help myself. "Because what you're talking about isn't loyalty to America. It's terrorism."

"It's protecting our brothers and sisters. Even the bleeding-heart, liberal ones who're too stupid to know they need it." He paused and turned his head to look directly into my eye. "Like you."

I discarded the notion of engaging him in an argument about that belief. You couldn't reason with zealots. I'd had plenty of practice trying. Instead, I spit out a mouthful of blood, deliberately making sure it landed in his path. He didn't react. He merely continued pacing. The glimpse I'd gotten of his face before he moseyed in front of me indicated he was deep in thought. But then he circled around behind me again, making the hairs on the back of my neck prickle and dance. I clenched my fist tighter and prayed with every fiber of my being he wouldn't realize something was clutched in it.

"I can't believe, after everything that happened to you, that you're not falling all over yourself to aid our cause."

"What can I say? I was never much of a joiner."

He completed his arc around my chair and stopped in front of me again, his gaze cold, calculating as he studied me. I tried not to tremble. It didn't work. "If those fucking Islamic terrorist bastards had taken a shot at me, you'd better believe I'd be getting my licks in, too."

Oh, here we go. I couldn't refrain from rolling my eyes this time. "*Islam* didn't take a shot at me. Some stupid assholes did, and it had nothing to do with religion. I doubt Islam as a whole has any idea who I am. If they did, I doubt they'd care."

"The guys who arranged it were Muslim."

"You know that for sure?"

"Are you saying they weren't?"

"I'm saying that even if they were, it doesn't matter. I do know this for certain, though: One of them was my fucking boss. And that pisses me off more than anything else, if you want the truth. You gonna take him out in your little holy war, too? Because I might be able to get behind that."

He refused to be dissuaded from his argument. "This country is in desperate need of a cleansing."

"I think they made a movie about that. I didn't see it." I lifted my good shoulder. "Not really my thing. I'm more of a Mel Brooks fan, myself. Did you like *Blazing Saddles*?" I paused and didn't bother to try to hide my smirk. "No. I'd imagine you didn't."

His expression darkened. "What the hell is that supposed to mean?"

Hmm. It appeared I'd touched a nerve. What were the odds I'd be able to keep him in front of me and talking long enough to get these fucking handcuffs off? "It means you're a racist," I told him in the same tone I might have used if we were talking about something innocuous, like a football game or the weather or how many licks it takes to get to the center of a Tootsie Pop. "And a xenophobe. And also a dick."

He scoffed, but I could tell his reaction was forced, that he wasn't as unaffected as he was pretending to be. "I hardly think that loving my country makes me a racist."

"You do realize that this country was founded on the premise of all different types of people finding freedom here, right?" I slowly relaxed my hand and went back to easing the shim out of the casing. I made it a point to wince and shift a bit in my seat as I did, trying to disguise the motion under the pretext of discomfort. Seth didn't even blink, which I was hoping meant it had worked.

"It's gone too far," Seth insisted, as though he needed me to agree with him for some strange reason.

"What has? Freedom?"

The shim was free, and I'd eased it into one of the handcuffs so slowly and carefully, it took me almost a full minute to be certain it'd slid home at all. My heart was racing, and I'd started sweating again, which only added to the mountain of things I was worried about now. Fuck, if he realized I was sweating because I was nervous or if he started his restless prowling again, I was toast. I licked my split and bloody lips and let out a painful, shaky breath.

He nodded emphatically. "We've reached a point where we're too politically correct, and everyone is too afraid to be themselves in case they offend someone. It makes me sick. If I want to walk around New York City in a full-body pig costume, I should be able to."

I frowned, surprised and confused. "Why the hell would you want to do that?" Was he a furry? Or just a Suidae enthusiast?

He rolled his eyes. "You hear about that barbecue joint? The one that was forced to take down their billboard because the picture of the pig on it was offending people?"

The way he said those last two words made me surprised that he hadn't employed air quotes when he'd uttered them. I shook my head. I hadn't heard. And I couldn't for the life of me make the leap between that and wanting to dress up like a farm animal.

"Why should that business have to lose money because someone doesn't like to eat pork? Why are my freedoms being infringed upon so someone else can be comfortable? Next thing you know, I'm going to be told I have to take the mud flaps with the woman's silhouette off my truck. It's a dangerously slippery slope, and we need to stop it now before it gets even more out of hand. Soon, this country will no longer be the land of the free."

Was he being serious? First of all, why did he have a truck in the city? And with mud flaps, no less. How much mud did he think he was likely to encounter in the five boroughs? But I was getting off topic. "If this is about to veer off into a lecture on how oppressed you feel as a straight, white male, I'm begging you to just kill me now and get it over with. There's no way I can sit through that."

Seth went back to glowering at me, and for a split second, I think he really was debating whether to shoot me. His hand twitched as though he wanted to reach for my gun. But in the end, he shook his head and settled for backhanding me across the hollow of my cheek. Hard.

I gasped sharply as the agony exploded white-hot behind my eyes, and it was a goddamn miracle I didn't drop the shim at the impact. My heart lurched, and my stomach roiled for an instant as I fumbled it, but I managed to keep it in place. I really hoped the relief I felt wasn't showing on my face.

I blinked against the new waves of pain the blow had sparked, and my vision blurred as tears sprang to my eyes. Since my arms were still bound behind my back, I had to allow them to trickle down my cheeks. The moisture stung a little as it ran, which caused more tears to well, and round and round it went. I sighed. This was not my day.

"Bobby was your son, wasn't he?" I blurted out, surprising myself at least as much as I'd obviously surprised Seth.

He blinked, and then his eyes got wide, and his face paled. "What?"

"Am I wrong?"

He narrowed his eyes as he glared at me, not bothering to hide his consternation. "What makes you say that?"

"So I'm not wrong?"

"You are, actually."

Oh. Well, crap. Still, there had to be something…"But I'm close, aren't I?"

"What?"

He'd said that a little too quickly.

"He may not have been your son, but he was a blood relative. Wasn't he?" I paused for a moment so I could try to work this out for myself. "Nephew?"

Seth's dark glare told me all I needed to know, and I couldn't help smiling, even though it made my entire face burn. The blood had started to dry in places, and the cracking that resulted whenever I moved my facial muscles was uncomfortable. I wanted a washcloth and a sink full of warm water in the worst way, and knowing I wasn't going to get one any time soon was grating on me, making my entire body itch. I tried to refocus my attention to the conversation at hand to keep my mind off it.

"Let me guess. Bobby's mom was your little sister. And Nathan beat her. That's why she left. That's why we couldn't find any record of her or Bobby when we searched for info about Nathan. She took off and changed her name." I stopped for a moment as something else occurred to me. "You helped her, didn't you?"

Seth goggled at me. "How could you possibly even…?" He shook his head. "You know what? It doesn't matter. Yes, I helped her. Of course I helped her. She was my sister."

Was? Hmm. That was news. "So what happened to her?"

Seth's face contorted into an expression of pure rage the likes of which I'd seen only on my mentally ill PI subjects. The effect was chilling, and a sliver of fear pierced my heart, causing me to redouble my efforts to get one of the handcuffs off.

"What happened to her?" he parroted, his tone dripping with venom. "What happened to her? She killed herself when she lost Bobby. That's what happened to her."

"I'm sorry," I said quietly, my apology sincere. I didn't really remember Reagan. I'd been so young when she'd died that her passing hadn't impacted me in any of the regular tangible ways. But I couldn't imagine losing any of my siblings now, especially Rory. I'd come close once, and it'd been like a part of me had spontaneously combusted and then turned to ash, leaving a charred wasteland in its place. "I didn't know."

"Fucking ragheads cost me my entire family," he said, not even seeming to see me anymore.

I winced at his heated use of such a derogatory term, but something told me now wasn't the best time to argue with him about his choice of adjectives. In fact, this was one of those rare times when I listened to the voice inside my head that was screaming at me to keep my mouth shut, though I had to physically bite my lip to manage it, which hurt like a sonofabitch. I held my breath as I worked, trying to conceal my triumph when I felt the lock on the cuff click open.

Seth had resumed his pacing back and forth in front of me, only now it was jerky and borderline frantic as he obviously attempted to burn off some of his frustrations. "Nathan was a part of Operation Desert Squall." He paused to glance at me, and I froze with the handcuff halfway eased open. I stayed still for the seeming eternity it took him to start speaking again. "Do you know what that was?"

All the air in my lungs rushed out of me in one giant gasp, and I nodded to cover up my relief. "Yes."

"I'm asking because it just now occurred to me that you probably didn't lose your father to an IED. Did you?"

I shook my head. "No. I didn't."

"Did you serve?"

"No, but I watched the news, and I read a lot. So I'm familiar with the situation."

He bobbed his head once, apparently satisfied, and went back to stomping around. "So I assume you're also familiar with Gulf War Syndrome?"

I licked my bloody lips and grimaced, praying that he continued to stomp in front of me. "A little bit."

"Nathan was like a brother to me. There was nothing I wouldn't do for him, and there was nothing he wouldn't do for me. Until that goddamn war. After that…well, between whatever he saw over there and what he went through after he came back, Nathan was a completely different person. He wasn't sleeping. He'd call at all hours of the night and just babble about nothing. And he was *so* angry all the time. He'd fly off the handle at the littlest things."

Seth paused in his narrative to take a deep, shaky breath and roll his shoulders, as though to relieve the tension that was collecting in his body. I felt a sharp stab of envy, as I'd have given anything to do the same with mine. Instead, I took advantage of his momentary inattention and opened the cuff that'd bound my left wrist all the way. I sighed softly and took a second to slip my ring back onto my left hand before positioning the free cuff in my right.

"The first time he hit her, she didn't even tell me. He did. He showed up at my house at almost midnight looking like he'd seen a ghost, and when I asked him what happened, he just started bawling. Took me almost five minutes to figure out what the hell he was trying to tell me." Seth's lips twisted in a bitter smirk, and he glanced at me. "I almost killed him that night."

"Why didn't you?" I asked, more to keep him talking than out of any real curiosity. I had to figure out a way to get him to come closer. I couldn't risk lunging at him at this distance. I was in horrible pain, and my entire body was stiff from sitting contorted in this uncomfortable position. I definitely wasn't at my best, so when I finally made my move, I needed it to count.

Seth looked away again after a moment and shrugged. "I don't know. I guess because my sister would've been crushed if I had. Besides, it wasn't his fault that he was struggling. Not after what he'd seen and probably done. He needed help, not judgment. And he swore to me he'd never do it again."

"But he did, didn't he?"

Seth swallowed and nodded. "Yeah. I honestly have no idea how many times. I only confronted Sadie about it once, and the way she reacted…let's just say I didn't have the heart to do it again. But I suspected. She'd make excuses not to see me sometimes, or she'd be wearing big, baggy clothing in the middle of the summer." He paused long enough to let out a bone-weary sigh. "I should've done something sooner. For both of them."

He lapsed into silence then, and watching him stare off into space as he drowned in memories of the past was unnerving. It also wasn't helping me achieve my goal of getting the fuck out of there. I endured it as long as I could before I decided I needed to kick-start the dialogue again. Anything to cover the subtle movements of my escape preparations. "What finally ended it?"

Seth blinked, startled. He gave his head a little shake and cleared his throat. "Sadie got pregnant. I think it was one thing for him to beat her. She loved him and wanted to stand by him no matter what. But once a baby was involved, I guess the idea became unbearable. She didn't want to keep Nathan from his son. Not really. But she didn't want Bobby to grow up around that violence without any escape."

"Understandable," I murmured, suddenly lost in thoughts of Allison and Rory.

He sniffed once and ran the back of his hand across his brow. "Anyway, back to my point. If Nathan hadn't gone through what he did, none of this would've happened. He and Sadie would still be together, Bobby would've grown up with a present, engaged father instead of someone who dropped in and out occasionally depending on his mental state, and both of them would still be alive."

I couldn't help raising my eyebrows as I contemplated his unique take on the situation. It made no sense. Like, at all. And I was tempted to point out any number of holes in his theory, but something told me I wouldn't gain much by that, short of making him angry enough to hit me again. And I wasn't sure I had it in me to withstand another blow. Although it would force him to come closer to me…Hmm…

I didn't have much time to contemplate the matter further. Seth's cell phone rang, and he threw me a quick glance before stalking a few feet away and turning his back on me before answering.

"What have I told you about calling me?" he snapped, running his free hand through his hair.

I hesitated, wondering whether his distraction afforded me enough of an opportunity to slide my ring back off and get to work on my other cuff. My heart was no longer pumping individual beats but was rather one solid, continuous roar, and my throat was dry. Did that have anything to do with the fact that I'd started sweating even more? Did physiology even work that way? I'd have to remember to ask Rory the next time I saw her. If there was a next time.

"Okay," Seth was saying, sounding a bit unhappy. "So what did you—?"

I swiped my sweaty palms one at a time against the back of my T-shirt, which I discovered a little too late was also damp. I hoped the moisture wasn't blood, but there was no way to tell. Grimacing at the thought, I set about trying to unlock the other cuff. My heart felt like it'd grown about six sizes and was now thudding painfully against the inside of my ribs. I held my breath as I worked, and each clink of metal that my movements produced made a lance of panic shoot through my chest. So far, Seth hadn't noticed, but it was only a matter of time.

"I see," Seth said. He nodded even though the person on the other end of the phone couldn't see him. "Okay, well, keep me posted."

Shit. Shit, shit, shit. I tried to speed up my movements, but the clanging of the cuffs against one another sounded as loud as a gunshot to my oversensitive ears. My lungs burned from lack of oxygen, and my fingers shook as I struggled. Just when I felt the lock give, Seth hung up and turned back around.

I froze and prayed as hard as I'd ever prayed for anything in my entire life that he wouldn't see my panic. If he did, he'd surely wonder why, and I didn't think it'd be long before he figured out what I'd been up to. I consciously tried to even out my breathing—or at least make it less gaspy—but I wasn't sure I managed it as well as I'd wanted to.

Seth walked back over to where I sat and stopped a few feet away, close enough to pin me with an oddly empty stare, but not close enough for me to kick. What a shame. Even without the space for a full wind-up, a foot to the balls probably would have surprised him just enough for me to get a jump on him. But with this much distance between us, there was no way. I'd have to come up with something else.

"Agent O'Connor," Seth said, his voice flat.

"Yes?" I asked when he didn't follow that utterance up with anything.

"It's time you and I had a talk."

I swallowed hard against the scratchy dryness of my throat and tried not to look as panicked as I felt. I couldn't imagine any scenario in which those words could mean anything good.

CHAPTER TWENTY-NINE

W e continued to stare at one another for a long time. My shoulder muscles were on fire from being stuck in that position, and I was dying to shake out my hands, to flex my fingers.

"Isn't that what we've been doing?" I asked with way more bravado than I felt. I may have been terrified, but he didn't need to know that.

Seth scowled at me and huffed. After a moment, he settled back onto his chair and resumed his inspection of me. "You've been distracting me, stalling me, in the hopes that someone will come rescue you. I've got news for you. Even if they knew where to look, they'd never get here in time."

I thought again about the agents who'd been in the bar with me. Surely they'd followed me through that sketchy door. But I suspected they'd waited for several long moments before they'd done it. Given that I was still here and not surrounded by government officials in an office being debriefed, Seth had probably had a car waiting for me in that alley, and the agents from the bar hadn't gotten a look at it. Which meant that all the other agents on the street had been looking for Seth and me to walk out and so hadn't paid any attention to any cars in the area. It'd been a clean getaway.

My heart turned to ash. Though he'd incorrectly guessed my motives for engaging, it was still devastating to hear that no one would find me.

"Sounds like we have plenty of time to talk, then," I said around the lump in my throat.

"You're Secret Service." His lip curled in a sneer as he spoke, and it seemed odd that he needed any further confirmation from me on the subject, but I didn't see any reason to deny it now.

I nodded. "I thought we already established that."

"Care to tell me how you stumbled onto us?"

I tried to smile, and white-hot stabs of pain assailed my face for my efforts. "A girl's gotta retain some secrets."

Seth was not amused. "Speaking of which, did you tell your little friends about our conversation at the bar the other day?"

"I assume you're referring to my coworkers."

"I am. Did you tell them?"

"Which conversation?" I asked, playing dumb.

"You know which one."

"You mean, the one where you said the president was going to get the bullet to the head that he deserved?"

"That's the one."

"Does it really matter?"

"Let's chalk it up to curiosity."

I narrowed my eyes as I pretended to think about my reply, but really I was studying his position and the distance between us and trying to gauge the odds that I'd be able to take him out before he could end me. I wasn't at all pleased with my answer.

"It might have come up."

Seth let out a long, noisy, overly dramatic sigh and made a show of dropping his head and clenching his hands on the back of the chair. "You shouldn't have done that," he said, his voice low, his tone menacing.

"It's kind of my job."

He lifted his head and opened his mouth to say something, but he must've changed his mind because he shut it again, then chewed the inside of his lips. "How much do they know?"

"About you?"

He nodded.

"Why do you ask?"

Okay, now I was just being a dick. I mean, I had no reason *not* to answer his questions. He knew everything. Or at least everything of any real importance. And having his attention focused on me like this was not at all conducive to my grandiose plans for escape. But I wasn't the sort of girl to go down without a fight, and if making him work extra hard to pull information out of me was the only way to rail against him, that's what I'd do.

The last thing I expected was for him to answer me. So imagine my surprise when he said, "Apparently, your friends paid my friends a visit a little while ago."

My internal organs melted and then solidified and took on the density of osmium. My ears started ringing, which made me doubt that I'd heard him right. "What?"

Something not unlike triumph flickered behind Seth's eyes. "Yeah.

Wonder where they got the idea to start asking my acquaintances whether I meant the president any harm."

I wanted to groan, loud and long and lusty. I wanted an outlet—any outlet—for the scalding feelings of frustration, betrayal, and disappointment that were having a battle of the titans in my gut. But I didn't want him to know he'd gotten to me, didn't want to give him any more of an upper hand than he already had. So I choked that groan down and swallowed hard against the pain denying its escape caused.

"Weird," I said after a moment, the word sounding as forced as it felt.

"Is it?"

I nodded as I debated how much to divulge. "It is. Considering I told them to wait until after I'd emerged to do that."

His eyebrows flew up in surprise, and he gaped at me for a moment. "You're admitting it?"

"No reason not to, right?" I tried to shrug, but that only resulted in sharp needles of pain raking through my shoulder muscles, and I hissed. God, I wanted to move my arms. This, knowing I was physically free to do it but having to bide my time until Seth provided me with an opening, was almost worse than having them bound. At least then, I hadn't had a choice.

"Since we're on the subject of admissions, are you going to cop to the fact that Tate's a fed, too?"

Holy fuck. That wasn't good. I had no clue where Tate was right now, so I had no guarantee he was safe. I needed to get Seth off that idea pronto. I threw my head back and laughed, praying I was convincing. "You're kidding me, right?"

Seth's expression was pure skepticism. "You expect me to believe he isn't your partner?"

I raised my eyebrows as best I could and tried my hardest to look incredulous, and when Seth didn't bite, I made a show of rolling my eyes. "Tate? Seriously? Come on. The man's easy on the eyes, but he doesn't have a whole lot going on upstairs."

"So, what? You just happened upon us by accident? I don't buy it."

Shit. I was going to have to come up with something plausible. I thought for a minute and attempted to make it look like I was weighing something in my mind. "You remember that time when Tate disappeared for a night and none of you could find him?"

Seth scratched his chin and nodded slowly. "Vaguely. Something about his mother being sick?"

He'd actually been briefing me, but I wasn't about to admit that. Instead, I snorted. "His mother wasn't sick. He was in lockup."

Seth's eyes widened a fraction. "What?"

"He got busted."

His eyes narrowed again, and his suspicion was back. "For what?"

"For trying to pass your piss-poor counterfeit."

I could almost see Seth's mind churning as he considered what I'd just told him and attempted to make it fit with what he thought he knew to be true. He shook his head. "No. Impossible. He said it passed fine."

It was my turn to show skepticism. "Are you high? That shit was terrible. And what I think he told you was he pawned it off on some punk kids who wouldn't know a bad knock-off if he shoved it up their ass."

Seth was still not convinced, and I was praying he wouldn't recognize my desperation. "So he...what? Gave me his own money to cover it?"

"No idea. I never asked. Maybe he thought that was better than telling you he got popped. And I think that's about when he also suggested to you that you try to get a better product."

Seth's lips twisted as he obviously attempted to recall the conversation. "He tell you all this?"

I shrugged as much as I could. "Some men think with their cocks. He'd have told me his Social Security number and bank account passcode if I'd asked."

Seth scoffed. "You expect me to believe you arrested him and then started blowing him to get intel?"

I wrinkled my nose. "Of course not. I never said *I* was the one who arrested him."

His brow furrowed, and he appeared confused. "I don't understand."

"Dude, I'm Secret Service. Counterfeit is our thing. How long do you think it took for the guys who interviewed him at the precinct to tell me what happened?"

"You were sent undercover to get stuff out of him on the sly?"

"Yup. Wasn't hard either. He was dying for some way to get into your good graces. Wanted to prove himself to you or something. God only knows why. But when I conveniently showed up at the bar he was getting hammered in with my graphic design degree and my print-shop job, he was so over the moon at his good fortune, it didn't even occur to him to consider I was a plant. Like I said, great to look at, not too bright."

"You played him."

"Like a dime-store kazoo. I just mentioned I was an artist, and the rest took care of itself. I didn't even need to lead him. He practically busted a nut at the thought that I'd be able to help him become your right-hand man or whatever." I shook my head.

"So…You literally whored yourself for your government?"

Hmm. When he put it that way, that is what it sounded like I was telling him. But let him think whatever he wanted. As long as it kept Tate alive. "Some assignments are more difficult than others."

He stared at me for a long moment, and I held my breath, waiting to see whether he'd bought my tale. It wasn't bulletproof. Not by a long shot. But I guessed I didn't need it to be. I just needed it to be probable enough that he stopped thinking Tate was a mole. I just needed it to buy some time until I could figure out what to do.

Finally, he said, "I'll say this for you: you've got some pair on you."

I tried not to either sigh or sag as relief washed over me. "Yeah, well…" I didn't have any follow-up to that. No witty retort, no snappy comeback, not even a poorly rhymed limerick. Nope, I had nothing, so I let the words just hang there while I tried to decide what my next move should be.

"Shame," Seth murmured, his expression almost thoughtful.

I clenched my teeth against the urge to ask him to clarify that comment, but as the silence stretched on between us, my curiosity eventually got the better of me, and almost counter to my will, I found myself asking, "What's a shame?"

"When I brought you here, I had been prepared to let you live. Now…"

Whereas my trailing off had been due to any lack of appropriate retort, his now was clearly a scare tactic. I had to give it to him. His attempt hit the bull's-eye. Hard. I started shivering, and while I initially started to hide that reaction from him, the effort turned out not to be worth it. I was in far too much pain to do that.

I licked my lips and tried to swallow again, only to discover that my mouth was completely devoid of all moisture, the gesture reminding me of the rough scraping of coarse sandpaper over tree bark. I didn't know why anyone would try to sand a tree, nor had I ever attempted it myself, but still, that was the image that immediately sprang to mind.

Okay, so this wasn't good. I mean, none of this had even remotely approached the definition of acceptable, but his words brought my situation into sharp focus almost too suddenly. My mind was having a hard time gaining any kind of traction now, which was bad. If I had any hope whatsoever of getting out of this alive, I needed my brain to stop freaking the fuck out and get in the game.

"Sucks to be me, I guess," I said.

He nodded as he studied me. "I guess it does."

"Tell me," I said, because I had to know. "The way you see it, am I just another casualty in your little holy war?"

Both his lips and his fingers twitched, and his eyes glinted with something cold and mad that made my blood crystallize. "Something like that."

"I don't suppose it would do any good to point out that none of what you're upset about—your sister, Nathan, Bobby—could be attributed solely to religion."

His hard glare was all the answer I needed, and my gut slithered under his intense gaze. I sighed and rolled my head to stare at the ceiling. Fuck, this was bad. He was so far past the point of reason, it was absurd. His knowingly kidnapping and beating a federal agent should have clued me in to that. Yet I'd still felt compelled to try. Stupid optimism. It always hurt to have it crushed like this, no matter how many times it happened.

"Grant a girl a last request?" I said, my voice shaking. I'd liked to have said that was on purpose, that I'd been trying to sell my fear, but nope. That was all anxiety leaking out.

Seth's eyes narrowed at me suspiciously before he nodded once, the gesture curt.

"Make it clean. Bullet to the back of the head. I don't want to suffer. I've already been shot in a non-fatal place, and it hurts like a motherfucker. I'd rather not have to endure bleeding out after being shot somewhere fatal."

He cocked his head and furrowed his brow, and I held my breath and tried to will my heart to slow its gallop as I waited. Time seemed to slow to the kind of crawl reserved for dancing in line praying for a bathroom stall to open up after you've had six beers, and it was a struggle not to fidget.

After what had to be an epoch—during which I estimated that at least *four* bathroom stalls would have opened up had I actually been in line for the restroom—he bobbed his head again. He pushed himself to a standing position and retrieved the pistol from the waistband of his pants.

"Far be it from me to let a woman suffer. I am a gentleman, after all."

"And they say chivalry is dead," I couldn't help quipping.

The corners of his mouth turned up in a small smile, and he took a deep breath. He walked over to me and stopped just to my right. Only a few scant inches separated us now, and my heart skipped several beats before resuming its Indy 500. This was it. This was my shot, no pun intended. Please, dear God, don't let what I'm about to do get me killed.

Seth towered over me for a few seconds, and I took the opportunity to adjust the grip I had on the free handcuff, ensuring that it was opened wide and the teeth were facing outward.

"Any last words?" he asked, his fingers flexing around the butt of the pistol.

I didn't bother to reply. Taking a quick, sharp inhalation of breath, I lunged forward and flailed wildly, my left hand reaching for the gun as my right hand swung in a madcap, uncoordinated arc in the general direction of his face. I hadn't counted on that move to work, so I was as surprised as Seth when I heard a guttural howl of pain. I took the opportunity his momentary distraction provided to follow up with a clumsy attempt at an elbow strike to the chin. While I did manage to clip him, it wasn't nearly hard enough.

The sharp report of a single gunshot reverberated, and my ears rang. The acrid stench of gunpowder filled the air and coated the back of my tongue, making me grimace. I realized after a second that he hadn't been shooting at me, that the shot had been a result of his hand clenching sympathetically in response to being struck. But it highlighted for me that he still had enough of a grip on the weapon to be able to pull the trigger, and that needed to change.

Quickly, I brought my right hand down and used it in conjunction with my left to trap his forearm next to my hip. My ribs were wailing at me now, so loudly they'd put the oldest, crankiest banshee to shame, and my shoulders were joining their vocal protest. The adrenaline careening through my veins like an old mining car in a cartoon muted the pain to an extent, but I still felt it.

I struggled against Seth's attempts to break free and tried to grab more of his arm. He wrapped his free one around my neck and pulled, trying to get me off balance. It worked. Sort of. Although I doubt it had the result he intended.

Instead of allowing him to force me into an awkward sort of backbend with him acting as a kind of support wall behind me, I abandoned the control I had over his gun hand so I could spin around in his grip. The scraping of my face against the fabric of his shirt as I went was agonizing, and I grunted through clenched teeth.

I braced my hands on his abdomen after I'd made a complete 180 and was facing him, then barreled directly at him as fast as my little feet would carry me, pushing against his stomach as I went.

He let out a yelp of surprise, and I could feel more than hear the *tap-tap-scrape* of his feet as he scrambled to back away while retaining his footing, and a small burst of triumph surged through me. But then I recalled that this landing was going to hurt like hell.

I was right. Tumbling on top of Seth was more akin to being slammed into by a Suburban than landing on a fluffy bed of freshly fallen snow. My teeth clacked together hard, and I bit my tongue on impact. A fresh spurt of blood filled my mouth, but that was the least of my concerns in the face of this fresh wave of pain. Stars danced behind my eyes, and my head swam. I took a deep breath and winced, willing myself not to pass out.

Seth's gun hand landed above his head when he fell, and I propelled myself bodily in the direction of that limb. I heard him grunt as I scrabbled my way up his body, probably because I'd inadvertently kneed him in the groin on the way. Whatever. It's not like he didn't deserve a jab to the nuts after what he'd pulled.

I dove headlong toward the gun, my pulse hammering in my ears as desperation pressed against the underside of my skin, fighting to break free. My fingers were fumbling as I frantically attempted to grip the weapon. I hissed as I scratched them against the concrete floor, breaking at least one nail in the process.

Then I shifted my position so I was kneeling on the inside of Seth's biceps in order to keep his arm still, and after what had to have been an eternity of fumbling and rooting and clawing, I managed to knock the gun out of his hand. The clattering of metal against stone provided a welcome relief. I'd much rather have it in my own hand, but at least he no longer had it in his.

I chanced a glance in his direction and noticed that his face was an unhealthy shade of red, and his eyes were sort of bugging out of his head. The cords on his neck stood out, and he looked panicked as he twisted and writhed.

Huh. Guess I'd kneed him harder than I thought. I wasted no time flipping him over and then dropping all my weight onto his shoulder blade as I wrenched his arm none too gently into a position of advantage. I torqued his elbow back against my inner thigh and put pressure on his wrist. Then I sat there for a long moment, panting through the pain, trying to catch my breath. Unfortunately, the deep, gasping breaths I was inclined to draw only exacerbated the ache in my ribs.

After a long moment of recovery, during which I tried to coax my heart into beating at a more reasonable rate, I looked at my wrists and frowned. Shit. One of the cuffs was still on. I'd started loosening it but had been interrupted before I could get it all the way off. Well, now what? I needed to get these off me and onto him, and I needed to do it fast, before he recovered, or before Crash returned. He had to have heard that gunshot, which meant he'd likely be back soon.

I scoured the floor around us, searching for my ring with the shim in it. It took a few too-long moments of serious searching, but I finally located it…on the other side of the chair, way too far away for me to reach. Fuck. I blew in the direction of the stray wisps of hair falling across my forehead—a long-ingrained habit from when I'd worn it longer—and shook my head. Now what?

I wasn't about to release my grip on him. Not even for the three seconds it would take me to dash over there, retrieve the ring, and rush back. And no way would I be able to drag him with me. He was too heavy, and I was in too much pain with not enough time. I tried searching his pockets for the key, but he either didn't have it on him— likely since he hadn't planned to let me go—or it'd gotten pushed to a part of the pocket I couldn't reach. As a last-ditch effort, I flagged his front pockets, but it didn't do any good. No key.

Sighing, I looked at my wrist. The cuff was slightly bigger now than it'd been when he first put it on. It dangled off me a bit more. I wondered… Biting my lower lip between my teeth, I adjusted my grip on Seth's arm so that his wrist was tucked into my armpit. It wasn't an ideal position, but I hoped I could get this over with faster than he'd be able to take advantage of the situation. Plus, the noises he was making led me to believe he was still recovering from the introduction of my knee to his balls. I had a few seconds at least.

A low, keening sort of moan emerged from deep inside my chest as I attempted to pull the cuff off the old-fashioned way. I just needed to get it over my thumb joint, and I'd be free and clear. I grunted with the effort of trying to yank it off and wished for some butter or olive oil or regular oil. Anything slippery or liquid.

I briefly debated trying to gather up some blood and smearing that over my hand to help make the task easier, but since my face already felt cracked and dry, I didn't bother. And seeing as how, after I'd swallowed the blood from biting my tongue, my mouth was somehow now more arid than the desert at high noon in the middle of summer, I forewent that route as well.

Okay. Muscle it was. I bit back the shriek of pain that bubbled up inside me as I redoubled my efforts to get the cuff off. Centimeter by centimeter I forced it until it came free with a pop that was so sudden, I momentarily lost my balance and my grip on Seth's arm. I struggled to retain it, my heart in my throat the entire time. It slithered down somewhat once I'd re-secured him. And it lessened its thundering when

I heard the sweet siren song of the cuffs clicking into place around Seth's wrists.

He groaned and sort of pulled at the restraints, and I rewarded his efforts with a quick elbow strike to the carotid artery. After that, he went still, and I was checking his pulse to make sure I hadn't accidentally killed him when I heard another click, this one behind me. And it wasn't the click of a handcuff.

I took a deep, shaky breath. What was that saying? Out of the frying pan and into the fire? Shit. This seriously wasn't my day.

CHAPTER THIRTY

Every muscle in my body went rigid, and the air turned to ice in my lungs and burned. The echo of the sharp click of a hammer being cocked reverberated inside my head, causing my heart to shudder. I was afraid to breathe, afraid to even twitch, lest I end up hearing a louder noise. One that could ruin my day.

The two of us sat there in silence for what had to have been an eternity. I could feel each millisecond dragging across the surface of my skin, scratching and prickling like a wool sweater. The spot between my shoulder blades tingled, and I wished I could see the look on Crash's face so I'd have some idea what he was thinking.

Unable to stand the weighty quiet for even an instant longer, I said, "You didn't need to do that, you know." I tried to keep my voice as steady and even as possible. He didn't need to know how on edge I was.

"Do what?"

Still on my knees on top of Seth's unconscious form, I twisted so I could look at Crash over my left shoulder. He was standing with his feet spread wide, arms out in front of him, pointing a pistol at me. I didn't even have to look hard to see that his hands were shaking. "Cock the weapon. That gun's a double action."

He frowned and glanced uncertainly at the pistol in his hands.

"It means you can fire it without pulling the hammer back first," I told him. I started to rise slowly, but he thrust the barrel at me several times in rapid succession, which I took as a hint that he didn't want me to get to my feet. I sank back down and shifted so I was resting all my weight on the heel of my right foot, which was tucked under me.

"So?"

"So, people only cock their weapons in real life for two reasons."

When I didn't go on, Crash rolled his eyes and sneered. "Oh, yeah?"

I nodded. "Yeah. Either they do it for dramatic effect because they aren't prepared to pull the trigger, and they're hoping the sound of the hammer cocking will be enough to ensure they don't have to. Or they don't have the proficiency to make an accurate shot with a double-action trigger pull." I paused and looked pointedly at his still-trembling hands. "In your case? I'd guess it's more the former, though I'm sure there's a dash of the latter mixed in."

His sneer became more pronounced, and his eyes flashed. "If you're so smart, why the hell am I the one holding the gun?" He waved the barrel at me again for emphasis, and I had to fight not to gasp.

Instead, I dipped my head once in acquiescence. "You're right. You are smart. Smart enough to know better than to pull some stupid television-crime-drama move and press the barrel of that gun to the back of my head. Which, honestly, I would've expected. But if you'd done that, we wouldn't be in this position having this conversation."

"Oh, no? And what position would we be in?"

"If you'd done that? I'd have taken that gun from you and pistol-whipped you with it until you were as unconscious as your friend here." I threaded my fingers through Seth's hair and lifted his head a couple inches off the ground before releasing my grip. His face made a dull thump as it slammed back into the concrete.

"I never liked you," Crash said. He adjusted his grip on the gun, and in doing so, his grip on the trigger tightened a hair. My eyes were drawn to the way the muscles in his hand and forearm tensed, to the miniscule twitch of the hammer. I held my breath waiting for the bang, but it didn't come. "I never trusted you either."

I let out a shaky breath when his grip eased and tried to smirk at him. "The feeling's pretty mutual. Bet you didn't see this coming, though, did you?"

Crash returned my wry grin. "No. Didn't see this coming."

"Are you a fan of surprises, Crash?"

He narrowed his eyes at me. "Why?"

"Because you're gonna love this one." I launched myself across Seth's body and made a grab for the gun he'd lost during our struggle. My gun. I'd just brushed my palm over it when the bang I'd been waiting for shattered the stillness. I felt more than heard the bullet impact the concrete a few feet to the right of where I'd landed, and the air around me was once again filled with the pungent scent of gunpowder. I couldn't help wondering what all these shots in such close proximity were doing to my hearing. It couldn't be good.

I established a firm grip on the handle of the gun and rolled over, bringing the muzzle up so it was pointed right back at Crash from between my bent knees. I was lying on my back, breathing heavily. My ribs were killing me, but I tried to push past the agony. Crash's eyes widened, and he licked his lips as we stared at one another over the barrels of our respective weapons, the haze of smoke between us slowly dissipating.

Maybe my coworkers were right. Maybe I was going soft. Because I had little to no doubt that if any of them found themselves in this position, they'd have just pulled the trigger and been done with it. Hell, if you'd asked me six months ago to describe my reaction to this very situation, I'd have insisted that I'd have done the same thing. I'd always believed that when it came to saving my own life, there was nothing I wouldn't do, no one I wouldn't shoot if I had to. Yet I'd just hesitated. I'd had the opportunity to end this—I could still end it—but instead I'd opted not to. I couldn't help wondering if everything that'd happened really had changed me that much or whether I'd been soft from the beginning and had just been deluding myself. Fuck. I so didn't need to be thinking about any of this now. Now I needed to try to find a way to talk myself out of this, so I didn't have to kill him.

"So," I said finally. "Where do we go from here?"

Crash adjusted his grip on the gun again, and I suspected he wanted to wipe his palms on his shirt but couldn't bring himself to do it. I took a deep, agonizing breath and let it out slowly, hoping it'd help calm my racing pulse.

"Put down your gun," Crash said, his voice wavering a little.

I tilted my head as I studied him, realizing for the first time that he wasn't much more than a scared kid who'd gotten in over his head and probably couldn't think of a way to get out. "You first."

"Don't make me kill you."

I didn't even try to hide my amusement. "Seriously? Your shot just now went wide by at least three feet."

"Maybe it was a warning shot."

"Maybe. But we both know it wasn't."

Crash scowled at me and shuffled his feet but said nothing.

I debated adjusting my position so I wasn't lying flat on my back, but I was afraid the resulting pain wouldn't be worth it. The last thing I needed right now was that sort of loss in focus. I dug my heels into the concrete to help solidify my prone stance.

"Look," I said after I tired of us just staring at one another in silence. "It doesn't have to end like this."

He laughed, and the sound was bitter and hollow. "Yes, it does."

"Why?"

His brow furrowed, and he seemed confused. "How the hell else would it end?"

"I don't know. Literally any other way?"

He shook his head, and his arms dipped. I took that as a sign that he was tiring, but that wasn't useful information. We were too far apart, and I was too injured to successfully take the weapon from him. I was going to have to talk him into putting it down.

"Come on," I said, trying to ignore the burning in the muscles of my core or the throbbing of my wounds. "You're in the best possible position now. Why ruin it?"

He let out another harsh, barking cackle. "You're fucking kidding me, right? I'm monumentally screwed no matter how this plays out."

"How do you figure that?"

"If I put this down, you'll arrest me."

I nodded. There was no point in lying to him about that. "I will. But you're looking at time either way. Right now, it's more a matter of how much. You put that down and let me cuff you, and I'll tell the AUSA you cooperated. He'll go easy on you. The other way? You won't be nearly as lucky."

Crash sneered, but his gaze was darting around like he was searching for an escape. "That's assuming they catch me. I'll have one helluva head start."

I raised my eyebrows at him. "Where are you gonna go? With what money? What ID? You'll be nabbed before you leave the borough. Don't kid yourself."

"Who's even going to know to look for me? You're not going to be able to call anybody."

I rolled my eyes. "Buddy, if you think I'm the one dying in this scenario, you're more delusional than I thought." I might not have wanted to kill him—might have wanted to do anything possible to figure out a way around it—but he didn't have to know that. And there was no way I was going to let him end me.

"You don't think I'll shoot you?" His voice cracked a little as he spoke.

I hesitated before replying, uncertain how to play this. "I don't think you can."

"I can!" He shrieked, though which one of us he was trying to convince, I'll never know. "I will."

"Let me rephrase," I said with exaggerated patience that I didn't feel. "It's not that I don't think you'll pull the trigger. I just don't think you have the skill to hit me. Even at this distance. Your grip is sloppy, and your arms are trembling. It'll be a miracle if you land a shot anywhere close to me. Me? I could make this shot in my sleep. So don't be an idiot. Put the gun down."

Why the hell was I even having this conversation with him again? I frowned and worried at the lacerations on the inside of my lower lip with the tip of my tongue, almost reveling in the ache the prodding produced. A couple months ago, when I'd opted not to shoot Walker in Prospect Park, I'd had good reason. I'd been running, so I'd been tired. He'd been farther away. And he'd been moving at the time. I could easily have missed him and hit someone else, including the president's daughter or my sister. The risk hadn't been worth it. Now, though, I had no real reason to refrain other than not wanting to kill him.

Again, I couldn't help ruminating on the questions that brought up. What did it mean, exactly? What did that say about me that I was trying anything I could think of to avoid making the hard call? Oh, God! Was I going to balk at other key moments in my career? And if so, should I consider turning in my badge for real? My head was spinning at the implications of it all, and my insides felt as though they'd become molten lead and were now hardening.

I shoved that thought away as hard as I could, willing it to fly far into the deepest recesses of my mind so it didn't come back up again. At least not any time soon. The last thing I needed was to dwell on this right now. It wasn't helping anything.

I forced myself to look at Crash, to take in the fear and desperation in his eyes, the tightness of his jaw. His hands were still shaking, and I watched in horror as he readjusted his grip on the gun. The muscles in his forearms tightened, and I shook my head.

"Don't do it, Crash." My stomach was knotted, and a shiver racked my body.

His lips twisted, and his teeth were bared. He took a deep breath and lifted his chin, as though physically steeling himself for what he was about to do. Sweat stood out on his brow, and one droplet made its way down the side of his cheek from his temple. And then I watched as the shutters came down on his emotions, and both his fear and his desperation winked out. All that was left was a soul-sucking hollowness that made me want to look away.

"Don't," I whispered, unable to make my voice any louder. "Please."

It was weird. Time once again did that funny thing it does when you're in the middle of a life-or-death situation. Now, for instance, it seemed to slow, and I could see each minute muscle twitch of his hand on the gun. I even had enough time to think *He's going too fast. He's going to jerk the trigger.* I saw the muzzle flash. And for the third time that day, my eardrums were assailed by the thunderous crack of a gunshot. Again, the shot went wide, and while it didn't hit me, I thought it might have been a little closer than the last one.

My shots, on the other hand, were right on target. And, unlike Crash's, which had seemed to take forever, all five of mine had been fired and hit home in the space it took to blink. And whereas I definitely heard his, my ears had decided to take a brief sabbatical during mine.

As soon as the last bullet had hit home, time slowed to a crawl again. Crash stumbled backward, and it took an eon for his arms to drop. Then he ducked his head just enough to inspect the damage. Watching his eyes fall to his chest and then rise back up to meet mine was akin to watching the second hand circle a clock face. And I was certain that I could've recited the Gettysburg Address in its entirety before he managed to blink that final time.

Then he was falling, and that, too, seemed to take a comically long time. As I watched, I had some inappropriate thoughts comparing his rate of motion to a cartoon I'd seen once as a kid, which weren't helped by the thud his body made as it finally hit the ground. It had reminded me of a movie sound effect. I half expected him to laugh or comment on it, but he did neither.

He was just still.

CHAPTER THIRTY-ONE

That had to be the most anticlimactic resolution to a situation ever. I continued to lie sprawled on the ground panting for a while, though what I was waiting for, I couldn't tell you. It wasn't until my arms started to tremble and ache that I even realized I was still clutching the gun—still had the trigger depressed, in fact—and I let out a huge, shaky breath as I slowly eased my grip. The sound of the hammer de-cocking was loud in the sudden stillness, and I looked around to be sure the noise hadn't roused someone else. I don't know why I even bothered. If the gunshots hadn't summoned anyone, I don't know what made me think that innocuous little click would. But I looked just the same.

I eased myself into a more upright position and tucked the weapon into the back waistband of my pants. It felt too warm against my skin, but that might just have been my imagination. After I was sure it would stay put and not fall out the second I moved, I unsteadily got to my feet. The process was sluggish and oh-so-painful, and I had to force myself not to cry out by clenching my teeth.

My breathing was labored, and my heart was pounding, but a sick, cloying sort of dread was bubbling up out of my stomach to splatter against the back of my throat. Oh, God, what had I just done? I glanced at Crash's prone body, but the only answer I received was his empty eyes staring at me accusingly. My gut rolled, and my mouth watered, and I heaved a little as though I were going to vomit.

"Okay," I whispered to myself. "Okay, okay, okay. You can do this."

I took as deep a breath as my aching ribs would allow and shifted my gaze back and forth between Crash and Seth, hyperalert for even the tiniest sign of movement from either of them. Crash was unnaturally still, which I supposed was to be expected after taking five bullets to center mass. The only sign of movement I saw from Seth was the gentle rise and fall of his back as he breathed. But I still didn't trust any of it.

Making sure to keep Seth in my field of vision, I shuffled over toward Crash's body. I kept expecting him to cough or gurgle or sit up and tell me to go fuck myself or something, but all he did was lie there. It was creepy as all get-out.

I gave both of them a wide berth—more than two arm lengths— as I moved. If they did try something, I wanted at least a little time to react. The suspense of expectation had me wound up tighter than a spool of dental floss, and I couldn't help reflecting that this was why I hated horror movies. This waiting for the proverbial other shoe to drop was driving me nuts.

It took me a bit, what with the obsessive checking on Crash and Seth and trying to keep my ears tuned for the slightest hint of motion anywhere in the warehouse, but I finally made it over to where the gun had landed after Crash fell.

This is it, I thought to myself. This is the part of the movie where we see that the guy's been playing possum. This is where he jumps me, and I scream like a small child and fall on my ass. My heart was lurching, and the air was lodged tight in my throat as I bent down to retrieve the weapon, making sure to keep my gaze on both men at once. I was sweating even more now, which made my palms slick. I wiped them on my pants as I reached out for the gun.

The instant my fingers brushed against the metal—still warm from Crash's skin—I snagged it as fast as the bounds of human physics would allow and scrambled back out of reach. I exhaled against the agony moving that quickly had wrought and then let out a relieved sigh when I registered that Crash hadn't tried to ambush me.

Okay. That part was over. I now had both guns. Well, both guns that I knew about. I narrowed my eyes and glared back and forth between the men suspiciously. Shit. Now I had to search each of them to make sure neither was further armed. I wrinkled my nose at the thought and took my time unloading the weapon I'd just retrieved off the ground. Then, for good measure, I dismantled it and tossed all the pieces as far as I could into different parts of the room.

Pursing my lips, I glanced back and forth between Seth and Crash, wondering where to start. Though I hadn't verified it yet, Crash was most likely dead. So, he'd probably be the easiest to search. However, it also meant he was the least likely of the two to try anything, so maybe I should leave him be for the moment. Hmm. What to do?

After considerable deliberation, I decided to start with Seth. He was still lying face down on the ground with his hands cuffed behind his back, just like I'd left him, and his eyes were still closed. But that didn't necessarily mean he was unconscious.

As quickly as I was able, I strode over and dropped the full force of my weight onto his right shoulder with my knee. He didn't react; not a grunt, not a groan, not a cry, nothing. I regarded that as a good sign, but I still didn't want to take any chances. Despite the pain in my torso, I leaned down and firmly gripped one of his cuffed wrists and torqued it back in an effort to control him should he attempt to move. I held my breath and waited. Still, he did nothing.

Keeping my eye on Crash, I executed the quickest search-incident-to-arrest I'd ever performed. It wasn't my most thorough, and I was positive that everyone I'd ever worked with would have something to say if they'd seen how sloppy it was, but in the interest of both time and physical comfort, I needed to do it as quickly as possible.

All the things I'd discovered during my previous search of Seth's pockets—change, a set of keys, a cell phone—were still strewn on the ground near his body. The change I left alone. The keys I tossed across the room. But the phone I slipped into my own pocket. I'd need it in a few minutes, since I had no idea what'd happened to mine.

Having completed that task, I struggled to my feet and took a moment to get used to, then absorb, the fresh waves of pain that washed over me. A part of me wanted to find some reflective surface—a mirror, a window, Seth's cell phone camera—to assess the damage that had been done to my face, but that would have to wait. First, I had to check on Crash.

Trying to watch Crash's body while keeping a wary eye on Seth's still form, I crept across the room. I was becoming colder and colder by degrees the nearer I got to him, and I was unsure whether the adrenaline I'd been flying on was wearing off or whether another, darker reason was at play.

I was trembling all over, and I stood there staring down at Crash for a long time, trying to summon the courage to touch him. I didn't want to, and I could probably get away with not doing this. Standing this close to him, gazing at him unable to look away, I could see that all five shots had truly hit him center mass. My shot grouping was the size of a half dollar. The odds that he could survive that damage were nonexistent. I'd probably have a better chance of hitting that billion-dollar jackpot than he did of making it out of this alive. But if I were wrong, if he had somehow managed to live and had a weapon, it could end very badly for me. At the end of the day, I couldn't compromise my own safety for the sake of my comfort.

Gritting my teeth against the sudden rebellion of my stomach, I took a huge breath and forced myself to kneel on Crash's shoulder and wrangle his limp arm into a position of control. Once I was comfortable that he wouldn't be able to do much damage even if he were alive, I frisked him in record time. Then I pressed my fingertips to his carotid artery and held my breath. Time seemed to crawl like a cartoon rabbit stranded in the desert who'd just seen an oasis. I kept waiting to feel a thump. Hell, even a feeble nudge would have been welcome. But there was nothing.

I dropped his arm, wincing at the dull thud it made as it hit the ground, and sank back on my haunches. I was still kneeling right next to him, and a part of me was internally screaming at myself to move, but nothing was happening. I wasn't sure why. But it was almost like I wasn't really *there* inside myself, like I was watching something happen from someone else's point of view. It was as horrifying as it was fascinating.

My skin felt cold and clammy and somehow too big, and an ominous buzzing was rattling the inside of my skull. I have no idea how long I sat there, but the tingling in my legs as they fell asleep finally compelled me to move.

Getting to my feet made me expend a great deal of energy. More than I would have thought possible. And I was suddenly completely wiped out. My ribs were killing me—I couldn't stop speculating whether they were broken and if deadly shards were shredding my delicate vital organs each time I moved or took a breath—and the skin on my face could easily have beaten out Death Valley as the hottest place on earth. I tried to push all that to the back of my mind as I took a few steps back to survey the carnage.

Satisfied—or was it sickened?—that neither Seth nor Crash was an immediate threat, I heaved a huge sigh, though it wasn't one of relief. Really, I think it was just the only way I could expel air at that point. I was shaking worse than ever, but perhaps I was now in some sort of shock. Emotional. Physical. Maybe some sort of super-hybrid of both. It was tough to tell. I became aware that I was light-headed, which I didn't think was a good sign.

I pressed Seth's phone to my ear with a vibrating hand and held my breath as I listened to the phone ring. It sounded so far away. And Jesus, this was taking forever. What the hell were all the operators—

"Nine-one-one. What's your emergency?"

I tried to speak through the sudden rush of relief, but the only thing that came out was a weird, hoarse sort of croak, so I cleared my throat and tried again. "Hello. My name is Special Agent Ryan O'Connor. I work for the United States Secret Service in the New York Field Office. I'm involved in an undercover operation, and it sort of went awry. I don't know where I am, but I'm going to need an ambulance."

"Okay, Agent O'Connor. We're going to get someone right over to you. Please just stay on the line. Are you injured?"

I paused as I considered that question for a moment. Technically, the answer to that question was yes, but that wasn't why I'd asked for an ambulance. I'd asked because I wanted transport for Crash's body, but I hadn't wanted to say on a recorded line that he was dead. I knew how this worked. I was already under investigation by the NYPD for one alleged murder. The last thing I needed was these 9-1-1 tapes surfacing and showing that I'd admitted I'd killed him, self-defense aside.

"I am, yes. But not that badly. I don't think. Okay. I guess I don't really know. I could be." Shit. I was rambling. I needed to get it together. I clenched my free hand into a fist at my side. "I've got two targets here who are unresponsive. One sustained several GSWs to the chest. Aside from putting pressure on the wounds, I don't see anything here with which to administer any sort of helpful first aid."

"That's fine, Agent O'Connor. Can you tell me how the victim sustained the gunshot wounds?"

No way in hell was I answering that question. Instead, I said, "I'm also going to need you to send marked units to secure the crime scene, but please make sure you tell them that there's an undercover federal agent inside, she has no identification on her, and she's armed. Can you do that for me?"

Sure, it sounded like I was talking down to her, but I needed to make absolutely certain she'd understood what I'd said and passed the message correctly. I'd once gotten into a minor fender bender and had specifically told the 9-1-1 operator that there were *no* injuries on scene. But the next thing I knew, an ambulance was rolling up, lights and sirens blasting. When I'd asked why, the driver told me they'd been informed by dispatch that there were people in need of medical attention. So I wasn't going to take any chances now. I could end up shot. Again.

"Absolutely, Agent O'Connor. I'm tracking your location now, and I'll be sending an ambulance and some marked units right away."

"Thank you, ma'am," I mumbled. Or at least I thought I did. I meant to, at any rate. But all the adrenaline that'd been sustaining me throughout this ordeal seemed to have vanished. I was baby-bird weak, and I just wanted to sit down. For a moment, I considered the chairs Seth and I had been using before, but both of them had been toppled during the struggle, and the idea of walking over there and setting one upright was exhausting. Better to just sit on the ground.

Immediately on the heels of the idea, I collapsed. My body seemed to have been awaiting permission, and the instant my mind had even deliberated giving it, my limbs took advantage. My legs buckled, and

I sat down. Hard. With all my aches and pains, I'd sort of expected it to hurt more, though perhaps the absence of pain should indicate something that I needed to pay attention to. Honestly, I was having trouble caring about much of anything now. No longer upright, I just wanted to go to sleep. But I couldn't. So, failing that, I stared through Crash's twisted body, not really seeing it most of the time, my mind adrift on a surprisingly tranquil sea of nothingness.

When I'd fallen down, I'd dropped my hand to my side. I'd felt the impact of knuckles against concrete, but the sensation had been numbed by what I could only assume was shock. Even though the phone was now on the ground, I could still hear the 9-1-1 operator talking to me, trying to get my attention, and while it occurred to me to answer, I didn't have the strength. Even sitting upright was becoming something of an effort. Was the room moving? Or was I? It was tough to tell.

As I continued to sit there, my eyes grew heavier and heavier, and each blink was longer and slower than the one before it. The floor—cold and dirty and debris-laden as it was—suddenly seemed so inviting. It couldn't hurt to lie down. Just for a second. I gritted my teeth against the moan I couldn't remember why I wanted to hold in and eased myself slowly to the ground, millimeter by agonizing millimeter. I couldn't decide whether I wanted to be on my back or on my stomach. Neither sounded appealing, so I settled for resting on my side. From the position, the phone was near my head, so I could hear the 9-1-1 operator much more clearly, though I still didn't have it in me to answer her.

Instead, I stared at Crash, memorizing the color of the stubble on his chin and the way his jaw had gone slack, the weird angle at which his limbs had fallen, and the glassy emptiness of his eyes. The longer I looked at him, the more I wanted to glance away and the less I seemed able to do it. It was as if my eyes were incapable of seeing anything else. My stomach rolled, and the only thing that kept me from vomiting was the knowledge that the sort of muscle contractions required for that action would hurt like a motherfucker.

And that was how the NYPD found me when they eventually arrived.

CHAPTER THIRTY-TWO

I don't remember a whole lot about their entry into the building, and what little I do recall is hazy at best. There was a lot of noise, a lot of shouting, but I couldn't seem to bring myself to pay much attention to it. When the ESU team flipped me over onto my stomach and cuffed me, I didn't even bother to protest. For an instant, I was annoyed that the 9-1-1 operator had not passed along my message, but then it occurred to me that even if she had, the ESU officers had no way to know I was telling the truth. From a safety standpoint, it made sense for them to cuff me until they could verify who I was. So I didn't fight them. I didn't say anything. I just closed my eyes and let out a contented sigh and made it a point not to wonder whether they were doing the same thing to Crash.

I don't remember much about the ambulance ride to the hospital, either. Or how I got in there, for that matter. One second, I was being shouted at and having my face ground into a concrete floor, and the next I'd opened my eyes and realized I was on a gurney that was being unloaded into the ER. I squinted against the bright lights as I was wheeled through the doors and then hissed at the sting the motion caused.

Orders were barked and status updates were given, though I couldn't imagine the din had anything to do with me. I mean, I was conscious. Well, more or less. And I could talk and move of my own accord. Or at least I had been able to earlier. Now it seemed like too much effort. For example, I didn't even have it in me to be too curious about what all the fuss was about. I just wanted to close my eyes and not open them again.

Which I must have done, and for a long time, too, because when I did open them again—or the one that wasn't swollen shut—I was in a private room. I frowned as I glanced around, inspecting my environment. I wasn't hooked up to any machinery, which I took to be a good sign. The last time I'd been here, the beeping had woken me up. No, wait. That'd been the time before. Maybe. I thought back. Hmm. Was it bad that my hospital trips were so numerous they were starting to run together? I didn't imagine it was good.

Regardless, I decided that not being hooked up to anything— whether good or bad from a medical point of view—would at least help get me the hell out of there. At least no alarms would sound as I attempted to make my escape. I let out a long, shaky sigh and tried to lift my hand to touch my face to assess the damage, but it wouldn't move. Instead, my efforts were rewarded with a harsh clang and a sharp pain in my wrist.

I glanced down as I tugged again with the same result. Sure enough, I was handcuffed to the bed. I groaned and let my arm fall. This was not my day. You'd think I would be content to just lie there until someone came in. I mean, it wasn't the most uncomfortable position I'd ever been in. It wasn't even in the top ten. But somehow knowing I couldn't leave only made it that much more imperative that I go.

Despite the pain the motion caused in my wrists, I rattled the handcuffs a few times, trying to summon someone. I waited several agonizing moments for the door to open, and when it didn't, I rattled again, harder, gritting my teeth against the discomfort. Either no one heard me, or no one cared.

Frowning, I cast around for some way to alert someone. I didn't have a phone. I tried calling out, but that didn't help anything. Finally, I settled for repeatedly jabbing at the call button that was supposed to beckon a nurse. Seconds dragged by with no response, but they underestimated my persistence. I had nowhere else to be, so I just kept at it until someone appeared.

It felt like forever, but finally an annoyed-looking woman in scrubs poked her head in my door. "Yes?"

I tried to smile, but that only made my face burn, so I quit and settled for attempting to look as innocent as possible. I held up my bound hand as high as it would go. "Any chance we can get someone in here to take these off?"

She rolled her eyes. "Not my department."

"I understand that," I said, making sure my tone didn't evidence the impatience burning a hole in my gut. "Would you mind sending in an officer who could? Please?"

She rolled her eyes again, harder this time, and a rude noise escaped the back of her throat. She disappeared without another word, and I stared at the doorway, waiting for someone to take her place. The longer it remained closed, the more anxious I began to feel. The skin all over my entire body started to itch, and I couldn't stop myself from yanking on the cuff, trying to pull it off. Panic was swelling inside me, and I was on the verge of dislocating my thumb so I could get this thing off when I heard a noise outside.

The door swung open, and a uniformed officer, who didn't look thrilled to have been summoned, appeared. I stopped fiddling with my bonds and shifted, trying to sit up straighter. "What?" he demanded, sounding pissed.

Despite the ache in my face, I frowned. I got that guard duty in a hospital sucked—I'd done it several times myself—but it didn't justify rudeness. Whatever happened to the NYPD motto "Courtesy, Professionalism, Respect?" Maybe if I were friendly first, that would help. "Hi. How are you today?"

He didn't even acknowledge my question. "What?" he said again, his tone somehow even harsher.

Okay. Pleasantries were out. Straight to the point it was. "My name is Special Agent Ryan O'Connor. I work for the United States Secret Service out of the New York Field Office."

He rolled his eyes and didn't even try to conceal his scoff. "Yeah, right, kid."

Kid? Come on. Who was he kidding? I knew I looked younger than my actual age, but how old did he think I was? "I'm serious. I'm a federal agent who was in the middle of a deep-cover operation. Hence my lack of identification. I explained the situation to the 9-1-1 dispatcher when I called. I'm sure she passed along the message." I wasn't sure about that, but voicing that opinion didn't seem like the best idea.

He shrugged, uninterested. "Dunno. I wasn't on the entry team. That was ESU. I was just told to guard you."

I had to remind myself to keep calm, but his refusal to take me seriously was starting to grate on my nerves. "I understand that. But I'm sure if you just call the New York Field Office, you'll be able to verify my identity."

"Not my department."

I ground my teeth together, ignoring the ache in my jaw. "Okay. Can you please tell me whose department that is, so we can get this cleared up?"

"No." Without another word, he turned and left, slamming the door behind him.

I stared after him for a long moment, feeling nothing before the reality of the situation set in. Shit. Now I was pissed *and* panicked. I'd never thought of myself as phobic before, but not being able to move from the bed was really starting to get to me. I'm sure it didn't help that this was happening so close to me being forcibly restrained to a chair. Fuck. I needed to calm down and think this through.

I sat very still and mentally inventoried my aches and pains. Most of my injuries appeared confined to my upper body, specifically my ribs and my face. And they'd cuffed only one hand to the railing. It was the hand I'd had to wrench the cuff off in the warehouse, so it was sore, but it wasn't incapacitating. Which meant I was free to stand. Okay. I could work with that.

Trying to be as quiet as possible so as not to call Officer Friendly back into the room, I eased myself off the side of the bed. I didn't like that I had to twist around to ensure that my back wasn't to the door, but it would do.

After holding my breath and remaining frozen for a long moment waiting to see whether anyone had heard me, I started taking stock of my available assets. A glance down told me that my shoelaces had been removed. Since that was standard operating procedure for a prisoner, I wasn't surprised. Those wouldn't have been useful anyway, so I discarded the information. I also checked my pockets, hoping to discover anything I could use to get someone's attention or assistance, but I'd obviously been very thoroughly searched, so there was nothing to find.

Huffing and scowling, I turned and started visually scouring the room. I didn't see anything in reach that would be at all helpful. Maybe that was for the best. I doubted the officer would be amused if he came back in and I was out of my restraints. But I was disappointed to note that they'd thought to remove the phone, as well. So much for trying to get ahold of Allison or Rico.

Feeling defeated, I flopped back onto the bed and returned to repeatedly pressing the button to call the nurse. She was either not at her station or she thought it would be a good idea to engage me in a test of wills because it took me pushing it a hundred and seventeen times for her to storm in.

"What?" she bellowed at me.

I smiled at her as sweetly as I was able. "I'd like to make my phone call now, please."

"Your what?"

"As a prisoner, I have a right to one phone call. I'd like to exercise that right now."

"That's not up to me," she snapped.

"Well, then, why don't you ask the officer standing next to you to get me a telephone so I can contact my attorney?" I made my voice a little louder. "And please remind him that I will be counting the seconds until he complies so I can pass along that information to my lawyer, the media, and his boss."

That'd been low, and no way in hell would I ever talk to the press about anything, but it'd seemed like good leverage to get him to act quickly. It must have worked, too, because barely thirty seconds had elapsed before he stomped into the room with a hospital landline in his hand and slammed it much harder than necessary onto the bedside table. He clomped out without a word and flung the door shut with a spectacular crash.

I grinned and shook my head at his theatrics before unwinding the cord and fighting to reach the port to plug it in. I wondered why he'd left me to my own devices to make as many phone calls as I wanted, but that wasn't my problem. I lifted the receiver, half expecting to hear nothing, and was relieved when the low hum of a dial tone greeted me.

First, I tried Allison's personal cell phone. When she didn't answer, I tried her work cell. And when that yielded negative results, I tried her desk. No answer. Hmm. I frowned. Where the hell could she be? Since I was so isolated from the rest of my normal life, I had no way to know. She could be in the bathroom or on a protection assignment or in a meeting or out to dinner. It occurred to me then that I didn't even have any idea what time it was, let alone what day. Shit. She could be anywhere doing anything. And I couldn't afford to just keep trying her until she answered. The phone could be taken away from me at any minute.

Next, I tried Rico's phones in reverse order: first his desk, then his work cell, and then his personal. With each ring that sounded in my ear that went unheeded, my panic ratcheted up another few notches. Where the hell was everybody? If I didn't get out of here soon, I was going to break something. I'd just about given up on him and moved to Meaghen when he finally answered. "Hello?"

"Rico, it's Ryan."

"Ryan?" I could hear his confusion. "Thank God. Are you okay? Where are you?"

I glanced at the phone where the hospital information was listed. Good thing it was on there, too. Otherwise, I wouldn't have known what to tell him. I doubted that calling either the nurse or the officer back in here to obtain my exact location would have gone well for me.

"I'm in Bellevue. The phone says I'm in room 312, but that could be wrong. I don't know."

"Wait. You're where?"

"I'm at the hospital, and I've been handcuffed to the bed."

"Why?"

I sighed and closed my eyes. "Things went pear-shaped, I had to call the cops, and they don't believe I'm an agent and won't let me out."

"I'll be right there," he said before he hung up.

I leaned over to set the receiver back into its cradle and snagged the TV remote before settling in for what I assumed was going to be a long wait. Traffic from Brooklyn was almost always a bitch, and I had to remind myself not to freak out and to just give him time. This would get sorted eventually.

I hadn't even made it through all the available channels in my search for a suitable distraction before I heard arguing outside my door. I sat up as much as I was able and focused all my attention on the conversation in the hall.

I couldn't make out any of what was being said, but it turned out not to matter. It wasn't long before the door to my room was flung open, and Rico was roughly shouldering the officer out of his way to get to me.

"That was quick," I said, surprised. What the hell? Had he helicoptered over?

He ignored me. "Are you okay?"

I shrugged and winced at the pain that shot through my shoulders. "I've been worse."

He shot a dark glare toward the officer, who was hovering in the doorway looking uncertain about how to proceed, and then moved to my side and reached for the handcuffs.

"Sir, you can't do that," the officer said.

Rico's expression stopped him cold. "I can, and I will. What the hell is wrong with you? You left an injured federal agent handcuffed to a hospital bed?" He shook his head and dug a handcuff key out of the pocket of his jeans.

The officer was distraught. "Sir, the ESU team found her in a warehouse with two other men, one of whom was unconscious, the other of whom was dead."

Rico shot me an astonished glance but kept whatever thoughts he might have had on that subject to himself for the time being. In lieu of comment, he undid the cuff around my wrist, and the second I was free, I started massaging the chafed skin.

The officer went on. "She had no identification on her, and there was no way to know what happened in that warehouse. We needed to cuff her. It's SOP."

Rico jabbed an angry finger in my direction. "Look at her. She's been through the wringer. Her face is an absolute mess, and she has abrasions on both her wrists, which suggests she was restrained at some point. I think even you could figure out what happened."

"We couldn't take any chances."

"Did she identify herself to you?"

"What?"

"Rico," I said, trying to stop him.

He ignored me and continued trying to incinerate the officer with the force of his glare. "Did she tell you she was a federal agent?"

"I don't know what she told the entry team."

"That isn't what I asked you."

"Rico." I tried again.

"Did she tell you who she was when she got here?" Rico demanded.

The officer took a deep breath and hesitated a beat before nodding reluctantly.

"Why, then, was she still handcuffed to this bed?"

"We had no way to verify her identity."

"Did you call the field office?"

The officer's face turned red, and he averted his eyes.

"Did she ask you to?" Rico asked, his tone icy.

The officer swallowed hard but didn't respond.

Rico let out a snort of derision. "What precinct do you turn out of?"

"Rico," I said softly, putting a hand on his arm as I stood. "It's okay. He was just doing his job."

"No. It is *not* okay." Rico snarled that comment, taking me by surprise. I didn't think I'd ever seen him so angry. "He should have tried to verify your identity."

"It doesn't matter. You're here. How'd you get here so fast, anyway? What's going on?"

Rico's anger evaporated and alchemized into something not unlike fear. His eyes grew wide. Now it was his turn to look away, and he cleared his throat. "Let me go get your discharge paperwork and talk to this idiot's supervisor to make sure he's not going to try to tackle you when we leave."

Warning bells were clanging loudly inside my head. "Rico, what happened?"

"Just give me a minute," he said as he fled the room.

"Rico," I called after him.

"I'm sorry," the officer muttered before he went after Rico, closing the door behind him.

I frowned at the door through which they'd just disappeared, and then I started pacing. Part of me debated just making an escape, but at least one of them was probably within eyesight of the room, so I doubted I'd get very far. The longer I was alone, the more anxious I became until I was almost ready to attempt to climb out the window.

The door opened just as I was considering seeing how much wiggle room the window would afford me and how far a drop it would be to the ground. I whirled around, a denial that I was up to anything ready to trip off my lips. It fell off and disintegrated when I was enveloped in a forceful hug before I even saw who'd just entered the room.

"Ooof," I wheezed as my sister squeezed my sensitive ribs. "Careful. I was maimed there."

Rory pulled back and scowled at me before poking me hard in the stomach.

"Ouch!" I said, rubbing the new sore spot. "What the hell was that for?"

"For being an idiot, that's what! And the next time you go undercover with a group of people who are going to try to murder you, you'd better tell them to finish the job. Because if they don't, I will."

I frowned. "Well, that's not very nice." But the rest of my words were cut off as Rory flung herself at me again and embraced me tighter than before. I coughed under my breath as the air was forced out of me.

"Don't you ever do that again," Rory whispered in my ear. "I'm serious. I'm tired of coming to work and finding out you almost died."

"I love you, too," I said, returning the hug.

Rory pulled back enough to be able to look at me and started shining a penlight that she'd produced from the pocket of her white lab coat into my good eye, the one that wasn't swollen shut. "Are you okay?"

I blinked and batted her hand away before taking a step back. "Stop that. I'm fine."

"You don't look fine," she said bluntly. "You look like shit."

"Nice to see you, too."

Rory was not amused. "Seriously, what the hell happened to you?"

I thought about how to explain it before going with "Difference of opinion."

Rory pursed her lips and then cupped my chin between her hands. She gently turned my face this way and that as she examined me. I didn't even want to know the magnitude of the damage. By her expression, it was extensive. "Must've been some serious difference of opinion to warrant all of this."

"It was." I started to say "You should see the other guy," but I stopped before I could get the thought out. I didn't want to go into how bad it had gotten because then I'd have to tell her about Crash, and I wasn't ready.

"You need to see someone from plastics."

"Hmm?" I murmured, my mind still on the warehouse. I knew Crash was dead—which meant I'd be getting a visit from the NYPD soon—but what about Seth? He'd made it, right? I wasn't even sure who to ask. I wasn't positive I cared.

"You don't want these to scar," Rory said.

I wrenched my mind back to the present. "Oh. That bad, huh?"

"Bad enough that they gave you stitches. Although I don't know why they didn't call someone from plastics down here to do that initially."

"How do you know they didn't?"

"The sutures would be better."

"Oh."

Rory released me, but she continued to study me without taking a step back. "Do you want to tell me why you look like you were beat to hell?"

"Probably because I was."

"Probably?"

I shrugged. "I was unconscious for most of it, so I can't really be sure. But it seems plausible. You know, considering how I feel."

"Great," she muttered under her breath, rolling her eyes.

"How did you know I was here?"

"Hmm? Oh, the nurse told me."

I raised my eyebrows in shock but dropped them again at the sting the movement caused. "Really? I'm pretty sure she hates me."

Rory shrugged. "She loves me."

I smiled wryly. "Of course she does. Seriously, how did you find out? I know the nurse didn't tell you because that would be a HIPAA violation. And I know how you feel about those."

Rory's expression was guilty, and my heart shuddered and dropped. Before I had a chance to press her on why she looked like I'd just caught her watching furry porn, the door banged open again, and Rico stalked back in. He exchanged an uncomfortable glance with my sister, and then both of them made it a point not to look at me.

"Okay, *what* is going on?" I'd reached the end of my patience with these cloak-and-dagger shenanigans.

"Did you tell her?" Rico asked Rory quietly, looking hopeful.

"Tell me what?"

Rory shook her head. "I was just about to."

"Tell me *what*?"

Rory did meet my eyes then, and the sadness and remorse I saw there almost made my knees buckle. Whatever she was about to say, I could tell I wasn't going to like it. She took a deep breath and licked her lips before taking a step closer and putting a gentle hand on my arm. The room around me started to spin, and the ringing in my ears almost drowned her out when she finally spoke.

"Ryan. It's Allison."

CHAPTER THIRTY-THREE

It took a long time for her words to sink in, and when they finally did, I doubted I'd heard her correctly. She seemed very far away, and I wasn't sure my voice was loud enough to traverse the distance when I whispered, "What?"

She put her other hand on my opposite arm, and I felt her fingers digging into my flesh, but the sensation seemed at a remove. "Let's get you a clean shirt," Rory was saying. "This one's covered in blood. Wait. Why is this even still on you? Why aren't you in a hospital gown?"

I didn't know the answer to that question, and I didn't care. "Forget my shirt. What happened to Allison?" My heart was heavy yet racing at the same time, and I was certain I was about to add vomit to the numerous stains marring my clothing. "Please tell me she's okay."

Rory slid her hands up my arms and cupped my jaw in her palms again, winding her fingers into the hair behind my ears. "Ryan. Look at me." She tightened her grip until I did as she asked, and then she nodded. "Breathe."

I knew she was trying to calm me, but she was only making me more anxious. I shook my head as I wrestled my way out of her grip, ignoring the stabbing pain inside my skull. My stomach was rolling, and I clenched my jaw against the nausea bubbling in the back of my throat. "Rory. Just tell me what happened."

Rory glanced at Rico, who I'd forgotten was even there. He cleared his throat and took a step forward, palming the back of his neck. His expression was as despondent as I'd ever seen it. He was clearly having trouble finding the words he wanted, and his hesitation wasn't helping my apprehension.

"Allison is going to be fine," he said, glancing to Rory. She nodded, and the knot in my chest loosened slightly.

"Where is she?"

"She's here," Rico told me. "That's how I got here so fast."

My legs went out from under me, and it's a good thing I was standing so close to the chair because I went down hard. The landing was forceful enough that my teeth clacked together, and I felt a definite sting in my tailbone. The air fled my lungs in a painful rush, and I put one hand to my side as though that would somehow lessen the ache. "Is she sick?"

Rico swallowed hard, and his brow furrowed. "She started bleeding at work. A lot."

I frowned as much as I was able without reigniting the fire in my face. "Bleeding? Why?"

Rico sighed and glanced at the ceiling, as though he could find the explanation he wanted to provide there. He shoved his hands into his pockets, his expression was thoughtful as he stared.

"There was a complication," Rory said, taking over. She stepped up next to me and rested a gentle hand on my shoulder.

"*Leis an leanbh?*" I whispered, trying to keep my voice low and asking the question in the childish Gaelic-hybrid she and I used as kids so as not to reveal Allison's secret to Rico. He might already know, but if he didn't, I wasn't going to be the one to tell him.

Rory nodded, her eyes brimming with sadness, and I tried to swallow through the lump in my throat. I took a shaky breath and wiped my trembling hands on the top of my thighs. I licked my lips and winced at the slash of pain. Then I set my jaw and stood.

"I want to see her," I said to Rory.

"I'm not sure that's a good idea," Rory said, her expression a mask of uncertainty.

I didn't even bother to reply. I just pushed her out of the way and barreled into the hall. If she and Rico weren't going to help me, I'd just have to find her on my own. I didn't care if I had to barge into every room in this godforsaken hospital to do it. I was going to see my girlfriend.

Rory caught up to me, but to her credit, she didn't try to stop me, for which I was grateful. I wasn't too keen on the idea of tossing my sister into a wall, but in that moment, I would have done it without a thought.

That didn't prevent her from trying to reason with me, though. "Ryan, please. Think about this."

"Think about what?" I demanded as I stalked over to the nurses' station and glared around, searching for anyone to assist me as my frustration threatened to scald me from the inside. Of course that damn nurse had decided now was the time for her break. That or she feared me and had hidden. Like that would help my mood. Making a rude noise in the back of my throat, I went around to the other side of the desk.

"What are you doing?" Rory glanced up and down the hall like she expected an alarm to sound.

"What does it look like I'm doing?" I grumbled as I studied the computer monitor. I narrowed my good eye as I perused the screen in front of me, trying to figure out which buttons I needed to push or tabs I needed to click in order to locate Allison. Too many things had been happening *to* me lately, not because of me. I hadn't directly influenced any of the recent events in my life. I was like a stick being tossed around by class 5 rapids. I'd lost control of my own existence at some point, and now I was determined to take it back. This step—making a deliberate attempt to find Allison despite other people insisting I shouldn't—might have been a small one, but it was a start.

"You can't be back there," Rory said, her voice only marginally louder yet somehow shriller.

"Clearly I can." Hmm. Maybe this was it. I began opening tabs in search of the one that would provide the information I was looking for.

"Do you have any idea how many laws you're breaking right now?"

"No. How many? I'd say probably at least three," I murmured as I read. No. This application wasn't helpful. I minimized the window and started scanning the icons on the desktop.

"Okay," Rory whispered as she grabbed me by the elbow and removed me from behind the desk. "Okay. I'll take you to her. Will you please just stop?"

I studied her for a moment as I attempted to determine whether she was sincere or trying to placate me. The offer seemed genuine, and when I detected no hint of deception in her expression, I bobbed my head once. "All right. Let's go."

Rory was silent as she led me down the hall, and I had only a brief instant to wonder where Rico had gone and whether we should retrieve him before a nearly crippling feeling of dread threatened to drown me. My head was spinning again, and I was sweating yet cold. I smacked my lips a few times to attempt to banish the horrible taste of blood from my tongue, but it didn't work.

Rory was striding down the corridor several paces in front of me, and I had to do a quick hop-step to get close enough to her to be able to snag her sleeve. My arm seemed way too long for my body as I reached out, and I couldn't feel the fabric underneath my fingertips. I tried to say her name as I grabbed her, but all that came out was a weak, pathetic whimper.

Rory spun around, her face pinched in annoyance, but she blinked when she looked at me, and I'm not sure what she saw, but whatever it was, it was enough to make her immediately soften. She took a step closer and cupped my elbow in her palm. "Hey."

I nodded at her unasked question, and the walls behind her danced and swayed.

"You look like you're going to pass out."

I kind of felt like it, too, but I wasn't sure I had it in me to form the words to tell her that. My head was swimming, but it seemed way too big for my body, like I was wearing a gigantic helmet and looking at my sister through the tiny eye holes. I wiped the beads of sweat from my forehead with the edge of my hand and licked my lips.

"Is she really going to be okay?" I managed to croak.

Rory's eyes filled with anguish, which was counter to her reply, which was to bite her lower lip and nod. "Yes. She will be. In time."

"What happened to her?" I asked, knowing that she was leaving something out. Something huge.

Rory hesitated and looked conflicted. "I think she should be the one to tell you."

I tried to swallow, but it hurt, and the air around me was too heavy and too moist to be able to breathe properly. Gasping like I was hurt like a bitch. Had my lung collapsed again? I thought I remembered someone telling me that because it'd happened once, it would be much easier for it to happen a second time. Or had I read that someplace? Hmm. They'd have looked for that, though, right? When I came in, even if they'd thought I was a perp, they'd have given me a thorough examination. Wouldn't they?

"Ryan?"

I started, and the resultant stab of pain I felt on the heels of my reflexive sharp inhalation did nothing to alleviate my concerns about the possible state of my internal organs. "Yeah?"

"You okay?"

Was I? I didn't know. Though, dreading it as I was, I knew that seeing Allison with my own eyes and confirming that she was more or less all right would help. "Sure. Just thinking."

"You don't have to go in."

I frowned at her, puzzled. "Huh?"

She nodded in the direction of the door to her right. "To see Allison. You don't have to go in right now if you're not ready. She doesn't know you're here, so she isn't expecting you. You have all the time you need to collect yourself. Besides, I'm not sure seeing you in this state is really going to help her."

"We're here?" Was it possible for a heart to both sink and soar at the same time? I wasn't sure. Maybe I had a concussion, and it was clouding my judgment. But they'd have mentioned that, too, I imagined. At least, they probably would have if I'd actually seen a medical professional. Since I'd regained consciousness, I hadn't spoken to anyone except that angry nurse, and she hadn't been in the mood to tell me anything. And unlike the last time I'd been here—or was it the time before that?—Rory hadn't even glanced at my chart, so I couldn't rely on her for that sort of information.

I was getting lost in my thoughts again, which I recognized as an unconscious stalling technique, so I cleared my throat and nodded. The room spun again, and I stopped just short of reaching out to steady myself on the wall. I hoped Rory hadn't caught that slip, hoped that I hadn't swayed on my feet or that my eyes hadn't gone glassy, because then she'd have forced me back to bed, and I wouldn't have been able to see Allison at all.

I held my breath and waited to see what her response would be. Her expression indicated that she was conflicted, wary even, and maybe a touch sad, but she didn't appear to be on the verge of ordering me back to my room, so that was something. She knocked lightly on the door before turning the handle and easing it open.

The inside of the room was dark. No lights were burning, the TV wasn't on, and I didn't see even an ambient glow from a cell phone or a laptop. I strained against the dimness to make out any shapes at all, and after a moment, I was able to spot the bed. And after a bit more scrutiny, I saw the crumpled form huddled beneath the covers lying on top of the mattress.

My heart began a slow and dramatic freefall that seemed to go on for eternity. I kept waiting for the splat that normally came at the end, but there was none. It just continued falling and falling until I was scarcely able to breathe through my near panic. I glanced at Rory for reassurance, but her knitted brow and wire-tight posture did nothing to comfort me.

I opened my mouth to say something, but she shook her head and placed one hand on the small of my back. The gentle pressure she exerted said more than any uttered statement ever could. With one last look and a deep breath, I followed her unspoken direction and stepped into the room.

Rory closed the door behind me, and I froze, unwilling to move lest I knock something over and startle or wake Allison. I struggled to force my eye to pierce the blackness that surrounded me, so I'd at least be able to move, but it wasn't working. To push past my frustration, I made myself concentrate on the noise of my blood rushing through my ears and the sound of my own ragged breathing, and after a time, beyond that, the whisper-soft sniffles that told me Allison was crying.

Ah. *There* was the shuddering, wet, bone-crushing splat of my heart that I'd been anticipating. My chest nearly caved in at the intensity of it, and I touched my palm to my breastbone as though to reassure myself it was intact. I took a few tentative, shuffling steps forward while trying to be as silent as possible. Allison hadn't acknowledged my presence, so I couldn't be certain whether she'd even registered it, and I didn't want to frighten her.

Allison sniffled again, and I heard a quiet rustle of cloth as she shifted positions slightly. I continued to creep forward slowly. It took nigh on forever, but eventually, the front of my thigh brushed the foot of the bed. I reached out and ran my hand over the blankets to get a feel for the parameters of it before I eased my way up so I could be closer to her.

The instant my fingertips made light contact with the planes of her back, Allison let out a strangled sob. My eye burned with the exertion of holding back my own tears, and it was a struggle not to sniffle, but I didn't want Allison to know I was on the verge of crying. That would only make her feel worse. Instead, I tried to pretend that her obvious pain wasn't excruciating to me. But in that moment, I would have given anything to be able to take it on for her.

I took a long, slow, deep breath. "Hey, baby."

Any other words I might have wanted to utter lodged painfully in my throat. What was there to say that wouldn't sound trite or force her to relive the atrocity of the situation? Or both? I struggled to come up with something but failed. Instead, I resigned myself to sketching random patterns on her back with my fingertips while I waited.

I'm not sure the motion soothed her at all, but it must have calmed me, because I sort of zoned out and lost track of time. I had no idea how long we'd been sitting there in strained silence before she took a deep breath that indicated she was getting ready to speak.

My motions on her back faltered, and I had to force myself to start tracing again. I was torn between wanting her to say something—anything—and wanting her to remain silent so we could pretend the horrors that had befallen us didn't exist for just a little while longer.

"It's weird, you know?" Allison said, her voice a sort of strained croak.

"What is?"

She rolled over to face me and took my hand between hers, gripping it tight as though she were using it to remain tethered to the world, and if her hold slipped, she'd fly away. Her gaze darted to mine and then just as quickly flitted away.

"I'd never really thought much about having kids," she said with a small sniffle. "I hadn't pictured having them in my life. I think I'd have been fine never having children. I *will* be fine never having children. But in a strange way, I'm a little bit sad right now."

Oh, shit. That meant that—I couldn't even bring myself to think the words. I clenched my jaw and tried to staunch the welling of tears by repeating the phrase "beige carpet" over and over and over again in my head. Someone had once told me that was a guaranteed way to stop yourself from crying. In this moment, I wasn't sure the theory was sound. At any rate, it didn't seem to be helping me.

"Oh, Allison. I'm so sorry."

Allison looked back up at me then, her dark eyes watery even in the dim room. "Placenta previa."

I'd understood only one of those words. "Huh?"

"That's what happened. That's why I lost the baby." She took a deep breath. "It's rare to happen this early in a pregnancy, but it's not unheard of, apparently. And usually it resolves itself without ending in…"

"Oh."

"But not this time." Allison tried to smile at me—though whether it was an attempt to be brave or to appear reassuring, I couldn't tell— but I knew she was forcing it. "My age probably had something to do with it. At least that's what they said. But I think they're really just guessing at this point. One of those things, you know? Sometimes they just can't pinpoint why this happens."

I used my free hand to stroke her hair. What the hell do you say to something like that? I couldn't think of anything, so I just kept quiet and let her talk.

"On the bright side, we don't have to worry about this happening ever again."

Shit. Did that mean Allison couldn't have children? Ever? I mean, she was older than I was, which meant she was definitely very near if not at the end of her childbearing years. But the news featured stories all the time about women getting pregnant long after doctors said they shouldn't have been able to. However, some medical intervention might have been required in those cases. Since I hadn't planned on ever getting inseminated, I'd never paid any attention, so I wasn't sure. I'd have to check.

At any rate, even I knew the difference between choosing not to have children and having the choice taken away from you. That was pretty much human nature in any situation. It didn't always matter if there was something you didn't want to do. The second someone told you that you couldn't do it, the rules of the game changed.

"Hey." Allison nudged me.

"Huh?" Oh, God. I still wasn't sure what to say. What would be the most sensitive response? The one least likely to make her burst into tears or try to choke me to death with all these tubes and wires?

"This is where you chime in and ask whether that meant I was planning on sleeping with a man anytime soon."

"Oh. Uh…"

Allison rolled her eyes and smiled at me. "Come on, Ryan. It's not the end of the world. I'm alive, right? My arms and legs still work. I can still do my job. Life isn't going to change because of this."

I suspected that she was trying to convince herself rather than convince me, so I played along. Anything to make her happy. "That is true. And you're not saddled with Beau for the rest of your life."

A tiny smidgen of light seeped into Allison's eyes. "That is a *huge* upside."

Silence settled heavy between us, and I watched as that slight twinkle faded and winked out. I tried not to let my despair show, but seeing as how she hadn't yet commented on the stitches on my face, I suspected she wasn't quite as present in the here and now as she might otherwise have been. Stress and heartache will do that to a person. Still, just to be safe, I turned away and took longer than necessary dragging a nearby chair to the bedside. Then I sat and resumed holding her hand.

"Do I want to know what happened?" Allison asked after I'd gotten settled.

Ah. So she had noticed. I shouldn't have been surprised. She didn't miss a thing. But I didn't think now was the time to tell her how close I'd just come to dying. Again. "I can tell you later."

That Allison didn't press me was a testament to how draining the day had been for her. Or the strength of the pain medication she was on. But instead of utilizing her interrogation skills, or just flat-out demanding that I start talking, she yawned and said, "I wish they'd discharge me already. I feel fine."

I suspected that was the result of whatever cocktail of narcotics they had her on, but I didn't say that. "How long did they say you have to stay?"

"I think I can go home tomorrow. I've been here for almost twenty-four hours already," she said, closing her eyes.

My heart might as well have been pierced by a javelin at her words. That's how much it hurt to hear that she'd been dealing with this for that long without me. I closed my eyes and rubbed my forehead with my fingertips. "I'm so sorry I wasn't here for you."

"S'fine," Allison mumbled, patting my hand with the one of hers I wasn't holding. "I know you'd have come if you'd known."

I swallowed hard against the painful lump in my throat and nodded. "I would have. Absolutely. Even if I'd had to break cover or leave in the middle of something, I would have."

"Are you done now?" she whispered.

It was clear she was fighting sleep, and I somehow doubted she'd remember any of this conversation later, but I answered her anyway. "What? With the op?"

"Mmm-hmm."

"Yes, baby. I'm done now."

The corners of her lips turned up in a small smile. "Good."

"Yes," I told her, leaning down to brush my lips across her knuckles. "It is."

CHAPTER THIRTY-FOUR

I sat with Allison for a bit while she dozed. I probably could've gotten away with sneaking out, but I didn't want to leave her. For me more than for her. This whole experience had highlighted for me just how much I hated being apart from her as well as how awful it was to find out that she'd gone through something so traumatic without me by her side. Lingering in her room wouldn't undo any of that, but it didn't make me any more eager to leave.

When I'd finally forced myself back out into the hall, I saw Rory leaning against the wall, gnawing on a cuticle, a faraway look on her face. I leaned against the wall next to her, but she didn't appear to have noticed me, so I bumped her shoulder with my own. "Hey."

Rory blinked and looked over at me, obviously startled. "Hey. How is she?"

What would the right answer to that question have even been? I couldn't begin to guess, so I didn't try. Instead, I asked, "When was she admitted?"

Rory blew her hair back off her face with a forceful breath. "I knew you were going to ask me that."

"And do you have an answer for me?"

"I do." She hesitated.

I rolled my eyes. "Is it really a HIPAA violation if you tell me? I mean, I can find that out at least seven other ways. Besides, it's not like I'll rat on you."

"If you can find out seven other ways, why ask me?"

"Rory, I am not in the mood for this right now."

She sighed. "Early yesterday morning. Based on her time of arrival, I'd say the bleeding started not long after she'd arrived at the office. But that's just a guess. I'm not basing that on any tangible information whatsoever."

I considered the info and tried to compare that timeline with my own movements for the day. Since the details were still vague, I couldn't be sure, but I thought I might have been getting dressed about the time tragedy had befallen her. Which meant that I could've been contacted. I could've been here for her, if only someone had notified me. Bitterness welled up in the back of my throat, and I pushed off the wall.

"Where are you going?" Rory asked, doing a shuffle step to catch up with me.

"To find Rico."

"Right, right. Cool. Uh…why do you look like you're going to murder him?"

"Why do you think?" Something occurred to me, and I narrowed my eyes as I turned my glare on her. "You weren't here when they brought her in, were you?"

Rory held up both her hands as though to keep me at bay, took a step back, and shook her head. "No. I didn't get here until a few hours ago. She was already out of surgery when I arrived. I wouldn't have even known she was here if I hadn't passed Rico sitting in the waiting area."

I quickened my stride, intent upon finding him and asking him what the actual fuck he'd been thinking when he'd decided not to let me know my girlfriend was in surgery. And if he gave me any pushback about the op or my duty or anything along those lines, I intended to ask him how he'd think Paige would feel after I *put* him in surgery and didn't call to tell her.

"Ryan, maybe you should take a minute to calm down."

"Not a chance."

"Do you at least want to hear about the extent of your injuries?" she asked, trying—and failing—once again to distract me.

"You know I don't."

I heard her sigh and mutter "Of course not" under her breath.

"Is it true? That Allison can go home tomorrow?"

"I'm not her doctor. And unless she listed you on her paperwork as someone with whom it was okay to share medical information, I couldn't tell you even if I were. So maybe we should go find her doctor and ask and save talking to Rico for another time? Like a month from now. Or maybe a year. Or never."

"This won't take long," I said as I slammed my shoulder into the door to the hall where I'd been held, ignoring the ache from the impact. I had no idea where Rico was, and I knew that calling him to get his location was a bad idea because he'd be able to tell how angry I was, and I didn't want him to have any advance warning that this storm was bearing down on him. It'd give him time to run, and I couldn't have that. So I decided to see if I could track him down first. I figured the best place to start was the last place I'd seen him.

He was there all right, standing in the middle of the hallway, smack-dab among a group of people, engaged in some sort of argument with Officer Friendly. I assumed it was about his treatment of me earlier, but I was past caring about that. What I did care about was having a witness to this premeditated murder I was about to commit.

"Listen, you fucking asshole," Officer Friendly was saying when I reached them. "Don't you tell me how to do my job."

Whoa. That was unexpected. It was so shocking that it was almost enough to put the kibosh on my own murderous rage. Almost. But not quite. I'd opened my mouth to lay into Rico when I saw the members of the rest of the group.

"Officer," one of the women in the group said, her tone firm and laced with displeasure. "I think you're out of line."

Officer Friendly rounded on her and pointed a stubby finger in her direction. "Lady, this doesn't concern you."

Never one to be able to resist poking a hornet's nest with a stick or making an already tense situation—especially one that didn't involve me—as uncomfortable as possible, I said, "What's going on?"

"Ryan," Rory whispered in my ear as she elbowed me.

I shrugged. "What?"

Everyone turned to look at me, and I was surprised to see that one of the women who'd had her back to me was Claudia. I frowned. "Claudia? What are you doing here?"

She pursed her lips and favored me with a tight smile that didn't reach her eyes by a long shot. I couldn't tell, though, whether that was because she was displeased because of the reason she was here or whether she was upset about the argument taking place around her. "Hello, Ryan. I don't believe you've met my wife. Ryan, this is Evie. Evie, Ryan."

I shook Evie's outstretched hand. "Nice to meet you."

"Likewise," she replied, returning her attention to the officer, who still looked annoyed.

My eyes went wide as I realized that he'd just talked down to her. Oh, shit. He didn't know who he was speaking with. Jesus, how did he not know? Shouldn't an officer of the NYPD have an idea what the police commissioner looked like? I shook my head.

"Oh, goodie," the officer said, not trying to hide his sarcasm. "She's back."

"I'm back. Wait. Was I missing?" I looked at Rico. "You knew where I was going."

He nodded, still glaring at the officer. "I knew."

"Okay. What's going on?" I asked.

The officer sneered at me. "Look. I don't know why everyone's making such a huge deal out of this. I didn't know who you were. I said I was sorry. You didn't have to sic your boyfriend on me."

"Boyfriend?" I said, glancing at Rico. "Ew. No. And I didn't sic anyone on you. I don't even know what's happening."

"What's happening is your buddy here needs to learn to let shit go," the officer said, scowling. "She's free. What more do you want from me?"

"I'm going to go wait for you in your room," Rory said softly into my ear, squeezing my arm as she fled. I didn't blame her. Part of me wanted to escape as well. Another part of me wanted to stick around, either to break up a fight or cheer one on. I was still undecided.

"What I want from you," Rico said, his voice low and even, a sure sign that he was about to blow his top, "is an answer regarding why you didn't bother to verify that Ryan is who she told you she is."

"Fuck you," the officer said.

"Officer," Evie said, her tone sharp. "That's uncalled for. And I'd also like an answer to that question."

"For the last time," the officer said, hardly sparing her a glance, "this doesn't concern you."

"Oh, God," I muttered. "Please stop talking."

The cop shot me a dirty look before returning his attention to Evie long enough to say, "Why don't you go on about your business, honey?"

I cringed. Jesus. He was going to get himself fired—or at least demoted to cop-in-a-box—if he wasn't careful. "I am begging you," I said under my breath, knowing everyone could hear me but feeling compelled to try to be sly about this anyway. "Please. Please, just stop."

Claudia looked as aghast as I felt, but Evie merely tensed her jaw muscles slightly. "What precinct do you turn out of?" she asked.

Nope. This couldn't go anywhere good, and I refused to stand here while my suspicions that I was an albatross to anyone I came into even fleeting contact with were confirmed. "Okay." I broke in. "We're not doing this." I pointed at the policeman. "You are going to shut your mouth and not say anything else that will get you fired until after we're all far, far away." He blinked, then frowned, then opened his mouth, but I went on, turning my loaded finger on Rico. "You are going to come with me so I can murder you without any witnesses."

Rico's expression of surprise was almost comical. "Me? What did I do?"

"It's what you didn't do that I have a problem with. And I'll explain it to you in great detail as the killing takes place. Try not to scream too loud." I turned to Claudia and Evie. "You two are going to pretend you don't know what I'm about to do to him. And will you please go get me some coffee? I have a raging headache."

Claudia was smirking at me. "Did you just give the SAIC of OPO an order, Agent O'Connor?"

"Of course not. It was a request. I said please. Besides, you're not my boss," I told her with a grin. I glared at Rico, who gulped. "You. With me. Now." I turned to go but then said to Claudia over my shoulder, "See? *That* was an order."

I stalked away, Rico close behind, and heard Evie say, "You were right. She's something."

Claudia's laughter followed Rico and me back into my room. Rory looked up from the chart she was reading when we walked in. I raised an eyebrow at her. "Mine?"

She nodded.

"Can I go?"

Rory hesitated. "Go where?"

"Where do you think? I want to get the hell out of here." I wasn't leaving the hospital. Not as long as Allison was here. But I also didn't want to have my movements constrained.

Rory shook her head. "Unfortunately, no. You can't."

"Why not?"

"You have a concussion. The doctors want to keep you under observation. At least for the night."

"That's ridiculous. I feel fine."

Rory snorted. "Really? No headache, nausea, dizziness?"

"Of course I have all those things. I was beaten up, and my girlfriend had major surgery without me."

"I rest my case."

"I could leave AMA, though, if I wanted to, right?"

"You could," Rory said. "But then you'd get kicked out of the hospital and wouldn't be able to sneak down to see Allison."

Ooh. Low blow. I narrowed my eye at her, feeling the pulling of the stitches in my face. "I hate you."

Rory smiled. "Of course you do. And since you're stuck here, I plan to see if I can get someone from plastics to come up here and fix that mess of a mug."

I stuck my tongue out at her as she turned to go, and she stuck hers out at me over her shoulder in response. After she left, Rico stood near the door looking ready to bolt as I went to the chair in the corner and picked up the jacket I'd been wearing in the warehouse. I wrinkled my nose when I saw just how bloody and dirty it was. I didn't think I'd ever be able to get the stains out. I wasn't sure I even wanted to try. So I checked the pockets to make sure I hadn't left anything in them and tossed it onto the bed for the hospital staff to dispose of.

I'd done that as much to have some time to gather myself before addressing my issue with Rico as to prepare to be discharged. It worked somewhat. But I still needed another minute or so to compose myself, so I asked him, "Where's my backup?"

Rico appeared startled, and his brow wrinkled. "Huh?"

I rolled my eyes. "The gun I wear on my ankle. Where is it?"

"Oh. Uh. I assume the NYPD has it."

"Would you please find out for me?" I'd said that to give him a legitimate reason to leave me alone. I was still furious, but I'd changed my mind about killing him imminently. As soon as this conversation ended, I needed him to stay as far away from me as possible until I calmed down.

Rico nodded and shoved his hands into his pockets before ducking his head.

I took a deep breath. "You know what I'm going to say?"

He nodded again. "Yeah. I should've called you."

Well, that was unexpected. "You're not going to try to offer me excuses or attempt to justify why you didn't?"

He glanced up at me from underneath his lashes. "Would it do any good if I did?"

"No. It'd probably just make me angrier." To be honest, I'd sort of wanted him to so I could have what I felt was a justifiable excuse to blow a gasket. If I did it now, after he'd just admitted he was wrong, I'd just look like an unhinged asshole.

"Then I'm not going to," Rico said.

Sonofabitch! "Good."

We stared at one another for a long moment before I said, "Find my gun." Then I brushed past him and stalked out into the hall.

CHAPTER THIRTY-FIVE

Rory was pacing in front of the door wearing a worried expression. Her eyes widened when she saw me, and she cleared her throat. "I didn't hear any gunshots."

"That's because I'm not armed."

She cocked her head like she was trying to decide whether I was joking or not before looking me up and down. "No signs of a struggle."

I shrugged and then hissed. Jesus. Was I ever going to be able to move my shoulders without searing pain? "It didn't seem worth the effort." I nodded at the papers in her hand. "Those for me?"

"Yup. Instructions and whatnot. They'll probably give you another copy before you leave, but…"

"Thanks." I reached for the papers, but she pulled them back out of my grasp.

I glared at her. "What?"

"I'd still like you to rethink this. But before I give you these, you're coming with me to get your face stitched up properly."

I rolled my eyes. "Is this really necessary?"

Rory smiled, her expression tight and devoid of all joy. "Humor me."

"Fine. Lead the way."

Rory waved her free hand for me to head down the hall, and I tried to restrain my frustrated grumble as I turned to comply.

"Oh," Rory said, calling me back. "There is one more thing."

Of course there was. "What?"

"I think this belongs to you."

I frowned and turned back around. Rory was standing behind Special Agent Anna Strom with one hand on her shoulder, pushing her toward me the way one might do with a small child who didn't want to hug their grandma. I looked from Anna to Rory. The former looked acutely embarrassed as she stared at the tile floor, and the latter was smirking at me.

"I wouldn't say she *belongs* to me. Though I am surprised to see her. Anna? What are you doing here?"

"Giving away classified information to who-the-hell-ever, that's what she's doing here," Rory said, rolling her eyes.

"What?"

Anna's head shot up, and she glared at Rory, still not looking at me. "The information wasn't classified. And I wasn't giving it to who-the-hell-ever. I thought you were Agent O'Connor."

Rory made a show of sweeping her arms up and down in front of herself. "Dressed like this? Really?"

"I forgot she had a twin sister," Anna replied, her face turning an even darker shade of red.

Rory wrinkled her nose and shook her head as Anna turned back to me. The instant her gaze landed on my face, her eyes went wide, and she gasped and put one hand over her mouth.

Before I could stop myself, I grinned, which hurt like a mother-fucker, so that didn't last long. "That good, huh?" I asked.

Anna dropped her hand and schooled her face into a neutral expression like a good agent. "I'm sorry, Agent O'Connor. You look fine."

I laughed and winced at the same time. "Uh-huh. Sure I do. But I doubt you came all the way over here to compliment my appearance."

Anna was looking uncomfortable again and helplessly glanced over at Rory, who shrugged. "No. I um…I wanted to check on AT Reynolds." A beat. "I was the one who found her."

Oh!

Poor Anna. She never even knew what was coming. I was surprisingly agile for someone in so much pain, and I launched myself at her to wrap her in the best imitation of a bear hug I could muster. She let out a squeak of surprise and became as stiff as an I-Beam as I squeezed.

"Thank you," I whispered in her ear, trying not to cry.

She patted my side with the palm of her hand and mumbled, "I didn't do anything."

I pulled back so I could meet her eyes, and when she refused to look at me, I placed my hands on her shoulders. "Anna, what you did was *everything*."

Anna flushed and dipped her head even lower as she muttered something I didn't catch.

"As touching as this is," Rory said, "we kind of have an appointment to keep."

I rolled my eye and kept my attention on Anna. "Are you busy right now? I'm sorry. I have no idea what time it is." I paused for a moment. "Or what day it is."

Anna shook her head. "I'm free. Why? What do you need?"

"Will you stay with Allison while I finish up? I don't want her to be alone if she wakes up."

Anna nodded. "Of course."

"Thank you," I said. "For that as well as for saving her life."

Anna's blush returned, and she mumbled again and took off down the hall without a backward glance. Rory stepped up next to me and watched her go for a moment before resting one hand on my arm. "Are you ready?"

I sighed. "As I'll ever be, I guess."

She canted her head in the direction of the other hallway. "Come on. This won't take long."

I let out a groan that a teenager would be proud of and shuffled off after her, dragging my feet to prolong the inevitable. I didn't want to get new stitches. I wanted to be with Allison. But Rory would never let me hear the end of it if I didn't get this done. Still…

"How long will this take?" I wanted to know.

Rory shrugged as she opened a set of double doors that led to a large room lined with what looked like triage bays. "I don't know. As long as it takes. Why?"

She didn't appear interested in whatever response I might've made. Instead, she continued about halfway down the row before choosing a bay and gestured for me to enter. I narrowed my eye at her as I complied, and she pulled the curtains shut around us so we'd have some illusion of privacy.

"I don't want to be away from Allison any longer than I have to. I want to be there when she wakes up. I don't suppose we can do this in her room?"

Rory pinned me with a look of disbelief and shook her head. "No. We can't. Hop up onto that gurney for me."

I did as she asked and swung my feet like an obnoxious child as I watched her gather some supplies and place them on a tray. Then she left our little curtained cocoon so she could wash her hands and pulled on a pair of rubber gloves. When she turned back to me and started to advance, I held up my hands and scrambled off the gurney as fast as my battered body would allow, being careful to land on the opposite side. I wanted to keep the bed between us because I thought it might buy me some time.

"Whoa there. What the hell do you think you're doing?"

Rory rolled her eyes. "Will you relax? I'm going to numb you, not peel your face off. Unless you'd rather get stitches without anesthesia."

I stared at her as I tried to determine whether she was telling me the truth and took a couple of shuffle-steps back. "You're not going to try to do this yourself?"

Rory blinked, looking indignant. "I do know how to suture, thank you very much. In fact, I've stitched you up several times after you've done something stupid, and you've never complained."

"This is my face, though," I pointed out as I inched back over toward the gurney and debated whether to get on it again.

"Yeah. I know. Get your ass back up there, or you're not going to like where I stick this," she replied, brandishing the syringe at me.

"You can go to jail for that," I told her as I resumed my spot on the gurney and tried to ignore the tightening of the muscles in my gut. "Threatening a law enforcement officer is a violation of title eighteen, United States code, section one-fifteen."

Rory appeared to be deeply concentrating as she stabbed me in several key places. I did my best to keep the hissing and wincing to a minimum, but it didn't work.

"I'll plead guilty," she murmured. "But if the judge has met you, even once, I'll probably be given leniency."

"You mean granted clemency?"

"Whatever."

I endured a long pause, punctuated by a few more pokes that I suspected were a bit more forceful than necessary. Then she laid the needle down on the tray next to some other sharp-looking instruments and retrieved something else I didn't recognize. It resembled a cross between a thermometer and a pregnancy test, neither of which seemed applicable, given the situation.

Rory raised an eyebrow as she held it up.

I frowned and pulled back. "I don't have a temperature."

"How would you know? And this isn't to take your temperature."

"Well, if not that, then it can only be a pregnancy test. And I think we both know there's no chance of that. Besides, I thought the hospital did their pregnancy tests via urine or bloodwork."

"It isn't a pregnancy test, either."

"That isn't what I think it is, is it?" I asked. Sure, sometimes it took my light bulb a little longer to turn on, and it wasn't always as bright as one might expect, but I did tend to catch on. Eventually.

Rory made steady eye contact with me. "I am not going to force you to take this test. But I would like you to consider it. You know as well as I do that pretending a situation doesn't exist does not make it go away. And the sooner you get answers, the sooner you can take actions. You know, if they need to be taken."

I really hated it when she was right. The whole undercover exercise had been an attempt for me to escape my life, which isn't a very good reason to put oneself in mortal danger, it turns out. I'd been avoiding taking this test because I'd been afraid of the answer. But the answer would still be there whether I knew it or not. I sighed, and my shoulders sagged. I nodded. "Go on, then."

"Open up," Rory said.

I hesitated a second before doing as she asked. She pulled a cap off the end before she ran the thermometer/pregnancy test across my gums. It wasn't long before she withdrew it and put the cap back on, and though it hadn't hurt when she'd been swabbing me, I rubbed my lips with the side of my index finger anyway.

"Stay here. The surgeon will be in shortly. I'll be right back."

And before I had time to formulate a witty retort, she was gone, leaving me alone in a hospital room with not very many fun things to play with. I understood now why she'd brought me here instead of to a regular room. I was less likely to make a mess in here. I was also less likely to lock myself in the bathroom. Though I thought I'd seen one down the hall on our way over here. I could always go hide in there.

"Hello, Agent O'Connor," a tall, brunet doctor said as he thrust the curtain out of the way and entered the little room, thwarting my escape plan. He pulled it shut behind him, but not all the way. I could still see what was going on in the main part of the corridor. "I'm Dr. Harvey. Your sister's told me a lot about you."

I bit the inside of my lip, trying to rein in the snarky comment that'd sprung to mind. I swallowed hard and bobbed my head once, my hands twitching under the urge to prod at my face to make sure the numbing agent had taken effect. "Nice to meet you."

"Nice to meet you, too," he replied as he turned to the sink Rory had used earlier to wash his hands. Then he grabbed a pair of latex gloves from a nearby box and started to pull them on as he turned back to face me. "Are you ready?"

I knew enough to realize that being sarcastic with someone who was about to sew my face up was not my best plan, so I concentrated on trying to determine whether I could feel my face without touching it. I needn't have bothered. Dr. Harvey started prodding me, and I tensed, expecting pain before relaxing and letting out a small sigh of relief when I realized there was none.

"Looks like you are," Dr. Harvey said. He turned to his instrument tray, and I busied myself selecting a spot on the wall to stare at while he worked. I didn't want to close my eyes, but I didn't want to see what he was doing either.

I'd been stitched up dozens of times in my life in about as many different places, and still I was unprepared for the strange pulling sensation that accompanied his motions. The wire might as well have been attached to my guts because I felt an unpleasant twinge there with each draw of his hand. Things got especially upsetting when he began to work on my lip. My head started to swim, and I had to focus very hard on not throwing up or passing out.

Time took on such a strange dreamlike quality that it was impossible to track its passing as he worked. I could've sat there trying to remain conscious for ten minutes or ten hours or ten days. It was tough to tell. And when Dr. Harvey finally spoke to let me know that he'd finished, it was as if his voice had pierced the bubble I'd been floating in, allowing it to begin slowly leaking reality back in on me.

I blinked and glanced away from my chosen spot on the wall to look at him. I could see his lips moving, but his words weren't reaching my ears at the same time. It reminded me of when an online video playback isn't synched properly. I grimaced and lost the thread of the conversation.

A hand on my arm dragged me out of my trippy hell and back into the present. I turned to see Rory staring at me with concern etched in deep lines across her face. "Are you okay?"

I nodded, but more because it felt like the thing I was supposed to do than because it was true. "Sure."

Rory appeared skeptical and shifted her attention to Dr. Harvey, who was removing his gloves. "Are you all done with her?"

"Yes," he said. "She's all set. Good luck, Agent O'Connor."

"Thanks," I mumbled as he left. Or at least I thought I did. Maybe. My lips were tingly, and I had no idea why. It was unnerving.

Rory was staring at me again, and her expression made me shiver. "Is something wrong with Allison?"

Rory frowned. "What? No. She's fine. She's still sleeping. Your little minion is with her."

"She's not a minion."

"Whatever. The point is, she's fine." A beat. "But we do need to talk."

Rory turned and strode out of the little bay without waiting to see whether I would follow, which under any other circumstances I might've considered rude, but which today wasn't even a blip on my radar. My stomach plummeted into the area around my knees. Fuck. Nothing good ever followed those words. Ever. I wondered if I still had time to go hide in the bathroom.

CHAPTER THIRTY-SIX

I took a deep breath, swallowed hard, and squared my shoulders. I did not want to do this. As far as I was concerned, I could wait until about a thousand years after the apocalypse to hear whatever Rory had to say. Unfortunately, I also knew that if I didn't emerge from this curtain fort in three seconds, she would come back in after me. I also knew there was nothing about that scenario I'd enjoy. So, after letting out the breath I'd drawn in a long, slow, noisy huff, I hopped off the gurney and forced my feet to propel me in the direction she had gone.

She was gnawing on her lower lip with a ferocity that made me afraid blood was imminent and glancing up and down the hall as though she were expecting to be overrun any minute. By whom or what or why wasn't clear, and I wasn't interested enough to inquire. Instead, I shoved my fingers into my back pockets and rocked forward onto the balls of my feet.

"What's up?" I asked, having just decided that if I had to do this, I wanted to get it over with. Something occurred to me, and my heart tried to fold in on itself. "Is this about my test?"

Rory frowned, clearly confused. "Huh?"

"My test. The pregnancy-test-thermometer thing." When she continued to stare at me like I had three heads, I went on. "The thing you ran across my gums." I swiped one finger across the dimple where my lip met my chin for emphasis. "I'm HIV positive, aren't I?" The words almost choked me, and I'd struggled to force them out, but now that they were out, the air around me seemed heavy and stagnant, as if it bore the weight of her answer.

"What?" Rory's frown deepened, and she was clearly having a hard time figuring out what I was talking about. But after several long seconds, she said, "Oh! Oh, no. No. That wasn't what I wanted to talk to you about."

Now I was confused. "So I'm not HIV positive?"

Rory shook her head. "Nope."

"Wait. What?"

"What?"

"Did you just say I'm not HIV positive?"

Rory almost smirked. "Of course you're not. You didn't really think you were, did you?"

I hadn't been sure, to be honest. But I guessed I'd been so afraid to hope for this outcome that maybe I'd started resigning myself to the fact prematurely. I was so relieved and so certain I hadn't heard her correctly that I replayed her words repeatedly in my mind. When I'd convinced myself that she'd said what I'd thought she'd said, I did the only thing I could do in that situation. I punched her arm. Hard.

"Ow! What the hell was that for?" She glowered at me as she rubbed her bicep.

"That was for making me think you had bad news. Jerk!"

"I'm sorry. It didn't even occur to me that you'd think that."

"What the hell else would I think?"

"I don't know. Maybe that your partner wants to see you."

Okay, she'd lost me again. "I thought Allison was sleeping. Did she wake up?"

Rory rolled her eyes. "One-track mind," she muttered under her breath. "I said partner, not girlfriend." When I continued to stare at her, she huffed. "Your undercover partner. I didn't catch his name. Tall guy."

"Tate? Where the hell did you run into him?" More important, what the hell was he doing risking the tenuous hold he had on his cover to come here and interact with me and half the Secret Service?

Rory gave the empty hall another once-over and stepped closer. I gritted my teeth as I forced myself not to step back. That became even tougher when she put one hand on my shoulder. "Ryan, I know you have a concussion, which makes it hard for you to follow conversations, but I really need for you to try to keep up."

I shook her off and scowled. "Keep up with what? You haven't told me anything that makes any sense."

Rory wrapped her fingers around my wrist and pulled me down the hall. "Just follow me."

I allowed myself to be led like a child, mostly because I was too tired to fight anymore. It had been a long, trying few days. And the touch of her hand seemed to sap what little energy I'd managed to hold on to, leaving me exhausted. I wanted only to curl up into a ball in the corner and go to sleep. As she tugged me along, I looked around, wondering where the bunk rooms were. They had to exist, right? If TV had taught me nothing else, it was that doctors always needed a place to hook up. Maybe I could crash in there for a bit. If I could find one.

Rory turned without warning, and my shoulder protested the sudden change in direction. She'd led us into an actual room with a door and shut it almost before I made it all the way inside.

"Jesus fucking Christ, Rory! What the hell?" I yanked my arm out of her grip and sidled away, trying to glare at her, though I suspected the lack of light in there dulled the intended effect.

"Oh, God! Sorry. Your shoulder. I keep forgetting." She did appear apologetic, and my anger at her flickered and died. She turned on the light.

I closed my eye against the sudden brightness and rubbed my eyelid with my forefinger and thumb. "It's fine. Would you mind just telling me what Tate wanted? I'd really like to go be with Allison, if you don't mind."

"Don't worry. I promise this won't take long," a deep voice said from behind me.

I jumped and shrieked a little as I spun around. "What the hell? Why is everyone being so fucking cagey? God!"

Tate stepped out from behind a half-drawn curtain on the far side of the room and looked like he couldn't decide whether to smile or look chagrined. But the horror on his face washed away both those expressions as he clearly registered the mess that my own had become. He raised his eyebrows and blinked before letting out a long, slow whistle.

"Yes. I know. I look like shit. What are you doing here?"

"Checking up on you, of course."

"Tate, you can't be here," I said. Rory moved to the other side of the small room to give us some privacy, and though I couldn't have cared less at this point, I still appreciated the gesture.

Tate snorted. "Why not?"

"They already suspect you aren't who you've said you are. I think I managed to throw up a smokescreen around that, but if they catch you here…" I let him finish that sentence however he saw fit. The more gruesome, the better.

"That's what I'm here to tell you. It's over."

I waited a few heartbeats for a punch line that never came. "What?"

Tate's brow furrowed, and his lips twisted. "Well, mostly over. We think."

I didn't have the energy to try to decipher that remark. "What does that even mean?"

"Seth's been arrested for kidnapping and attempted murder. That was a given, considering what he did to you. That allowed us to get warrants for his house and several of the group's safe houses that we were able to connect to him. The man was smart, but he wasn't smart enough to follow the most basic rule of being a criminal: Never leave a paper trail."

"He didn't!"

"I mean, not a literal paper trail, since no actual paper was involved. No. That's not true. There were some maps. But by and large—"

"I get it. Can you get on with the story?" I was listening to him. I really was. But also, Rory was rummaging through all the drawers in the room and slamming them shut, which distracted me. I had no clue what she was looking for, and I couldn't decide whether I wanted to ask.

"Right. Sorry." He took a deep breath. "We don't have to get into all the specifics right now. To be honest, we're still trying to sort out a couple of things. We can go over all the nuts and bolts in a few weeks when we start talking to the AUSA about the preliminary stages of trial prep. You know you'll have to testify…"

I waved my hand at him while trying to see what Rory was up to without appearing inattentive. Did a concussion truly make you more susceptible to distraction? That didn't sound right. "That's fine. Whatever. I don't care."

"We definitely want to make sure this organization didn't have any other facets we hadn't accounted for. We sure don't need another group of these nuts crawling out of the woodwork to pick up where Seth left off."

"Uh-huh," I muttered, watching Rory smile triumphantly at the Sharpie marker she'd managed to locate.

"And of course you'll have a security detail until we can establish that you're not in any danger," Tate said.

"Mmm." I was only half listening. Rory had removed the cap of the marker and was now coloring on her white lab coat. I was so busy trying to figure out what she was up to that it took a bit longer than usual for Tate's words to sink into my brain. I snapped around to stare at him. "What?"

Tate looked both concerned and fearful. I hoped it was fear of me. "Just until we know for sure that—"

"Absolutely not."

Tate gave me a sharp look. "Alex."

"No and no," I said, putting my hands on my hips. "I am not

having a security detail. And if I didn't know better, I'd say *you* were the one with the concussion for even suggesting it."

Tate rolled his eyes. "This isn't a negotiation. And even if it were, I wouldn't be the one to take this up with. I'm just the messenger."

"We'll see," I muttered under my breath.

Rory, who either hadn't been paying attention or couldn't have cared less about the news that I was about to be treated like a protectee, replaced the cap on the marker, tossed it onto the nearby countertop, and grinned at me. I was drawn to the dark ink that was like a beacon on her white coat. She had drawn a thick line underneath where her first name had been stitched onto the fabric and some accent lines off the top of it, reminiscent of how a child would draw rays of a sun. Then, beneath the line, she had scrawled "(NOT RYAN)." She looked very proud of herself.

"I don't think that'll help as much as you think it will," I told her.

She frowned and glanced down at her handiwork.

"The long and short of it," Tate went on, "is that Seth is going away for a very long time."

That remark jogged something in me, something that'd occurred to me earlier that I'd forgotten, and I returned my focus to him. "He's going to be okay?"

Tate glanced at Rory, who held up her hands. "That's not my case. And if it was—"

"I know. You wouldn't be able to talk about it."

"But I can if I know something, right?" Tate asked.

"I can't control what you do. If you aren't trying to pump me for information, go for it," Rory said.

Tate shrugged. "I think he'll be okay. He's handcuffed to a bed upstairs, and the doctors are observing him to make sure he has no residual effects from the fight you had before letting him go to central booking."

I nodded, but my mind was too much of a jumble to make much sense of my thoughts. "And everybody else?"

"Some have been arrested. Some are still just being questioned. We still have to do a lot of work on this case, but it's mostly evidence gathering and taking statements at this point. And I don't want you to worry. Anyone we don't have in custody yet, we won't let them get to you."

Maybe I should've been more concerned than I was, but I was buckling under the weight of a lot of conflicting emotions that I wasn't truly feeling. I just nodded again. My energy was coming and going in waves like the tide, and now we were in the ebbing part of the cycle. I wanted to sit down, but the bed looked clean, and I didn't want to get it dirty, and the chair was too far away to try to reach it. I settled for leaning against the counter.

My thoughts drifted from Seth to Crash to the other people in their group—both the ones I'd met and the ones I hadn't—and I wondered how they'd all gotten there. Obviously, some of them had wholeheartedly believed in the cause. But what about the rest of them? Had it been all playing and make-believe? Had they been searching for a sense of belonging and gotten swept up in the stampede? I didn't understand. I probably never would. Perhaps I didn't want to.

"Okay," Rory said, taking a step closer to me and putting a hand on my back. "That's enough for today. You guys can hash out some of the other details another time, I'm sure." Rory was speaking more to Tate than to me, and her meaning was clear. I didn't think I'd ever been more grateful for her.

Tate dipped his head once. "Of course. I'll let you rest. Give me a call when you feel up to it. I'll do my best to keep the jackals at bay in the meantime."

"Thanks, Tate." I knew I'd never be able to find the right words to express what I was trying to say.

Tate looked at me for a long moment. "I know things went horribly off track with this op, but at the end of the day, we saved a lot of lives. You're kind of a hero."

I tried to smile before he left, and I couldn't help thinking that for all the lives that'd been saved, at least one hadn't been. That didn't feel heroic to me at all.

CHAPTER THIRTY-SEVEN

After Tate left, I stared at the doorway for a long time, torn between laughing and crying. I reached up to rub my eyes but then yelped and drew my hands away immediately at the sting.

"Do you think I'll ever be able to move like a normal person without having to worry about pain?" I asked Rory. It seemed like I'd been dealing with aches and twinges forever, both residual and not so much.

Rory paused. "No," she said, her tone and her expression very serious. "You're the clumsiest person on earth. You'll always be injuring yourself somehow."

I blinked at her, and she smiled at me. "I want to argue with you…"

"But you know you can't." Her smile widened, and she held out her hand. "Come on."

I narrowed my eye at her. At least I tried to. "Nothing good ever happens when I follow you anywhere."

"It'll be different this time. I promise."

"I feel like you've said that to me before."

"No. I don't think I have."

"Mmm." I pretended to grumble under my breath even as I was falling into step behind her as she led me out of the room. "If you're taking me someplace horrible, I'm never going to forgive you."

Rory scoffed. "Sure, you will."

"Not if needles are involved, I won't."

"That's fair. And there shouldn't be any needles where we're going. At least not for you. Well, at least not right away. I can't promise about later."

"That doesn't make me want to come with you any more than I did a second ago."

Rory chuckled.

We walked in silence for a moment before my concussed little brain remembered what it was like to be a compassionate human being and think about someone else. Shame washed over me in burning waves, and I had to swallow it back so I could speak. "Hey. How are you doing?"

Rory looked surprised. "What?"

"I've been so caught up with Allison and the case and my injuries that I completely forgot to ask about you. Are you okay?"

Muscles rippled in Rory's face in configurations I didn't realize were possible, and for an instant it was tough to tell whether she might call me an asshole or cry. She cleared her throat and dragged one palm down her cheeks the way she always did when she was drained. "You know. Hanging in. What choice do any of us have?"

I was pretty sure that was what she'd said the last time I'd asked. How long ago had that been? I couldn't recall. I also didn't know what to say to her now.

"Do you...wanna talk about anything?"

Rory's eyes grew a little glassy, like she was thinking really hard or remembering. Or maybe she was trying not to remember. "Eventually," she said after a beat. "When all of this is over."

I put a hand on her arm to stop her. "Hey. Listen. Just because my life is a shitstorm doesn't mean you take a back seat. If you need to talk, I'm here. We don't need to wait for anything."

Rory tried to smile, but her attempt wasn't convincing. "Tell you what. You go a month without landing in the hospital, and we can talk all you want."

I recognized the need for an out when I saw one, so I was willing to let it go. For now. I played along. "Do you mean at all? Or just due to work-related injuries? Because I'm pretty sure I can manage that."

Rory's smile looked more genuine now. "We'll see."

We stopped outside the door to a room, and Rory gestured me inside. It didn't look familiar, but the hospital was a maze, and all these corridors tended to look alike to me. Plus, with all my recent visits, all the various hospitals and trips were a jumble, and I was starting to mix them all up.

"Who's in here?" I asked, reluctant to just see for myself, which would've been the easier thing to do.

"You are."

"No. I said I was leaving."

"No. You said you *wanted* to leave. It wasn't officially decided. And

I told you that if you left, you wouldn't be able to spend the night with Allison. But I arranged it so you can."

"I don't understand."

Rory gestured to the opened door again. "See for yourself."

I shuffled through the doorway and glanced around, uncertain what I was walking into. Anna, tucked into a chair in the corner, looked up from the book she was reading and stood. She glanced from me to Allison and back again, and I took the opportunity to check in on my girlfriend as well. She was sound asleep, and her deep, even breaths somehow soothed me.

"Did she wake up at all?" I asked Anna.

Anna shook her head. "Not really. She sort of mumbled a bit and kind of fidgeted some. Her heart rate monitor spiked a couple times, but mostly it's been quiet."

"Thank you. I appreciate everything you've done for her today. And for me."

"It wasn't a problem."

"I'm sure you want to get going, but can I trouble you to do me one more favor? It's a quick one, I promise."

"Anything," Anna said.

"There's a Dunkin' up on Twenty-third and Lex. Would you mind popping up there and grabbing a half dozen doughnuts for me? Rory will give you the money."

"I will?" Rory asked.

"You will."

Anna waved a hand. "Don't worry about it. You can get me later. What kind of doughnuts do you want?"

"You can get an assortment, as long as one of them is the powdered kind with the chocolate cream in the middle."

"Sure. I'll be right back."

Once Anna had gone on her errand, I took a moment to really examine the room. Two hospital beds stood side by side. Allison was in one, but the other was empty.

Rory must've sensed what I was thinking, because before I had a chance to open my mouth, she said, "That one's for you."

"What?"

"I had you transferred so you could spend the night with her. I knew you'd want to."

I didn't think I'd ever been so happy to hear anything. I was barely holding myself together at this point. I didn't know if it was the concussion or the trauma of the events in the warehouse or seeing Allison all drugged up in that hospital bed. Maybe it was all of it. Maybe it didn't matter. But I did know that I wanted nothing more than to curl up in that bed next to my girlfriend and fall asleep looking at her and holding her hand. I sighed.

Rory brushed one hand across my shoulder. "I'll check in on you later," she said.

I nodded, fixated on climbing into that bed. "It's okay if I go to sleep?"

Rory gave me a puzzled look.

"With my concussion," I said.

Rory took the penlight out of her pocket and tried to pry open the less battered of my two eyes far enough to shine a beam into it. I winced and pulled back. "Of course. You're fine. Get some rest."

Rory gave me a small smile, glanced at Allison, and then left.

My eyes were burning now, but that could've been from the beating I'd taken as much as it could've been from fatigue. Either way, I was looking forward to closing them for a while. Careful not to make too much noise, I slipped off my shoes and crawled into the bed next to Allison's. It took some maneuvering, during which I had to bite my lips to hold back the grunts and groans of pain, but I settled onto my side so I could study my sleeping girlfriend.

Rory had very thoughtfully had someone arrange the room so the beds were right next to one another, and though it took some agonizing scooting to the very edge of the mattress and some additional uncomfortable stretching, I was able to rest my hand on top of Allison's. I lost myself in drawing gentle patterns on the soft skin of her knuckles as I thought about everything that'd happened and nothing at all.

Allison murmured, and I froze, feeling like an asshole for waking her. She needed her rest, and it'd been selfish of me to do anything that would take that away from her. I held my breath, hoping she would drift off again. Her brow furrowed, and she frowned as her eyes fluttered open.

She blinked at me and moved her hand out from under mine so she could wrap her fingers around my wrist. "Hey."

"Hey," I said softly back. "I'm sorry. I didn't mean to wake you. Go back to sleep."

"It's okay," she said through a yawn, stretching her legs out straight and shifting so she could touch me with her other arm as well. "I'm okay. How are you?"

"Better now," I told her, which was true. My gut twisted with guilt because I'd woken her, but I was happy to speak to her. "How are you feeling?"

Her expression turned pensive, and if we'd been in a cartoon, I'd have been able to see the cogs and gears twisting and turning in her head as she considered my question. "There's some pain. But it's better than it was. I think."

I placed the tips of my fingers against her breastbone and stroked. "And here?"

Allison smiled, the saddest smile I'd ever seen. My heart cracked at the sight of it, and it broke apart altogether when she took my hand, lifted it to her lips, and kissed it softly. "I don't know yet."

I tried to smile back, but the muscles in my cheeks were trembling. "That's okay," I told her, struggling to force the words past the tightness in my throat. "You don't have to know. Not now. Maybe not ever."

She sighed and let go of my hand in favor of tracing the stitches on my face. For an instant, I was transported back to the day I'd woken up in the hospital after I'd been shot, when she'd done the same thing. The feeling of déjà vu disoriented me.

"Are you starting a collection?" she asked.

"A collection of what?"

"Scars. You'll probably have a few new ones after this."

If my heart weren't so heavy, I might've teased her about having a thing for me in stitches or liking women with scars, but I couldn't even bring myself to joke. "Yeah."

We stared at one another intently for a while, and I wondered a lot of different things. What she was thinking. What she needed from me now. If I could do anything to make this better for her. Whether she would ever fully recover from this and how long it might take until things felt happy and normal again. In a moment of selfishness, I even wondered what the sight of my face made her think and feel. But while her expression was earnest and searching as she looked at me, it revealed nothing of her thoughts.

I ran the pad of my thumb across the hollow of her cheek and smiled at her. "Always the perfect Secret Service agent."

My words shattered her stoic veneer, her confusion plain. "What?"

I opened my mouth to explain, fearing that I was about to dig myself into a hole I'd never get out of, but Anna's return interrupted my explanation. She stopped at the foot of Allison's bed clenching the Dunkin' bag, her eyes wide. She averted her gaze as though she'd walked in on us having sex—or at least well on our way to it—and blushed.

"Thanks, Anna," I said, struggling to push myself up to a sitting position. "I appreciate it."

Anna tossed the bag at me, then looked horrified by her own behavior. I grinned at her discomfort and started to tease her, but Allison smacked my arm and gave me a warning glare. I huffed and opened the bag.

"No problem," Anna said after the longest, most awkward pause in history. "AT Reynolds, I'm glad you're feeling better."

Allison smiled warmly, and I frowned at the doughnut in my hand as I realized that my jaw hurt too much to open it wide enough to take a real bite. Just my luck. I tore off a piece of powdered dough with my fingers and shoved it into my mouth. The sweetness made me a little less petulant about the fact that I couldn't enjoy my doughnut as I normally would, which was inhaling it in four bites or less.

"Thank you, Anna," Allison said. "I can't tell you how much everything you've done means to me."

I chewed and watched with interest as Anna's face somehow became even redder. Was she having a stroke? Some sort of breathing issue? Maybe a heart attack? No. She'd grab her arm or her chest if that was the problem, wouldn't she? I glanced to the side of my bed to get eyes on the button that I knew would summon a nurse, just in case.

"You're welcome, AT Reynolds," Anna said, still looking at the foot of the bed rather than at either of us. "Since Agent O'Connor is here with you now, I'm going to take off."

"Of course. Have a nice night, Anna," Allison replied. "And take the day off tomorrow." Anna's head shot up, and she did look directly at Allison, her expression indicating that she was inclined to protest. But Allison beat her to it. "That's an order."

Anna nodded. "Thank you." She seemed to want to say something else but instead went with "Good night."

"She needs to stop calling me that," I said to no one in particular after she'd gone. I tore off another chunk of doughnut and started to bring it to my lips, but Allison's hand on my arm stopped me.

With the ghost of a mischievous twinkle in her eye, Allison leaned forward while tugging on my arm so she could pop the piece of doughnut into her own mouth instead.

"Hey!"

Allison's lips twitched as she chewed, and when she'd swallowed, she stopped trying to contain her smile. "I don't know why you insisted on sending her to get those."

"Because you never eat them," I said.

"Exactly," she said, snatching the bag out of my hands and stealing the rest of the doughnut I'd been picking at.

My heart swelled as we sat side by side on our respective hospital beds, me eating doughnuts and her insisting that she didn't, even as powdered sugar dusted her lips. This time my smile felt genuine and underscored by joy. Things were shit right now, and it'd be a while until they felt right again, but bickering over breakfast snacks as we always did turned my hope into certainty.

Everything was going to be all right.

About the Author

Kara A. McLeod is a badass by day and a smartass by night. Or maybe it's the other way around. Or quite possibly neither. A Jersey girl at heart, "Mac" is an intrepid wanderer who goes wherever the wind takes her. A former Secret Service agent who decided she wanted more out of life than standing in a stairwell and losing an entire month every year to the United Nations General Assembly, she currently resides in Hove Actually and is still searching hither and yon for the meaning of life, the nearest comic con, and a shiny Shuckle.

If anyone has any leads on any of the above, she can be contacted at kara.a.mcleod@gmail.com.

Books Available From Bold Strokes Books

Across the Enchanted Border by Crin Claxton. Magic, telepathy, swordsmanship, tyranny, and tenderness abound in a tale of two lands separated by the enchanted border. (978-1-63679-804-2)

Deep Cover by Kara A. McLeod. Running from your problems by pretending to be someone else only works if the person you're pretending to be doesn't have even bigger problems. (978-1-63679-808-0)

Good Game by Suzanne Lenoir. Even though Lauren has sworn off dating gamers, it's becoming hard to resist the multifaceted Sam. An opposites attract lesbian romance. (978-1-63679-764-9)

Innocence of the Maiden by Ileandra Young. Three powerful women. Two covens at war. One horrifying murder. When mighty and powerful witches begin to butt heads, who out there is strong enough to mediate? (978-1-63679-765-6)

Protection in Paradise by Julia Underwood. When arson forces them together, the flames between chief of police Eve Maguire and librarian Shaye Hayden aren't that easy to extinguish. (978-1-63679-847-9)

Too Forward by Krystina Rivers. Just as professional basketball player Jane May's career finally starts heating up, a new relationship with her team's brand consultant could derail the success and happiness she's struggled so long to find. (978-1-63679-717-5)

Worth Waiting For by Kristin Keppler. For Peyton and Hanna, reliving the past is painful, but looking back might be the only way to move forward. (978-1-63679-773-1)

All For Her: Forbidden Romance Novellas by Gun Brooke, J.J. Hale & Aurora Rey. Explore the angst and excitement of forbidden love few would dare in this heart-stopping novella collection. (978-1-63679-713-7)

Finding Harmony by CF Frizzell. Rock star Harper Cushing has to rearrange her grandmother's future and sell the family store out from under her, but she reassesses everything because Gram's helper, Frankie, could be offering the harmony her heart has been missing. (978-1-63679-741-0)

Gaze by Kris Bryant. Love at first sight is for dreamers, but the more time Lucky and Brianna spend together, the more they realize the chemistry of a gaze can make anything possible. (978-1-63679-711-3)

Laying of Hands by Patricia Evans. The mysterious new writing instructor at camp makes Grace Waters brave enough to wonder what would happen if she dared to write her own story. (978-1-63679-782-3)

The Naked Truth by Sandy Lowe. How far are Rowan and Genevieve willing to go and how much will they risk to make their most captivating and forbidden fantasies a reality? (978-1-63679-426-6)

The Roommate by Claire Forsythe. Jess Black's boyfriend is handsome and successful. That's why it comes as a shock when she meets a woman on the train who makes her pulse race. (978-1-63679-757-1)

Seducing the Widow by Jane Walsh. Former rival debutantes have a second chance at love after fifteen years apart when a spinster persuades her ex-lover to help save her family business. (978-1-63679-747-2)

Close to Home by Allisa Bahney. Eli Thomas has to decide if avoiding her hometown forever is worth losing the people who used to mean the most to her, especially Aracely Hernandez, the girl who got away. (978-1-63679-661-1)

Innis Harbor by Patricia Evans. When Amir Farzaneh meets and falls in love with Loch, a dark secret lurking in her past reappears, threatening the happiness she'd just started to believe could be hers. (978-1-63679-781-6)

The Blessed by Anne Shade. Layla and Suri are brought together by fate to defeat the darkness threatening to tear their world apart. What they don't expect to discover is a love that might set them free. (978-1-63679-715-1)

The Guardians by Sheri Lewis Wohl. Dogs, devotion, and determination are all that stand between darkness and light. (978-1-63679-681-9)

The Mogul Meets Her Match by Julia Underwood. When CEO Claire Beauchamp goes undercover as a customer of Abby Pita's café to help seal a deal that will solidify her career, she doesn't expect to be so drawn to her. When the truth is revealed, will she break Abby's heart? (978-1-63679-784-7)

Trial Run by Carsen Taite. When Reggie Knoll and Brooke Dawson wind up serving on a jury together, their one task—reaching a unanimous verdict—is derailed by the fiery clash of their personalities, the intensity of their attraction, and a secret that could threaten Brooke's life. (978-1-63555-865-4)

Waterlogged by Nance Sparks. When conservation warden Jordan Pearce discovers a body floating in the flowage, the serenity of the Northwoods is rocked. (978-1-63679-699-4)

Accidentally in Love by Kimberly Cooper Griffin. Nic and Lee have good reasons for keeping their distance. So why does their growing attraction seem more like a love-hate relationship? (978-1-63679-759-5)

Frosted by the Girl Next Door by Aurora Rey and Jaime Clevenger. When heartbroken Casey Stevens opens a sex shop next door to uptight cupcake baker Tara McCoy, things get a little frosty. (978-1-63679-723-6)

Ghost of the Heart by Catherine Friend. Being possessed by a ghost was not on Gwen's bucket list, but she must admit that ghosts might be real, and one is obviously trying to send her a message. (978-1-63555-112-9)

Hot Honey Love by Nan Campbell. When chef Stef Lombardozzi puts her cooking career into the hands of filmmaker Mallory Radowski—the pickiest eater alive—she doesn't anticipate how hard she'll fall for her. (978-1-63679-743-4)

London by Patricia Evans. Jaq's and Bronwyn's lives become entwined as dangerous secrets emerge and Bronwyn's seemingly perfect life starts to unravel. (978-1-63679-778-6)

This Christmas by Georgia Beers. When Sam's grandmother rigs the Christmas parade to make Sam and Keegan queen and queen, sparks fly, but they can't forget the Big Embarrassing Thing that makes romance a total nope. (978-1-63679-729-8)

Unwrapped by D. Jackson Leigh. Asia du Muir is not going to let some party-girl actress ruin her best chance to get noticed by a Broadway critic. Everyone knows you should never mix business and pleasure. (978-1-63679-667-3)

Language Lessons by Sage Donnell. Grace and Lenka never expected to fall in love. Is home really where the heart is if it means giving up your dreams? (978-1-63679-725-0)

New Horizons by Shia Woods. When Quinn Collins meets Alex Anders, Horizon Theater's enigmatic managing director, a passionate connection ignites, but amidst the complex backdrop of theater politics, their budding romance faces a formidable challenge. (978-1-63679-683-3)

Scrambled: A Tuesday Night Book Club Mystery by Jaime Maddox. Avery Hutchins makes a discovery about her father's death that will force her to face an impossible choice between doing what is right and finally finding a way to regain a part of herself she had lost. (978-1-63679-703-8

www.ingramcontent.com/pod-product-compliance
Lightning Source LLC
Chambersburg PA
CBHW021951010726
47494CB00003B/691